Praise for N. J. Cooper

'One of Cooper's strengths is her ability to unpack ideas and issues . . . A fascinating, splendidly atmospheric read' *Guardian*

'N. J. Cooper's chilling new novel shines . . . the plot is convincing' *Times Literary Supplement*

'A departure in mood, setting and issues, but successfully achieved . . . an altogether satisfying novel' *The Times*

'A probing psychological book that reaches out to the reader on two levels, that of an interesting mystery and a deeply fascinating psychological insight into family relationships. Highly recommended' *Eurocrime*

'The combination of a well-described setting in the Isle of Wight and Cooper's sensitive understanding of human behaviour lend conviction to an intriguing, enjoyable puzzle' *Literary Review*

'An excellent novel . . . Informative and entertaining' *Telegraph*

Also by N. J. Cooper

No Escape
Lifeblood
Face of the Devil

N.J. COOPER

VENGEANCE IN MIND

**SIMON &
SCHUSTER**

London · New York · Sydney · Toronto · New Delhi

A CBS COMPANY

First published in Great Britain by Simon & Schuster UK Ltd, 2012
A CBS Company

1 3 5 7 9 10 8 6 4 2

Simon & Schuster UK Ltd
1st Floor,
222 Gray's Inn Road
London WC1X 8HB

www.simonandschuster.co.uk

Simon & Schuster Australia, Sydney
Simon & Schuster India, New Delhi

A CIP catalogue record for this book is available
from the British Library

Hardback ISBN 978-0-85720-680-0
Paperback ISBN 978-0-85720-681-7
Ebook ISBN 978-0-85720-682-4

Typeset by Hewer Text UK Ltd, Edinburgh

Printed and bound by CPI Group (UK) Ltd, Croydon, CR0 4YY

For
Roland and Julie Johnson

Acknowledgements

As always, I have been helped and supported by a great team. I should particularly like to thank Suzanne Baboneau, Mary Carter, Stephanie Glencross, Jane Gregory, Isabelle Grey, and Emma Lowth.

Chapter 1

1 February
Day One: Before dawn

Something crashed into Karen's dream. She heard the ring of smashed glass falling on a hard surface. Fear pinned her to the mattress and kept her swollen eyes closed as she lay, heart hammering, breathing high and quick, listening for clues.

Behind the almost musical sound of broken glass came the roar of wind and heavy drumming from rain on the skylights overhead. A wetter, splashier noise told her the rain was inside her bedroom, too. Traffic coughed and grunted from further away, split by shrill insistent sirens. Linking all the different noises was the continuous low-level grumble of the sea. But there was nothing human.

Opening her eyes to star-lightened darkness, Karen slid out of bed and felt the cold tighten her muscles and scrape at her skin. Her brushed-cotton pyjamas were no match for the savagery of the February weather, and she was shivering as she stumbled towards the French doors that led out to the balcony.

The patchy light glittered on broken glass all over the floor, but the warning came too late. Her bare foot had come down on one sharp piece and she felt it slice into her skin.

Backing away on her heels, she dropped onto the bed again, seeing she'd left a trail of scarlet blood drips. Starlight caught on them too and made them look like jewellery. Gusts of wind kept sucking the doors shut, then smashing them open against the walls. She'd have to fix them before any more glass broke, but she couldn't do that until she'd dealt with her foot.

Careful probing with her fingers suggested the shard hadn't cracked inside her flesh. She pulled at the protruding piece, gritting her teeth against the small pain as the glass moved. The warm rush of blood that followed comforted her. She let it flow unchecked for a while, hoping it would be strong enough to wash out any dirt or tiny chip left behind.

The sweet metallic smell of the blood mixed with hints of lavender from her crisp linen sheets and the muddle of petrol, seaweed and salt that always rose to her top-floor flat from the city below.

While the French doors continued to swing back and forth, expelling more chunks of broken glass each time, she reached for the box of Kleenex by her bed and made a pad of tissues, tucking the edges between her toes, then stuffed her feet into her old leather slippers for safety. Her dressing gown was draped over the chair at the foot of the bed, and she dragged it over her shoulders.

Thick Shetland wool, woven in a mixture of greys and blues, it wasn't beautiful or alluring, but it had been made in a place where wind and cold were a lot worse than anything Southampton could offer, even on a night like this. Karen hoped it would be enough to keep her from hypothermia. As she tied the cord around her waist, her engagement ring caught in the coarse fabric.

Diamonds glittered like the broken glass. Karen looked down at the stones for a second or two before pulling the ring painfully over her knuckle. If Will no longer wanted to marry her, why should she wear this uncomfortable symbol of his ownership?

Naming him, even in silence, opened the way to a dark cold patch in her mind, but she couldn't deal with it now. Not when she had to do something with the French doors, clear up the mess, put a proper dressing on the cut in her foot, and warm up enough to get back to sleep.

Thick towels and some masking tape should cover the gaps in the glass, Karen thought, and she ought to be able to knock out the last few splinters from the glazing bars without cutting herself again now that she was properly awake.

When she crunched over the broken bits in her sturdy slippers, she saw why the doors had blown open. She hadn't clicked down the catch properly, let alone turned the keys at top and bottom of the frames, as she would once have done. A grim little laugh forced its way out from between her bitten lips.

That was the trouble with being a psychologist. You could never let your own motives alone.

Sometimes analysis helped; more often it made you feel even worse.

Karen had had to fight a long battle with her fears of how marriage might confine her and how Will might try to impose his sometimes weird world-view on her. She'd won, but the victory had been hard. Then yesterday, barely a week after he'd given her the ring, he'd told her he'd changed his mind and didn't want to commit himself. Hurting and angry, she could see any number of reasons why her subconscious might have set up this icy mayhem for her new solitude.

'Freedom,' Karen muttered to herself as she crouched with the dustpan and brush to scoop up all the nuggets, splinters and chips of glass she could find. 'Cleansing cold. Rebirth. Cracking through the barriers. Opening the way to a new life. Destruction. Fury. *Punishment.*'

But who did she want to punish? Will? Or herself? In that moment, she couldn't be sure.

Ten minutes later, standing under the powerful jets of her shower and revelling in the sensation of wet heat melting her gelid skin, she stopped being a psychologist and let go once again. She hadn't cried in front of Will when he'd said he was leaving her. Nor had she sworn at him. She was still glad of that. But now, with the shower washing away the evidence as quickly as it emerged, she tipped back her head and let go. Hot water coursed down over her throat, which still felt tight and sore from the stress of keeping back the words she could never have said to him.

Later, when the water pouring down from the over-sized shower head was cooling and her tears had stopped, she yanked the handle to turn off the flow before it undid all its earlier good work. Her thick towel was warm from the pipes when she hugged it around herself. She even smiled a little as she dragged off the ludicrous plastic shower cap she would never have worn in front of Will, dropping it onto the floor.

If he'd seen it, he'd have pounced at once to pick it up, shake off the water, and fold it away on a shelf. He was a neat-freak, as well as a control-freak.

Is it the control-freakery that drove him away? Karen asked herself as she rubbed the towel across her slim back. Maybe he has to be the strong one, the successful one, the rich one, in any partnership. Maybe he can't bear the thought of owing me anything. Taking's harder than giving for some people, and it needs a lot more grace. Maybe he just hasn't got that grace.

Anger was always easier to bear than vulnerability. Karen felt more like herself as she towelled the last of the water off her long legs, surprised at the way some of last summer's tan was still there, even though it was mid-winter now and she hadn't been out of jeans or thick black tights for months. She should probably moisturize her legs to keep the faint golden colour going, but that would have to wait until tomorrow.

Back in her pyjamas, she shook out her hair and stuffed her feet into the slippers again for safety. She had switched on the electric blanket before she'd showered, so there was more warmth awaiting her under the duvet.

She glanced at the clock and swore. Three-thirty. Only four hours until the alarm woke her again.

She did not get even four hours. Hugging one of Will's pillows and breathing in the fading lemony smell from his skin, she was torn out of sleep, this time by the buzzing of her intercom. Swearing and pushing a tangle of hair out of her mouth, where she must have been chewing it in her sleep, she rolled out from under the duvet and stumbled across the cold floor to pick up the receiver.

'Yes?' she said, letting herself sound tough enough to frighten off any unauthorized caller.

The clock over the kitchen worktop told her it was only

six-thirty. Less than three hours since she'd turned off her light for the second time. No wonder she felt as though she'd been drinking all night, with burning eyes, headache, and a throbbing nausea to add to her sore throat and puffy eyelids.

'Yes?' she said again.

'It's Charlie.' The voice was so familiar and so dangerously welcome that Karen sagged against the wall as though someone had cut her tendons.

The last thing she needed now was an encounter with DCI Charlie Trench of the Hampshire Police Major Crimes Team.

'I need you over on the Island,' he said. 'Buzz me in. I'll brief you while you dress.'

Karen had worked with him several times before, liked him more than she cared to admit, and had come perilously close to the kind of involvement that could have destroyed her peace for ever. And that was before Will had left her.

'Karen.' His Geordie voice was rough with urgency. 'Let me in. This is important.'

'So's my sleep,' she said, fighting all kinds of emotions she hadn't time to sort out.

'Not now it isn't. We've got a body. Bad one. Crucified and castrated. I'm the SIO and I need you. Now buzz me in.'

Karen weakened. Once she knew something of the victim's life and character she would have to fight off all the normal human feelings about what had been done to him, but now all she could think was how well a body killed and violated in such an extreme way could fit into her new research project into post-mortem mutilation. Besides, the case might provide just the kind of distraction she needed to put all her feelings about Will into a virtual box, where they couldn't contaminate her life. And with Charlie as the Senior Investigating Officer, she might even be able to do the work he wanted in a way that suited her own timetable, switching in and out of his inquiry when she had to be somewhere else.

Her cold finger pressed down hard on the door-release button for long enough to admit half a football team. Then she crashed down the receiver, unlocked the door of her flat for Charlie and ran back into her bedroom, planning to pull on jeans, T-shirt and a warm sweater before he arrived. He had five flights to climb if he ignored the lift as usual. That should give her enough time.

Her right foot ached, reminding her of the night's dramas, but the pain was dull enough to reassure her that there was no glass left in her flesh.

'What the hell happened here?' Charlie's deep voice was sharp with shock as he stood in her bedroom doorway. 'You're not . . .'

Karen turned to face him as she zipped up her skinny black jeans and tucked the soft cream T-shirt into them. The unmade bed and her half-dressed state were far too intimate, but Charlie hadn't even noticed. His attention was riveted to the trail of blood that led from the broken window to her bed, where it had broadened into a fair-sized puddle. Who would have thought a smallish cut in a foot could produce so much? Karen had forgotten to wipe it up last night.

'It was the wind, not a human being,' she said and watched his tense face relax.

His dark eyes were very round under the strong eyebrows, and he looked more than ever like a taller thicker version of Robert Downey, Jr.

'Thank fuck,' he said, rubbing both hands over his face and through his spiky dark hair. 'For a minute I thought . . . Never mind. Hurry up.'

'What's so urgent?' she said, bending down to zip up her red ankle boots.

'I told you: I need you,' he said, sounding so impatient that she might have thought he was angry with her if she hadn't known him so well. Before she could do more than look at him, frowning, to work out why he was in such a state this time, he added more calmly: 'It's Sir Dan Blackwater, see. Body found just over an hour ago, lying on the kitchen table, knives driven through his wrists and ankles right into the wood of the table. Like I said, he was castrated.'

'Who found him?' Karen asked, hoping it wasn't the dead man's wife or child. That kind of trauma would be hard to heal.

'Woman called Sheena Greves.' Charlie's voice was unemotional. 'No help at all. Claims she doesn't know anything. Not even what she was doing in his house or what made her go down to the kitchen in her pyjamas at dawn.'

'Sounds like post-traumatic amnesia,' Karen said, even more interested. 'The sight of a body like that could shock anyone's brain into all kinds of self-protective denial. What's her connection with the deceased?'

'Worked for him in London but claims she'd never been to the Island before and doesn't know why she was there this time. Or if he said anything before he died. Or if she heard anything in the night. Or where his wife was, or why there was no one else in the house. You can see how that's all going down.'

'So you want me to assess her condition?' Karen suggested,

pulling on the long soft scarlet cashmere sweater that had been Will's last Christmas present.

Charlie wagged his head from side to side in a way that was so familiar it made her heart drum in her chest.

'And help with the interview.'

'But you've got specially trained officers for that,' Karen protested.

'Yeah. They're good too, but they're not psychologists. I need *your* skills. You'll know how to get round the memory loss – if it's real – or tell us if she's faking. We've got to sort this quick.'

'Quicker than usual? Why?'

Karen was dragging a brush through her hair as they talked, feeling the bristles catch in more tangles than she usually had.

'Don't you know who Sir Dan is?' Charlie sounded surprised, and impatient.

'Businessman?' she said vaguely, much more curious about what had been done to the man – and exactly when and why – than how he might have earned his living.

She finished dealing with her hair and rummaged in her cupboard for the old flying jacket she'd bought from an army surplus shop years ago. It was going to be freezing on the ferry across to the Island, and none of her usual clothes would be warm enough. She reached past them, then felt the hard, cracked leather graze her palm. Pulling out the old jacket, she registered the strong smells of lanolin and petrol and something spicier that was probably no more than ancient dirt. She hadn't worn it for a while because Will had hated its shabbiness and had often begged her to get it dry-cleaned.

Charlie didn't seem to notice the smell, or the shabbiness, as he grabbed it from her and held it out so that she could stuff her arms into the thick sleeves. She realized she hadn't concentrated on his answer and asked her question again.

'Giant of the high street,' he said, the impatience sharpening his voice into an attack. 'Not as big as Philip Green but nearly. To make it worse, he's just agreed to "spearhead the government's new charitable-giving taskforce". Got that now?'

Karen nodded, offering a guilty smile to placate him.

'Great,' Charlie said with all his familiar sarcasm. 'He's also one of the richest men in the county. Powerful. Important. Supporter of a whole bunch of charities himself. Hobnobs with the Prime Minister and all that, which is why he's leading this new quango thingy.'

'Ah, him. Yes. I know who you mean,' Karen said, zipping up the jacket. 'But I still don't understand this extreme rush.'

'Somebody kills a bloke like that and castrates him, we got to find out who quick. Before the press start harassing us and whipping up the public so we lose it and bag some poor inadequate who didn't do it and makes us look like vindictive arseholes. Come on.'

'I can't leave the flat like this.' Karen pointed to the smashed glass in her French windows, where her makeshift repair looked even more pathetically inadequate in daylight than it had in the night. 'Anyone could get in.'

Chapter 2

Day One: 7.00 a.m.

Twenty minutes later Charlie parked on the ferry's almost empty car deck and the two of them climbed the steep companionway to emerge into the freezing wind for the twenty-minute voyage to the Island. However cold it might be, the fresh sea-smelling air was preferable to the stuffiness indoors, scented as it usually was with throat-catching cleaning-fluids.

Karen tugged the flying jacket more tightly around her body and leaned over the rail to stare down at the grey sea. Churned up by low fat waves, it looked uninviting and grubby. The idea that it had ever sparkled in bright sunlight, decorated with the dancing yachts of rich visitors, seemed impossible to believe. Karen raised her head to watch the slowly approaching Island she knew so well.

Through the woods away to the right, she could almost make out the plot of land where her own small house was being built on the site of her late grandmother's shabby bunga-low. It was supposed to be finished by the summer, but the project had taken so long to get this far she couldn't believe the house would ever be ready for her.

Straight ahead was Cowes itself, with its yacht clubs and marinas and sharp boundaries between rich and poor. Charlie had once lived in a flat on the outskirts of the town, with a great view over the Solent towards the green Hampshire country-side. Then he'd been promoted to the Major Incident Teams, which were based on the mainland, and he'd rented a place in Southampton, quite near her flat.

'Tell me the truth about why we're in such a rush.' Karen turned away from the wind as a particularly vicious gust blew her hair across her eyeball, scratching it and making both eyes water. 'And don't pretend it's because the corpse is such a celebrity. It's still not seven o'clock. You could have waited a couple of hours to break into my sleep.'

Charlie turned his back to the wind, too, leaning against the rail with one heel hooked over to the lowest bar.

'It's Eve,' he muttered, not looking at Karen.

'This is Detective Sergeant Eve Clarke, I take it,' Karen said, laughing with real amusement. 'What's she done now?'

A vivid picture shot into her mind of the resentful, scrawny woman, who disliked her so much. Eve was thinner than Karen and had far better legs and was always flaunting both attributes when they were anywhere near each other, unable to believe Karen wasn't interested in the competition.

Charlie glowered. Embarrassment had flicked a little colour across his broad cheekbones. He knew as well as Karen that Eve had some powerful fantasies about him and believed she would make them come true if she could only make him look at her properly.

'What's her part in all this?' Karen added, even more amused to see how much irritation Charlie was trying to suppress. He'd always been loyal, but Eve was enough to test the most patient of colleagues.

'Sheena found the body around 5 a.m. and phoned us.' His voice was clipped, but informative, too, even though he kept leaving out words he thought irrelevant. 'Eve's on nights; responded as the most senior officer around. All doors to Sir Dan's place bolted from the inside. Security alarm on its night setting. No sign of forced entry. No one else in the house. When Sheena unbolts the front door for Eve, she sets off the alarms. Housekeeper has to come up from her cottage to turn 'em off. Whole thing so obvious Eve arrests Sheena, and . . .' Charlie broke off, apparently unable to speak and control his feelings at the same time.

'Started interviewing her?' Karen suggested, knowing all about the strict time limits the police were given to dealing with suspects.

The clock started with the first question asked, however casually. If Eve had set it off before calling in help from the mainland, she'd gone a long way to screwing up the whole process. No wonder Charlie was so irritable.

He caught Karen's sardonic expression and smiled reluctantly. The affectionate light that crept into his black eyes made her stomach contract and she had to look away again for safety.

'She just didn't think,' he said, anger fighting his usual tolerance of Eve. His voice and speech patterns were easing up a little. 'Brought the suspect into an interview room, set the video and recording equipment going, and asked her questions about who'd bolted the front door and when. Makes me want to grab her by her hair and chuck her in the sea. But I can't. Got to make the best of it. Which is why I had to drag you from your bed like this. Lucky Will wasn't with you.'

'I'll do what I can this morning,' Karen said, keeping her professional mask intact with care, 'but after that you're on your own.'

'I told you before we left that I'd get your windows fixed. Hurry up and phone your mate Stella to warn her we'll need the keys, and I'll sort it. You won't even need to be there.'

'I can't disturb Stella till at least eight. But that's not the point. This has nothing to do with my windows. I've got to be somewhere else.'

'Bollocks to that. You're needed here.'

'I'm not employed by the police,' Karen reminded him. 'You call when you need me, and if I have time I'm happy to help. But I've got students . . .'

'Who can wait a day or two,' Charlie said, as though discussing something wholly trivial. 'They usually have to.'

'And the last chunk of my book, which is due to go to the publishers in June, and some research for the next one,' Karen said, hiding from the guilty conscience her students always generated.

She never had quite enough time to give them all the attention they wanted. The thought of the debts they were clocking up to study with her made her conscience even sharper.

'I'll lose my job if I don't publish at regular intervals, and I can't publish if I've nothing to say. I've spent weeks building up a relationship that's just got a result, and I'm due to set off for Norfolk this afternoon. I can't chuck the chance even for you.'

'Relationship with who?'

'Your colleagues in Norfolk caught a particularly interesting serial killer a couple of years back,' Karen said, adding more lightly: 'I've been stalking the Chief Constable for permission to ransack his records and grill his people. He's succumbed at last.'

'I'm not surprised.' Charlie put his big, rough-skinned hands on either side of her cold face for a second, then let her go. 'But he can't have you. Not yet. I need you here.'

'But . . .'

'Shut up, Karen, and . . .' He broke off, his dark-brown eyes losing focus as though he were listening to some interior voice, then they sharpened again. 'No, first tell me, why the Norfolk killer?'

Karen was reluctant to say any more, but she knew Charlie too well to think she could fend off his curiosity for long. He could always tell when she was withholding information – or lying.

'He mutilated the bodies after death,' she said casually, as though the statement could have no possible relevance to this urgent new case. 'I've always been interested in that. Why bother, when you wouldn't get any sadistic satisfaction from the victim's pain? What's the psychology behind that kind of drive? What's the pay-off? Obviously there's the release of some kind of anger, but is it cowardice that makes them wait until their victims are dead? Or conscience? Surely not. If they had any kind of conscience they couldn't kill . . . You can see how much there is here – and how useful it could be. If I can analyse why they do it, then that's going to help your colleagues whenever they're faced with a body mutilated after death. I can point them towards the likeliest suspects. Well, the likeliest kind of suspects.'

Charlie's face looked as though he'd been fattened on satisfaction, even though he'd obviously stopped listening long before she got to the end of her explanation. 'First impressions say Sir Dan's killer did the castrating and crucifying after death, so you'll get a hot fresh case instead of cold records. Hang with me, and you'll get everything you ever wanted. You'll be closer to your students, too.'

The ferry hooted; its deep roar lifted Karen's spirits a little. What he'd said was true enough. So long as she could phone the chief constable in East Anglia and explain, she shouldn't lose anything too important. She'd have to cancel the B&B she'd booked, of course, and that would mean writing off her £25 deposit. Not much to most people maybe, but every pound counted for her now that she'd taken on huge debts to buy the land for her new house and have it built. Maybe she could charge the deposit to Charlie's investigation.

'You have got enough in the budget to pay me, I trust,' she said, following him down the companionway to the car deck. 'I can't afford to do *pro bono* work any longer, even to raise my profile or help my research.'

'I can pay,' he said, without looking at her.

Thinking of the money she owed made her grateful she wasn't taking her own car to the Island. The ferry charges had always seemed extortionate. Once her little wooden house was ready, she would probably have to keep a beat-up old banger over there and travel as a foot-passenger until they finally got round to building a bridge across the Solent.

One of the tattooed deck hands waved them forwards and

Charlie's quiet dark-grey car rolled off the ferry ahead of the small queue that had built up behind it.

Eve was nowhere to be seen when they walked into the old police station in East Cowes. The desk sergeant's face lit when he saw Charlie and he leaned across the counter to wring his hand.

'Great to see you, boss. You here for Sheena Greves?'

'That's right. Along with Doctor Taylor here. I'm the SIO this time. Can you tell DS Clarke?'

'Will do. I'll buzz you in, and get her up out of custody to the interview room, soon as you're ready to start.'

The automatic lock clicked open on the door between the public and official parts of the building and Charlie pushed through, leaning against it to allow Karen to walk past him. The space was too narrow for comfort and she caught the familiar smell of the Pears soap he always used and something more exotic that might be rosemary shaving oil. His breathing changed and she could feel herself responding. You're at work, she told herself furiously, speeding up to get properly past him and focus on the coming interview.

'I'll let you talk to her alone,' he said from behind Karen, before reaching over her shoulder to shove open the next door. The leather sleeve of his jacket brushed her cheek. 'That way you'll get a better feel for her state than if she's being scared off by a cop. OK?'

'Fine.' Karen took off her own jacket and hung it over the back of one of the bentwood chairs to the right of the table. She pointed towards the recording equipment. 'Presumably I don't have to tape this session?'

'Yup, you do. Everything better be on record. That way no wanking defence brief can cause trouble. Don't fret, I'll set it up before I leave you to it. You'll be on camera, too.'

'What will you do?' Karen asked and saw his face tighten. She assumed he was planning what he'd say to Eve.

The door opened again and a uniformed constable brought in a woman of about Karen's own age of thirty-six. She was considerably shorter than Karen, though, and must have weighed a good twelve pounds more. Her face was strong and square, although one cheek had an ugly pink mark, as though she had been lying on her side with her skin pressed into some harsh fabric. Her black wide-legged trousers and loose camel-coloured woollen top were creased too, but they hadn't come from any high street store like the kind Sir Dan had owned.

Karen was surprised the woman was still wearing her own clothes. Surely Eve would have been professional enough to take any suspect's clothes for scientific testing, even if she had been careless enough to start the questioning too soon.

Filing her own question for later, Karen stood up to introduce herself to Sheena and offer her hand for shaking. The other woman touched it briefly with a palm that was damp and cold.

'I'm DCI Trench,' Charlie said in his kindest voice, which surprised Karen. 'And I've asked Doctor Taylor here, who is a psychologist, to talk to you to see if she can help you with your memory problems. She won't be interviewing you about Sir Dan's death, and you'll be alone with her. If at any time you want to stop the discussion, all you have to do is say so. She'll call the officer and he can take you back downstairs. OK?'

The woman turned to peer into his face. After a while, she

sighed as though something had reassured her, and nodded. Her unbrushed brown hair swung across the stain on her face.

'Sit down now,' Charlie said, looking over her head towards Karen with his eyebrows raised, clearly asking whether she felt comfortable enough for him to leave.

She nodded. He walked out without looking at her again. The click of the closing door sounded very loud, but it released Sheena Greves from her submissive expression and she faced Karen, revealing hazel eyes and long, thick, dark lashes. Blobs of yesterday's mascara clung to them and smears of it marked the skin, but her eyes were clear and intelligent.

'Where do you want to start?' she asked in a voice that suggested she came originally from the East End of London but had worked to make her accent softer, less identifiable.

'Maybe you could tell me who you are?' Karen said, with a warm smile. 'That's usually the easiest way into a blocked memory.'

'You know my name. I'm Sheena Greves. I am . . .' She stopped, clenching the muscles under her eyes for a second, as though she had a sharp headache as well as everything else. 'I was Sir Dan's personal press officer.'

'I don't understand,' Karen said, careful to put herself in an unfrightening and subordinate position. 'What do you mean by "personal press officer"?'

Sheena's lips twitched in a gesture that suggested impatience rather than amusement or politeness. 'He has other people who deal with the media over his work and over his and his wife's charities. My job is to manage his personal profile and field press enquiries that have nothing to do with his professional life or the actual work his charities do.'

'Right. I see now. Thank you.' Karen wondered whether the
job description included any more intimate contact with Sir
Dan. Something about the possessive confidence with which
Sheena had talked about fielding the press enquiries suggested
a closer link. If there had been anything, her shock at seeing
what had been done to his body would have been even more
acute. 'How long had you worked for him?'

'This is all on record,' Sheena said, still impatient. 'Why
d'you need to ask me?'

'I don't have access to any records,' Karen said in a peace-
making tone. 'And I'm here to see if I can help you remember.
Talking about yourself may be a useful way in to whatever is
blocking you.'

'Sorry.' Sheena's shoulders lifted under the camel wool. 'I
started working for him, in the main PR office, nearly seven
years ago. Then he gave me this new job about a year after that.'

'Is it just you in the personal PR office?'

'No. I have a secretary these days.'

'So you're quite senior,' Karen said, letting admiration seep
into her voice.

'That's right.'

'Which means Sir Dan must have relied on you. Trusted
you, too.'

A hint of colour warmed Sheena's cheeks for a second. As
she brushed back her hair, Karen could see that when she was
not in a state of shocked distress she must be quite attractive.

'Did you often come to see him here on the Island?'

'Never.' Sheena lowered her head again and began to pick at
her cuticles. The nails themselves were well kept, Karen saw,
neatly shaped and unvarnished. 'That's why I don't know what

I'm doing here. You see, I . . . can't . . . I can't remember getting here or deciding to come here, or anything. All I know is that I was standing in that huge kitchen, staring at . . . at his dead body.' Tears welled in her eyes.

Karen felt her own ache in sympathy. It was easy to imagine how you'd feel if you'd had to look down at a stranger lying naked and castrated, spread-eagled on his kitchen table with sharp knives through his wrists and ankles. If it was a friend or lover . . .

'What did you do then?' Karen asked, pushing her own feelings out of the way.

'I looked round for a phone. There was one on the worktop – on its docking station. I grabbed it, then dropped it because my hands were so sweaty. I felt sick when I bent down to pick it up. I can remember all that, you see. I was silly too – you know, stupid. I couldn't remember how to get a dialling tone. Then I did and I phoned 999 for the police. They told me to wait where I was, so I did. Till I heard them banging on the door.'

'Right,' Karen said. 'This is great. Do you remember anything about the hours before you got to the kitchen this morning? Were you in his house last night?'

'I must've been, mustn't I? That policewoman said *all* the doors were bolted from the inside. The security alarm was on its night setting, too. Someone must've locked me in and set up the alarm. But I can't remember anything. And they haven't found anybody else in the house, so I don't understand how it can've happened. I don't . . . I can't see why . . . Oh, you know.'

'Could it have been Sir Dan's wife?' Karen suggested. 'She's the natural person, isn't she?'

Sheena's face paled. 'Olga? No. It couldn't have been. The

officers wouldn't have missed *her*. She's not the kind of woman you could overlook.'

'OK. So tell me what happened when you heard the police banging on the door.'

'I ran out of the kitchen and unbolted the front door to let them in, and all the alarms went off. I screamed when the noise started. It was such a shock. I didn't expect it. You could've heard the alarms in Cowes, I should think, but still nobody else appeared inside the house. And when the police looked, they couldn't find anybody. Not anybody, anywhere in the house. I can't understand how . . .'

'Had you been sleeping there?' Karen asked, filing away for later a question about why a man as rich and powerful as Sir Dan would have had no staff living in the house. It seemed unlikely from the little she knew of the super-rich.

'I don't know.' Sheena sounded defeated rather than obstructive.

'What were you wearing when the police came?'

'Pyjamas,' Sheena said quickly, as though she was glad to be able to help with something. 'Not mine. Striped cotton. You know, superfine cotton. Thick, expensive. From Turnbull & Asser. With the bottom of the legs rolled up. I don't remember ever seeing them before. The police told me to change into something else, and they took the pyjamas away.'

'Were they his, the pyjamas? Sir Dan's? Had you borrowed them?'

Sheena shook her head, looking agonized for a second. 'I don't know.'

'All right. Forget the pyjamas for the moment. Whereabouts were you in the house when you phoned the police?'

'In the kitchen.' Sheena's voice was shaking and very quiet. She looked as though forcing the words up through her throat hurt her physically. 'I already told you: I was standing in the kitchen. Bare feet. They were cold. It's a tiled floor. Quarry tiles, I think. Dark red anyway.'

'Great.' Karen noted the fact that Sheena's story was consistent in its details, even when she was answering a differently phrased question. 'You're doing really well. What could you see?'

'Dan . . . He was . . . I can't.' Her voice rose and lengthened into a wail.

Karen waited. Sheena covered her face with both hands and gave in to tears. Her shoulders heaved.

'You can't what?' Karen said, after a pause, fighting her sympathy. She knew just how those tears felt. 'Can't remember? Or can't tell me what you remember?'

'I can't do this.' Sheena pulled her hands away from her face, disfigured with tears and snot.

The distress was clearly genuine. But Karen was still not sure about the memory loss: Sheena's story seemed too coherent in spite of its artful gaps, and rather too convenient, to be real.

'That inspector said you wouldn't ask me about the crime and I could stop at any time,' Sheena added. 'I want to stop now.'

'Are you sure?' Karen let a little steel into her manner. 'Giving yourself permission to tell me what you remember seeing might help you.'

'No.'

'If you fight it, you could be storing up all kinds of trouble for yourself in the future,' Karen said. 'I've heard a little of what it was you saw in that kitchen and I can understand how horrific the mental pictures must be. But if you hide from them, they will do the emotional equivalent of festering, and you may . . .'

'He said I could stop at any time and that you'd get me taken back to my cell. I want that now.'

'Well?' Charlie said when they were alone again. 'What do you think?'

Karen grimaced. 'It's definitely not organic amnesia, i.e. anything to do with the physical brain. There's no damage there. She knows precisely who she is and if there were organic memory loss it's unlikely that she would. It is possible she's suffering from functional amnesia, which is relatively common in cases of violent crime. Purely psychological in origin, and often designed as a defence mechanism.'

'From the shock of finding Sir Dan's body?' Charlie asked in a way that suggested he wanted Sheena to be innocent, which was one of his most engaging habits whenever he was faced with a new suspect.

'It could be,' Karen said, with some pity because she thought this time his target was more complicated than he believed. 'But there are plenty of cases in the literature of people who can't allow themselves to believe they're capable of perpetrating any violence, which means their minds won't allow them to remember what they did.'

'So they're faking memory loss?'

'No more than people suffering psychosomatic illness are faking that,' Karen said patiently. She was fairly sure Charlie was ensuring that he had all the information he might need in the future. She could see the machine was still recording, so she kept her voice cool and informative. 'The symptoms are real, but they're caused by psychological factors, not infections, viruses, or any kind of organic damage.'

Charlie reached across to switch off the machine.

'Bugger,' he said with such feeling that she looked at him with sharp curiosity.

'Do you know her?' Karen asked, feeling her way. 'Had you met her before?'

He shook his head, then grinned like a shamefaced school-boy. 'I don't want Eve to have the satisfaction of getting this right. She exceeded her authority, and . . . you know how she sometimes thinks she owns me?'

'I do,' Karen couldn't resist touching his hand, just above the point where his over-large watchstrap hung over the bumpy bone in his wrist. Her fingertip felt more sensitive than usual and she withdrew it with regret. 'But I don't think you'll cure her fixation like this. You'll have to take it head on and tell her you'll never be what she wants.'

His thick eyebrows twitched and his lips turned inwards, whitening as he pressed them together to display his absolute determination not to comment. Whether it was a subconscious message driven by his loyalty to Eve or a straightforward dislike of being touched in such a public place, Karen accepted it and went back to work.

'What Sheena saw this morning was clearly horrifying and, given how closely she'd worked with the man, there could be bereavement in the mix as well as horror. I also think they might have been more than employer and employee. But . . . '

Charlie watched her with a wary expression in his eyes. 'But what?'

'The functional amnesia might have been caused by the shock of seeing the body, or by her inability to admit that she had killed him. But it could also have been caused by something that happened before the crime. He could have shown her something – or told her something – that was so traumatizing she went into a kind of fugue state, from which she emerged only at the point when she focused on the body and called 999. Was there blood on the pyjamas she was wearing?'

'Not visible to the naked eye. They're on their way to the lab now in case there are microscopic traces. Can I safely interview her in this state?'

'I'd have thought so, yes,' Karen said. 'She's in control, functioning, articulate, and shows no sign of confusion or other-than-expected distress. But she'll need a lawyer.'

'No,' Charlie said in a tone of mock amazement. 'I'd never have thought of that.'

'Sorry.' Karen met his laughing eyes and smiled back at him.

Another of his endearing habits was the way he sometimes implied she was in charge while she was working for him. Her particular speciality was giving evidence in court about the psychology of defendants or witnesses, but Charlie had come to respect her ability to pinpoint behavioural markers in his suspects and to interpret the evidence their actions had left on the spaces where they had lived or worked.

He often made her feel that the success of any investigation hung on her skills, while she knew perfectly well that he and his team carried out a clearly planned and minute examination of all kinds of evidence she never got to see. She assumed he gave everyone in his team the same feeling that they were the key to his success, which probably explained why he got such consistently good results. You didn't get made SIO on the murder of a man with a profile like Sir Dan Blackwater's if you'd had many failures.

'I know you've investigated even more murders than I've had student essays to mark,' she added with real affection. 'I get carried away sometimes.'

'D'you want to sit in on the interviews? I made Eve call for the duty solicitor. Sheena says she doesn't know of any lawyers and doesn't want to phone anyone else.'

'Which doesn't sound much like someone who came here to commit a premeditated crime, does it?' Karen said. 'Which suggests the amnesia might *not* be faked.'

'Don't ask me. You know I can't see into anyone's mind. Even my own. Specially my own.' Charlie brought his hands out from behind his back and handed her a pile of photographs. 'You'd better look at these. The printouts just came through.'

From the little he had already told her, Karen knew more or less what to expect, but the reality was hard to face. Even in black and white, these pictures would have been shocking. In full colour, they were stomach-churning.

But this was Karen's job. If she were ever to finish her current research paper on the motives for post-mortem mutilation, she would have to look at others that were worse.

Sir Dan had been a big man, barrel-chested and slim-hipped. His beak of a nose jutted up from a well-defined face, and the thick mass of hair still had some gold strands among the grey. The curls on his chest and between his legs were the same. He must have looked magnificent in life. A strange, bruise-like mark crossed the centre of his stomach in an almost straight line.

'Well?' Charlie said again, when he had grown bored waiting for her to comment.

'Could she have done it physically?' Karen asked, pointing to the big, black-bladed chef's knives that pinioned him to the table. 'This must have taken a lot of force. I've tried to cut through a duck carcase with knives like these and had to use a mallet to get through the cartilage. To hammer knives right through a man's wrists and ankles and into the wood of the table is going to need a lot of strength. Where's the . . . the rest?'

Charlie's lips relaxed, as though he was amused by her reluctance to name the body parts. 'In the kitchen bin,' he said, handing her another photograph.

The lid of the expensive heavy stainless-steel rubbish bin had been propped open for the photographer. Nestling on a pile of packaging, two wine corks, a clutch of broken eggshells and some cheese rinds were Sir Dan's hacked-off penis and testicles, along with the knife that must have been used: a heavy, serrated bread knife from the same range as the chef's knives.

'Presumably that's gone for finger-printing,' Karen said, pointing.

'Of course. The CSIs are doing their thing right now. But look there.' Charlie's blunt finger, with its badly cut short nail, rested on a small muddle of cream-coloured material. 'Gloves. Rubber gloves.'

'DNA from the inside? Sweat?' Karen suggested.

'Who'd be stupid enough to chuck those in a bin so close to the victim? I bet this killer was double-gloved. We're checking, obviously.'

'So you think it's a set-up?' Karen said and watched his shoulders rise up to his neat ears.

She'd never noticed how small they were. Now she couldn't see anything else, remembering an article she'd once read that suggested ears with tiny lobes were the mark of a psychopath. She hadn't believed it then; she didn't believe it now. But his ears were amazingly small.

'How do I know?' Sounds of an arrival outside made him turn his head. 'If this is the duty brief we can get going.'

Chapter 3

Day One: 8.30 a.m.

'What are *you* doing here?' Eve's voice was harsher than ever, and there was a hint of a whine behind the anger. 'Charlie said the other day that you're getting married. I'd have thought you'd be concentrating on your wedding plans.'

Karen slipped her left hand into the pocket of her jeans. She didn't want Eve to see the naked ring finger, with its tell-tale dent where Will's diamonds had once gripped her.

'He needed a forensic psychologist,' Karen said, determined not to join in with any of Eve's games. 'And I was available. When's the rest of his team arriving?'

Eve shrugged one thin shoulder and yanked the thin, dry red hair she'd pushed behind her ear. 'Nothing to do with me. I'll be off duty in another hour.' She must have realized how pettish she sounded because she added in a more adult tone: 'They're getting the first floor ready for his incident room now. You . . .'

Karen's phone rang, which made Eve sigh heavily. Karen offered an apologetic smile, then looked down at the screen to see the name of Stella Atkins, her best friend, the architect in charge of her new little wooden house on the Island, and the holder of the keys to her Southampton flat.

'Hi,' Karen said into the phone, smiling. 'What are you doing up so early? I was going to ring you, but thought I'd better wait. I know how you love your sleep.'

'Why? Something the matter?' Stella's voice sounded different, as though speaking took less physical effort than usual.

Karen quickly explained about her broken windows and heard Stella's instant offer to meet Charlie's emergency glaziers with the keys or do anything else that might help, adding: 'I'm in an unbelievably good mood today.'

'I can tell.' Karen's smile widened and her own voice relaxed. She heard Eve's sharp intake of breath and took in the implied criticism without doing anything about it. 'What's up, Stella?'

'Heaven,' she sang. 'I'm in . . . you know.'

'Work or play?'

'Real life. My bloody mother will never believe it.'

'So who is he?' Karen said, remembering all the confidences Stella had offered over the years about the way her mother taunted her with her lack of success with men.

She'd had a string of relationships, none of which had either satisfied her or lasted very long. Karen's private view was that Stella shared her own terror of being in someone else's power, so that the moment any of her blokes had started to trespass on her private space she lost interest in them.

'Everything my mother has always told me I'll never get because I'm so "squat and freckly",' Stella said in a lilting voice. 'Clever and funny. Good-looking. Even rich. Well, richer than any academic like us. He's in insurance. But respectable. Shipping insurance. Big stuff. Seriously yummy.'

Yummy, Karen thought with a smile. Who'd have thought any forty-year-old professor of architecture would use a word like that – or still be at the mercy of her jealous mother's taunting?

'Fantastic!' Karen said aloud, hoping she sounded as enthusiastic as she felt. 'I'm really pleased. How long's it been going on? And why have you kept him so quiet?'

A movement to one side caught her eye and she turned to see the door of the interview room opening.

'I wanted to be sure,' Stella was saying, 'before I let you see him. But I am now. So can we fix up a foursome with you and Will and go somewhere really nice to eat?'

'Can I phone you back?' Karen said, relieved to see Charlie beckon so that she wouldn't have to explain about Will quite yet. 'I've got to go.'

'OK.' Stella's voice had deflated and sounded much more normal. 'Where . . . ?'

'I'm at work, Stella. Sorry.' Karen clicked off the call, flipped the phone shut and stuffed it in her pocket, before scribbling Stella's number on a piece of paper from her bag. 'Here's Stella's number, Charlie. She's happy to deal with your glaziers. In the meantime, I'm all yours.'

He held open the door for her, completely ignoring Eve. Karen listened to the clatter of her high heels as she hurried down the long corridor to the outside world.

Charlie announced Karen's arrival to the tape while she smiled first at the solicitor, a young man wearing a cheap suit, greyish cream polyester shirt and over-bright tie, and then at Sheena. She nodded back, as though they were old acquaintances rather than the enemies they had seemed only half an hour ago. Someone had lent her a comb and she'd made good use of it. Her messy hair had been reduced to something much sleeker.

'Now, Ms Greves, can you describe everything you can remember from this morning?' Charlie said.

In a voice that sounded heavy with boredom, Sheena repeated everything she had said to Karen, almost word for word, right down to the dark-red colour of the quarry tiles on the kitchen floor, and dropping the phone from her sweaty hand and feeling sick as she picked it up.

'What was your relationship with Sir Dan? You were more than his private PR, weren't you?' Charlie said.

Karen noticed the solicitor's quick interest. She was impressed with the way Charlie had picked up her hint and made his question sound as though he knew what the answer was going to be. Or did he actually have information he hadn't shared with her?

Sheena reached for the mug of tea someone had made for her and choked down a mouthful, wiping the back of her hand under her lower lip a moment later. Then she shrugged and pulled at the neck of her camel cashmere top. The pink mark on her face was fading.

'You obviously know, so why deny it?' she said in a voice equally full of tiredness and resentment. 'But I promised him I'd never . . .'

'Never what?' Charlie said, still with all the kindliness that had so surprised Karen.

'That I'd never tell anyone, or suggest I ever saw him in a non-work context, or come here. This place, the Isle of Wight, was always off limits,' she said a little more easily. 'I was part

of his London life. This is where Olga lives when she's in the
UK. Dan and I agreed it all. It was the deal. I never broke it
till now.'

'Olga?' Charlie said, glancing at the solicitor, who looked
curious but waited for his client to give the answer.

'Dan's wife,' Sheena said with a brisk practicality that offered
no clue to her feelings about the woman.

'Did . . . ?' Karen began, then realized she should have
asked Charlie's permission before doing anything more than
observing his interview. He gave her a brief nod, which she
took to be general permission to ask questions. 'Did Olga
know about you?'

Sheena's hazel eyes welled. 'I don't know. We always
tried . . .' She looked at Charlie with a pleading expression and
pushed her fingers through her mousy hair. 'I don't know how
much of it all you know, but Olga's not well. She hates London
and all the . . . you know, the stuff about being such an influ-
ential man's wife, all the entertaining and so on. Can't cope. So
she spends most weeks in Switzerland and comes back here
two weekends a month, while he goes there for the other two.
She knows I've always acted as his hostess at official parties he
held, and accompanied him to other people's receptions; like a
kind-of paid consort. She never minded that, and there was
never any secret about it.'

'What was secret?' Karen asked, fairly sure but needing
confirmation.

The other woman sat straighter, and her hands rose to
smooth her hair down again and then rub one finger along
each of her eyebrows. In its way it was an impressive perform-
ance. After only a few moments, she had ceased to look like the

victim of a disaster and was projecting an air of confidence and something Karen could only think of as authority.

'That I loved him. And he me. And how if she hadn't been so fragile, he would have divorced her and we'd have been married in the ordinary way.'

'How long . . . ?' Charlie asked.

'Over five years,' Sheena said, her voice low and warm. 'At first, it was just what he told her: I acted as his hostess at receptions and stuff. Then . . .' She blinked away tears. 'Then it was more.'

'And were you happy with the arrangement?' Karen asked. 'Made to keep away from his home and friends – his real life – always hiding the truth about your relationship?'

'There wasn't any option.' Sheena didn't seem resentful, which amazed Karen. 'Dan couldn't leave Olga; not when she needed him so much. If he had . . . or if I'd made any kind of fuss, or confronted her or anything like that, she might have had another breakdown. The last was nearly catastrophic. She tried to kill herself, you see. He couldn't have lived with himself, if we'd . . . I mean, if she'd . . . You know.'

'When was the first breakdown?' Karen asked.

Sheena's eyes looked vague. 'A while ago. Maybe six or seven years. Anyway, before he and I . . .'

Bastard, Karen thought, sitting back in her chair. Most of her sympathy over his appalling death had been overtaken by dislike. So he wasn't just a magnificent-looking man with a wildly successful business and an international reputation, she told herself, but an exploitative bastard, who kept this much-younger woman besotted and on a string. Second place. Subordinate.

Could the trauma that had sent Sheena into a temporary fugue state have come from something Sir Dan said that exposed the full meanness of what he'd done to her?

'Doctor Taylor?' Charlie's voice, sharper now, brought Karen back to the present.

She told herself to forget the way Will had first begged her to marry him and then dumped her so soon after she'd given in. Knowing she mustn't let anger fog her mind, she breathed with deliberate care, expanding her ribs, and felt more in control of her own reactions.

'So why did you come to the Island this time?' she asked and watched Sheena glance briefly towards the recording machine, then up towards the right-hand corner of the room, before scratching her neck and staring down at her own knees.

'I don't know,' she said, mumbling a little. 'That's what I don't remember.'

'What is the last thing you *do* remember?' Karen wanted to know what had so interested Sheena in the top corner of the room, but she'd have to wait to find out.

'I was at home, watching television,' Sheena said.

'Where's home?' Charlie asked, as though he wanted to regain command of the session.

'Spitalfields. You know, in east London. I have . . .' Sheena was blinking again. 'Dan bought us a weaver's house. Early eighteenth century. In Wilkes Street. Really beautiful and incredibly light. It wasn't just mine. It was *our* home. Together.'

Karen watched her with as much calculation as pity, then said: 'And did you really feel that he was at home with you when he was there?'

Sheena's face contracted as she frowned. 'What d'you mean?'

'When the two of you were there together, did you feel you were playing a role? Kind of acting as his wife. Or did you feel you were part of a genuinely equal relationship?'

The frown didn't shift. Karen couldn't be sure whether it was supposed to convey puzzlement or anger.

'When he was with me during the week, he was with me,' Sheena said at last. She looked as though she was trying to find words simple enough for an alien to understand. 'He loved me.'

Karen thought for a moment, then asked casually: 'Who did the washing up when you ate together?'

'Me, of course.'

QED, Karen thought, carefully not looking at Charlie. She didn't want Sheena to think the two of them were conspirators, ganging up on her.

'And I loved him,' Sheena added, clearly understanding exactly what Karen was thinking. 'I'd have ironed his shirts too, if he'd let me. But he never did. He worked so hard, you see, and he had so much to worry him, that I'd have done anything I could to make his life even a tiny bit easier. He was always so tired when he was free of work commitments and receptions and things that he liked us to be in bed by half ten. I'd wash up after dinner, while he had a bath, and then I'd join him. We . . .' Her eyes filled again and she looked away.

'Did you fight?' Charlie's Northumbrian accent could sound harsh, but now it was soft and inviting.

'No,' Sheena whispered. 'Never. There was never any need.'

'Because you never challenged him?' Karen suggested. 'Or disagreed with him? Or disappointed him? Or asked for something he didn't want to give you?'

Sheena sat up and looked first at Karen, then at Charlie, then back at Karen again. She looked dignified and in command. 'You're misjudging him, Doctor Taylor. I never asked him for anything because I never had to. He loved me, and he gave me things I never even knew I wanted before he showed them to me. He would have given me the whole world if it could have been bought.'

'He wouldn't divorce his wife for you.' Karen knew she sounded unkind, but her job was to get at the truth for Charlie, not to comfort this woman, however terrible her recent experience.

'I've told you why.' Sheena's dignity was unshaken. 'I would have loved him less if he had been capable of doing that much damage to an already damaged woman.'

So much love, Karen thought, with a certain amount of envy muddling her other feelings; and how much self-deception? If self-deception made you happy, was clear-eyed unhappiness really so much better?

'Yet you broke his rule yesterday and came to the Island,' Karen said, pushing at the only inconsistency she had been shown. 'Why?'

Sheena met her gaze with eyes that did not waver or well with tears. 'I told you: I don't remember.'

Outside the interview room, Charlie gripped Karen's elbow so hard she was afraid for her bones.

'Careful,' she said, 'I do break, you know.'

'Sorry.' He grimaced like a small boy in trouble and let her go. 'I never did know my own strength. Come upstairs.'

They walked up to the empty, stale-smelling incident room in silence. Computers had already been set up on the scarred tables, and empty litter bins stood like miniature sentries beside each one. Once Charlie's team arrived from the mainland, the whole room would be full of noise and movement, coffee cups and screwed-up balls of waste paper. Now it looked sad: waiting and pointless.

He kicked the door shut behind them and pulled a couple of chairs out from under one of the tables.

'Sit. And tell me: did she do it?'

Karen resisted the temptation to shrug. How could she know yet?

'I'm still worried about the physical force she'd have had to use,' she said aloud. 'And on the face of it, she doesn't look a likely prospect, but there have been plenty of intelligent, pleasant, and attractive female killers. As you know perfectly well. Until we know why she came, and what he said to her when she came, I can't tell you any more. Except . . .'

Karen saw Charlie's arm reaching out towards her. Mindful of her aching elbow, she moved her chair backwards and said quickly: 'Except I don't think this is her first time as a suspect in a police station.'

Charlie let his hand fall to his side. 'What?'

Karen analysed her instinctive reaction and said slowly: 'I think she's faced this kind of interview before.'

'Why?'

'For one thing, she kept looking up at the ceiling, as though she expected to see a video camera there. For another, she was taking it all so calmly. Think of the way she admitted to being Sir Dan's lover: most people facing a murder charge are silent, or aggressive, or gobbling out words as though the more they say the more they'll display their innocence.'

Charlie gave her a quick nod, admitting he knew what she meant, this far anyway.

'Think about it,' she added, encouraged. 'Have you ever interviewed a murder suspect who talked as though she were in a board meeting? She gave up the information about their relationship because she knew it wouldn't be hard for you to find it. This way she was in control. I'm sure she's done this before.'

'Which makes her what? Unlucky? Or a serial killer?'

Karen smiled. 'You tell me. You must have someone accessing the PNC for her background. And all the post-Soham Impact stuff,' she said, referring to the information-sharing systems that had been set up after the murder of two young girls in East Anglia. 'Funding for that hasn't been cut yet, has it?'

'Not yet. Almost.'

'Great. Now, I need coffee. You get me the answers, and I'll . . .'

'Eve's got a kettle and some coffee downstairs. They'll make you some if she's already gone off duty.'

Karen was a connoisseur and never drank anything freeze-dried or powdered if she could help it.

'I'll nip out and get some. What d'you want? A latte?'

Charlie shrugged. Over to me, Karen thought. Fine.

Will turned over in his sleep, waking himself as his broken leg drove pain shooting up his spine. The bones had begun to heal, but the damage done to the soft tissues and to the distorted joints would take a long time yet. He stopped himself from groaning, then remembered he was alone and let the pain out in a long ugly grunt. There was no Karen to disturb. He could give himself the luxury of showing what he felt, just for a second or two. A knot in the muscles below his shoulders loosened and he found a way to turn on his back without pain screeching through his brain.

One day all this would be gone and he would be himself again. He wasn't a hysteric. He knew he would mend. He was doing everything his physios wanted. But the process was a lot harder than he'd expected, in every way, and it was taking much longer than he'd planned.

He did his best to shut out all thought of Karen. He shouldn't have let her make love to him the other night. He'd known even then that he'd have to break off their engagement. He should have admitted it straight away, instead of trying to pretend he was going to stay with her. But he'd had enough to do controlling the pain as she moved over him.

The sight of her face when he had told her he was leaving was even more painful, as was the knowledge that she was still hurting. He could feel that now, as clearly as if it were his own emotion. He was sorry, but he couldn't do anything about it. He hadn't the strength to cope with anyone else while he was in this state. Karen was a psychologist: she'd understand.

She would. In time, she would see why he'd had to leave her and she would accept it. He had more than enough faith in her to be sure of that. Then the hurt would go for her, too, and she'd be able to remake her life. In the meantime, he just had to keep her out of his mind, cut the links, so that he didn't have this weird sensation that he was monitoring her feelings at long range. Otherwise he'd go mad.

Light was seeping around the edges of his bedroom blinds. It was time to get up. The prospect was daunting but he had to do it. He got his mind in order, then began the roll that would eventually get him off his mattress. As soon as he was on his feet, he would start the whole laborious business of dressing and shaving. In pain he might be, but he wasn't going to loaf around in stubble, pyjamas and dressing gown, swallowing analgesics, just because it would be easier. That was a recipe for self-pity and mess: everything he most hated.

The old-fashioned Italian café produced a better cup of coffee than anything Karen could have bought from one of the modern chains. She sat on an uncomfortable wooden chair, sipping her double espresso, revelling in the complex scent as well as the kick it gave her and the almost chocolatey taste behind its bitterness. Her heart beat faster and she felt her brain firing more effectively, like a tuned-up engine. Tempted to order another to take away, she drained her cup and stood up to pay for that and the latte she'd ordered for Charlie.

The moment she walked back into the incident room, she knew he'd found something, but he made her wait for it. He thanked her elaborately for the coffee and made a great show of taking off the plastic lid and licking its inside before flicking it into the bin.

'Come on,' she said, half-amused and half impatient. 'What've you found?'

'Four years ago, she had a child: a boy. He suffocated at three months old and she was charged, tried, and . . .'

'Exonerated.' Karen couldn't wait any longer. 'Or she'd be in prison. Sir Dan's son?'

'That was never established,' Charlie said. 'Although . . .'

'Four years ago was soon after he bought her the house in Spitalfields, wasn't it?' Karen said.

'Yeah. Paid for her lawyers, too. Best money can buy. Cleverly picked: a woman QC best known for *prosecuting* child abusers, with a hunky young bloke for her junior. The jury loved them, and Sheena.'

'So she got off.'

'Went back to her old job with Sir Dan two months later. Makes you think, doesn't it?'

Karen nodded and felt her hair swing forwards over her face. She pulled it back, twirling it up into a topknot, which she released at once.

'Especially when you remember she said she didn't know any lawyers. Or maybe that was just to add verisimilitude to faked amnesia.' Karen licked her lips and felt them smart. The cracks she'd made as she bit them last night hadn't had time to heal yet. For a moment she had forgotten Will.

'What did he say to her when she got to the house yesterday?' she asked.

'No idea.' Charlie was looking cross again.

'Haven't you got the CCTV films yet? If he's that rich he must have a good security system at the house.' Karen didn't think she should have had to explain anything so obvious.

'They're on their way.'

'Good. We need to see them before we talk to Sheena again.'

'We?' Charlie repeated with a wicked glint in his black eyes. 'You mean you're in? You're dumping Norfolk for me?'

Karen felt an answering smile stretch the tight muscles around her mouth as she recognized how neatly he had manipulated her. 'Sod off, you cocky bugger,' she said.

'Which means "yes", yes?'

Karen nodded and Charlie grabbed her hand with both of

his, making her wince again. He let her go and reached for the phone. But it rang before he could make his own call. Karen turned away to give him some privacy, walking over to the windows to stare out above the other buildings towards the clustered masts of the yachts at the marina.

'It's started already.' Charlie's voice made her turn, eyebrows raised to invite him to say more. 'That was the ACC. Number Ten's been on the phone.'

'The Prime Minister is bullying your Assistant Chief Constable about this case already?' Karen looked down at her watch. 'Sir Dan's only been dead a few hours.'

'Not bullying,' Charlie said. 'Offering help. Anything we need. Christ! Talk about pressure.'

Chapter 4

Day One: 10.30 a.m.

The sight of Sir Dan in life was shocking after the photographs of his corpse. Karen watched the amazingly clear, full-colour pictures on the security film in awe. Standing under the grandiose portico of his big white house, he was as she'd imagined him: magnificent and powerful. Even in this short footage it was clear he'd had charm as well as force. The smile that lit his face as he looked down at his visitor showed surprise, but there was a lot of delighted welcome too, and his arms stretched out towards her.

Sheena's facial expression was equally clear on a separate film, recorded by a differently angled camera. She looked impeccably dressed, with perfectly smooth hair in spite of the rain, but very anxious. She had with her a big umbrella, a small trolley suitcase and a neat, expensive-looking handbag. She'd obviously come to stay.

Karen wheeled back through that film to the point at which the cameras first picked up Sheena's figure hurrying up the drive through the rain, with her suitcase bumping along behind her, the handbag slapping into the case's handle, and the umbrella wobbling in her other hand. In the background was a taxi from one of the Island's most respected firms. Karen laid her finger on the screen and looked round at Charlie, opening her mouth.

'We're on it,' he said before she could speak. 'The driver'll be interviewed as soon as his wife's woken him. He was on nights and went home at six thirty this morning. If you've got any technical questions about Sheena's behaviour, give me a list and we'll add yours to ours.'

'Fine.' Karen knew Charlie's team would ask all the obvious questions: how did the suspect appear? What did she say? Did she take or make any phone calls in the taxi? Did she seem confused or ill?

She set the film going again from the beginning, looking for markers, watching the awkward way Sheena ran towards the house, stumbling, pushing herself, as though time were very short indeed. She pressed the front-door bell, holding it down for much longer than necessary. Not even that was enough for Sheena; she started banging the heavy brass knocker almost at once. Whatever had brought her to the Island had been urgent. Anyone could see that.

Karen flicked a glance at the time running along the bottom of the screen and saw that it read, '22.23'.

When the door opened, Sir Dan had his shoes off, revealing soft-looking dark-red socks. His trousers were well shaped and made of thick, dark-blue corduroy. Both cuffs of his discreetly checked cream shirt were dangling open, as though he'd just removed the links, and he'd undone most of the buttons. Under the shirt he was wearing a dark T-shirt instead of a vest. But his silver-and-gold hair looked immaculate, with the pristine shape achieved only by a weekly cut.

Sheena did not look so immaculate, in spite of her tidy hair, and her first moves were to drop the umbrella and let go of the suitcase to fling out her arms sideways, palms towards him, as she looked up into his face, obviously saying something sharp, and very short. Karen was no lip-reader but it seemed clear enough. Sheena was asking, 'What? What's happened?'

'He sent for her,' Karen said, convinced.

'Can't have,' Charlie said. 'Think how surprised he looked in the other film.'

Karen turned to him, full of pity for his wish that Sheena could be innocent.

'That could've come from anything. The clumsy way she was running up the drive. The sight of the taxi. The way she'd both rung the bell and banged the knocker. No. Look again at her face when she's asking her question.'

Having re-run the short, clear but soundless film, Karen put it on pause and touched the screen. 'Here. She doesn't know why she's here. He sent for her, as he had never done before, if what she told us just now was true. What happens next?'

Charlie's face darkened a little as blood rushed into his cheeks.

'The next section shows her get something small – like a phone or BlackBerry – out of her bag and show it to him. He lets her in, bangs the door behind her. Then the films stop. No camera records anything till he resets them three-quarters of an hour later. After that it's only foxes and badgers sneaking across the lawns. Got any insights into what could've happened between them?'

Karen licked her sore lips. 'Sorry. I can see that with no cameras inside the house and no witnesses you need something. But I can't help. Not yet anyway. Sheena's the only one who can tell us and till we've got round the amnesia . . . But I'm *sure* she thought he was expecting her. Haven't their phones got anything useful?'

'I'm waiting to hear. I'll chase it up. Don't go anywhere.'

Karen watched the tape again, trying to see in the body language of both parties something that would give her clues to their feelings. Nothing she saw contradicted her first impression: Sir Dan was welcoming, if surprised; Sheena was afraid and rushed and wanted to know why she was there.

Charlie's hand touched her shoulder and she looked up to see he was holding an evidence bag in the other. The transparent pouch held a BlackBerry.

'It's PIN- and password-protected,' he said. 'If her memory's really dodgy and she can't give us the info, our geeks can crack it, but that'll take for ever. I'll be back.'

Karen waited, assuming that even if Sheena's short-term amnesia was genuine, she would not have forgotten the passwords. Whether she would give them up was a different question.

Charlie was soon back, looking triumphant, waving the BlackBerry.

'Like a lamb,' he said. 'Here.'

The small screen of Sheena's BlackBerry showed an email that answered a lot of questions:

Come to the Island now. Don't tell anyone. I'm alone. I need you. Dan

It was timed at 18.15.

'She took that "now" seriously, didn't she?' Karen said, looking up at Charlie and doing the sums. 'She got herself from Spitalfields to Waterloo and over here to the Island in the shortest possible time. I'm amazed there was a train at the right moment.'

A faint smirk tweaked at his lips. Karen looked away. She hated seeing that Charlie could be enjoying the idea of a pliant, attractive, intelligent woman ready to drop everything and race across the south of England because of an email from her married lover. Years ago she'd overheard a friend of her father's saying that every man's dream was an affair with 'Fifi from Typing', who would be uncritically adoring when you had time for her and entirely silent and undemanding when you hadn't. No one had typing pools any longer, but that clearly didn't change the basic fantasy.

Charlie's phone rang. He said his name, listened for a second, then said: 'Incident room on the first floor. Bring you up to speed when you get here.' He clicked off the phone and turned to Karen to add: 'The whole team's here now. I'll be briefing them on the facts, but I want you to say where we are from the psychological angle.'

'The whole team?' Karen said with a wary note in her voice. Charlie nodded, his expression showing he knew why she was doubtful.

He was a rarity in respecting her profession. Most detectives mistrusted psychology and disliked its practitioners. There had been one or two disasters in the past with investigations that had gone badly wrong because of the psychologist's over-confident interpretation of the crime scene and its likely

perpetrator. Even without those, the caveats good psychologists had to make convinced many police officers that they
were a waste of time and dangerous with it. More than one
had said to Karen, 'You just make it all up, don't you?'

'There've been cock-ups,' Charlie said with an interesting
lack of passion, 'when shrinks weren't used till all other leads
had failed. By then half the evidence that could've helped had
gone or been confused. I'm not going down that route. I need
you in at the start.'

'You've got me,' she said with a grin.

'That's m'lass.' He whacked her lightly on the back.

She squared her shoulders, braced herself and planned to
talk to his team as though they were eager students and not
cynical doubters, outlining the already established reasons why
some killers mutilated their victims' bodies after death.

'You can get the very organized type of killer, who plans
everything down to the last detail,' she explained a few minutes
later, 'and who rarely leaves the weapon behind. Those who
do leave the weapon – as our perpetrator has – tend to be the
more hopeless, disorganized killers, who have a low IQ, live
near the victim and often act on impulse, sometimes hiding –
though not burying – the body, so that they can come back
time after time to make more cuts or take more trophies from
it. Ears, that kind of thing.'

Karen saw obstinacy and dislike on several of the faces in
front of her. She smiled back at them, glanced at Charlie, who
was standing beside her and not looking much more friendly.
After a moment, she pressed on with her small lecture, trying
to choose words that wouldn't be off-putting but still meant
what she wanted them to mean.

'That kind of rather pathetic, privately minded individual doesn't fit with the crime scene we have here, which looks to be the work of someone *highly* organized and proud of what he's done, even though he did leave the castrating knife behind, as well as the ones used to fix the body to the table. The way that pinning was done is like an exhibition, a grand display, typical of one kind of serial killer, but not limited to serial k . . .'

She felt Charlie touch her arm and looked back at him.

'All this theory is interesting, but the other stuff's more urgent. Can you explain about our suspect – Sheena Greves – how she claims she's lost her memory, and how the things she said in her first interview make you think she's faking the amnesia?'

'Fine. But one last point about killers who go in for post-mortem mutilation. Neither the organized nor the chaotic kind would normally dump the trophy – in this case Sir Dan's genitals – in a local bin. They'd take it with them.'

'We'll remember that,' said a thin-faced middle-aged constable, who had been introduced as Richard Silver. His tone suggested he was one of the army of doubters about her profession. 'But what about this suspect? Like the boss says, *that's* what we need to know now, with the clock ticking like it is.'

DS Annie Colvin came over to Karen at the end of the briefing. They'd known each other for a couple of years now and were more than acquaintances but less than friends. What linked them was a similar protective affection for Charlie and a determination to get at the truth behind any crime under investigation, rather than achieve a conviction at any cost.

'That ended up pretty clear,' Annie said.

Karen breathed more easily. 'D'you think the team will accept what I said?'

'Some did.' Annie's smile was kind. 'Some never will. Don't worry about it. Charlie's asked me to look into Sheena Greves's personal life, work and friends. Anything you think I should specially go for?'

Touched by Annie's trust in her judgment, Karen tried to think of a useful angle. 'Obviously the child, his death, and the trial. Not many people have to deal with anything that tragic – dramatic – and it would be useful to know how she coped. She seems so calm now, even with the memory loss. Was she always like that? Or has she learned how to use serenity as a defence? Who does she talk to? There must be someone.'

'Maybe only Sir Dan,' Annie suggested.

'Maybe.' Karen smiled sadly at the thought of Stella's excited call about her new bloke this morning. 'But most of us have at least one good girlfriend, who'll go through the thrills and spills with us. Or sisters. Brothers even. If you can find Sheena's confidantes, you'll be half-way there.'

'OK. You've got my number. Text me if you think of anything else.'

'Will do.'

'Karen!' Charlie's voice was crisp and official. She turned away from Annie to answer his summons.

'The taxi driver's got zilch,' he told her, while a very junior detective constable stood in admiring silence beside him. She looked to Karen's eye to be about fifteen, but must have been ten years more than that. 'Denise here says he claimed Sheena was normal and polite, if a bit rushed, when she said where she wanted to go. Didn't talk on the journey. Gave him the fare and a precise ten per cent tip, didn't want a receipt, and left him with a brief "thank-you".'

'So nothing there.' Karen smiled at the baby constable, who didn't respond.

'Nope,' Charlie agreed. 'Denise, start getting hold of some background on Sir Dan's life here on the Island: who he talked to, what he did, who could tell us more?'

'Of course, boss. I'll get right on it.'

Charlie's smile was warm with amusement as he watched her hurry off. Karen had to wait only moments before he turned back to her.

'We need another crack at Sheena. I want more on that email he sent, and a lot more about this memory loss. Exactly when her brain shut down and all that.'

'If it did,' Karen said.

'Right.'

'Can I suggest getting at that by a roundabout route?' Karen said, careful not to make him obstinate by sounding bossy.

'Like?'

'The story of the dead child.' Karen wasn't sure how easily Sheena would talk about her tragedy, but it was the obvious way into something difficult and painful that she could not possibly have forgotten. 'Sir Dan had a crucial part in getting her such good defence at the trial – and was probably the father of the baby – which means that story could lead us to where we need to be now.'

Charlie took his usual time thinking through her request, then shoved a hand in the small of her back, saying: 'No time to waste. You lead on those questions. But stop if I tell you to. OK?'

Karen just looked at him. They both knew she didn't submit well to any kind of authority. But she liked the feel of his impatient hand on her spine.

Someone had given Sheena and her solicitor more tea. She was turning her empty plastic mug round and round between her hands when Charlie led Karen back into the interview room. The solicitor looked bored but resigned, as though they'd been sitting in silence for some time.

'Doctor Taylor here has some more questions to ask you,' Charlie said, as the two of them sat down.

'To help loosen your memory,' Karen added, with a smile. 'I wanted to ask you about the very sad death of your child.'

Sheena drew in a breath so sharply Karen was surprised she didn't choke herself.

'I'm sorry to . . .'

'How is this relevant?' asked the solicitor, waking up and setting about his job.

Karen turned briefly to look straight at him. 'It's all a question of how trauma affects the memory in different individuals. Nothing could be as traumatic as the death of so young a child, and . . .'

'And being accused of murdering him.' Sheena's voice held so much anger that Karen felt the interview room was too small to contain it safely. 'And standing trial for it.'

'What happened?' Karen asked, wanting to like her. 'I know we could get all the court records, but it would help to hear about it from you.'

Sheena closed her eyes briefly, then opened them and said in a voice of cold, controlled bitterness, as though she were re-dictating a statement she had made many times in the past: 'I was taking Andy for a walk in his pram. It wasn't a buggy. I don't like the way I've seen babies slump in those. It was an old-fashioned horizontal pram, so that he was facing me. I pushed it along, looking down at him. He was asleep. It was a gorgeous day, sunny and warm but not harsh or dazzling. You know.' She paused, as though she expected an answer.

'I know,' Karen told her gently. Sheena smiled as though to acknowledge the kindness, but her eyes were dull.

'We'd been awake for most of the night because he'd been crying and I was tired. Very tired. There was a bench under a tree and hardly anyone else around. Just the usual pensioners pottering on their sticks and Zimmer frames, and a few kids playing, but they were far enough away for the noise to be kind of muted. I sat down for a minute and fell asleep. I don't know how long I was out but it was heavy sleep. When I woke, my neck was aching because of the way my head had been hanging, and I'd been dribbling. For a moment or two I didn't know where I was. When I looked in the pram, I saw Andy had rolled over, which surprised me because he was so little. But he was asleep and that seemed so important that I didn't try to disturb him. He must've been worn out like me. That's what I thought, anyway.'

'But you were wrong?' Karen suggested, as Sheena sat in silence. She gave a little jump, as though she'd been drifting off again and had been suddenly woken.

'After I'd got him home again and lifted him out of the pram to change him, he was all floppy. I knew then that it wasn't sleep at all.' Her throat clicked with the effort of saying the words. 'He was . . . dead.'

Sheena paused again, swallowing hard. When she'd got control of herself, she went on in an even more formal voice: 'They found petechial haemorrhages in his eyes and fibres in his throat and saliva on the pillow. They said I'd smothered him with it. I hadn't.'

'As the court established later,' Karen said, making an assumption. 'Did your lawyers find out what *had* happened?'

Sheena nodded. All the colour had left her face and she looked ill.

'Like I said, he'd rolled over and got his face stuck in the pillow. The expert witness explained how it's possible for even tiny babies to do that, and how an adult would've woken and rolled back again to breathe, but Andy couldn't. It was just a terrible accident. No one's fault. That's what they found. It's hard to believe, but it's the truth.'

'Thank you,' Karen said. 'That can't have been easy. How did Sir Dan take Andy's death?'

Sheena's eyes filled with tears that spilled over the lower lids, bringing more mascara with them. Soon she had thick grey streaks down her pallid cheeks.

'He was so kind to me,' she said in a voice that betrayed wells of unhappiness. 'You can't imagine how kind. He knew how I felt, like . . . like something in me had broken. Maybe for ever. He couldn't have . . . He was even more loving and gener-ous than before. Never blamed me, even though he'd longed for Andy's birth as much as me . . . And he never complained when I didn't get pregnant again. Month after month we hoped . . . and once I thought it had happened. But I miscarried five weeks later. Andy had been our only . . . '

Sheena found a tissue up her sleeve and wiped her eyes before looking at Charlie and then back at Karen as though she was more likely to understand.

'Not that we'd given up. Of course not. In fact . . . ' Sheena stopped.

Charlie's heavy dark eyebrows twitched. He leaned towards her across the table.

'In fact, what?' he said, with an urgency that had been missing at the start of this session.

Sheena's face took on a little colour again. She looked as though she were trying to make a hard decision, perhaps even debating it with herself. After a moment, she shrugged and said in a much tougher voice, 'Oh, what does it matter now? What does any of it matter? I'm ovulating at the moment. Dan knew. I thought . . . when I got his email, I thought he'd discovered at the last minute that Olga wasn't going to be here this weekend after all, so that he'd be safely alone when he hadn't expected to be, and it was a really good chance for us to . . . so he and I could . . .'

'So he was keen to have a child himself,' Karen said, wanting a clear confirmation. 'I mean, he wasn't just doing what you wanted?'

Sheena nodded, then put it in words: 'He really did want a child. He often said it – until he saw how it worried me, when I couldn't get pregnant again.'

'His wife, Olga: has she ever had any children?'

'She couldn't at all. I don't know why not.' Sheena watched Charlie sitting straight again, as though he was less interested now. 'Dan trusted me to leave that part of his life alone.'

'I don't see,' said the solicitor, reminding them all of his presence at last, 'how this is helping the investigation into Sir Dan's death.'

'Perhaps not.' Karen made sure she sounded polite and without even the slightest hint of smug triumph. 'But I hope it's helping your client realize how effective her powers of memory actually are.'

Sheena sent Karen a glare of fiery resentment. Karen smiled blandly back, adding: 'We just need to find a way to free them for what happened last night and early this morning.'

A knock at the door gave her time to plan her next question. Charlie got up to answer it, spoke briefly to the tape and left. Karen waited in silence for his return. Sheena sat very upright in her hard chair, fiddling with her hair and not looking at anyone. Moments later, Charlie was back. Ignoring Karen, he said to Sheena: 'Tell me about the security system.'

'Where? I mean which one? Spitalfields or the office?'

'Here, on the Island, at Sir Dan's house.'

Sheena looked genuinely confused. And worried. 'I don't know anything about it. I'm sorry. He never told me. You see, it's like I said: we – he and I – never talked at all about his life here.'

'Did he say anything about the system when you arrived last night?' Charlie asked.

'No.' Suddenly Sheena's voice was hoarse. She coughed, as though to clear it. 'Why?'

'Security films show you arriving, you and him talking, you showing him something, then him grabbing your arm and more or less pulling you inside the house. After that, nothing. The whole system shuts down. Did he do that?'

Sheena's hair swung back across her face as she nodded. 'I suppose so. I didn't . . . didn't know what he was doing. But if the film stopped that must've been it. There wasn't anyone else here to do it.'

'What did you see?' Charlie asked, his voice cool now. Karen thought he might have stopped wanting Sheena to be innocent.

'After Dan let me in,' she said, 'he opened a door in the panelling of the hall wall. I couldn't see inside. I was on the door side, if you see what I mean. But I heard a few bleeps, so he could have been changing the alarms. He didn't explain.'

Charlie glanced at Karen, nodding, as though to tell her to ask anything she wanted to know. She smiled at Sheena.

'What was it that you showed him, just before he pulled you into the house?'

'My BlackBerry,' Sheena said at once, as though she'd given up any idea of claiming amnesia.

'Why did you want him to see it?'

'Because of the email. He asked me why I'd come in such a rush and I said "because you sent for me and said it was urgent." And he looked, well, kind of shocked for a minute.'

'Shocked?' Karen repeated. 'Are you sure?'

Sheena thought for a bit, perhaps trying to decide what would fit best with the story she had concocted, then nodded decisively. 'I think so. Then I showed him the email and he laughed a bit, though he didn't sound as if it was funny, and . . .' Her voice tailed off as they waited.

'If he didn't seem amused when he was laughing, how do you think he was feeling? You must know him well enough to tell,' Karen said.

Half Sheena's lower lip disappeared between her teeth, which were enviably white and even. After a moment she released it and covered her whole mouth with her hand. Her eyelids fluttered and her face paled again, as though she might faint.

'He was angry,' she said at last. Her soft brown eyes were full of pain and her voice sounded far more hesitant than it had been. 'At least I think so, although I was too worried to realize at the time. He never . . . He always . . . I mean he always used to say, "anger's a sign of inadequacy", so he tried to hide it whenever he felt it.'

'What happened then?' Karen asked, curious and impressed. Anger was one of the emotions she found most difficult, both in herself and in other people. Forgetting half her rage at what he'd done to Sheena, she found herself wishing she'd had the chance to meet him.

Sheena closed her eyes, leaned back in the chair, and Karen held her breath. At last, Sheena gave them what they wanted.

'He said there were things we'd have to talk about, but it was too late to deal with them now. We were both too tired and so we might get cross wires and things. We'd talk in the morning. Then he told me to wait in the hall while he found a bed that had been made up in one of the spare rooms. He asked rather formally if I'd brought nightclothes in my suitcase. That worried me because I . . . he knew I . . . Sorry.'

'Take your time,' Karen said when she saw that Charlie wasn't going to offer any reassurance at all.

'Thanks,' Sheena said, dabbing at her lower lip with a shredded tissue. 'I couldn't understand why he was asking because when we were together I never wore anything in bed. I said I hadn't got anything, so he said he'd lend me some pyjamas. He wasn't like himself at all. I couldn't think why not. I still can't. Except, when I first woke next morning I thought maybe he could've been frightened. D'you think that could be it?'

Karen couldn't answer sensibly, so she said nothing. After a moment Sheena went on:

'It was the idea of how he could've been scared and me not understanding that made me . . . I couldn't bear to think about it, about me failing him like that, and I suppose that's why my memory went.' This time her expression was full of pleading, as though begging Karen to accept this explanation of the now unconvincing amnesia.

'Could be,' Karen said as a way of moving them all on.

'Anyway, yesterday evening Dan was gone, out of the hall for quite a time, and I just had to wait, like a . . . like a kind of beggar. At last he came down again and told me to go upstairs and through the open third door on the left after the stairs on the second floor, where I'd find a bed made up and a bathroom I could use. I was to stay up there till half eight this morning, dress before I came down and . . .' She broke off, as though just becoming aware that her story didn't tally with the facts. 'And then we'd talk.'

Her solicitor was looking worried. He could do the sums too.

'So why did you go to the kitchen, still in pyjamas, at five fifteen?' Charlie asked.

'I heard . . . I thought I heard . . . I thought I heard him calling me,' Sheena said, but as she spoke her eyes moved fast from side to side, as though she was looking for help. Sweat was visible on her forehead and her upper lip. Her hands twisted around each other. 'I couldn't fail him again, so I went to see if I could help him.'

Karen had rarely seen anyone displaying the fact that she was lying quite so clearly. Charlie said nothing, waiting for more. Karen looked quickly at him and saw a familiar ruthless gleam in his eyes. After a moment, he uncrossed his legs and sat up straighter in the hard grey plastic chair.

'Not the first time you'd disobeyed him and come downstairs, was it?'

'What?' Sheena sounded genuinely surprised.

'Oh, come on.' Charlie was allowing more roughness into his questions. 'Sir Dan reset the security system when he went up to bed, didn't he?'

Sheena shrugged. 'How would I know? Like I told you, he sent me to bed. Alone. He was waiting downstairs in the hall, watching me go upstairs. I didn't understand . . . didn't see why he wouldn't . . . We were on our own, after all. But if that's what he wanted, it's what I did. Like always.'

Charlie looked remorseless as he went on, 'The security system shows three failed attempts to turn it off again at 2.30 a.m. before it locked you out. Why did you try to deactivate it?'

'I didn't. I don't know what you're talking about.'

'You'd killed him by then, hadn't you?'

'No.' The word came out as a kind of scream.

'You'd planned to turn off the alarms and cameras so you could leave the house undetected,' Charlie said, still harshly.

'You're mad,' Sheena said.

'When the system locked you out and you knew it would record every movement you made outside the building, you had to think on your feet, didn't you? You didn't do very well, did you? This memory-loss idea. Did you really think we'd buy it? You must've realized your arrival would've been recorded and we'd see that.'

Sheena's face was blank, as though she'd withdrawn so completely that she'd made herself deaf to everything Charlie was saying. Karen could see the solicitor twitching in his chair, as though he thought he should intervene but wasn't sure how.

'Chief Inspector, I think . . .' he began at last, but Sheena interrupted him, her eyes focusing again and her face hard.

'It's OK,' she said. 'I can do this. It's like before. Because all I've got to tell is the truth, in the end they'll believe me, however unlikely it sounds. I should have remembered and . . . better late than never, though.'

Sheena looked first at Karen and then at Charlie, then reverted to her earlier dictation speed to say, 'I did not wake at 2.30 a.m. or any other time until I went down to the kitchen and found his body, whenever it was – soon after five this morning. I was so upset by what happened when I got here, and the way he talked to me, as though we were nearly strangers, that I took two sleeping pills, which must be why I didn't hear anything in the night.'

Waiting for a moment, as though to make sure they could keep up, Sheena looked expectantly at Charlie.

'OK?'

He nodded, his expression unhelpful.

'OK. Then when I did wake it was because I heard his voice.' Sheena's eyes leaked a few more tears, but her voice was still firm. 'At least that's what I thought. Now I know it couldn't have been. I must've been in a dream. I thought he was calling out to me for help. I ran downstairs and looked for his bedroom. It wasn't hard to see which it was: the only one with an open door. The bed was rumpled and his slippers . . .' Her voice broke. They waited. She coughed and started again: 'His slippers were lying waiting beside the bed. That's how I knew something was really wrong. He always left them like that, toes pointing away from the bed so that he could put his feet right in them the minute he swung his legs out of bed. You see, I knew then.'

'Knew what?' Charlie asked.

'That someone had done something to him. That's when I started to think he must've been scared last night and that's why he was so brusque, so . . . so unloving. So unlike his real self. And then I thought someone must be in the house, someone who'd hurt him. I didn't think of Dan as dead. Not then. But I knew something was terribly wrong. He would never have left his room without slippers. It was the kind of thing that was almost like a kind of religion for him. No bare feet in the house. Ever.'

Now, Sheena was wringing her hands, almost like Lady Macbeth, trying in her nightmares to clean the remembered blood off her fingers. 'For a bit I was too scared to move,' she continued, 'but, like I said, I couldn't fail him again. I looked for something I could use as a weapon – a poker or something – but there wasn't anything. I thought if I could find the kitchen I'd be able to get a knife. Something like that.'

Karen saw that Sheena was hyperventilating and looked towards Charlie, as though to ask him to stop. He raised one of his hands a little way off the table in a holding gesture. Karen said nothing. Sheena rushed on, panting and sweating:

'I didn't know I'd find Dan . . . But that's what I saw . . . His body, like that. I was so muddled by the dream I'd been having, or the after-effects of the sleeping pills, I suppose. At first I thought I really had heard him calling and the killer must still be there in the house, and I was . . . I was . . . I tried to pull out one of the knives so I could fight off the killer.' She choked and pulled a balled tissue from her sleeve to hold against her lips. 'I wanted something to protect me. But I couldn't make it move at all. It was stuck fast. They all were.' Tears poured out of her eyes. She didn't even try to stem them, keeping the tissue near her mouth as though she thought she might vomit.

Karen wasn't surprised. Faced with a body mutilated as Sir Dan's had been, believing yourself alone in a huge house with someone capable of that kind of violence, anyone would feel terror. But, her cold professional internal voice also told her, it's a brilliant explanation of why Sheena's fingerprints would be on one of the knives, if not all of them.

'Then when I got a bit of sanity back, I looked at Dan's wounds,' Sheena went on, a little more in control of her breathing. 'At the blood. I saw how it was clotted, blackening already, and I knew they must have killed him hours before and escaped. That's when I phoned you.'

Once more she looked straight at Charlie and this time there was heavy accusation in her expression.

'I phoned for help. I never thought I'd get arrested. Be accused of killing him. That's why I panicked and said I couldn't remember anything.'

'Even after your experience with the police last time?' Charlie was taunting her, as though he thought that might push her into a confession. All his kindness, all his longing for her to be innocent had gone. The solicitor looked poised to intervene again but still said nothing.

Sheena took her time planning her answer. The delay gave Karen more than enough time to think: I don't care what you say; your body language tells me you're lying about something.

Chapter 5

Day One: 12.15 p.m.

'You don't need me now,' Karen said to Charlie after Sheena had been taken back to the cells and her ineffectual solicitor had left the station. 'No question of amnesia any more. It's a straight investigation. I could still get to Norfolk.'

'Don't be so worky-ticket.' He grabbed her wrist, luckily not squeezing quite so hard this time and pulled her out of the interview room. 'Get on upstairs. I need you to give the team an update. And then I'll need full profiles of both victim and suspect. Psych profiles.'

'What does worky-ticket mean?' Karen asked, trying to tug her arm out of his grip.

He grinned as he let go. '"Annoying" is what you'd say in your prissy southern kind of way.'

'Thanks, Charlie.' She enjoyed these flashes of the friend she liked so much bursting through the urgency of the investigation, but she wasn't going to let him push her around. 'Be serious. What can I contribute to the work you'll all be doing now?'

'Plenty, if you concentrate. And we can help you. Think of
Sir Dan's body. It's the right kind of mutilation for your paper.
You heard of any other examples of this kind of castration?
Extreme or what? Plus you've got all the excitement of the
killer chucking away the trophy instead of keeping it.' His
voice changed as he added in an unconvincingly casual way,
'Castration points to a woman, doesn't it?'

'Why?' Karen looked at him in surprise. 'It's just an indication that the perpetrator wanted to humiliate as well as kill Sir
Dan. Fairly common and not gender-specific.' Knowing how
much he hated her professional jargon when he was under
pressure, she picked deliberately casual words: 'Think of all
those Old Testament accounts of men mutilating beaten
enemies – foreskins and all that.'

They'd reached the incident room door and Charlie shoved
it open with his right foot and urged Karen to go in first.

He waited till all the members of the small team had put
down their phones and gathered at his end of the shabby
room.

'Great,' he said with a brief smile. 'Doctor Taylor here has
some more things to say about our suspect. Karen.'

'Thanks, Charlie. OK. Not surprisingly Sheena Greves is
denying any responsibility for the death of her lover, Sir Dan
Blackwater.' Karen took a deep breath to steady her voice.
'Psychologically, her denials could be a form of self-protection,
like the amnesia she claimed at first but has now dropped . . .'

'Or got over,' Charlie said, with the air of one who wanted
to be fair, however hard that might be.

'Indeed.' Karen could have done without his intervention.
She could see some of his officers still weren't impressed with

her, even though Annie offered an encouraging smile. 'Or she could be telling the truth.'

'In other words,' said the middle-aged DC Silver, 'you're telling us that *psychologically* she might have done it or she might not. That's helpful.'

Three other people laughed. Karen could have kicked Charlie hard for putting her in this position for the second time in only a few hours.

'At least we've now got past the amnesia, real or otherwise,' she said, without, she hoped, sounding ingratiating. 'It's not for me to tell you how to conduct the investigation, but I should have thought finding out whether there are other means of ingress into the house, bypassing the security system, would be essential. I'd also want to find out whether there is or ever has been a meat-tenderizing mallet in the kitchen or any easily available hammers. This suspect doesn't look to me like someone with enough strength in hands, wrists and upper body to drive those knives through the victim's joints and into the kitchen table without some kind of heavy tool. Then I'd want to know whether Sir Dan had any . . .'

'Any enemies?' said DC Silver in the same thin, sarcastic tone. 'I guess we'd have managed to think of that one on our own.'

'I was going to say any unusual problems in his personal or professional lives. Anything that was making him peculiarly worried or angry. The key to Sheena's behaviour is – clearly – her relationship with him, and the only way to access the truth of that now is to find out more about him.'

'But . . .' The interruption came from Annie, then she

thought better of it and kept her mouth shut, waving her hand as though brushing away a fly to show she'd changed her mind.

'On the face of it, the relationship was unequal and exploitative,' Karen said. 'But Sheena's view is that it was full of trust and honesty. Sir Dan claimed his wife was too emotionally fragile to bear a divorce, or even the knowledge that he might have a girlfriend. She'll have to be interviewed, and her movements established, with . . .'

'She's been in Switzerland for the past six weeks.' Charlie nodded to Annie. 'That's right, isn't it?'

'Yeah. They have a chalet there, where she spends a lot of her time. Partly for tax reasons and partly because she doesn't like the Island in winter, and . . .'

'Not surprising,' said DC Silver. 'Grim and grey and dull beyond bearing. How long are we going to have to be here?'

'As long as it takes,' Charlie said sharply. DC Silver looked as though he'd swallowed a spoonful of vinegar. 'Great, Karen, thanks. I think that's it for the moment. When we've got more I'll phone you.'

Without saying another word, she turned and left the room. She heard DC Silver's voice, saying, 'Typical bloody shrink. Telling us nothing we don't already know, and being paid five times what we . . .'

'That's enough, Rich.' Charlie's sounded sharp and hard. 'She's had more success in identifying killers than you know. Trust her. I do.'

That's something, Karen told herself, bitterly amused that the superannuated detective constable thought freelance psychologists earned so much more than he did.

Footsteps from behind her warned that someone was following her out of the incident room. She didn't look back and
picked up speed.

Out in the street, Charlie caught up with her.

'Don't sulk,' he said, with a laugh of his own.

'I'm not. But I don't enjoy humiliation. So I thought I'd
do your profiles at home in private, well away from all that
sneering.' Karen looked down at her watch and winced at
the sight of its restrained and expensive elegance. Yet
another present from Will. In due course, she'd have to get
all his presents together and pack them up and send them
back to him. But that was for later. Thank God she had
work to do now.

'Don't do that, Karen. I may need you here on the Island at
no notice. Tell me what you need from us and I'll get it for you.
You've got your laptop. I'll give you a desk. You can work on
it in the incident room.'

'With that lot? That thin sarcastic bastard, who thinks I'm
rich and who's just waiting for me to trip up and fall flat on my
face? No way. Anyway, I need to get home to sort out my
windows.'

'Stop banging on about your boring windows. You know
they're being sorted. You try and work in the flat now and
you'll be making cuppas and listening to hammers and chisels
all morning. You can do everything here on the Island.' Charlie
paused for a second, then added, 'I need you.'

Karen couldn't admit how much she liked hearing him
say it.

'Oh, all right,' she said, pretending to be grudging. 'I'll stay,
but not in the incident room. I'll go out to the Goose, work

there. Peg will give me houseroom. If you haven't come up with anything you need me to do by three, I'll head over to the site to see how my builders are getting on, and then I really will get back to the mainland.'

'I thought they weren't starting on your house till spring,' Charlie said, looking through the window at the grey, lowering sky. 'That's what you said before.'

'Remember how weirdly sunny the beginning of January was? They decided to make a start. Now they can't get any further till the weather's better again.' She tried not to see a parallel in her plans for a life with Will. 'If it ever is.'

Charlie looked at her with such an openly curious stare that she was afraid she must have sounded bitter. Or mad.

Karen found a cab to take her the eight miles out of Cowes to the Goose Inn, which had always been Charlie's favourite pub on the Island and had now become a kind of refuge for her too. The licensee was a woman whose husband had dumped her and their small son. Karen liked her, and admired the grit with which she toughed out the bleak winter months, when trade was so quiet as to be almost silent.

One of Peg's principles was that if you were running a business that depended on customers, you made yourself available whenever they wanted you. She would definitely open her doors, even though at ten forty-five in the morning most of the rival pubs would still be shut.

The place looked its usual charming self as Karen's cab dropped her in the small car park. Built of white cob, and thatched, it must once have been a farmhouse, but Peg's family had run it as a pub for at least four generations. It stood on ground high enough to see the sea, over towards Ryde. From this distance the waves looked just as grey and soupy as they had first thing. The fat white geese that gave the place its name waddled up to the fence to greet Karen with their clucking, squawking cries.

She wasn't sentimental enough to believe they could remember her, but they were always curious and liked to investigate all the comings and goings at the pub. Watching them, she could well believe in the ancient story of the geese that had saved Rome from attack by bellowing a warning at the arrival of a threatening force.

Peg must have heard these ones because she opened the door, recognized Karen at once and called a real greeting, waving.

Karen saw that Peg was looking her usual casual but ravishing self in a calf-length skirt of sea-coloured patchwork and a well fitting dark-green top. Karen felt a load lifting off her shoulders. She hurried across the crunching pea gravel and wanted to fling herself into Peg's arms.

'Hey, what's up? I've never seen you in such a tizzy before,' Peg said in the soft Island accent, with its 'oi' sounds for 'I', that always reminded Karen of her grandmother, the one safe figure in her difficult childhood.

'Nothing much.' Karen got hold of herself and smiled in an ordinarily pleasant way, keeping a proper distance. 'Charlie got me out of bed at dawn this morning because of a case he's got, and for various reasons I'm all over the place. He wanted me to work in the incident room but I said I wouldn't. Can I set up my laptop here? Will I be in your way?'

'Course not. We're not technically open yet, but you're

more than welcome. Come on in. Coffee's on. D'you want breakfast?'

Acceptance, Karen thought with gratitude. Instant acceptance and the offer of sustenance. What more could anyone want?

'Breakfast would be great. Whatever you've got. And I'm working, so I can charge it. If not to Charlie, at least against my own tax.'

'It's OK,' Peg said, with the wide smile that lit up her whole face. 'I know you're a proper customer. I know you know I need to earn my profits. Come on in. The fire's lit, too.'

'And your boy?' For a shaming second, Karen couldn't remember his name, then luckily the information swam into her mind. 'Your Johnnie. Won't he mind a stranger hanging around while the pub's technically closed?'

'He's with his nan today. Come on. Make yourself comfortable. I'm cooking for a big coach tour booked in for lunch on their way to the Roman Villa at Brading tomorrow, so I won't be in your way.'

Karen set up her temporary office at a table between the fire for warmth and one of the small windows for light, switched on the laptop, knowing Peg had Wi-Fi, and downloaded the morning's emails.

Before she did anything else, she thought she ought to send one to Stella to make up for truncating her excited call this morning. Karen quickly tapped in her message, blessing the fact that she'd learned touch-typing during her disastrous first marriage, long before she'd even thought of becoming a psychologist:

Sorry about this morning. As I said, I had some urgent
work to finish. But I'm really really pleased about your
bloke. Can't wait to meet him. Am on the Island now.
Thought I might nip over to the site later to see how
they've got on with the house. Kxxxx

In her in-box was an email from Max Pitton, the head of
her department, who was also a great friend in spite of his
monstrous teasing and occasional pretence of dinosaur-like
attitudes towards young women. Today Karen hesitated
before opening the email. Friend of hers though Max might
be, he'd known Will even longer. In fact Max had introduced them.

'Don't be such a coward,' she muttered aloud and clicked.

Karen, Will's told me. Can't be easy for you at the
moment, so phone if you need me. And let's go to Mario's
as soon as you feel like it. Love, Max.

She bit her lip, recognizing each of the emotions that jumbled
together in her mind: anger, feebleness, humiliation, regret,
and straight misery.

A bit like butter being churned, she thought in an attempt to
lighten her mood. As a child, she'd once watched a teacher
shaking a little milk in a jar to show how the stuff was made,
first curdling the milk into a disgusting-looking mess, then
making it coagulate into something useful. Delicious even.

This won't turn into anything useful, she thought, still trying
to understand why Will had left her so suddenly. As far as she
could see, she'd neither done nor said anything she hadn't been

doing and saying for as long as he'd known her. Was he the
kind of bloke who wanted only what he couldn't have so that
once she'd agreed to marry him he'd quickly got bored with
her? Was he taking revenge on her for all the doubts she'd had
when he was begging her to marry him? Or was this some kind
of test of her devotion, to see whether she'd wait for him to
change his mind again? Or crawl to him? Surely not. How
could she have loved anyone capable of that kind of manipula-
tive cruelty?

The squeak of the swing door beside the bar stopped her
miserable questions. She looked up to see Peg walking towards
her with a heavy tray.

'Grilled bacon, egg, tomato, mushrooms,' Peg said. 'Didn't
think you'd want sausage and black pudding and all that stuff
Charlie likes. I poached the egg. You don't look like a woman
who eats much fried stuff. And I know you like your coffee
black.'

She was unloading the tray as she talked, and putting everything in front of Karen. When it was all done, Peg stood up
straight, with the tray dangling from her left hand. With her
right, she pointed at Karen's finger.

'Did you lose it?' she said, her lovely face crunched into a
mask of sympathy. 'Or have you . . . ?'

Karen felt her own features tightening, as though the skin
and muscle were being shrunk against the bones.

'Sorry,' Peg said at once. 'I shouldn't have asked.'

'It's OK. Don't tell Charlie. I probably shouldn't have taken
it off yet, but . . .' Karen pushed the heavy blonde hair away
from her face, then looked down at the betraying finger. The
imprint of Will's ring was still visible, even though she'd been

wearing it for only a few days. 'Will's thought better of it. But I can't . . . Just now, I don't want to . . .'

'Not a problem. No questions asked here.' Peg's radiant smile came again. 'Never are. It's like a refuge. You can talk or not. Hunker down for as long as you need. When you want something, you give me a shout. I'll answer.'

Peg took the tray back to the kitchen, leaving Karen to feel thoroughly ashamed of the days when she'd been so jealous of Charlie's devotion to this professionally generous woman. No wonder he liked being here so much.

Work, Karen reminded herself. You're here to work and it's the one thing that will get you through.

Ignoring her breakfast for the moment, she typed Sir Dan's name into Google and saw that there were more than thirty million entries. A grim laugh escaped her. They'd keep her busy enough until long after three.

She pushed the laptop aside, poured her coffee, and set about eating the beautifully cooked food before it got too cold. At first it was wonderful, the saltiness of the soft bacon moderated by the delicacy of the egg yolk and the sweet fruitiness of the tomato, then her appetite left her completely.

One of Will's pleasures in the early days of their relationship, before he'd started to nag her into agreeing to marry and have children with him so that everything had got difficult, had been to arrive early on a Saturday morning at her flat when she was still asleep, cook some elaborately delicious and unlikely food for breakfast and bring it to her in bed. She picked up Peg's plate and put it down on the table behind her, revolted now by the mess of tomato and egg yolk, and all the crime scenes and operating theatres they suggested.

She'd never been seriously squeamish, but today all her perceptions were heightened and her defences lowered.

'So use it,' she muttered, pulling the computer nearer and hoping to learn enough about Sir Dan, high street genius, to banish every thought of Will Hawkins, who had been a consultant neurosurgeon before he'd been injured in her car, driving to the site of her new house here on the Island. Perhaps all he'd been doing since had been intended as punishment for that.

Her phone rang. Charlie's name was on the screen.

'Yes?' she said. 'What now?'

'Olga, Sir Dan's wife, is flying in on their private jet. Due to arrive at the airfield at Bembridge by half three. Says she'll see me an hour later. Help me interview her?'

Karen hesitated.

'Come on, pet. I'm doing you a favour. She'll give you insights you won't get anywhere else. Say yes and let me get back to work. I've been told I've got to phone in a fucking report for the ACC at five every day so he can pass it on to Number Fucking Ten. And I've got to do a TV appearance tomorrow morning, so I need something to throw the press by then. I'm under the microscope here, Karen. So are you.'

'OK. Fine.' Karen hated to think what would happen to her career if she screwed up a case as public as this one was clearly going to be. Failure to publish often enough in the academic journals would be nothing to the kind of scandal the press might whip up over any mistakes here. Good university jobs were hard to find, and since she was clearly going to be single for ever, she needed to earn as much as she humanly could.

'Great,' Charlie said, without sounding as grateful as he

should have. 'I'll swing by and pick you up at the Goose at four-fifteen on my way to the house.'

Karen typed Olga's name into Google and found only a fraction of the entries her husband had. She was on the board of a variety of charities. She had presented the prizes at a big Swiss sporting gala, but there were no photographs. And there was nothing anywhere about her mental state or any suggestion of nervous breakdowns or anything remotely illuminating. Karen was disappointed. She hated going into a meeting without fully briefing herself on the people she was about to encounter. All she had to go on now were the few comments Sheena had made. As Olga's secret rival, Sheena was hardly a disinterested witness.

By four o'clock, Karen could see exactly why Sheena had fallen for Sir Dan. Everything she read about him made her wish she'd known him. A loyal friend, a brilliant businessman with vision and courage admired even by his rivals, he had owned properties in five countries, a private jet, and an unrivalled art collection. More importantly, he had also clearly been moved by the vulnerability of anyone who did not have his resources. He had poured money into charities concerned with lost and damaged children, trafficked women, and the victims of any kind of sex crime.

He'd had a sense of humour, too. Karen found three letters he'd sent to broadsheet newspapers protesting about lack of official funding for his causes, and each one had made her smile in spite of the anger that had obviously driven them.

Finishing Peg's second pot of fragrant coffee, Karen made a mental list of what she'd learned about him in practical terms.

He had been born fifty-one years ago and had had no health problems. He had been married to Olga for eighteen years and had no children. His wife was his co-trustee on many of the ventures, and had a few of her own as well.

That needn't necessarily mean much, Karen knew, scrabbling for reasons why anyone might have disliked Sir Dan. As it was, she couldn't see how anyone could have hated him enough to kill him, let alone visit such dramatic mutilation on his body.

All the old saws about 'a woman scorned' and 'deadlier than the male' rang in her mind, but she couldn't believe that, even if Sir Dan had summoned Sheena to tell her their affair was over, she'd have been angry enough to attack him like this.

What if Olga had found out about their affair? Could she have been in the house all along, in spite of everything Sheena had said, overheard them, seen them together, and decided to take this dramatic revenge?

It didn't seem likely. Nothing in the photographs of Sir Dan's body suggested any kind of struggle. There'd been no bruises or scratches on his skin, except that thin straight mark across the stomach.

In any case, the Blackwaters' living arrangements, with Olga spending most of her time in Switzerland, suggested a semi-detached relationship that was unlikely to have generated the kind of fury and desire to humiliate that castration indicated.

Even more curious than usual about the way people managed long marriages, Karen wondered exactly how the Blackwaters' curious arrangement had developed. Her vivid imagination always needed controlling when she was interviewing suspects or witnesses in case she planted ideas in their minds, but here on her own she could let rip.

Olga's name suggested she might have come from Russia or Eastern Europe. Adding that to her inability to have children, emotional fragility, refusal to appear in public and the nature of the charities she and her husband had supported, Karen wondered whether Olga could have been the source of her husband's interest in rescuing trafficked women. But where would she ever find evidence of that?

One of the few encouraging things Karen had learned so far was the fact that the legal affairs of Sir Dan's Island-based charity were dealt with by Antony Quiggly, who had once been her grandmother's solicitor. Now the senior partner of the firm, he was far too grand for such minor clients, and Karen herself dealt with a newly qualified member of his staff, but she'd met him often in the past and was fairly confident he would remember her. She opened her bag to get her phone and find out for sure.

But the phone was already ringing. Expecting Charlie again, Karen didn't even look at the screen, merely saying: 'You ready then?'

Her mother's voice answered her, sounding puzzled. 'Ready for what?'

'Oh, hi, Dillie,' Karen said. She'd rarely called her mother anything else since her teens. 'I thought you were going to be someone else. How are you?'

'Terrific!' Dillie said, with all the over-dramatic bounciness that was a crucial part of her public persona. 'We've just finished a colossal project and the client's over the moon. Which means I've got a tiny bit of spare creative energy to get going on your wedding. So, tell me . . .'

'What?' The word burst out of Karen's mouth like a bullet from a gun. Even if she and Will hadn't broken up, her mother would not have had any part in organizing anything to do with either of them.

'Your wedding, Karen. You only had a register office last time, which means now we can push the boat out. Church. Fizz. The whole hog. I've already talked to the marquee firm, who are going to give us a *brilliant* deal – less than fifty per cent of the usual retail price – but they need the date. I thought June 28th would be ideal. Probably decent weather and before the schools have broken up, so . . .'

'Dillie, stop! Just stop it.'

'Why? What's gone wrong?'

Karen took enough time to ensure that her voice would be steady and unemotional enough to lie. She hadn't the strength yet to tell her mother what had happened.

'Nothing's wrong. But a) we're far too old and experienced for that kind of froufrou ceremony and b) we will be organizing – and paying for it – ourselves. When we have a date, I'll let you know, because obviously we'll want you and Dad there, but . . .'

'You are *such* a spoilsport.' Dillie could have been a six-year-old bilked of a promised birthday treat. She even produced the hint of a sob. 'You're my only daughter, and this is my one chance to do a 'proper wedding. I didn't have one and I've always dreamed of yours.'

A car horn blared outside. Unable to believe that even Charlie would summon an independent expert in such a peremptory way, Karen didn't look out of the window to see who was making the horrible noise. Then it came again.

Peg pushed her way through the swing doors, saying: 'It's Charlie. You said he was coming to pick you up. Looks in a right state to me. Even worse than you were when you got there this morning. Better get going.'

'Dillie,' Karen said into the phone. 'You and Dad have told me enough about the wedding you did have to make that sad story a complete nonsense. Remember the vicar dropping the ring and the cat who got at the wedding cake?'

Guilty laughter bubbled in her mother's voice. 'Darling, you know how advertising's trained me to make sales out of whatever meagre facts I have?'

'I certainly do.' Karen's voice was grim as she remembered the way her mother had manipulated her into paying a fortune for her grandmother's ramshackle wooden chalet and the two acres of muddy unproductive Island woods on which it stood. 'Anyway, I have to go now. Sorry, but it's work. Please, don't go all mother-of-the-bride on me.' She paused for a second, then added with some of the affection she was only just allowing herself to feel: 'Yellow polyester frills and a cartwheel hat just wouldn't suit you.'

Dillie laughed, sounding positively joyous. 'As I said, you're a rotten spoilsport. We could have fun with a grand bash, you and I. If you think better of it, let me know. And don't forget to give me notice of whatever date you do choose so that I can order my polyester in good time.'

Karen laughed back, and felt a lot better as she said goodbye.

'Don't go, Karen darling.' Dillie's voice was more serious. 'There's something else I need to say. It's a bit important. About your building project, and a story about one of the odder locals I . . .'

'Charlie's waiting,' Peg reminded Karen, just as he hit the car's horn again, making it blare out with angry urgency.

'Can't stop now, Dillie,' Karen said into her phone before clicking it off. She wasn't going to jump to Charlie's orders, but phone conversations with her mother could go on for hours. She looked up at Peg, saying, 'I need to pack up my stuff. And have a pee.'

'OK.' Peg sounded unconcerned and cheerful. 'I'll tell Charlie you'll be out in a minute.'

When Karen emerged, she saw that Charlie had wound down his window and Peg was leaning both arms on it, talking animatedly. At the sound of Karen's steps on the gravel, she extracted herself from the car and stood up to turn her usual blinding smile on Karen.

'Thanks, Peg,' Karen said. 'You hadn't given me a bill so I've left some money on the table. If it isn't enough, tell Charlie and he'll tell me. You've been great. Thanks.'

'No problem, chicken.'

Charlie leaned across the passenger seat to open the door for Karen. As she slid in and clicked her seatbelt into the socket, he said: 'You look as if you've seen a ghost.'

'I nearly did,' Karen said slowly. Then she smiled. 'She called me "chicken". I haven't heard that since Granny died, even here on the Island. So, tell me: how far have you got today, while I've been working?'

'We found another way in and out of the Blackwaters' house. Apart from the four doors and all the windows, I mean.'

'Oh, great! So maybe it *wasn't* Sheena who killed him. Where?'

'The old coal hole and a chute down to it from the back

yard. Not so great though. No sign anyone's been up or down it. I've got people going over it with all the kit; not just tweezers and sticky tape.'

'Then we just have to hope they find fibres of some kind,' said Karen. 'Or human skin or something. And a kitchen mallet? Any sign of the inner pair of rubber gloves?'

'No to both.'

'Any results yet for the pyjamas Sheena was wearing?'

'They can't find any blood.'

'So?'

'So unless we come up with something soon, or she confesses to something, we'll have to let her out on police bail,' Charlie said, sounding as pissed-off as Karen had ever heard him. 'What was it you told me at the start of all this about how Sir Dan could've given her such a shock she went into a fugue state and forgot everything before finding the body? Did you mean you think she could've killed him and not remember doing it?'

'That is what I meant, and it's possible from a psychological point of view, although from what I've seen of her and learned of him I don't think it's likely. I mean, he was a big man and she doesn't look especially fit. How would she have overpowered him?'

'There are ways. Could the shock of him sending her away to a second-rate bedroom more or less in the attic without him, have been enough?' Charlie's voice was edged with a cold anger that was new to Karen. Rage was familiar. Passion, too. But not this kind of chilly distaste. She wondered whether Sir Dan or his mistress was its cause.

'It's possible,' Karen said again, ignoring all the good things she now knew about the victim as she recalled every bit of her own angry response to his apparent exploitation of Sheena.

Maybe there were other ways to look at his interest in abused children and trafficked women. Charitable coverings could hide some very unhealthy drives. Had Sheena discovered something about her powerful lover that destroyed her picture of him as all good and made her challenge him when he sent for her? Had he admitted to her something she could not accept in the man she thought had loved her for so long?

Chapter 6

Day One: 4.30 p.m.

Olga, Lady Blackwater, looked like royalty as she waited for Karen and Charlie in her enormous drawing room. She stood in front of the ornate white marble fireplace, wearing a black suit with such a perfect shoulder line, neat waist and impeccable bell-like skirt that Karen was sure it had to be Chanel.

'Detective Chief Inspector Trench and Doctor Taylor,' said the middle-aged housekeeper, announcing them from the doorway.

'Thank you, Mrs Brown. That will be all,' Olga said in a husky voice that seemed surprisingly hesitant for the owner of all this luxury. It held only the slightest hint of a foreign accent beneath the drawly vowels of the British upper classes.

As Karen walked towards her over the antique Brussels weave carpet, she nearly laughed at her own misjudgment. Unlike the rescued victim of her fantasies, this woman appeared to have everything, including one of the most beautiful faces Karen had ever seen. Even the tearstains and swollen eyelids couldn't hide that.

She was also tiny, barely five feet two, and very slight. Her age could have been anything between the mid-thirties and late forties. If she had had work done, it had been of the highest quality. Her face had none of the stretched blankness too many women mistook for youth.

Her honey-coloured hair was put up in a complicated knot that looked as though it had only just been arranged, and, in spite of the tears, her discreet make-up was as perfect as her slim legs and understated shoes. Not for her anything as identifiable as Louboutins with their scarlet soles. The only jewellery she wore was a plain gold wedding ring. Her scent, the expensive Eau d'Hadrien by Annick Goutal, with its unmistakable citrus and cypress notes, overcame the wood smoke from the fire and the furniture polish.

When the door had closed behind the housekeeper with a soft sound like a chicken's cluck, Olga held out one hand towards Charlie. There was no varnish on her short nails.

'Detective Chief Inspector Trench,' she said, still with that odd hesitancy in her voice.

Charlie took her hand, holding it as gently as if it were a nestling bird. After a moment, he gave it a tiny squeeze, then let it go.

'I'm sorry for your loss,' he said, sounding more uncomfortable than an investigator of his experience should. 'You must be feeling very . . .'

Olga trembled, then grabbed hold of the mantelpiece as though afraid she might fall.

'Thank you,' she said after a moment, 'but I cannot bear to . . .' Her eyes welled and she bit her lip, then let go of the mantelpiece so that she could pull a handkerchief from her sleeve. She wiped her eyes, then blew her nose loudly.

Karen forgave her the queenliness and the luxury.

'What have you discovered about this . . . this atrocity, Chief Inspector?'

'We haven't got very far. There hasn't been much time,' Charlie said.

'Has this woman not confessed yet?' Olga coughed, as though her throat was as painful as her reddened eyes. 'The one they found in the house.'

'I think to say "they found" her is not quite right,' Karen said with great care. 'She herself called the police when she discovered the . . . the body of your husband.'

'But what was she *doing* here? She was one of his London employees.' Olga looked a little dazed, as though grief was making her brain work more slowly than usual. 'Quite a junior employee. He never invited such people here, and he cannot have wanted this one because he sent her to bed on the servants' floor. So why did she force her way in?'

'We're still not sure,' Charlie said, gesturing to Karen to ask her to take over.

'I really think it's possible you're misjudging her,' Karen said obediently. 'It doesn't look as though there was any "force". She had an email from your husband, telling her to come here urgently.'

'Are you sure, Doctor Taylor? It seems most unlikely.' Olga glanced towards a satinwood side table, where a large silver-framed photograph of Sir Dan stood with a black band tied around the top right-hand corner.

'We have actually seen the email on her BlackBerry. All she was doing when she left London was obeying an order from her employer.'

Olga lifted her shoulders in a shrug. Her bird-like collar-bones looked very prominent as the neckline of her jacket shifted with the movement. 'How can you be sure she did not fake this email? Is it so hard to do?'

'I don't know,' Karen said. 'Do you?'

An expression of surprise distorted Olga's face. 'Me? Of course not. But I cannot imagine that it would be so hard for someone in his office to gain access to his email password. With this, it must be possible for anyone to fake such a message, no?'

'You're right about that,' Charlie said. 'Anyone with the password could do it. Did he have enemies, Lady Blackwater?'

Again the shrug. 'Of course. What man of his stature does not? There are those among the rent-a-mob who believe he is evading his taxes and they think it is their right to punish him for this.' Her faint accent was growing stronger, as though stress was making her forget the language that had come so easily at the start of the interview. 'Which of course he never did. He believed absolutely that it is the duty of the rich to pay for the rest, even for these most feckless, who will not work and lie about eating until they grow like baboons. No, I am forgetting my English: balloons.'

'Good for him,' Charlie said, taking care not to catch Karen's eye.

'Then there are his rivals in business. They could be enemies, I suppose. You know there was what he called "a contested takeover" last year?'

'We're still waiting for details of that too,' Charlie said. 'The attempt failed, didn't it?'

'It did. Dan saw off the raiders, as he always does. Some of them lost a great deal of money. One of the big investment bankers was sacked.' Olga smiled suddenly, revealing hints of a stronger personality and the possibility of a sense of humour that might have matched her husband's. 'And some just don't like him. But not many people commit murder for dislike. Or do they, Chief Inspector? You will know this much better than I.'

'Are you talking about Islanders?' Charlie asked, frowning. 'Have you had trouble here?'

'Not at all, but . . .' Olga broke off to look around her magnificent room, with its world-class paintings and ravishing furniture. 'Seeing how much we have, someone might resent us. Like the Jacobins. It happens to other people. Why not to us?'

'Are you suggesting one of the locals might have killed your husband out of jealousy of his wealth and success?' Karen asked, not sure that Olga herself could believe such an absurdity.

'I accept that this seems most unlikely. All the neighbours I have met are good people. So many of them already have sent flowers. All these flowers! What can I do with them? Mrs Brown has them in the kitchen, but if there are more . . .' Olga shuddered, then smiled a little. 'So, no: I do not think we are hated.'

'Doesn't sound like it,' Charlie said with real warmth. 'Not if they're giving you flowers.'

'Exactly. After all, we do bring employment here – quite a lot of it – and we never hire overners.' Olga paused for a moment, flicked a glance in Karen's direction before offering an explanation. 'What you would call outsiders. The Islanders have always seemed to appreciate this, and they seem also to like the glamour that attaches to anyone with a private plane or a helicopter. But why should we even be discussing them? You have the killer already. This young woman, who was here inside a bolted house, alone with my husband's body.'

'We're still not sure about her,' Charlie said casually. 'There's been a suggestion that she could have been his mistress.'

Karen was shocked at the way he was revealing Sheena's secret, guarded so closely for so long in order to protect this woman's frail sensibilities. But Olga's colour did not change. Nor did her expression carry any surprise or anxiety. Instead a faint laugh emerged from her lips, and she looked anything but fragile.

'Do not be ridiculous,' she said. 'Did she tell you this?'

Charlie shrugged, saying, 'She hasn't denied it.'

Olga's laugh sounded again, then she coughed, covering her mouth with her right hand, and closed her eyes. After a few seconds she blew her nose again, then stuffed the handkerchief back up her sleeve and faced them with a small brave smile.

'For a moment this absurdity made me forget what has happened. But . . .' She broke off and turned away to compose herself once more. A moment later she was standing with her arms by her side again, politely smiling. 'I must not let myself think about what I have lost until you have completed your investigation and no longer need me. Until then I will always try to help you, but you must forgive me if sometimes I cannot speak so easily.'

She took a step towards Karen and gestured to the long low cream-coloured sofa, which was filled with cushions made of ancient tapestry, glowing in the subtle raspberry tones of the hangings she'd seen in the Cluny Museum when Will had taken her to Paris one weekend

'You see how I forget myself. Please forgive my bad behaviour and take a seat.' Olga herself chose a gilded French elbow chair, upholstered in thick gold-coloured silk, sitting with a very straight back and crossing her legs at the ankle.

'Thank you.' Karen settled herself in the soft, deep sofa, with relief, pulling three of the cushions behind her aching back for support. 'So you do not believe there was any personal connection between your husband and Sheena?'

'I am absolutely certain there was not.' Olga sounded as though only a fool would have doubted her husband's fidelity.

'But . . .' Karen began, only to be silenced by the pain in the other woman's large brown eyes.

'Men of his achievements – as well as looking the way he does . . . did – always attract these emotionally incontinent young women,' Olga said, with a kind of detached pity that impressed Karen. 'This one has probably been fantasizing about him for years. Perhaps this will be why she faked the email, pretending to herself that he loved and needed her. I understand how these things happen. So did Dan. We often talked of it. It is "one of the hazards of success", he said when he told me about the first of them. There have been many during the eighteen years we have been married. He always told me when it happened. I have felt sorry for most of the women. They do not often cause much trouble when he has gently explained to them the realities of all our lives.'

When she had finished speaking, she sat in silence, back as

straight as a pane of glass. Charlie looked interested. After a while, he turned to Karen.

'Is that possible in this case?' he asked.

'Plenty of erotomaniac stalkers have persuaded themselves that the object of their fantasies secretly loves them back,' Karen said, with the coolness professional certainty always brought her. 'It occurs often in the literature. I must say that Sheena Greves did not strike me as the type. But there'll be no difficulty checking her story.'

'True,' Charlie said. 'Officers are going through her statements right now. By the time I left, everything she said checked out. Not least the fact that Sir Dan bought a house in Wilkes Street, Spitalfields, for her. It's in her name, Lady Blackwater, but the money behind the purchase was his. And he paid for her defence when she was in the dock for killing her child. Both those facts mean she . . .'

'Aah, she's *that* one,' Olga said, visibly relaxing. Her voice warmed up too. 'I could not understand why you had even contemplated believing such a nonsense. Now I see. It is no problem. Yes, my darling Dan paid for the lawyers and yes he bought the house. He – we both – felt so sorry for *her*.'

'Did you?' Karen allowed herself to sound doubtful. 'May I ask why?'

'She came from the same very poor part of London where Dan's mother lived when he was a young boy. She was one of those heroic single mothers from the underclass, you see, and there was so little he could do for her when he was young. She died when he was about twelve, I believe. He feels he owes a debt to people like her. Sentimental, perhaps, but charming, no?'

Karen didn't look at Charlie, who had also grown up believing he had failed to protect his mother as he should have done.

'I think he felt that this . . .' Olga's impeccably threaded eyebrows flattened over her eyes as she frowned. 'Remind me of her name?'

'Sheena Greves.' Charlie's voice was unemotional. Either he had not made the link between his own experience and that of the victim or he had already discounted it.

'This is it. This Sheena.' Olga's smile warmed a little. 'I think she reminded him of his poor dead mother. She came to him when she fell pregnant and begged not only to keep her job – which she would have anyway with all this terrible legislation you have here in the UK – but also for an interest-free loan so that she could afford to keep the child. Dan consulted me and we came to the conclusion that we should help her.'

'When was this?' Karen asked, finding the scene hard to imagine.

'Oh, when? I should remember. It must be six years ago? Five, perhaps? I cannot be sure. He felt so sorry for her. After he had explained, it was easy for me to agree that we should help.' A faint delicate pink flush made Olga look even more beautiful. 'To buy a house and settle some money on her was a kind of fleabite to us. I know it may seem shocking to someone on a policeman's wage, but it is how it is. Like one of our charities, no?'

As Karen watched, assessing tiny changes in Olga's body language and differences in the timbre of her voice, her face hardened until all the warmth and tolerance disappeared.

'We had no idea, you see, that she was so emotionally unstable that she would build this charitable generosity into some kind of personal link and make believe my husband belonged in some way to her and then kill him when she realized the truth.'

'The truth?' Charlie repeated, making it a question.

Olga produced another tiny smile and bent her head to examine her perfect nails. 'That he did not care about her as a person; only as a symbol,' she said, looking up again. 'He felt as he would about any one of his employees, either at work or here in the house. Loyal and so to be well treated and supported, but always a member of his staff.'

'Talking of staff,' Karen began and watched Olga's expression turn haughty.

'Yes, Doctor Taylor?'

'Do you know why your husband was alone here last night – apart from Sheena?'

'This is also easy to answer,' Olga said, the hauteur overtaken by another faint smile. 'My husband never liked to have the servants living in. While we are both away or when I am in residence, the housekeeper stays here in the house like a French *gardienne*, although the others still come in by the day, but my husband, always surrounded by people in his London life, craved solitude here. When he was here alone at weekends, Mrs Brown moved out to sleep in the cottage she and her husband have – he is our gardener – and then she would come up to the house between eight o'clock in the morning, when she prepared my husband's breakfast, and half-past nine in the evening, when she finished clearing away his dinner.'

'And so she knows all the codes and passwords for the security system?' Karen asked.

Olga shrugged her elegant shoulders. 'But of course. How

else could she do her work? None of the other servants know. She is always here to let them in and is the last to leave at the end of the day. We pay her for carrying this responsibility. She is completely trustworthy, has been with us for many years.'

'I see. Thank you,' Karen said. 'Just one more question: when your husband was in London, where did he stay?'

'There is a flat in the penthouse in his office building.' Olga's laugh sounded like the tinkling of a tiny silver triangle. 'It is not a beautiful part of London, but the view is fabulous. And we have had our favourite decorator there . . .' She broke off to look around her drawing room, with its paintings by Kandinsky and Paul Klee. Turning back to face Karen with a self-depre-cating smile, she went on: 'So it is elegant and very comfortable. And, of course, convenient for a workaholic like my husband. No commuting.'

'I see, thank you,' Karen said, thinking her way around a much more difficult question. She never got the chance to ask it.

Olga had risen to her feet and glided back to her position in front of the fire to press a discreet bell beside it.

The door opened instantly, almost as though the house-keeper had been just outside, eavesdropping. Karen glanced at her and was glad to see no sign of resentment in her square face. Her eyes were a clear grey and her whole demeanour was of sensible efficiency. She looked about Sir Dan's age, and was more solidly built than Olga but barely an inch taller.

'Ah, Mrs Brown,' Olga said, clearly untroubled by any possibility of having been overheard or any suspicion of this woman. 'Thank you. Will you show Chief Inspector Trench and Doctor Taylor out?' She didn't offer her hand again, but she did add to Charlie alone: 'You will keep me informed of your progress towards charging the killer of my husband, won't you?'

'I will,' he said, adding after a moment, 'but may I suggest that when the media come – and they will – you do not tell them anything beyond the fact of his death.'

An expression of supreme disdain made Olga's face look as though it had been carved out of stone. 'Do you seriously believe I do not understand how the press work in this country? Dan and I have taken out so many injunctions over the years, I can organize our lawyers in my sleep. I would not speak to a journalist if I were drowning and he the only possible rescuer, and my servants here know better than to discuss my affairs with anyone also.'

'Great,' Charlie said, making no comment on her contempt. 'Our press department can help, and if you're prepared to help them, then . . .'

'I do not speak to the media.' All the hauteur was back in Olga's voice and she even managed to make herself look taller, more substantial.

'Fine. Right.' Charlie seemed disconcerted. 'Well, then the only thing left is the DNA. We will need samples from you and everyone who works in the house, for elimination purposes. Will you come to the police station, or shall I send an officer up here?'

'I would prefer you to send someone.'

Karen followed Charlie out of the house and back into his car. Sitting in the driving seat, he turned to look at her, an expression on his face that suggested sympathy, but also some amusement, awe, disbelief, all at once.

'I know,' Karen said, adding, *'plus royale que la reine.'*

'Don't flaunt your education over me, lass,' he said with a grin. 'D'you think it's possible Sheena is a – what did you call it? – an erotomaniac stalker?'

'It's possible.' Karen stared at the great white house with its neo-classical portico and pompous urns on either side of the front steps. 'But think what Olga's just told us about his dislike of living-in staff. Could it be that he didn't have quite such a highly developed taste for grandeur as she has? Maybe he wanted a more ordinary kind of woman, someone he could relax with. Put on his slippers and all that. You're a bloke; what d'you think? Could you relax with Olga?'

Charlie's face lightened for a moment, but he didn't comment. He didn't need to. The very thought of him lolling about after work in a room like the one they'd just left made Karen smile.

'OK, but say you're wrong about that and Olga's right,' he said, 'how would the child, Andy, and his death fit in with the erotomaniac syndrome?'

'Easily enough,' Karen said sadly. 'If Sheena were the kind of lonely early-middle-aged office devotee, fantasizing about the boss, she could have had a baby by some random pick-up and persuaded herself it was Sir Dan's. When he and Olga bought her the house, that would have added a lot of fuel to her mental furnace.'

'But the death?' Charlie was impatient.

Karen felt even sadder and more reluctant to follow the proposition through to the end. But this was her job.

'If she is the kind of woman who lives in her head, making up stories to keep herself happy, then she might have found the real-life existence of a baby more than she could manage.' Karen looked sideways at him and saw that he was frowning through the windscreen. 'She could have been as happy as anything with her story of how Sir Dan couldn't leave his wife ...'

'Yeah,' Charlie said. 'And that's something I can definitely believe, can't you? Didn't you see the way Olga had to hold on to the mantelpiece to keep upright, poor little thing? Talk about vulnerable.'

'I did,' Karen said, trying to keep the dialogue cool enough to avoid missing important ideas in a wave of sympathy. 'But she may not always be so fragile. After all, her husband has just been killed in a revolting way. That would make anyone wobbly. But whether it's true or not, Sheena could still have invented the whole story, dreaming of Sir Dan coming to spend happy evenings in the house he had actually bought for her, giving her a baby. She could have believed every word of it, even though none of it ever actually happened.'

'Then trying to feed the kid, keeping it quiet, not getting any sleep, doing its nappies, having it howling ... Yeah,' Charlie said again, 'I can see how that kind of reality would screw the dream. But could it make her kill the child?'

'Infanticide is the most common cause of death in babies,' Karen said. 'And post-partum psychosis isn't rare. It's possible she did it.'

'So are you saying you think she's still psychotic, that she *did* kill Sir Dan herself?'

'I don't know.' Karen saw how she was irritating him, but she could never pretend a certainty she didn't have. 'No evidence yet. But that pattern does work in its own terms.

Whether it applies to Sheena or not . . . We'll have to talk to her again. And when your officers are back with statements from her colleagues and family we'll know more, and be able to frame better questions.'

'OK.' Charlie turned the key in the ignition and the powerful engine of his Audi purred into life. 'On the way back to the nick you can fill me in on how far you've got with Sir Dan's psych profile.'

He swung the car round and down the gravel drive towards the main road.

'What Olga said fits with the published biographies,' Karen said, pulling out the notes she'd made at the Goose this morning. 'He never knew his father. Mother died when he was twelve. He survived a couple of years in a children's home, then went out to work in a small shop in Chelmsford. Classic rags-to-riches story. He spends a lot of those riches now on charities protecting abused children and also trafficked women, which suggests . . .'

'His mother could've been a tom?' Charlie said. 'That's what Olga was on about, wasn't it?'

'It's the obvious conclusion to draw.' Karen enjoyed the times when Charlie's mind worked in parallel with her own. It didn't happen often and she planned to make the most of it, adding, 'Couldn't save mum when he was a boy, so once he's grown up and made billions he does whatever he can to save other women like her.'

'In which case, there could be plenty of people who'd want him dead.'

'Pimps and traffickers, you mean? Yup. Known to be exceptionally violent, as a type. Punitive; vengeful, too. Although, somehow the Island doesn't seem an enormously likely place for pimps and traffickers to operate, does it?'

Charlie gave a brief cackle of laughter, which made her move closer to him for a second.

'Right. But maybe that was the appeal of the place for the killers.'

'Although it would be a weirdly elaborate set-up, wouldn't it?' Karen said. 'For some trafficker who resented the way Sir Dan had been stealing his "product" to summon Sheena, mess about with the burglar alarm to implicate her, and . . . ?'

'What? You saying you think they fitted her up?' Charlie's voice was like a guard dog's bark. 'No way. Her arrival must've been coincidence.'

'Bloody convenient coincidence,' Karen said, turning her head so that she could watch the changing expressions on his face.

'Are you going back to the mainland tonight?' he said, his tone barely changing from the earlier sharp aggression. 'Will expecting you?'

'Yes. And no.'

Karen realized she must have let some of her feelings out in her voice when Charlie braked hard, bringing the car almost to a stop. Luckily there was no one behind them.

'Why isn't he expecting you?' he said in a quite different voice as he signalled into a lay-by and slid to a halt beside a tattered rubbish bin with evidence of long-past picnics scattered around it.

Karen turned away and stared out at the bare sticks of the winter trees. Only the clinging suffocating ivy that twined around their trunks still had green leaves on it.

'Karen, what's up?'

'He's dumped me,' she said, still concentrating on the trees. She was proud of the way her own voice sounded: calm, not angry, and without a single quiver; unlike her mind, which was still a churning mass of miserable weediness and fury.

Charlie was silent. She couldn't turn to face him because she wanted him to tell her Will was a fool, that he himself would always . . . She had to stop herself there because she didn't know what she wanted from him except comfort, and he didn't really do comfort. After a moment, he switched on the engine again and drove in silence until they reached the police station.

'Denise!' he bellowed as soon as they walked into the incident room. 'Any tea going? Two cups. Milk. No sugar. Annie?'

'Sir.'

'What've you got for us?'

Annie's eyebrows rose, and she looked from Charlie to Karen and then back again with clear curiosity. Karen wondered what Annie could see in their faces and she fought to forget everything except the work she should be doing.

'Not a lot,' Annie said, in a voice that gave no clue to her thoughts. 'I talked to the secretary in her office, who denies all knowledge of any friendship – let alone anything more – between Sir Dan and Sheena. Said Sheena was a good boss to work for, occasionally got agitated and sure she'd cocked up something important but never had. Made the odd mistake, but never anything that couldn't be corrected. Never blamed Terry – that's the secretary – for her own mistakes, which is rare in Terry's experience.'

'Rare and appealing,' Karen said, chalking up another

mental credit to Sheena. She hoped they'd find another, like-lier, suspect soon. 'What else? Any friends?'

'None I've found so far. Occasionally went out to eat or drink with the other women in the publicity office, but the general view is that she had to do so much formal enter-taining for Sir Dan, and going to launches or shows of one sort or another, that she wanted to hunker down on her own at weekends. No whisper of gossip about an affair anywhere.'

'What about the baby?' Karen said. 'Any suggestion of who the father was?'

'None.' Annie dropped into a seat. 'They weren't interested. Assumed it was a holiday romance. She'd had a couple of weeks off in the Dodecanese a few months before she announced the pregnancy and told them she wasn't going to have any contact with the father, so I think they had a mental picture of a Greek fisherman. Something like it anyway. But they revelled in the drama of the death and the trial and all that.'

'Did they like her?' Karen asked.

'So-so, I think. An easy colleague but not a close mate.'

'Right,' said Charlie. 'Any family?'

'None that we can find. Only child. Both parents dead. There must be aunties or cousins somewhere, but none in her immediate circle.'

'You'll be checking out the house in Spitalfields, I assume,' Karen said to Charlie. 'Can I see it, too?'

He looked at his watch. 'I've borrowed a CSI from the Met, who's probably there now. You can see it when they've finished, Karen. Bit late to go tonight. Let's have another crack at her now and go to London together first thing tomorrow.

I've an appointment with Sir Dan's chief executive, Gilbert Tackley. OK?'

Karen shrugged. She clearly wasn't going to get to Norfolk until they'd solved this killing.

'Come on.' Charlie's smile had some of the old wickedness she had always enjoyed. 'See where you get with Sheena when you suggest erotomania and stalking, before I make my report to the ACC.'

Chapter 7

Day One: 7.00 p.m.

'Well?' Charlie asked as they emerged into the dim evening light and fresh salty air outside the police station after the fruitless final interview of the day. 'What do you think?'

'I think your DC Richard Silver is a seriously good interviewer, and I can quite see why he was pissed off that you'd brought me in on the investigation.'

Charlie's dark face split into delighted grin. 'He is good, isn't he? Did all the special courses.'

'Why's he still a constable? He must be, what? Past forty?'

'Yeah. But he's exam-phobic or whatever you'd call it. Fluffed the sergeant's exams too many times. Won't try again. Gives everyone a hard time, but it's worth it for what he brings to the team.'

'Like what?'

'Good ideas,' Charlie said, shrugging. 'Insights. And he's a worker. But that's not what I meant. What about *Sheena*? I brought you in for your psych insights. I need them now.'

'All I know so far is that she has a lot of natural dignity and

is convinced she was Sir Dan's lover. That doesn't necessarily
mean it's true. But, as she said, there'll be no evidence because
they both worked so hard to ensure that there never would be
anything to alert – or worry – Olga.'

'Bummer.'

'The house may tell us more. It's hard to fake a man's habit-
ual presence. Are you driving tomorrow? Will you pick me up
in the morning on your way?'

'I'm going by train after my stint at the TV studio. Just as
quick, if not quicker, and I can work during the trip. I could
pick you up on my way to the station,' Charlie said, concentrating hard on a seagull that was pecking at a discarded burger
in the gutter. 'Or I could put you up in my flat here tonight and
you could come to the studio with me. The flat isn't let at the
moment. Not much call for rented accommodation in Cowes
in February.'

'I haven't any luggage,' Karen said quickly, without even
thinking about what she wanted. 'Not even a toothbrush.'

'Boots is still open,' he said, not looking at her. She appre-
ciated the way he was being so businesslike, when the
drumming of her blood told her that neither of them felt
remotely cool.

'And I ought to check on the glazier,' she added so fast that
she jammed the words together. 'Make sure the windows are
secure and he's double-locked the door. I need . . .'

'Karen,' Charlie said in a voice that amazed her: full of
tenderness and acceptance. 'Don't make excuses. You don't
need to. Just say yes or no. I won't . . . Either way, I won't
make life difficult for you.'

Her teeth came down on her already cracked lip, hurting

her. The bird went on feeding from the burger. Charlie's arm settled around her shoulders and his hand curled around her arm.

'Hmm?' he murmured gently. 'What do you think?'

Karen leaned against him and felt his hand tighten. All the humiliation of Will's desertion disappeared in a wave of tingling pleasure.

'Come on,' Charlie said, taking her gesture for consent. 'Twelve minutes' walk at most.'

They didn't talk, but he hung on to her all the way. She found walking beside him easy, with no clumsy bumps or lack of rhythm. Even when there was a deep puddle, or an uneven paving stone, they worked out how to get round it without words, always in step. Her only problem was increasing breathlessness and a light-headed dizziness that had nothing to do with low blood pressure.

At last they arrived outside a neat double-fronted red-brick house with a wide white front door in the middle and a narrower side door painted black. Charlie took her there, let them in, pressed a light switch and shuddered.

'I didn't think of the cold. So romantic!' He tried to laugh. 'Come on up, I'll turn on the boiler as we go.'

Karen's teeth were chattering. She followed him up the narrow staircase at the end of the little hall. He paused at the turn of the stairs to open a tall cupboard door and pressed some switches. She heard the clicks and whoosh of a gas boiler firing up.

'First go,' he said, emerging from the cupboard with a triumphant look on his face. 'Wonders of modern technology. Don't look like that, pet.'

'Like what?' Karen said, teeth still clattering against each other.

'Like you're facing a psycho with an axe.'

She laughed. 'I'm cold. That's all. We should've gone back to my flat. It's warm as anything there.'

'No ghosts here, though,' he said, taking her hand and leading her into a large room overlooking the sea. 'Which makes it better.'

The moon had risen and was almost full, making the sea look like black silk with silver lace edging. The star-spattered indigo sky above it could have been a theatrical backdrop. Charlie made to pull the curtains shut.

'Don't,' Karen whispered. 'No one can see in if we don't put on the lights and it's so . . . gorgeous.'

He came back to the centre of the room and took her face between his hands. She could feel the roughness of his skin and the strength of his fingers as he drew her towards him. She didn't fight it, feeling a sense of luscious relief as his lips touched hers. Softness and warmth and slow gentleness.

Moments later she pulled him towards the bed, aware that there'd be no sheets on it and not bothered, knowing it was far too cold to undress but wanting him too much to care. He pushed up the scarlet cashmere tunic as she lay on the bed, and tugged the cream T-shirt from under the belt of her jeans until he could slide his hands up against her skin.

'No bra,' he murmured against her lips. 'Perfect.'

Moments later her shiver had nothing to do with the cold, and she moved against him urgently.

'Patience, pet,' he said, taking his hands away.

'Charlie!'

'Shhh,' he said, smiling down at her. 'We've waited a long time. No rush now.'

He straddled her and pushed both tunic and T-shirt right up under her armpits. She raised her arms above her head, knowing he wasn't going to make her wait longer than she could bear.

He was still asleep when she woke, feeling the weight of his head pressing down against her breastbone, feeling the steady beat of his heart and the warmth of his breath on her skin. Her racing mind was still for once, filled with a sense of rightness that left no room for questions or any ideas at all. She was at home here. There were no monsters hiding in the corners of the moonlit room. And for once there was nothing for her to analyse; only to feel.

Her arms were lying flat against the bedcover. She brought them up around him, with one hand cupping the back of his head. He moved closer, still sleeping, and she stroked his hair, remembering every word, every move, every sensation they'd just shared. She slept again.

When she woke for the second time, he was gone. The sides of the thick old quilted bedcover had been brought up to cover her body with plumply stuffed warmth. When she sat up, clutching it against her, she heard and felt something crackling. Letting go of the cover, shivering in the blast of cold air that took its place, she saw a piece of paper fluttering down and caught it just before it hit the floor.

Torn from the front of a paperback cookery book, it carried

a brief message in Charlie's characteristically impatient black handwriting:

Gone back to the nick. Phone me when you wake. You'll need to eat. Water should be hot now.

Karen read the terse instructions three times, searching for the feelings she wanted them to express, then she looked at her watch. Astonishingly, it was only half past ten. She picked up her phone.

'Hi,' he said and she could tell he was smiling. 'I thought it was time for food, but I wanted to wait for you. It'll have to be a takeaway at this time of night on the Island in winter. Indian or Chinese?'

'Whatever,' she said. 'I'll go and shower and make up the bed. How long will you be?'

'Twenty minutes? That long enough for you?'

'Plenty. Charlie?'

'Yeah?'

'I . . . no. You . . .'

'Save it. Twenty minutes.' He was still smiling, she knew, when he added: 'I've bought you a toothbrush.'

Sitting opposite him on the train to London next day, taking the route Sheena had used in reverse, Karen felt as though something that had been knotted inside her for as long as she could remember had been untied. Charlie had emerged from his stint in front of the television cameras in an edgy mood that saddened her, but now he was reading peacefully and his facial muscles looked as soft as they had when she'd first woken beside him this morning.

She watched as he steadily made his way through a thick wodge of printout. After a moment he looked up as though she'd called his name. He grinned a secret private kind of smile and went back to work, breathing more deeply than before.

Karen looked back at her screen and tried to forget about last night and her new freedom, concentrating instead on her psychological profile of Sir Dan Blackwater, and the huge gaps in her knowledge of his wife. The ping of an arriving email was a welcome distraction and when she saw it was from his Island lawyer, Antony Quiggly, she was even more pleased.

Dear Karen, Good to hear from you again. Naturally I can't tell you anything about my work for Sir Dan, but his charitable venture on the Island isn't secret and I'm more than happy to give you any leads you need. What I've read of his death in the papers this morning is appalling. A dreadful loss of a fine and generous man. I am particularly sorry because we were about to meet for the first time in at least a year.

She quickly typed a reply:

Dear Antony, Thank you. I'd be grateful for anything you can tell me, both about the man and about his charities. Was he a friend?

The answer came quickly:

Not a friend, no. We moved in very different circles. But I liked him enormously. You can tell a lot about a man from the way he deals with his advisors and their staff. Sir Dan was the soul of courtesy and patience, when patience was required. He did not tolerate mistakes, but then who would? I don't myself. His main Island charity is Clagbourne House, a refuge for women who have been rescued from violent pimps. They spend however long they need here. There's a resident counsellor and house manager. They use the local doctors' practices. And there has never been the slightest trouble. He hasn't taken an active part in the day-to-day running of the place, although Lady Blackwater has a role in encouraging those of the young women who are not English to learn the language, brush up their general education and training for the jobs that will consolidate their rescue. She's a great role model.

Karen emailed back:

Will his death cause problems for the funding of the charity?

The answer came almost as soon as she'd hit 'send'.

That comes under client confidentiality. Sorry.

Karen was interested, assuming that Sir Dan must have set up a trust to fund Clagbourne House. Otherwise, why would he have used Antony, who was a specialist in wills and trusts? With the donor dead, why would Antony try to hide behind client confidentiality?

'Is something going on?' she said aloud, surprising the

strangers in the other two seats at the table. They both looked away at once, embarrassed, but Charlie raised his eyebrows, obviously asking her to explain what she meant.

'His charities, and their funding, and his motives,' Karen said, believing that so long as she avoided using Sir Dan's name it would not matter who overheard her. 'I wish I'd met him.'

Charlie's smile widened. ''S what I always feel, faced with . . .' he glanced at the strangers next to them and went on, 'this kind of thing. You think: come you on, you bugger, talk to me.'

'Maybe the house will help.'

'And the CEO,' Charlie said.

The recorded voice of the train's guard interrupted, telling them they were approaching Waterloo Station. Karen switched off her laptop and unplugged it from the socket in the train's wall.

'What's the best way from here?' she asked, knowing Charlie would have worked it all out. He could be lavishly careless with some things, but time was never wasted and he always knew where he was going.

'The Drain to Bank,' he said, referring to the dedicated tube line that took commuters from the rail terminus at Waterloo directly into the heart of the City of London, 'then one ordinary tube stop to Liverpool Street, then a short walk. If Sheena *was* his girlfriend, he must've picked Spitalfields for her house because he could walk there from head office in five minutes flat.'

Gilbert Tackley, Sir Dan's Chief Executive, was immediately impressive. Not quite as tall as his late boss, he exuded authority without arrogance. He looked shocked and almost as unhappy as Olga, but he found a polite smile to greet Karen and Charlie, and his palm was warm and dry as he shook their hands. To Karen, he seemed comfortable in his own skin, which was the quality she most envied in anyone.

His office was a lot more luxurious than the grey concrete-and-glass exterior of the 1960s building had suggested, and it was furnished with some of the best of modern Scandinavian design. His various screens were almost as thin as paper, and there was a beautiful Bang & Olufsen sound system on a side shelf.

Money called out to them, in its most restrained and tasteful way, from everything in the big room, but Gilbert poured their coffee himself from a tray that was already waiting. Karen took a sip from the cup he offered her and smiled at once. This was an excellent light Kenya Peaberry blend, which suited the hour and their surroundings. She gave him full marks, which was rare when it came to coffee.

'Don't let us waste time exchanging comments on Dan's death,' he said in an East End accent he hadn't bothered to moderate, which fitted oddly with his elaborate sentences. He leaned down to take his own cup from the tray. 'I haven't the time, and you didn't know him. Please take a seat.'

'Fine,' Charlie said, as one professional to another. He chose the corner of an L-shaped upholstered unit near the big glass desk, while Karen sat a few yards away in an Arne Jacobsen egg chair that she guessed was probably an original. She saw a pile of today's papers on a side table, and even from her chair could read the first lines of the piece in the most respectable of the tabloids:

Sir Dan Blackwater brutally murdered on holiday island.
Police call for witnesses even though a woman is already
helping with their enquiries.

'I've brought Doctor Taylor with me,' Charlie added,
'because she's working on a psychological profile of the victim
in order to point us towards the most likely suspects. Karen,
d'you want to start?'

'Thank you.' She turned away from the papers and faced the
CEO. 'Can you sum him up in a few words?'

'Loyal. Hardworking. Generous. Tolerant of everything
except laziness and deceit.'

'Wow!' she said. 'Quite a testimonial. How did he display
his intolerance?'

For a second Gilbert's expression changed into a flashing
smile of such informality and affection that Karen almost
doubted she'd seen it.

'We used to call it WOL,' he said, adding a quick transla-
tion, 'the withdrawal of love.'

'Who's "we"?' she asked.

'Dan and me.'

'How did you meet?' Karen would have asked the question
in any case, but she was increasingly interested in their
relationship.

Gilbert's face stiffened a little and some of his healthy colour
left his cheeks.

'At the children's home where we did time,' he said in a
voice that hinted at all kinds of pain. Karen was about to ask
for more, but he gave her enough of a clue without any prompting. 'He was always bigger than the rest, and he made himself

my protector. When he left he promised he'd give me a job as soon as he'd made enough money to need anyone. It only took him four years. We've worked together ever since. He's the best friend I could have had.'

And were you *his* best friend? Karen wondered, but she didn't ask the question aloud. Instead she put it more tactfully, saying, 'Did you socialize much outside the office?'

'A bit. My wife's always believed she's not in Olga's league and didn't like feeling . . . well, she called it "being put in my place", so Dan and I tended to go out on our own: you know, snooker in the pub, pie-and-mash in one of the old shops. Just the two of us, enjoying a boys' night out and looking back at the distance we'd come.'

'Yeah, I do know,' Charlie said with feeling. Gilbert flicked him a glance that hinted at hostility, as though no one should presume to understand the full importance of his relationship with Dan Blackwater.

'How did the WOL manifest itself?' Karen asked quickly, seeing that Charlie was taken aback by the implied aggression. She was interested, too, amused by the term and knowing exactly what it meant. What she did not know was how the tactic could have affected some of Sir Dan's victims.

'Just that,' Gilbert said, looking at something on the wall above their heads. 'He'd withdraw himself from them in every way.'

Karen turned to see what interested him so much and found a small pencil portrait of Sir Dan, very slight in outline and yet vividly expressive of great strength and a lot of the humour she'd seen in his few published letters. She glanced back at Gilbert, whose face was now a mask of polite competence. What exactly did it hide?

'He sent them to a kind of emotional Siberia,' Gilbert said, still looking at the portrait. 'He hardly ever sacked anyone, because he didn't like throwing people out of work, knowing how it felt to live without means of support. But he'd move them away from him, into some position where he didn't have to see them, and he'd wait to hear from their line manager about their chances of earning their way back by effort and demonstrable loyalty.'

'Any of them ever get back?' Charlie asked, with a sharpness that must have had more to do with the other man's attitude than his own interest in this particular question.

'Quite a few. You'd be surprised.' Gilbert's smile looked more convincing again. 'Being part of the inner circle was . . . amazing. And the goal of everyone in the company. Well, group of companies.'

'Who didn't work their way back?' Karen asked.

'I can probably give you a list,' Gilbert said. 'But it'll take a while. OK if I email it to you later this afternoon?'

'Fine,' Charlie said. 'But say now if there was anyone in particular.'

'The saddest case was a bloke in the accounts department. Hand in the till. He did get fired. Nearly three years ago now.'

'Reported to the police?' Charlie's voice was that of someone who expected the answer 'no'.

'Dan didn't think the police would be appropriate. Calling them in to investigate a staff member would not be good for the companies' image. But he did sack him. Name of Trevor Fieldsham. My PA can get his last-known address for you later. But he was a pathetic individual. Unlikely to be able to do something like this, even if he wanted to.'

'Any other enemies?'

Gilbert repeated what Olga had said about the recently failed takeover, filling in more details than she had given them about the bankers in question and the officers of the company that had dared to mount a raid on Dan Blackwater's companies. While he was talking, a buzzer sounded outside the office. Gilbert pushed his left wrist forward, well beyond the cuff of his immaculate shirt, and glanced at his Longines watch.

'Don't think I'm not prepared to talk for as long as you need to catch his killer,' he said, looking up at Charlie. 'But, as you can imagine, we have a hell of a lot to do here, with the press besieging us and everyone we do business with needing reassurance, so . . .'

'Who takes over now?' Karen asked.

'In the short term, me,' he said, looking surprised at her intervention. 'But it'll have to go to the shareholders, and they may want more of a figurehead. Dan . . . well, he knew my strengths better than I did, but I'd be the first to admit those have never been the public side of things. We'll call an EGM as soon as is practicable and get the right man. Or woman, I suppose, although . . .'

'And the shareholders are?' Charlie said, picking up Karen's lead.

Gilbert laughed. 'We're a plc. I can't give you all the names off the top of my head. Although it's public knowledge. You can find the list.'

'You know what I mean. *Sir*.' Charlie showed his teeth.

'The majority shareholders are – or were – Sir Dan and his wife, with fifty-four per cent,' Gilbert said, chastened but not apologetic. 'I have a ten per cent stake. Institutional shareholders have approximately thirty per cent, and the rest belong to grannies and suchlike, some of them holding only a few hundred quids' worth.'

Karen saw that the pink *Financial Times* lay in the heap below the tabloids.

'What's happened to the share price since his death?' she asked.

'Fallen by eight and a quarter pence.' Gilbert's expressive face was now blank of everything except courtesy.

Lightning calculation had never been among Karen's talents, but she assumed that a ten per cent stake must amount to several hundred thousand shares, and the loss of even eight pence on each of those added up to some people's annual salary; all gone in a single day.

'It'll go down a lot further once more details of how he died get out.' Gilbert sounded resigned. 'I must say, I'm impressed they haven't yet. How've you managed to keep such a tight lid on it?'

Charlie shrugged his big shoulders. 'Everyone on my team knows not to leak and both Blackwaters are famous for taking out every kind of injunction. You must know that's why the media's wary enough to accept what our press department's telling them. But it won't last long. We have to use it while we can.'

'Talking of injunctions and secrecy and such,' Karen said. 'What can you tell us about Sheena Greves?'

'Sheena?' Gilbert's face and voice both expressed complete surprise. 'Why? She's not the woman helping you with your enquiries, is she?'

'Just answer the question, sir.' Charlie didn't often fall back into traditional copper-speak.

'Excellent employee.' Gilbert's eyes were cold now, and his voice was distant, as though his attention was distracted. 'Never subject to WOL. Worked hard. Came back after the tragedy of her child's death in an exemplary way. Dan really rated her. Again: why?'

'Any more than that?' Karen asked with a sympathetic note in her voice. 'Any out-of-office relationship between them?'

'With *Sheena*?' Gilbert's surprise intensified until he was concentrating fully again. 'Have you ever seen Olga?'

Karen nodded.

'Then you know how gorgeous she is. Why would Dan . . . ? Sorry.' He laughed, sounding genuinely amused. 'Only someone who didn't know him could think Sheena was ever more to him than an efficient, hard-working, loyal employee, who earned every penny of her generous salary. While I'm in charge we'll definitely keep her on, and, if I have any influence after the EGM, for the foreseeable future. Now, unless there's anything else, I really do have to get on. I've a meeting with the FD. He's waiting outside.'

'Before we go, sir.' Charlie was back in cop mode. 'Who do you think could've killed Sir Dan, crucified and mutilated his body?'

Karen knew why Charlie was trying to shock all the potential suspects, but she didn't like it. Gilbert's colour fluctuated again and his eyelids closed for a second. But he showed no sign of the slight sly satisfaction Karen had seen in the eyes of several killers who had thought they'd got away with it.

Gilbert drew in a breath and stood taller than before,

glanced at the pencil portrait and spoke directly to it. 'He was a great man. And generous to his very bones. Only a truly sick individual could have done something like this. All I can hope is that it was a case of mistaken identity. No one who knew Dan – really knew him – could have done this. If it turns out to be anyone I've ever met, I . . .'

He paused, stared at the drawing again, then looked back at Charlie. 'All I can say is it'll be lucky for him that justice is in the hands of the law these days and not individuals like me.'

'Sir Dan did like to keep his life in compartments, didn't he?' Karen said, as she and Charlie left the dull concrete-and-glass building to walk to Spitalfields.

'Sounds like it,' Charlie said, stopping to jab a finger on the button for the pedestrian crossing. They waited for the lights to change. 'What does that tell you?'

'He enjoyed intense relationships,' Karen said slowly, 'but only in bite-sized portions, which would fit with his upbringing.'

'Like how?'

'Any boy who'd loved his mother but thought he'd failed her would find it hard to commit himself a hundred per cent to anyone else. At some level he'll think: what if I can't make it work again? What if the love I have for this person turns out to be unearned? How do I know it's safe to trust anyone? Was my mother the woman I thought she was? Did she deserve what I felt for her? What if I'm hurt again? Left in the cold again like I was when she abandoned me?'

Charlie said nothing, and Karen was once more reminded of the life he had lived as a child, defending his mother against his brutal father, once even having both arms broken as he tried to stop her being beaten. Karen put on her most professional voice to add, 'So Sir Dan may have subconsciously ensured that he could enjoy devotion but never risk abandonment by becoming too devoted himself. From what we've heard, it sounds as though he could suck up the adoration of his boyhood mate and close colleague, then move on to the unthreateningly besotted Sheena (if what she claims is true), then the beautiful but fragile Olga, then back again: always keeping himself above the others. Sprinkling their lesser lives with his glory and leaving them wanting more, so that they'd never think of dumping him.'

'Poor buggers,' Charlie said with real sympathy, as they got the green sign for the walking man and crossed the road. 'So could one of 'em have got so angry they killed him?'

Karen knew the question was rhetorical. No one could possibly say yet.

The two of them were moving from the sad grubby streets east of Brick Lane towards Spitalfields, with its glorious Hawksmoor church and wonderful eighteenth-century domestic architecture. The route took precisely seven and a half minutes, and Karen had a vivid sense of Sheena walking to and fro this way every day, dreaming of her boss. Was she also inventing a whole fantasy life with him?

When they reached Wilkes Street, Karen thought it looked like a film set: ravishing but unreal, in its slightly bleak brick-and-gaslight way, with the early eighteenth-century houses towering on either side of the narrow street. They found Sheena's, and Charlie took out the keys she had left with the custody sergeant. When he'd told her that they would have to search the house she had looked sick, but she'd made no protest. Her past experience had clearly warned her this would happen.

Charlie opened the door and held it for Karen, saying, 'You go in on your own. Look and feel. I'll wait till you've had some time to pick up any . . . vibes there are.'

'Have your borrowed CSIs taken anything?' Karen asked, as she stood with one foot inside the house and the other on the well-scrubbed step.

'Man's razor and ivory-backed hairbrush. Both showed signs of blond and grey hair or stubble. We'll test it and if it's his DNA we'll know where we are. An erotomaniac stalker could've faked something like this, but it doesn't sound likely here.'

Karen walked into a hall that felt surprisingly wide, with panelling painted a subtle quiet duck-egg blue. Down the centre of the polished treads of the staircase ran some plain, inexpensive buff-coloured carpet. A dining room took up the front of the house to the right of the stairs, with kitchen behind, and beyond that a glass door leading into a small walled garden.

Everything was calm in colour and style. Nothing jarred. Nothing shouted 'look at me', as Olga's ornate and glamorous drawing room had done, with its art, gilt and silks. Here there was comfort and peace, and the atmosphere was easy and warm. Karen could imagine coming here after a day filled with people and argument to find rest.

Upstairs, a well-proportioned, light sitting room ran the full width of the house, furnished with a couple of ordinary sofas, a big soft chair and well-filled bookshelves. Behind it, on the garden side, was a small study.

Was this Sir Dan's private lair?

Unlike the rest of the house, which had all been painted in light colours, this room had been decorated to suit a very traditional idea of masculine taste. The walls were a strange mustardy ochre and the wooden floorboards had been stained to a walnut darkness under the Persian rugs. A sturdy mahogany bureau-bookcase took up half of the wall opposite the window, its shelves full of dictionaries and directories and leather-bound classics. In front of the window was a plain pedestal desk, with a folding blotter on it.

'Can I open the desk drawers?' Karen called down the stairwell.

Charlie came up after her and looked round the door. He offered her a pair of rubber gloves, which she pulled on, before opening the central drawer.

'He might have come here,' she said, looking down at it. 'But these are her bank statements, not his. We'd better look through the rest of the house.'

They found one bathroom filled with female cosmetics, tampons, and pink and white towels and another with dark-blue towels, an electric razor point, a bottle of Penhaligon's Blenheim Bouquet aftershave, and, hanging on the back of the door, a man's dressing gown of thick navy-blue silk, dotted, piped and corded in crimson.

'It certainly looks as if a man did come here on a regular basis,' Karen said. 'As you say, if the brushes have Sir Dan's DNA on them, we should be able to believe that part of Sheena's story. Although even if it is true, that doesn't mean we have to believe everything else she claimed.'

'No,' Charlie agreed. 'By the way, according to Mrs Brown,

the housekeeper, there never was any kind of meat-tenderizing mallet in the kitchen, but there's a tool room in the basement – near the old coal hole – stuffed with hammers of all sorts. She doesn't think any are missing. We're having them all tested.'

'What? For blood?' Karen said. 'That's not likely, is it? Would there be splatters that far above the knife points as they hammered down into his joints after he was dead?'

'Prints, dafty. DNA.'

Karen nodded, thinking of the double-glove theory. 'Do you yet know exactly how he was killed? You said you thought the wounds and the scene-setting were all done post-mortem?'

'Petechial haemorrhage in his eyes, fluff in his throat: he was smothered, probably with a pillow, probably as he slept, which would be why he didn't struggle.'

'Oh, shit!' Karen said, remembering the way the baby had died, then she brightened. 'He was a big bloke. If Sheena were the killer, how would she have got him downstairs? It's the upper-body strength thing again, isn't it?'

'There's a lift in the house, just outside the master bedroom,' Charlie said sadly. 'She'd have had to grip him under the arms and pull him off the bed, then drag him out of the bedroom door. Someone did exactly that; there are marks of his heels in the carpet pile and wool from that on his skin. Then she'd have had to drag him to the lift, then from the lift to the kitchen.'

'And up on to the table? A big bloke like him? She couldn't have.'

'They think the body was draped over the table, face down, then the legs lifted and the whole thing turned over so it was lying on its back.'

Karen thought of the straight bruise-like line that had

marked the body's stomach. That could easily have come from the impact of the table edge.

'It would take a fair amount of strength,' Charlie added. 'But we haven't given her any physical tests yet. Lots of women do weights these days. Bench press, too. She's, what? About ten stone, d'you think?'

Karen wagged her head from side to side, just as he did whenever he wanted to express modified agreement. She saw him smile the same secret smile he'd used on the train and felt her own lips part.

'Work!' he said, in the tone of a general giving an important order. 'A ten-stone elite bench-presser could lift . . . ooh, maybe 165, 170 pounds. She could shift a body like Sir Dan's, given enough leverage.'

'If she's a bench-presser,' Karen said with a certain amount of tartness. 'No evidence of any such thing in her bedroom or bathroom. Either of the bathrooms.'

'Even so.'

Karen glanced upwards. 'It's a non-starter, Charlie. Think! Don't you remember her bathroom? All pink and white and frilly. Have you come across many bench-pressers with that kind of taste? Sheena clearly chose everything here. Don't forget: it was bought for her.'

Charlie was looking as stubborn as he ever had. Karen tried to laugh him out of it, saying, 'Come on. It shouldn't take a psychologist to see that.'

'Maybe there's a gym in the basement. Come on down.' He led the way to a door under the stairs, opened it gingerly, felt around for a switch and then flooded the place with light. The steps were stone, but well cleaned and clearly often used.

Charlie led the way. The first space they came to was lined with wine racks. Karen pulled out a few bottles at random and raised her eyebrows.

'This is fantastic stuff. Just the kind of thing a man like Sir Dan would have.' She offered a bottle of Corton Charlemagne to Charlie. 'White Burgundy. Retails at around eighty, ninety quid a bottle. Not your average girls'-night-out tipple from the totty-rack.'

Charlie pushed on, bending his head to cross into the next vault through a low arch, and they both saw neat piles of old wine cases and boxes of all sorts. When he flipped the first few open they saw there was nothing stored in any of them.

'Bugger,' he said. 'Why would she keep . . . ?'

'Hang on,' Karen said, interrupting him as a memory surfaced. 'She talked about this being a "lovely light house". It's the weavers' lofts that are so light. Will once showed me round one of these houses when he was thinking of taking a job at the Royal London. Let's see what she's got up at the top.'

Charlie left her at a run and before she'd reached the first floor she heard him shout, 'Bingo!'

Karen was breathless before she'd caught up with him and found the last flight of stairs steeper than was quite comfortable. Straight ahead of her, mounted on trestles, was an antique settee in the process of reupholstery. It was being rewebbed, preparatory to springing and stuffing. Karen walked forwards to test the tension of the grey-and-cream straps. She almost bruised her hand before it bounced up off the webbing.

Upholsterer's tools were neatly laid out on the work table beside the trestles: hammers, stretchers, mallets, webbing and tacks. Piles of clean horsehair stood in one corner, and the paper sacks in which feathers were supplied covered the whole of one wall.

'She has upper body strength all right,' Charlie said in a dry voice. 'And bloody strong hands. And a lot of experience in hammering stuff in exactly where she wanted it. Did she take one of the hammers with her?'

'If this is her work,' Karen said, feeling as though she were fighting a hopeless battle.

'Who else would be doing this sort of thing in her house? Must be her hobby for the weekends and the nights when Sir Dan's not here.' Charlie looked at Karen with eyes that were rounder than ever. His smile showed how hard he was trying not to laugh at her. 'Come on, pet. It shouldn't take a shrink to see that Sheena has to have something to do, and there's no telly anywhere that I can see.'

'OK, OK,' she said, laughing back at him. 'You win. And I do know what you mean. Most long-term mistresses are like old-style politicians' wives and have screens in their bedrooms for all those long nights of lonely waiting.'

'Yeah. Right. And Sheena told us she has no social life outside her work for Sir Dan. She must've looked for a hobby that needs lots of time.'

'Poor woman,' Karen said with feeling. 'But, apart from the razor and the brushes, we still . . . Hang on a moment.'

'What?'

'There was a big bureau-bookcase in the study,' she said slowly. 'So?'

'So: they sometimes have secret drawers . . .' Karen broke off, seeing more mocking gleams in his eyes.

'Where d'you think you are, Karen? 221B Baker Street? Any clues to her dealings with Sir Dan will come off her laptop, which she took to the Island with her, and which is being examined by our techies, byte by byte, as we speak.'

'Come on, Charlie. Humour me. I can't believe the woman we talked to yesterday could have kept nothing of her lover to look at when she was alone – but she'd definitely have had to hide it from any casual visitor – or any curious cleaner. And this place is professionally cleaned: you can always tell.'

'Can you?' Charlie's black eyebrows looked like inverted v-shapes as he raised them.

'A secret drawer would be an ideal way to protect something from other people's curiosity.'

Clattering down the first steep, uncarpeted, flight of stairs and the next, which felt softer, Karen arrived back on the first floor, where she examined the handsome piece of furniture in the study. Drawing out the heavy central drawer, she unclicked the front flap that would turn it into a desk. As she'd expected, there was a row of pigeonholes and smaller drawers ranged at the back of the desk part, with a small cupboard in the centre.

Its door was inlaid with a beautifully carved nautilus shell, and it was locked. Karen didn't bother even looking for a key, having been shown something very like this in the past, when her dead husband had insisted on buying expensive antiques they couldn't afford for the big Yorkshire house she'd usually inhabited alone.

She slid her hands into the two pigeonholes either side of it and felt about, pushing and tapping, until she found a small hinged flap in each. Behind the flaps were small bolts. She undid them and watched the small central cupboard pop out whole. She drew it gently away from its moorings and tapped the back. A hollow sound rewarded her, with a rattle in it.

'See, Charlie? A secret compartment.' Karen found the slide cover she expected, pushed it open and saw a thin framed photograph in the narrow drawer, along with two small leather jewellery boxes.

Charlie opened them, revealing a superb square-cut diamond set in a pretty arrangement of smaller brilliants in one and a thick Tiffany eternity ring in the other.

'Somebody loved her,' he said, flicking a glance at Karen that made her breathing catch for a second. He looked away, adding with an edge: 'Somebody fucking rich, too.'

'Talking of your techies,' Karen said, controlling herself with difficulty, 'I hope they're looking for the true source of the email summoning her to the Island.'

'Of course,' Charlie said, pointing towards the frame, still in the secret drawer. 'No answers yet.'

Karen took it out, and looked down at a black-and-white photograph of Sir Dan, holding a shawl-wrapped baby in his arms, gazing down at its face with absorbed and besotted attention, which reminded Karen of innumerable portraits of mothers and their new-born infants. Sir Dan was wearing a spotted dressing gown, exactly like the one that hung on the back of the bathroom door upstairs.

Karen picked up the frame in her gloved hands, turned it over and saw that the backing was held to the frame with the easiest of swivelling pins. She looked up at Charlie.

'May I?'

He nodded and she slipped the backing off the photograph, to see in unfamiliar writing:

'S, you have made me the happiest man in the world. Danny.'

'If you can get the writing authenticated,' Karen said, hiding all her satisfaction at having been proved right in the face of his scepticism, 'Olga's going to have a bad time when her illusions about her husband are smashed.'

'Poor little cow,' Charlie said, with what sounded like genuine sympathy. 'Listen, I've got an appointment in half an hour with an old colleague who worked on the baby's death. Shouldn't take too long, but it's one I'd better do on my own. You'll be OK, won't you?'

'Fine,' Karen said, but she felt a little chilled that he hadn't warned her about the meeting. Still, it wasn't anything to get too hung up on.

'Great. I'll meet you back at Waterloo in good time for the train.'

'What about your daily call to your ACC? Or are you going to Number Ten itself while you're here?'

'Here.' Charlie handed her a train ticket, without answering her question. 'In case anything goes wrong. This'll get you back OK, even if I'm late.'

Chapter 8

Day Two: afternoon and evening

'He *is* moving up in the world,' Karen muttered to herself, disliking the sensation of hanging about while Charlie met the great and the good in Downing Street. 'I should have asked for more information yesterday and made plans of my own.'

She was sitting, shivering, on a bench in Trafalgar Square, looking at the white water of one of the fountains crashing down into its light turquoise basin. Two pigeons fought over a scrap of greyish bread on the fountain's coping. One had a club foot, the red claws bunched into a useless mass. That one fought hard but was not nearly as manoeuvrable as its adversary and eventually it had to hobble away, foodless. She saw it hunch up under the next bench to hers, fluffing up its feathers to make itself look bigger and more threatening. No other bird went near it, but a child in a red coat wandered over and flung some crumbs in its direction. Karen had to look away from its ungainly gobbling haste.

There was no reason for her not to be sipping coffee in a warm café or even eating something, or phoning a friend, or dropping in to her parents' advertising office to catch up on the news of their rackety lives, or any of a hundred other time-using activities. But she didn't want any of them.

Alone, she had a chance to work out why she felt so troubled by Charlie's disappearance into meetings to which she had not been invited, and just exactly what she thought she'd been doing when she'd made love with him, and why the knots were back in her mind, and why she was so vulnerable again, as though she were a lot younger than her thirty-six years.

For a few minutes, she persuaded herself that she was creating an empathetic pathway into the way Sheena must have felt every time Sir Dan was too busy to see her or treated her like an employee instead of a surrogate wife. But it wasn't true. Karen was coming to feel queasy about the significance of her night with Charlie.

She'd longed for comfort, and he'd given her that, along with all the reassurance she'd needed that she wasn't hideous. He had made her feel desirable, desired, and free. Now she couldn't help thinking that she'd used him.

She was also missing Will and blaming herself for just letting him go when he'd said he couldn't marry her, instead of fighting for him. In the days when she had been so wary and reluctant to commit, he hadn't worried about his dignity: he had nagged and pleaded with her to marry him. Shouldn't she have done the same?

Like the survivor of a shipwreck, she felt cold and frightened, trying to keep her head above a wild sea, and without any familiar landmarks to guide her to safety.

An idea shot into her mind, like a hunting shark appearing

through the waves. When she had agreed to marry Will and try for a family, she'd come off the pill at once. At thirty-six she was way past her maximum fertility, and, after so many years of chemical contraception, it might be a year or more before she could conceive. They'd made love, she moving with infinite care to avoid hurting him, only two nights before he had decided to leave her.

She tried to work out dates and times and to calculate whether she could have been ovulating, and she felt the cold even more sharply.

Her cycle had never been regular and she had never bothered with where, exactly, she was in it. Sheena's certainty of her own moment of fertility had seemed odd at the time. Now, Karen wished she had been as obsessive as the other woman. If she'd been ovulating when she'd been with Will, then it wasn't likely she'd still be in that state last night. But what if . . . ?

There was a chemist just across the square, in the Strand. There'd be morning-after pills there. She wouldn't even need a doctor's prescription.

Her feet felt icy and seemed incapable of movement. Everything in her mind slowed down until there was almost nothing in it but a memory of the photograph she had found in the bureau-bookcase's secret drawer.

Thinking of the image of Sir Dan looking down at the son he cradled on his lap led to sharp memories of the passion with which Will had talked about his own longing for children. Karen ground the nails of her left hand into the palm of her right.

'Pliz?' said a foreign voice, as a shadow fell between her and the bright, clear winter sun.

Karen looked up to see a very young blonde woman with an enormous rucksack rising high above her head, stooping and holding out a tattered map and a handwritten address.

'Are you lost?' Karen said, enunciating her words with care. The woman nodded and pushed her map closer to Karen.

The address was in Kilburn. Karen took a few moments to think of the best way of directing her and fell back eventually on pointing to the Bakerloo line on the tube map and then to Kilburn Park station on the street map, and adding:

'Go there and ask again at the station. OK?'

The young woman looked as though she might burst into tears, but she nodded slowly. Her skin looked grimy and her eyes were red-rimmed. She might have just emerged from a cheap laborious over-night journey, but she looked like an escaper from somewhere scary. Karen hoped she would find refuge and pointed to the nearest tube station, saying with as much warmth as she could manage, 'There. You go down there.'

The young woman turned, staggering a little under the weight of her rucksack and stumbled off towards Charing Cross Station. Karen thought of what it must be like to be lost, exhausted, in a vast city, whose language you did not speak. It must be just as bad for young men, she told herself, and every statistic showed that it was they who were at greater risk of violent attack from strangers, but she was feeling so wobbly herself just now that she was sure that it was worse for women.

Another reason to admire Sir Dan and his wife, she thought, for all the money they'd poured out on projects to rescue sex slaves and brutalized children.

In that moment it seemed absurd that Charlie, the Senior

Investigating Officer, should have abandoned the incident room for most of a day to look into Sheena's background, when it was so much more likely than Sir Dan's appalling death had been caused by someone whose cash-cows he had removed through one of his charities.

Karen's phone whimpered as a text arrived. She pulled the phone out of her pocket, saw the message came from Charlie, and opened it to read: *Caught up here. Will miss train. You get it as planned. Talk later.*

'Fine,' she said in a loud, crisp voice that fluttered a few pigeons, and didn't make her feel any better herself.

Walking to Waterloo would take about twenty minutes from Trafalgar Square, so she set off down Whitehall, past the high, whitish-grey stone facades that hid all the great ministries of state, then crossed the river Thames at Westminster Bridge and made her way into the station, picking up a ham and cheese baguette as she went. She was glad at the prospect of going home, of being in her own flat, where she might be able to think more clearly than by the fountains in Trafalgar Square, surrounded by warring pigeons and lost young women, and memories of a father's devotion to his baby son.

Her ticket had been booked right through to the Island. There didn't seem any point going back there alone, unless she could make good use of the time. Opening her laptop and plugging it into the socket at her side, she emailed Antony Quiggly, saying:

Could we meet? I'll have a couple of hours or so on the Island this afternoon, and I'd love to hear more about Sir Dan's charities.

She waited, watching her in-box for nearly fifteen minutes, trying not to think of anything very much, until she saw Antony's name popping up.

Am on the mainland today. Will be in Southampton by five thirty. Booked on the seven thirty ferry. We could meet for a quick drink near the port. Any idea where would be best?

My flat, she typed, adding the address, and promising tea, coffee, wine, or whatever he wanted.

Coming out of her email, she clicked on to Facebook, wondering whether she would find a page for Will that might give her some clues to her own private mystery. It seemed deeply unlikely, somehow, and she had never even looked before.

Several Will Hawkins appeared, but none were him.

Her French doors had been perfectly mended. Whoever Charlie's glazier was, he'd done a great job, even sweeping up every dangerous, foot-cutting crumb of glass. But her blood still marked the polished wooden floor. Dumping her laptop case and handbag on one of the sofas, she filled a large bowl with hot soapy water and set about cleaning away the evidence of her small midnight drama. She would have to re-wax the boards, and even then marks would probably still show, but they might fade one day.

The flat felt strange, and she knew what Charlie had meant when he'd talked about 'no ghosts' in his. Here Will's presence was very strong. Wherever Karen looked, she could remember watching him doing something characteristic, or making her laugh, or feeding her something delicious and unexpected, or letting her see – just occasionally – the terrors inherent in his work. No one dug a scalpel into a patient's brain without awareness of the damage he could do. How much else had he hidden? And why had she never even thought of drawing up a psychological profile of him to make educated guesses? If she'd done that, would she have some idea of why he'd decided to abandon her? If she'd understood him better, would he have wanted to leave? What *had* she done to him that had made him hate her?

Kneeling on the floor with her hands in the pink-tinged foamy water, she also asked herself why on earth she had fought him for so long. And why she had let Charlie . . .

'Not a question of letting,' she said aloud, wringing out the cloth and applying it hard to the last of the bloodstains. 'You were more than up for it.'

The floor was still damp by the time Antony rang her bell, but it was clean, and he wouldn't be going anywhere near her bedroom in any case.

He looked tired, she thought, when she let him in and saw how pale his face was above his formal dark pinstriped suit and crisply ironed white shirt. A heavy-looking black-leather briefcase dangled from one gloved hand. She offered him a drink.

'Tea would be great,' he said, putting down the briefcase just inside her front door and stripping off his gloves. 'I've got a pile of documents to deal with in the office when I get back.'

'Fine. Have a seat. I'll be with you in a minute.'

Karen went to switch on the kettle and was surprised when

he followed her into the narrow kitchen, leaning back against the fridge to watch her as she collected mugs and tea bags.

'It was good to hear from you,' he said after a companionable silence. 'What can I do for you?'

'It's Dan Blackwater's Clagbourne House,' Karen said frankly. 'I need to know more about it. You emailed this morning, saying there'd never been any trouble there. Is that true?' She looked over her shoulder and caught a puzzled expression on Antony's face.

'As far as I know. Occasionally one of the girls – sorry, women – turns out to be more damaged than anyone realized at first. Sometimes it's agreed that they can't be cared for in such an informal way.'

'So what happens to them then?'

He shrugged his big square shoulders. 'They're referred to specialist care on the mainland.'

'What specialist care? Mental health? It barely exists.'

'That depends on your resources.' Antony's voice was as dry as blotting paper. 'Sir Dan can . . . could pay for anything they needed. Is this all you wanted to ask? We could have done it by email.'

He produced a short, embarrassed laugh before adding: 'Not that it's not good to see you again. I was very fond of your grandmother.'

'I didn't actually mean trouble of that sort,' Karen said, fishing out the tea bags and handing him his mug. 'Let's go and sit down. I meant trouble from the pimps or the traffickers, or old clients of the women. Anyone who'd lost profit because of the charity's intervention. Anyone trying to abduct one of the women. You know, like the violent husbands who try to get at their brutalized wife and children after they've run to a refuge. That kind of thing.'

'Ah, yes. I see what you mean.' Antony took a sip of boiling tea, then set his mug down on a coaster on the pale polished beechwood table at his side. 'Not that I know of. But I'm hardly the man to ask. Wouldn't your police friends know all about that side of it?'

'Only if they'd ever been called in to help.' Karen had long ago grown out of her first need to placate and agree with older authority figures who threw impatiently critical comments her way in the way her elder brother once had. These days she was quite able to fight back.

'Knowing a little about Dan Blackwater and his business methods,' she went on, 'I am quite sure that he would choose to handle anything short of – well, say – murder on his own. Come on, have there ever been any break-ins at Clagbourne House, or any instances of the girls or the staff being harassed?'

Antony picked up his tea and spent a long time taking another very small sip. He was clearly deciding how much to tell her and which words to use.

'I doubt it,' he said at last. 'There's efficient "security" there. You know, muscle. But what makes you ask?'

'Oh, come on, Antony,' she said, losing patience with his lawyerly discretion. 'Sir Dan's been murdered in a particularly brutal fashion, and on the Island. You must see that the perpetrator is likely to be physically powerful, enraged about something local, and violently inclined. As far as I've been able to discover, Sir Dan did nothing on the Island except chill, offer a little very high-level corporate entertaining, and finance

Clagbourne House. It's hardly pushing any envelopes to suggest a link.'

The solicitor's handsome face under the thick, dark-brown hair looked thoroughly surprised, perhaps at her slangy language.

'But they've already caught the killer,' he said. 'A disgruntled female employee.'

'Who told you that?' Karen asked. 'Or did you see it on the internet? None of the newspapers I've seen have said anything like it – just that a woman is helping with enquiries. The old cliché.'

He shoved a hand through his hair. Ruffled, it made him more attractive than the earlier smoothness.

'Caught out,' he admitted. 'I saw his widow this morning, before I went to London. She told me how pleased she was the police have acted so fast, and with such discretion, keeping the worst of the mutilations out of the papers in consideration for her position.'

'Ah.' Karen could easily imagine Olga taking that line. 'You saw her at her instigation or yours?'

'I'm not sure that's within your remit to ask, Karen,' he said, putting down the tea and getting to his feet. 'She's a client, and therefore her affairs are not for discussion, any more than yours would be if someone wanted to know what you're doing with your grandmother's house and garden. Look, sorry to have drunk your tea without giving you anything, but that's how it is. I'd better head off. Things to do before I catch the ferry.'

'Before you go: how's your wife? I heard she was having a second round of chemo.'

His face took on the bleakness of an arctic winter. 'Do you need to ask?'

'I'm sorry,' she said quickly. 'And I'm even sorrier that I've got to press you about Sir Dan. In your email this morning, you said you'd been about to meet him. Yet you also said you weren't friends. What was he coming to consult you about? And why did his widow send for you?'

Antony's expression was that of a giant about to squash an impertinent slug. 'I have already told you, I do not discuss my clients' affairs.'

'Fine. Presumably you'll be very busy now, dealing with his estate. Getting probate and all that,' Karen said, still hoping to provoke a more illuminating reaction.

'My firm has nothing to do with his will.'

Antony turned smartly, as though on a parade ground, and let himself out of her flat. Rarely had she seen a more perfect picture of a man under discipline.

So what, Karen asked herself, was Sir Dan going to ask him to do? Was he cutting the funding to Clagbourne House? Or to some other more private, more discreet charity? And why did Olga follow up the meeting that never happened with one of her own?

Karen heard the ping of the lift arriving and then the complicated series of clatters and whooshes of its doors opening and closing.

'Stella,' she said aloud as soon as she was certain that he had gone. She picked up her phone and dialled her friend.

'Sorry for being so fraught when you phoned yesterday,' Karen said, as soon as Stella picked up the call. 'But I've got a gap now. I don't suppose your lovely bloke is here and free tonight for that dinner you talked about?'

'Funny you should say that,' Stella said, her voice light and flirty in a way Karen had never heard. 'He is here and we were just wondering where we might go and eat later. But can Will come in the middle of the week like this?'

Karen felt her heart thud and fought for an equally chirpy tone as she said, 'Won't I do on my own?'

A short silence warned her she'd failed.

'I really would love to meet him,' Karen added. 'And diaries get so clogged-up now the post-Christmas recovery is over.'

'Of course,' Stella said, with all her old warmth. 'We'll have a threesome. Where shall we go? What about that funny little place you and Max love so much?'

'Mario's?' Karen felt herself relaxing at the thought of the inexpensive, old-style Italian restaurant where she and her professor, Max Pitton, had eaten hundreds of meals over the years she'd worked in Southampton. 'Why not? But do you think it's sophisticated enough for a man like this one?'

Stella's snort of laughter reassured Karen. 'He'll do as he's told,' she said. 'Half seven?'

'Great. See you there.'

That answered the question of how to fill this evening. Karen put on Mozart's piano concerto no. 9 in E flat major, which was one of her favourites. She had once read that his music had a particularly stimulating effect on the brain, which was why she had started listening, but she was now an addict.

With the clear, exuberant notes ringing all around her, she stripped off the dark suit and subdued shirt she had put on for the London trip while Charlie had been doing his appeal for witnesses at the television studio. When she'd had a shower, she pulled on her old standby L K Bennett jersey dress, which hung well on her tall slender figure and added an intensity to her eyes with its particular, almost peacock blue.

Memories of how badly she had wanted Will to like and admire her friends when she had first introduced him made her take extra trouble with her hair and face. A sudden drumming on the skylights above her head warned her that heavy rain was falling.

She swore. Mario's was only about twelve minutes' walk from her flat, but that was more than enough to make her arrive at the restaurant dripping. In the hope that the storm might stop in a few minutes, she took out her phone and sent Charlie a text:

Safely back. How was yr meeting?

She stood in front of the newly mended French doors, watching the rain drops hitting the glass, clinging and dribbling down, muddling the view of the docks, the Solent and the Island beyond them, until they looked like an Impressionist painting.

How interesting, she thought suddenly, that the Blackwaters had not gone for the obvious rich-man's Impressionists but had looked to the more austere, Bauhaus-inspired artists from a few decades later. Whose taste had informed their purchase? His or hers? Or an expensive decorator's?

Karen's phone whimpered. She looked at the screen, saw the envelope icon and Charlie's number and opened the text.

Still in London. Lots to say. Drop in later?

Full of remorse for making love with him to make herself feel better before she knew whether she really wanted to be with him, she was tempted to make an excuse, but her fingers moved, almost against her will, to write:

Out for dinner. Back around 10. CU then?

Back came the answer.

I'll B there.

Mario's Pasta House was its usual welcoming self, with candles leaking hot wax down their Chianti-bottle holders, hissing from the espresso machine by the bar, scents of garlic and oil and Parmesan, and a friendly buzz of chatter from a room so full that Karen was worried there might not be space for the three of them. But Mario himself, dressed as always in tight, high-waisted black trousers and a shiny maroon shirt, waved at her as she stood in the doorway, then pointed towards a desirable corner table, where red-headed Stella was sitting. Not for her the faded carroty colour she'd been born with, but a rich dramatic dye she had specially mixed. Karen had occasionally thought that if you whizzed beetroot and oranges together in a juicer you would come up with something like it. Opposite her was a tall, intelligent-looking man in glasses.

They both got to their feet as Karen approached, which impressed her. Stella, shorter than she by a good three inches, hugged her close.

'Karen, this is Martin Fieny,' she said, as she pulled away. 'Darling, my mate Karen Taylor.'

'How d'you do?' he said, in an old-fashioned way in an

old-fashioned voice. 'Forgive me if I'm a bit nervous. Stella's told me all about how you're able to see right through anyone to all the bits they most want to hide.' He laughed. 'Not that *I* have anything to hide, of course.'

'Stella's been talking nonsense,' Karen said, smiling as she pulled out one of the free chairs at the table and sitting down. 'You're thinking of palmists and fortune-tellers. All people like me do is gather data and statistics about behavioural markers and the emotional damage that can result in crime. No personal stuff at all.'

'There's a relief.' Martin chuckled as he leaned across the table to pour some red wine into her glass from a tall decanter. She caught a slight hint of violets among the more obvious alcohol and cherry scents and realized he must have sprung for Mario's most expensive Chianti. That was good: Stella deserved a generous man. 'I thought you might start asking me about my childhood and my mother.'

'Wouldn't dream of it,' she assured him, glancing round to smile at Stella. 'That would be like asking a fellow diner who happened to be an architect about rolled steel joists or drains or something. What's *your* line of work, Martin?'

He laughed. 'Dull, dull, dull. I'm in insurance, I'm afraid.'

'So how did the two of you meet?' Karen knew she had to keep the conversation going artificially until they found a subject of shared interest.

'Oh, friends of friends. Here's a menu. I couldn't believe places like this still exist, but I'm glad it does. Makes me feel young again.' He laughed once more, still not sounding wholly at ease. Karen could see he was working as hard as she was to get the evening going.

'Us, too,' Stella said, leaning sideways so that her shoulder touched his. 'And the food's good, not just nostalgia-inducing retro.'

'How did you find it?'

'My professor introduced me to it,' Karen said, 'and his mother's Italian, so I had faith in the food right from the start, and now Stella and I use it all the time.' Karen rather liked Martin's smile and willingness to produce civilized chat.

'I wish I'd known about it when I first discovered Stella's bizarre devotion to modernist architecture,' Martin said, before kissing the top of her head. 'The austerity of that made me so afraid I'd be eating raw fish and the odd bit of seaweed for ever that I nearly ran away from our first date.'

'Luckily we share pretty much all our other tastes,' Stella said, obviously wanting Karen to like him.

'Except for my equally bizarre enjoyment of golf.' Martin laughed much more naturally, and Stella joined in happily. 'You're a sweetie to put up with that so patiently, darling.'

All went well through the starters and Karen's assault on a huge main-course-sized dish of her favourite spaghetti puttanesca, while the others applied steak knives to large veal chops cooked in butter and capers, but then Martin put down his knife and fork and gestured with his chin to the other side of the room.

'What?' Stella said, wiping a smear of butter from her chin with a thick pink napkin, which clashed with her bright red hair. 'What's the matter, Martin?'

'Much as I'm enjoying my grub,' he said, 'I do wish you'd warned me this is a pick-up joint.'

Karen frowned. She wasn't going to turn and gawp.

'I don't know what you mean,' she said, disliking the way her voice sounded as though someone had stuck a poker down her throat.

Martin wiped his hands on his own handkerchief, as though he'd suddenly decided the cutlery – or the food – might contaminate him. 'There's a couple of men over there, salesmen on expenses probably, who've been eyeing up a couple of tarts all evening. They've just sent over a note and the girls have joined them, all giggly and preening. Your friend Mario acts as pimp as well as maître d'? How much does he rake off their earnings?'

'Oh, do shut up,' Karen said, forgetting her urge to placate and flatter Stella's new bloke. 'This isn't that kind of place at all. And what makes you think they're "tarts"? Much more likely to be students scenting the possibility of free food. With all the cuts and the debts they're taking on, you can hardly blame them.'

'They're tarts,' he said, with an air of total certainty. 'You can always tell.'

'How?' Stella's voice was a little cracked and higher than usual, which warned Karen how much she disliked what was happening.

All ready to pull back and distract Martin by asking about his dreams or his mother, or whatever he'd been expecting from a psychologist, Karen watched in astonishment as a patronizing smile made his face look impossibly smug. He leaned across the table towards Stella, saying: 'Fake tits, and quite well done; permatan; skirt no bigger than a large pair of knickers, and under the skirt no more than a thong. D'you want me to go on?'

Stella opened her mouth, then shut it again, then looked towards Karen as though she couldn't decide whether to lose her temper or cry. Karen took that as a plea for help and said distantly, 'I'll have to take your word for it. But how come you have such a close acquaintance with the markers for prostitution?'

Once more he laughed. 'Don't be naïve.'

'*Martin.*' Stella's protest was heartfelt. 'What do you mean?'

'Darling, for God's sake!' he said. 'I'm bloody nearly fifty. Eight years out of a marriage that had been going sour for fifteen before that. So: twenty-three years of not getting it at home. D'you really think I've never . . . ?'

'Never what?'

'Come on, Stella,' he said, now sounding almost as angry as she did. 'I hadn't put you down as sentimental – or a bra-burning feminist. You must know blokes pay for it sometimes.'

'But not respectable, intelligent . . .'

'Of course we do. Don't you read the papers? Look around you? Talk to men who've had stag nights?' Gradually he realized she was serious and his tone changed to one of hectoring impatience. 'You don't have to look so shocked. It's not dirty slags off the street we're talking about here; it's expensive, well-maintained, safe girls. And condoms, of course. You needn't think, you . . .'

Karen glared at him with such a ferocious warning that he stopped in mid-sentence.

'But, Martin,' Stella said, her voice high and tight, 'you can't . . .'

'Everyone's always done it. If we'd been part of our fathers' generation we'd have hidden it, but not now. It's no different than ordering a takeaway.' He looked at them both with such a clearly punitive expression in his brown eyes that Karen wanted to whisk Stella right away as quickly as possible. But she didn't have time before he started again.

'If you're paying enough, you can have anything you want. You don't have to go through all that dreary "of course I love you" nonsense either. Or listen to her banging on about her crap day when all you want is to be allowed to forget your own.'

Stella looked sick and pushed her chair away from the table. 'I'm off,' she said. 'Karen?'

'Right behind you.' Karen grabbed a couple of twenty-pound notes out of her bag and dumped them on the table, hurrying after Stella and hearing Martin's outraged protests echoing behind her. They became cruder and louder the further away she got.

'Fucking bitches,' he said at last, just as Stella reached the door.

Karen brushed off Mario's attempt to offer help with a muttered apology for bringing such unpleasantness to his restaurant.

'You wan' a taxi?' he said, all sympathy. 'I call for one. On the house. The professore he would be expectin' me to takea care of you. You wait. I call.'

Stella was already outside, running away through the rain. Karen ignored her carefully blow-dried hair and told Mario she had to follow her friend. He let her go. She'd caught up with Stella by the end of the block and grabbed her arms.

'Stella, it's OK. You're safe. He can't . . .'

Stella turned a despairing face to Karen, tears and rain carrying dark trails of eye make-up down her freckly cheeks.

'I'm so, so sorry,' she said, clearly agonized. 'I had no idea he was . . . Oh, God! Why did I ever think . . . ?'

'Come to my flat,' Karen said. 'Get dry and warm up and we can open a bottle and you can tell me all about it. And we can laugh at him. He's not worth all this angst.'

'I couldn't laugh. Not after that.' Stella turned away, hanging her head, then faced Karen again. 'It's all my fault. I was so angry after my bloody mother's latest round of insults that I went on the net. Joined a dating site. He seemed . . . Everyone said it would be safe. I checked he does work for the firm he claims to. He's never been like that before; always perfectly OK. Manners, you know.' She shuddered.

Karen felt the rain trickling down through her hair and over her scalp, chilling her. She urged Stella into the nearest doorway that would provide a little shelter.

'We've . . . I let him . . . Oh, Karen, we've been having wild sex for the past three weeks, and he . . . I feel . . .'

'What do you feel?' Karen asked as gently as possible.

'Disgusted. Disgusting. Hating him. Hating myself. Sick.' She waved over Karen's shoulder and yelled, 'Taxi!'

Looking back at Karen, Stella forced a smile, wiping the back of one hand under her snotty nose and the heel of the palm against each eye in turn. 'I need to get home and have a boiling bath full of Dettol or something. Sorry about that exhibition. Sorry for putting you through all that. Sorry to have . . . I'll phone you when I can.'

The taxi had pulled up at the kerb. Karen had to let her get into it and go. Somewhere a clock chimed. She paused in the rain, counting the bongs. Ten o'clock. Charlie was due at her flat. She wasn't far away, but she didn't want to miss him. Especially now. She turned back the way Stella had led her and ran, feeling the rain splash up the backs of her legs and leak in between the uppers and soles of her good leather boots.

Chapter 9

Day Two: 10.30 p.m.

'I was just giving up on you,' Charlie said, as Karen let herself in at the street door of her building. But he was smiling and not at all tetchy. 'Luckily one of your fellow tenants let me in or I'd be as wet as you by now. You look like you need a king-sized bath towel and probably a shower first. I'll come in with you and scrub your back if you like.'

Rocked by his assumptions, even after last night, she stood where she was, feeling the water draining off her clothes and pooling around her icy feet.

'What's the matter?' he said, still smiling but with worry edging into his eyes.

Karen shivered, then pulled herself together. 'I've just been with Stella and her new bloke – well, her new ex-bloke now, I should think, and he . . . Ugh! You don't want to hear it. And I don't want to tell you. But it'll take a while before I'll ever be able to show my face in Mario's again.'

Charlie reached behind her to press the button for the lift. 'Don't fret, pet. You don't have to talk about anything if you don't want to. I'll tell you all about my meetings while you dry off and change.'

She felt better at once and flashed a smile at him. He put his arm around her wet jacket, then pulled back as he realized just how soaked she was.

'You so need a towel.' The lift arrived and he hauled back its well-sprung gates. 'In with you.'

Once she'd let them both in to the flat, he offered to put on the kettle while she changed. Touched by his quick under-standing as much as his solicitude, Karen ran into the bedroom, leaving the door open.

'Tea or coffee?' he called out.

'Green tea, I think,' she said, feeling that anything more powerful might make her sick.

If she'd met someone like Martin in the course of her work, she wouldn't have thought twice about his horrible ideas. But in the context of what he had done – and was doing – to her best friend, she had none of her professional armour.

Emerging from her bedroom in her favourite skinny jeans and layered tops in a variety of pinks and reds, with a face scrubbed clean of rain-smeared make-up and her damp hair hanging in elf-locks around her face, she found Charlie sitting at his ease on one of her sofas with a mug of builders' tea warming his hands and a porcelain cup of green tea awaiting her on the coffee table.

Standing, looking down at him as he relaxed in the corner of her sofa, she said abruptly, 'Is it true that all men pay for sex?'

Charlie didn't flush or frown. Instead he turned his head slightly so that he could look straight at her. 'That why you went all cold on me when I offered to have a shower with you? Come on, Karen, don't you know me better than that?'

'I didn't mean you,' she said, lying. 'I meant in general. This man of Stella's has just said everyone does it, no one's ashamed of it any more, and you just order what you want.' She swallowed, then recovered herself. 'It doesn't seem to have crossed his mind that the prostitutes who provide it are human beings, with feelings; not . . . not ingredients of some kind of takeaway meal, to be used and scraped down the drain when you've had enough.'

'He's not alone,' Charlie said, quickly adding: 'Don't look like I'm a fiend. I'm not talking about me. Frankly, what I've seen since I was first on the beat in Newcastle, I wouldn't go near a working girl for . . . oh, for fifty million quid.'

Karen felt her shoulder muscles slacken at once.

'But I've been talking to a woman from SOCA for most of the afternoon, and . . .'

'Serious organized crime?' Karen said, astonished. 'I thought you were seeing someone who'd dealt with the case of Sheena's dead baby and then going to Number Ten.'

'I was. But it was the SOCA meeting I couldn't take you to. They'd been so cagey about talking even to me I wasn't going to push it by introducing a civilian.'

'What did you find out?' Karen felt half the afternoon's angst melt away, but only half. 'Was Sir Dan . . . ?'

'They know all about him and really rated him for his charities. Things he funded are all well run and doing good. They don't know of any trafficker he'd specially pissed off. And they haven't heard of any contracts put out on him. All the current known contracts are to do with a war that's going on between some of the biggest players: Albanian, Eastern European, Turkish.'

'But?' Karen said, already forgetting the scene in Mario's. 'There's definitely a but in there, Charlie.'

'But they're always short of intel. So it's thought possible this could've been a hit.'

'Which would fit with the strength needed,' Karen said, thinking as she spoke, 'and the nature of the display they made of his body. A kind of warning. Except...'

'What?' he asked when she faltered. Her nose wrinkled as she thought but she couldn't understand why he suddenly smiled. 'Pretty face,' he said, in ironic explanation. She relaxed it at once.

'I'd have expected that kind of warning to be offered in a more public place,' she said seriously. 'After all, you've managed to keep the worst details from the press, which, as Gilbert said this morning, is amazing, but...'

'Not so amazing.' Charlie's voice was as dry as it had ever been. 'Both Sir Dan and Olga have taken out so many injunctions and super injunctions over the years and he's been to the libel courts on at least three occasions and won every time that all the media are going to be... well careful.'

'Even so, in the privacy of his own home, and in the kitchen... He can't have cooked his own meals, a man like that. The kitchen is the unlikeliest place for his corpse to be placed as any kind of public threat, revenge, punishment, warning... Anything really.'

'You heard Olga say he liked the servants out of the house at night,' Charlie reminded her. 'Late night cups of tea, midnight feasts – he must've known where it was and how to get his own scran and that. Maybe he had cosy, secret, meetings there, too. Maybe he had someone in there when

Sheena arrived and that's why he sent her off to the top floor and told her to stay out of the way. You're letting your filthy tea get cold.'

Karen swung away from him, grabbed her cup and drained it in two large swallows. Then she stood at the French windows, staring out through the heavy rain towards the Island again. A ferry was steaming its way in to Southampton, lights blazing like the headlamps of all the traffic that crawled unceasingly along the roads so far below her flat. Lorries brought who-knew-what to and from the port.

'Why don't SOCA have enough intelligence on pimps and traffickers?' Karen asked, still staring out, trying to imagine how it must feel to be a human being smuggled under the legit-imate cargo of one of those international juggernauts.

'Isn't it obvious?' Charlie said, his voice harsher now. 'It's one thing for a male spook to join the tree-huggers or the bunny-snugglers and have it off with any willing female he finds. Quite another to ask a woman to go undercover as a tom. It's not a controllable trade. Never has been. Never will be.'

'Too many willing customers, I suppose,' Karen said, remembering Martin with an unpleasant lurch of her stomach. 'Couldn't some of the customers help you? Couldn't you get your blokey undercovers to pretend to be punters?'

'That happens, but it's not easy to learn much of any use. Most trafficked women are so terrorized they won't talk.'

'What about the ones in Sir Dan's refuge?' Karen asked. 'Clagbourne House on the Island. Have you talked . . . ?'

'What do you think?'

'Of course you have, Charlie,' she said quickly, remember-ing all the cases he'd successfully solved.

'I sent Annie, who's usually good with troubled women. But these ones aren't saying much. Some aren't so hot in English and we're waiting for a bunch of translators. Moldovan, Latvian, Ukrainian, Belarusian. Like the rest, these girls are mostly far too scared to tell us what little they know. My SOCA contact says they often haven't a clue where they've been held or who their pimps were.' Charlie looked sick as he added, 'They're bought and sold so many times in so many countries before they get here, bundled into this vehicle and that, beaten, threatened, de-passported and de-phoned.'

Karen shuddered. The horror of being in someone else's power had been one of her nightmares for years.

'So even when they're brave enough to talk,' Charlie went on, 'they can't help us much.'

He rubbed his hands through his hair in a way that was very familiar to her. 'SOCA are sending us a specialist interviewer tomorrow.'

'Not the Border Agency?' Karen said, surprised.

'Not yet. They'll come in later. At the moment SOCA want intel on this war between different sex trafficking gangs. I'm hoping their woman and her translators will get somewhere with the Clagbourne House inmates, find some link that could explain a professional hit on Sir Dan.'

'Can I sit in on the interviews?'

'I'll try and get you in.' Charlie drained his tea and got to his feet. 'But SOCA may . . . Either way, you'll get to see the written report. Better be off now. See you tomorrow?'

Karen nodded, relieved he wasn't planning to stay the night. She couldn't make love with him again until she knew for certain what she wanted – and that she was not pregnant with a child of Will's.

'What time d'you want me?'

'Eight thirty,' he said. 'We won't have much more than an hour or two left with Sheena by tomorrow morning, so I want you, as well as Rich Silver, to have one more crack at her and get everything you can. OK?'

'Fine. Goodnight, Charlie.'

He walked across the floor to take her by both shoulders. She didn't know how to trust him or herself. It would be so easy to blot out all her thoughts in pure physical sensation, but it wouldn't be fair. Not again. Not while she was missing Will so much. Charlie looked right into her eyes, his own soft and worried still.

'We're not all like Stella's bloke, you know,' he said, leaning forwards to kiss her.

She liked the sensation of his lips – so much softer than the rest of him – and longed for more but forced herself to resist. He pulled back.

'Sleep well,' he said casually.

'I'll do my best.'

'Great. I want you firing on all cylinders tomorrow.' He walked towards the door and the way he moved through her flat reminded her all too vividly of last night. For a moment she couldn't think of anything else, then he put his hand on the latch, and she remembered.

'Before you go,' she said. He turned, his eyebrows lifting to invite her to carry on. He looked so hopeful that she felt even more guilty about wanting only to ask a work question: 'What did your mate say about the case of Sheena's baby?'

Charlie's face almost disappeared into itself as he grimaced. After a moment, he looked normal again, and said, 'That's one reason why the communications director at Number Ten's so interested in our case and why he wanted to see me today. The Met are all still sure she was the killer last time. Number Ten don't want a scandal over the man they've been publicizing as one of the few unimpeachably decent billionaires. I've promised to give them the heads-up on any dirt we find before the press get it.'

When Karen had eventually got Charlie out of her mind and written notes of the next set of questions she would have to ask Sheena, she checked the time, then picked up her phone to find out how Stella was coping. The phone rang and rang until the voicemail message kicked in. Karen said nothing. It would be so easy to get the tone wrong in an oral message. Instead, she fired up her laptop, opened the email program and typed:

Dearest Stella, How are you? I know nothing I can say could possibly help, and you may well want to be on your own for a bit. But if you don't, I'm here. And if you want to talk I'm here. Or on the mobile anyway. Lots of love, K.

She looked at the screen for a while, then added:

PS It's not just you. Will's dumped me. So we're both single again. Should we celebrate some time? Or commiserate? Kxx

'What now?' Sheena's voice was so harsh next morning that Karen didn't think she would cooperate with any more questions. The texture of her skin and the baggy grey circles under her eyes showed that she had not slept much.

Karen wasn't surprised. Police station cells were always noisy places, with drunks shouting and doors banging close by, and phones ringing and cars coming and going as the work of the station carried on all night. But she felt guilty that she was sitting here after an unexpectedly good night's sleep, dressed in indigo jeans and her favourite kingfisher-coloured shirt under a bright yellow cashmere sweater. Sheena cast a resentful glance in her direction and then concentrated on Charlie.

Her solicitor didn't look much better than Sheena, with his face more or less the same colour as his greying cream-coloured polyester shirt. A powerful miasma of Aramis aftershave hung around him, as though he'd become conscious of his own shabbiness and grabbed the first thing that might distract them from his clothes.

'Doctor Taylor has one or two more questions for you,' Charlie said to Sheena, adding a little cruelly, 'now that you've dropped the whole memory-loss charade.'

Sheena dragged her head round to glare at Karen with all the frustrated hostility of a losing cage-fighter.

'It was never a charade. I can see now that I panicked when I found Dan's body and my brain just kind of shut down. But now it's working again. That can happen, can't it, Doctor Taylor?'

'Certainly can,' Karen said, watching her carefully. 'But now I need to ask you about Olga Blackwater's breakdown.'

Surprise pushed everything else out of Sheena's expression. 'Why me? I know nothing more than I've told you.'

'When did Sir Dan tell you about it?' Karen asked.

'When I first went to work for him and he wanted me to accompany him to a big reception,' Sheena said, frowning. She licked her dry-looking lips. 'Long before we were together. Why is this important?'

'Did he fill you in on details of her progress over the years?' Karen went on.

'No. I told you: he's – he was incredibly loyal. I never asked about her and he never talked about her, except that one time, and then again on the day I told him I was pregnant.'

'What did he say then?' Karen was keeping her voice low and gentle. She could tell from the tight alertness of Charlie's body that he had no idea what she was doing and wanted her to get on with something more important.

'Just that he would always look after us but that he could never divorce Olga to marry me because of her state of health.'

'Have you ever met her?' Karen asked and felt Charlie relax.

Sheena shook her head. Her hair had been combed, but it was greasy now and hung down either side of her face like grubby curtains. But her hands were clean and she'd scraped out whatever had been left under her nails when the scientific examiner had done with them.

'Never. Why?'

Charlie squared his shoulders, making himself look bigger and even more powerful than he was.

'If I'd been in your shoes, I'd have wanted to check her out, make sure he wasn't lying to me.'

Sheena sighed heavily and turned to Karen, hunching her shoulders to make a barrier between herself and Charlie.

'Of course Dan didn't lie,' she said. 'Never. Not to me; not to anyone.'

'That's good to know.' Karen nodded. 'Tell me something. Sir Dan looked after you financially. How was that organized?'

'There's a trust,' Sheena said, without any hesitation or embarrassment. 'I have the house for my lifetime and an income, a good income. Before Andy . . . before our son died, there was an extra trust for him, but after . . . Well, it all had to get sorted out, of course.'

'Who acted for you both when Sir Dan set it up?'

'No one acted for *me*,' Sheena said, frowning again, as though she had difficulty understanding why Karen was curious about her financial affairs. 'Why would they? The trusts were set up by his private lawyers, here on the Island, so that they didn't get muddled up with his work affairs, or cause any kind of talk in London. Quiggly and Partners, the lawyers are called. Why does it matter?'

'I just wondered,' Karen said, 'whether it might explain why Sir Dan summoned you here. You see, he'd made an appointment with Quiggly's senior partner for the day after he died.'

She glanced at Charlie with an 'over-to-you' expression on her face. He nodded and picked up the questions, taking them further and faster than Karen would have.

'Did he tell you he was going to break your trust?' he said. 'Like he'd broken the one set up for your baby, for Andy? Was that what shocked you so much that you lost your memory for a bit?'

Sheena just looked at him, but her expression was enough to

show what she thought of him. Medusa could have taken lessons, Karen thought. Charlie only leaned forwards, more keenly interested, saying, 'Shocked you enough to make you lay that pillow over his face and lean on it till he'd stopped breathing?'

'What?' Sheena's frown had no anger in it; only perplexity. 'What are you talking about? Dan was stabbed, in the kitchen. That's where I . . .' She coughed, rubbed her eyes, sat up straighter, and carried on: 'That's where I found him. Stabbed. There wasn't a pillow. Not . . . not this time.'

'Not in the kitchen,' Charlie agreed, looking encouraged, 'but that's because you left the pillow upstairs after you'd killed him with it. Then you put your arms under his and dragged him off the bed, across the carpet, picking up fibres on your slippers, into the lift, where you left some of those fibres and some of your own hairs.'

'Me?' Sheena looked down at her own body, then stroked her upper left arm with her right hand, as though the muscles were aching. '*Me*?'

'Yup. You with those impressive biceps that you developed hauling furniture about to reupholster it. You dragged him out of the lift in the same way when you got to the ground floor, then levered him up, face down on to the kitchen table, turned him over and hammered those knives through his dead joints. It must have . . .'

'Chief Inspector!' The mild-mannered solicitor sounded outraged as he butted in at last. 'I must protest. This is right out of order. What evidence have you for these accusations?'

'Plenty. You know how easy it is for the labs to identify hairs and fibres these days.' Charlie's voice allowed no doubt. He looked away from the lawyer to stare straight at Sheena. 'Well?'

The solicitor leaned sideways and whispered into her ear. Sheena adjusted her head around his so that she could speak into his ear. Then they reversed their positions, looking, Karen thought, like swans performing a mating dance. At last Sheena straightened up.

'No comment,' she said, which made Charlie look even happier. Karen assumed it was because that deadly little phrase was the one used by the experienced guilty in all their police interviews. But he said nothing, only looking at Karen, as though asking for her help.

'Was it a revocable trust?' she said, again using memories of her first husband's affairs. He had been a conman, working under the pretence of being an independent financial adviser. She'd picked up a lot of the language.

'What?' Sheena's face grew pink, and her eyes glistened. 'I don't know what that means.'

Her solicitor leaned towards her again, and whispered. The colour left her face and the glistening eyes leaked tears. Dumbly she shook her head.

'It means he could change his mind whenever he wanted and cut you out of all the money,' Karen said, thinking of the house in Spitalfields, with its atmosphere of generous quiet welcome. She hated what she was allowing Charlie to make her do.

'No,' Sheena said, drawing out the vowel into a long quiet wail. 'I mean, no comment.'

'That's what happened, wasn't it?' Charlie said, picking up the baton again and wielding it with all the aggression that was part of his nature: sometimes hidden, but always there, making him a dangerous man to trust. 'Was it because he was only prepared to pay your bills if you had his kids? Had he had enough of you when he could see you weren't going to get pregnant again? Did he tell you he'd fixed this meeting with his lawyer to take away your money?'

'No comment.'

'Did he warn you he was thinking of doing it when you were both in London?'

'No comment.'

'What did you say to him that made him so angry? Because he was in a rage, wasn't he? You said he was angry when he let you into the house here, even though he tried to hide it.'

'No comment.'

'What did you think when he sent you up to sleep in a servant's bedroom? He was showing you in every possible way that your relationship was over, wasn't he?'

'No.' This time Sheena didn't complete the phrase. She just said the word over and over again. 'No. No. No. No.'

'I'm not surprised you got angry,' Charlie said, pushing on hard. 'All those years of giving him what he wanted, hanging about, sitting up and waiting for him, having his kid and going through hell, and then he turns round and kicks you in the teeth and takes away your financial support.'

Charlie paused for a moment, but Sheena was looking bewildered, and didn't speak at all.

'A lot of us can see why you wanted to kill him,' he said, hesitated for a second, then added, 'but not why you took a bread knife and sawed off his penis and testicles. Can you explain that bit to me?'

'Bastard!' The word emerged from Sheena's lips like a snake's warning hiss.

'How long did it take?' Charlie said, making Karen hate him. But she knew why he was doing it: they were nearly out of time. He had to get anything he could by any legal means, however rough. 'Five minutes? Ten? Did the knife go in easily? Was it sharp, or did you have to hack and saw? How did it feel? Did you think about the times he'd made love to you when you were hacking at his . . . ?'

'Get him out of here,' Sheena shouted at her solicitor before burying her face in her hands.

He took hold of her arm in warning, but she shook him off so violently that he overbalanced and had to hold on to the edge of the table to keep his chair from rocking right over.

Charlie waited, smiling slightly, raising his eyebrows in his usual invitation to talk.

'Get him out of my sight before I fucking kill him,' shouted Sheena, pointing her sharpened nails straight at Charlie's eyes.

Chapter 10

Day Three: 10.00 a.m.

'Mission accomplished,' Charlie said, when he and Karen were well away from the interview room. 'Don't look at me like that, pet. We had to get her to lose her rag. See how she'd act.'

'You haven't accomplished anything. All you did was trample about on a woman suffering an appalling bereavement, and . . .'

'Shut up, Karen.' Charlie sighed, then added in a more reasonable tone, 'She threatened to kill me. First sign of violence we've had from her, and . . .'

'That means nothing. You know as well as I do that the CPS wouldn't even contemplate going to court on something so trivial. I might have threatened to kill you if you'd done that to me.'

His face darkened as he scowled. 'I had to crack that sweet, reasonable shell of hers. It's the reason she got off last time. My mate at the Met says the jury fucking loved her.'

'Maybe she was innocent then as well, and that's what the jury saw,' Karen said, then listened to a quiet voice from her subconscious, suggesting: or maybe she really does respond to trauma with temporary amnesia and that's what happened after the baby's death too. She didn't voice the thought.

'Not in the eyes of the investigating team, or the pathologist.' Charlie was at his toughest. 'Like I said last night, they're all still sure she did it. But she's devious. Clever too. Makes anyone like her enough to give her whatever it is she wants off them.'

'Like Sir Dan?'

'Mebbe. Now, how did you know her trust was "revocable" – or was it a guess, Karen?'

They were walking up the shabby stairs towards the incident room and had got near enough to hear the buzz of talk from inside. Karen stopped on one step and made Charlie wait with her.

'It was a genuine question. You see, I happened to be talking to Antony Quiggly yesterday, but he wouldn't . . .'

'You just happened to talk to him? Forgetting your place in this investigation, Karen?' Charlie was sounding dangerous again. Karen saw that she'd taken some of his apparent dependence on her judgment too literally.

'Never,' she said, hoping she'd be able to make peace. 'I did email him and we met. Just casually. But you don't need to look at me so crossly. I didn't do any harm or share any secrets, and he wouldn't tell me anything. All he'd say was that he'd been due to see Sir Dan on the day after his death. They're not friends. All they have in common, as far as I could gather, are the arrangements for funding Clagbourne House and Sheena. I thought the idea of his revoking her trust was worth trying.'

'You should've left him to us.'

'Think back to the way she reacted, Charlie.' Karen wasn't going to apologize for this, even to make peace. 'There was nothing but "I don't know what you mean".'

'And "No Comment".' He wasn't ready to forgive her yet. Well, that didn't matter. It would give her time to get herself under control again and stop thinking of their one night together.

'But she wasn't angry or threatening until you tortured her with that horrible picture of her castrating her lover,' Karen added. 'That session got us nowhere. When you talk to Antony yourself, make sure you ask him . . .'

'You think I need you to teach me my job?' Charlie said, with fury, before turning away to run up the last few steps to the room where his team waited.

Karen felt suddenly dizzy and flung out a hand to press against the wall to hold herself up. Waves of ringing blankness poured over her, frightening and blinding her. She couldn't stand upright, couldn't see, couldn't think of anything except the way she kept enraging the men she loved.

At last the waves receded, leaving her panting and sweaty, not sure exactly what had happened. She was used to powerful emotions and they'd never done this to her in the past. The only helpful thoughts in her mind were, 'I didn't feel sick. It wasn't nausea. It's not pregnancy. It's not. It's not.'

She knew too well from a couple of past scares that there was no point taking a test for another couple of weeks. Even if she were pregnant, her body would not yet have produced enough human chorionic gonadotrophin to register on any test. And now she was too late for a morning-after pill, as well. All she could do was wait and try not to think too hard about all the possible consequences – or the choices she would have to make – if she were pregnant.

'Karen!' Charlie's bellow pulled her away from the wall. 'Where the fuck are you? We've got work to do.'

And thank God for that, she thought, dragging herself up the last few stairs, not remotely ready to face any more of his anger – or his team.

Inside the incident room everyone was buzzing. Karen saw at once that someone had made progress.

'The housekeeper – Mrs Brown – has made a statement,' said the thin, derisive Richard Silver, 'which includes the fact that two carpenters with what she called "foreign accents" came to mend a split window frame on the morning of Sir Dan's arrival. She'd been warned to expect them in an email from him.'

'OK,' Charlie said. 'And?'

'And Mrs Brown admits it was unusual. In fact, she can't remember Sir Dan ever organizing anything like that at all. Normally he'd just leave her a note if he'd noticed anything that was broken, or a dripping tap or something like that, and let her choose the tradesmen she wanted and get them to mend it, pay them and add the cost to the monthly accounts she prepared for Olga.'

'So?'

Karen couldn't decide whether Charlie was being deliberately obstructive or whether he really did not see where this was going.

'Although Mrs B signed the worksheet for one of the foreign blokes and saw him get back into his van, she admits she didn't actually see the second man get in, and agrees it's possible he never actually left the house.'

'You mean, he could have hidden in the basement with the hammers and waited until Sir Dan was asleep that night, committed the murder, hid again and left the house ... when?'

'After DS Clarke went round in answer to Sheena Greves's call, they got Mrs Brown in to switch off the security. That's when they arrested Greves. The house was unsecured. There are lots of doors – and windows. Anyone could have wandered out while Eve Clarke and co were arresting Sheena.'

'True,' Charlie said. 'Anything useful on the CCTV?'

'Bugger all, boss. The van arriving is there. Two blokes get out, both wearing beanies and two- maybe three-day-old stubble. They don't look up at the cameras and I don't see how we'd ever identify them from that. Mrs B may give the e-fit boys something they can use, but she says she didn't look closely at either bloke and isn't sure she could identify them.'

'Registration number of the van?' Charlie asked.

'Yeah. We got that on film,' Silver said. 'But it belongs to a stolen fourteen-year-old red Ford Fiesta, so that doesn't get us anywhere.'

'Bugger. The existence of these chippies means we've got less than nothing to hold Sheena any longer,' Charlie said.

Karen couldn't keep back one question, although it had nothing to do with her own expertise in the investigation, and he'd already warned her off interfering.

'Have the techies discovered where the original email summoning Sheena was sent from?' she said. 'Could this one from Sir Dan about the window-frame menders have been sent from the same place? By the same person?'

Charlie looked impatiently across at Annie Colvin, who was

in charge of the technical aspects of the hunt. She shook her head.

'We haven't heard back yet, but whoever sent Sheena's email had his email account details and password. They're hoping to find the geographical position of the terminal that sent it. They'll let us know as soon as they've got it.'

'Having the password is more or less what Olga Blackwater said when she accused Sheena of sending the email herself. Could she have organized these so-called window-frame menders too?' Karen asked, before answering the question herself. 'But why would she put herself in so much danger of suspicion if . . . ? No. It has to have been someone else.'

'We'll have to . . .' Charlie began, until one of the phones interrupted him. Annie picked it up, listened, then said to Charlie,

'Maureen Ely's downstairs for you. From SOCA? Along with a couple of translators.'

He grabbed his leather jacket and pulled it over his powerful shoulders, saying, 'Come on, Karen. Off to Clagbourne House.'

Surprised he'd changed his mind about including her, Karen noticed the resentment on DC Silver's narrow face. She smiled briefly in his direction, then led the way out of the incident room, vaguely hearing Charlie give out instructions to the others about pursuing their enquiries into the failed takeover of Sir Dan's businesses last year, and about releasing Sheena on police bail and explaining how she'd have to surrender herself the moment they needed to ask her more questions.

'Will you have her followed?' Karen asked over her shoulder, as Charlie joined her running down the shallow stairs.

'Why would I?'

'To find out what she does so you can collect evidence,' Karen said, amazed he'd even asked the question. 'You were so sure she was guilty this morning, after she threatened you.'

'You any idea how much full surveillance costs? If it's her, we'll find out in other ways, without crashing all my budgets.'

'But you said Number Ten had offered you any help you wanted, and that people in the Met think she's a killer. Doesn't that mean . . . ?'

Charlie's laugh had a bitter edge. 'Offers like that need taking carefully. You start spending their money without getting a good result quick and it's a recipe for the scrap heap.'

'OK. How are your daily reports for the ACC going down?'

All temptation to laugh disappeared as he gritted his teeth. Then he relaxed and asked Karen how her students were taking her prolonged absence.

'Bastard,' she said, before lightening her tone. 'You want me to go and concentrate on them? More than happy to do that, as you know.'

He cuffed her gently, and she felt a lot better.

Clagbourne House turned out to be a large and ugly Victorian villa, sprawling across a wide expanse of land and surrounded by evergreen trees. Laurels, Karen thought, of the most depressing kind, with large shiny-leaves that hung on to both dust and water. From the road, you could see only the shrubs, peaks of the tiled roof and a tall wrought-iron gate with a path beyond it, leading to a black front door.

Charlie knocked, standing beside the SOCA interviewer, while Karen and the two translators waited a few steps behind like large bridesmaids. The door was opened by a heavy-set man dressed as a gardener, who looked them up and down, before checking their warrant cards with extreme care. This must be the security muscle Antony Quiggly had mentioned.

Inside, the small party was met by a friendly-looking English woman in her sixties, who shook hands briskly and said her name was Gilda Wilkins, and that she was the house mother.

'What exactly does that entail?' Karen asked.

Gilda smiled. 'Running the house itself – you know, making sure there's enough food and linen, paying the fuel and staff bills. Then welcoming the girls when they first arrive, deciding which need medical and which psychological help – it's usually both – and just being a friendly older woman while they get over what's been done to them and gather enough strength to decide what they want to do with their lives. You know: do they want to go home or stay in the UK? If they want to stay here, we have lawyers who look into the legal questions of residency; if they want to go home, we facilitate that.'

'Sounds admirable,' Karen said, but she could see that the woman from SOCA wasn't looking particularly impressed.

'Come on through,' Gilda said, taking them into a sunny sitting room, which smelled strongly of the deep-blue hyacinths that filled a large Delft bowl in the bay window.

Seven much younger women were waiting, some reading, two sewing, and one staring into the bleak garden outside. All of them were beautiful, with smooth blonde hair and long legs, high cheekbones and white teeth. Thinking of what the revolting Martin Fieny had said, Karen realized these women must have generated serious amounts of cash before they'd fled their pimps or brothels.

Looking around the clean, light, blue-and-white room, she

thought of the relief they must have felt when their escape had ended here. A place of true asylum.

Charlie nodded to the woman from SOCA and her two interpreters, as though to say 'over to you.'

Only one of the Clagbourne House residents showed any sign of fear as Maureen began to speak, explaining that she needed to talk to each of them separately because she was trying to identify an individual who had been involved in a serious violent crime. The frightened woman was the youngest, probably still in her teens. She was introduced simply as 'Vera', and she wouldn't meet anyone's eyes. Even when she reacted to the second of the translations of Maureen's explanation of how the interviews would be organized, making it obvious she understood, Vera did not show any sign of relaxation.

Karen watched her glancing towards Charlie, licking her lips and looking shiftily from side to side. But she didn't speak. After a moment, she tugged a packet of Marlboro cigarettes out of her jeans pocket, together with a small red plastic disposable lighter.

'You know the rules, Vera,' said Gilda kindly, speaking in English but slowly and articulating her words with great care. 'Only in the garden.'

The second of the translators spoke in a guttural language Karen didn't know. Vera flushed, nodded, and tapped her own chest before gesturing towards the garden with the hand that held the cigarettes. Maureen said something quietly to the translator, who smiled in reassurance and obviously gave Vera permission to go outside to smoke.

Charlie's gaze met Karen's for a second. She knew what he wanted, and she waited until everyone was distracted by organizing who would be interviewed first and who would sit where. While they were all talking to each other, and Maureen was helping one of the rescued prostitutes to push a small sofa out of the way, Karen slid quietly out of the room, walked through the hall and let herself out of the front door.

At first she couldn't see Vera, but a column of smoke hung in the cold air just above one of the biggest and ugliest of the laurel bushes. Karen walked round it and saw the teenager leaning against the gnarled trunk, sucking on her cigarette as though she were a starving baby and it were the first bottle she'd been offered in her life.

Not sure how they would communicate, Karen smiled and held her hand up to her mouth, gesturing with two fingers to show she wanted a cigarette. Vera understood and nodded, offering her packet and the lighter to Karen.

'Who you are?' she asked in a heavy accent, still looking scared.

'I am a psychologist,' Karen said, copying Maureen's clear articulation. 'And the others are all from the police. We are here to help.'

'Pliz?' Vera said, reminding Karen of the young woman lost in Trafalgar Square.

'Psychologist,' Karen said, digging in her bag for one of her cards. It held her title, her address at the university and her mobile phone number. She'd never wanted to give out details of her flat.

She held the small cardboard rectangle out to Vera, pointing to the words: 'Dept of Forensic Psychology.'

Vera nodded, although her eyes still looked blankly uncomprehending and scared, and stuffed the card in the pocket of her jeans. She sucked on her cigarette again. Karen didn't think she was going to get anything much to help Charlie here. In order to increase the mateyness she hoped to establish, she shook a cigarette out of the packet for herself and lifted it to her mouth.

It was fifteen years since she'd last smoked, but she still hadn't forgotten the ritual or the pleasure. She felt the old comforting dryness of the paper between her lips, and she inhaled the scent of non-burning tobacco, sweet and enticing. At last she lifted the flame, drew in the first, tremendously familiar mouthful of smoke and taste.

The cough took her by surprise, wrenching her whole body, rasping her throat, making her eyes water and her head spin. She could think of nothing but the nauseating sensations. How could she ever have enjoyed this?

Footsteps rustling through dry leaves brought her to her senses and she opened her streaming eyes to see Vera disappearing through the wrought-iron gate at the end of the garden path.

Letting all the smoke out of her mouth, still coughing, Karen dropped the cigarette, before taking a moment to grind it out on the paving stone before running after Vera.

The road was empty of traffic. Nothing had got in Vera's way, and she was off, belting through a field gate opposite, then running diagonally across the edge of the field by the time Karen reached the garden gate. She could see Vera's vivid green sweater and flapping golden hair, both much brighter than the winter grass or evergreen leaves all around.

The field gate had been tied up with twine in knots that looked as though they'd take hours to undo. Vera must have climbed. Karen followed suit, stumbled as she reached the ground and felt one foot slide into a cowpat. Only its surface was hard. An acrid miasma rose from the greeny-brown mush beneath. She felt its dampness through her sock, grimaced, and wiped her foot on the grass as well as she could and ran on.

Vera had pushed through into the next field, but by the time Karen reached the hedge she could not see how she'd done it. Brambles with tiny soft greyish buds and vicious long red spikes covered every gap in the trees.

The trees had their own spikes, Karen saw as she tried to force a way through. Blackthorn. The name came back to her out of the past. There'd be white flowers soon and hard little black sloes next autumn. She ran sideways, parallel to the hedge, searching for a gap and saw it at last. A loop of bright green wool clinging to one of the blackthorn's spikes showed Vera had been here too.

Karen got through in the end, but not before leaving fibres from her parka, clumps of her hair, and some skin from her scalp on the wicked thorns. She hoped her yellow cashmere sweater hadn't suffered too much. Straightening up on the far side, panting and furious, she saw Vera climb yet another gate at the far end of the new field.

As far as Karen could see, it was the only sensible way out, and she was not going through any more hedges if she could help it. She ran on, trying to ignore the stitch developing in her side. Her throat rasped as she heaved for breath, her lungs were on fire, and her heart was banging. She cursed herself for even that one puff of Vera's cigarette.

Another thunderous sound overtook even the crashing of her heart and blood and she realized she was running next to a road. Heavy lorries were passing her. The hedge was well over ten feet high here and she had no way of seeing through it, but the clanking roars told her the vehicles on this road were huge. The field gate seemed further away than ever. None of the traffic sounds suggested any vehicle had braked, which meant Vera was still on foot: faster than Karen and with a good start, but not impossible to catch.

The gate at last. Karen's brain offered relief and triumph, but she was too tired to accept either. She slammed into the metal bars much faster than she'd meant and this time the gate opened. Brakes squealed. Karen got her breath back and emerged on to the edge of the road just in time to see Vera climb the mountainous side of an enormous container lorry. Karen rushed forwards, shouting out Vera's name. The lorry driver took off his brake again and the great monster eased out into the traffic. Karen ran forwards, caught her foot in a disguised badger's hole and fell face down into a muddy puddle that felt as though it was filled with broken glass.

Chapter 11

Day Three: 11.20 a.m.

Will felt the thin winter sun on his right cheek as he picked up his ringing phone.

'Will Hawkins,' he said.

'Will?' A familiar voice. Stella. Karen's best friend. But sounding angry instead of warm and giggly in her usual, slightly irritating, way.

'Stella, hi. How are you?'

'Outraged, you bastard! What the hell have you done to Karen?'

'Stella, I don't wish to be rude, but this is nothing to do with you. I must go. Goodbye.'

Will clicked off the call, knowing Karen must still be hurting badly if she'd confided in Stella, but absolutely certain he had to leave her to get on with healing in her own way and in her own time until he knew where he was. He put the phone back on the table.

If he should ever get back to full fitness, and be able to work again, he could go back to her. If not, not. He knew what became of people in relationships where one was the carer and the other the victim-tyrant of the household. He'd never turn her into a resentful drudge or himself an equally resentful demander of her services, however much he missed her now.

A sudden impatient banging made him drop his phone. Then came his elder sister's voice: 'Will! Will! Are you there? Forgot my keys.'

Sighing, he reached for his sticks, levered himself up from the chair by the window, straightened his back and forced himself to walk almost normally towards the front door. Freya insisted on shopping for him, instead of letting him order what he wanted over the internet. And he knew why. She'd been his surrogate mother since his eleventh birthday and she still took her responsibilities seriously.

He pinned a smile on his face, feeling his muscles stretch, and opened the door. She looked exactly as he'd expected, maroon-dyed hair shrieking at her oversized shocking-pink tunic, which in turn shrieked at the orange jeans she wore beneath. Not many fifty-year-olds had such a taste for strident colour.

Five straining plastic bags nestled around her ankles, sprouting greenery and pasta packets at their tops. When she leaned across the step to kiss him, he smelled the familiar sweetness of the scent she'd always worn. Diorissimo. He knew that's what it was because he'd saved up to buy her some for her twenty-first, the year of their mother's death, when he'd been eleven.

'How is it today? The pain,' she said, hauling all five bags up to waist height again. He'd seen the red welts on her palms and took both sticks in his right hand so that he could reach out to save her the weight of at least two bags. 'Don't be silly, Will. I can manage. Let me past.'

He flattened himself against the wall, knowing silent obedience was the only way to stop her when she was in this kind of steamroller mood, shut the door when she'd passed him, and walked slowly after her, concentrating on getting his heels right down on the floor at each step, however much it hurt.

'I'll let you put it all away,' she called from the narrow kitchen, with its view towards Lewes Castle. 'Because I know you'll only rearrange everything after I've gone anyway. Now, a cuppa? Or a drink?'

'Freya, for heaven's sake, it's far too early.'

She laughed at his horrified protest, with the same rollicking guffaw she'd always used to hide discomfort of any kind. He lowered himself back into his chair, not fighting the pain because resistance only made it worse and longer lasting. But he was still grateful for the sun's warmth on his cheek. He hoped it would give him a little colour. His shaving mirror had shown him how pale his face became when his legs and hips did this to him, and he didn't want Freya worrying about him any more than she already was.

When she came back she had a couple of mugs in her hands and looked around for somewhere to put them. To his silent fury she dumped them on the paper cover of a medical journal he'd been reading. He knew she wouldn't have dried the bottoms of the mugs, so that he'd find wet brownish rings on the journal. She dragged a delicate ebonized chinoiserie table next to his chair and went back for the mug.

'Coasters on the windowsill,' he said and heard her give the biggest, most theatrically resigned sigh.

'You really are a pernickety old woman,' Freya said, not

sounding affectionate any longer. 'No wonder your relationship foundered.'

'Don't go there, Freya.' he said. He'd specifically avoided introducing her and Karen because he didn't want his sister explaining what he was really feeling or what it signified or how he should change it.

He saw a great lump of red paint under her nail and hoped she wasn't going anywhere near his pristine walls with that finger.

'Sorry if I'm talking out of turn,' she said, not sounding remotely apologetic. 'But there are things that have to be said.'

He didn't comment, but that didn't stop her.

'I've watched you for the past year or so, actually looking happy. Now, here you are stuck, alone again, with a broken leg and god knows what other injuries. And you're back with your old "I can take it, whatever it is" look. Did she dump you because of the sticks?'

'Certainly not.' Will knew he sounded distant, but he couldn't help that.

'Then why? What kind of woman is she?'

He just looked at his sister, thinking: you're a psychotherapist, who's always been certain she knows what I feel; work it out for yourself.

'Not another alkie, is she?' Freya said, then quickly corrected herself. 'No. Too obvious. All men marry their mothers in one way or another, but probably not in quite that straightforward a way. So who is she? *What* is she?'

'She's a forensic psychologist,' he said, still keeping his distance even when Freya burst into gust after gust of belly-trembling laughter.

'Oh, Will. My poor Will,' she said when she could speak again. 'Did she describe one of your neuroses a bit too accurately? Did you sack her? I bet that was it. You'd never put up with someone else commenting on your emotions.'

Suddenly he was angry, not just pissed-off or irritated, but deeply retrospectively furious with Freya for years and years of over-interpreting every little thing he'd thought or said or done. Getting it wrong every single time and driving him even further into the dark silence that was the only true defence he'd ever found against anything.

'She is far too intelligent to think she could accurately analyse my psyche from any external signs,' he said coldly, 'and in any case she's far too generous to lumber me with self-serving interpretations of my mental state.'

Freya stepped backwards so fast she tripped over the indigo and saffron Kangxi rug. He watched, powerless, as she went back, tea flying up out of her mug to splatter down on the early eighteenth-century carpet, around which he had arranged and decorated his quiet and recherché room.

'Shit!' she said, righting herself long before she'd come anywhere near falling right over. 'Sorry, Will. About the rug I mean.'

Dumping her mug back on his medical journal, she dashed into the kitchen for a roll of paper and plumped down on her knees to soak up as much as she could of the spilled liquid. At least she drank her tea without milk, which would have made the stain much harder to shift.

'I promise I won't rub it,' she said, laying sheet after sheet of absorbent paper over the wet patch. They'd had carpet experiences before, and she didn't forget. He had to give her that. 'Is it very valuable?'

'Moderately,' he said, thinking of the sixteen thousand pounds he'd paid at Sotheby's five years ago. 'But that's fine. You've done enough. Thanks. Leave it now.'

She knew him well enough to understand he meant what he said. Chastened, she took the pile of tea-soaked paper out to the kitchen. But she was like the float on a fishing line: never below the surface for more than a second.

'Is she a neat-freak too?' she said, bouncing back out of the kitchen. 'Your girlfriend.'

Will thought of the supreme self-control he'd needed not to rush around after Karen picking up the things she'd dropped or left out of place in her flat and his, and the way she left onion and garlic peelings scattered around the kitchen floor when she'd been sliding a heap of them from the chopping board into her small brown recycling caddy. He laughed at the memories.

'Hardly,' he said. 'My tidiness drives her nuts.'

Freya relaxed. 'She sounds OK, then. What does she look like? You must have a photo. Even you. No point pretending: you know I'll get it out of you in the end. It'll be more dignified to give in without a struggle. Where is it?'

'Steamroller!' he said, with a small smile. 'There's a photograph in the top drawer of my desk.'

He watched her fetch it, look down with almost popping eyes, then stare at him, saying: 'Wow! She's gorgeous.'

'She doesn't think so.' Will looked out of the window, remembering yet more. 'She thinks her face is too small for her height. Five foot nine, in case you want to know. Size 12.'

Freya laughed, but Will couldn't share in the amusement. He said, 'I'm worried about her.'

'I can see that. Which is why I don't understand why you're here and she isn't if you feel like this.'

'I can't . . .' He looked down at his sticks.

'At the risk of not being generous enough to keep my ideas to myself,' Freya said with enough bite to warn him that he'd hurt her, 'you're still as terrified of any kind of weakness in yourself as you are of mess – your own or anyone else's. Don't look at me like that, Will. I know you hate my job, but it's necessary and it helps people, and for once you have got to listen.'

He kept his head turned away from her, which was invitation enough in its perverse way.

'You've always known you were conceived in a last-ditch attempt to save a failing marriage and it didn't work. You've blamed yourself for that for years, nearly as much as you've blamed Dad for leaving us all.'

'Haven't you?' The question was out of Will's mouth before he could stop it. He knew Freya saw their father and his new family, an act of disloyalty he didn't think he would ever be able to forgive.

'Yes, but I've gone beyond blame now.' There was gentleness as well as implacability in her voice. 'Because it's the only way to salvage anything from the wreck. I know you've got yourself a brilliant career and have worked harder than any human being should work, but that's not enough. There's more to life than work. You have to forgive him, too, or you'll never get it.'

'Does he yet accept that, because of his selfishness, we had to live in squalor?' Will asked, keeping most of his feelings out of his voice.

He heard Freya trampling across his treasured carpet like a navvy in dirty work boots, but he felt her hand on his head, too, as he'd felt it in childhood.

'It wasn't squalor, Will.' She sounded sad. 'Or only for those few weeks. I'm sorry I didn't realize what would happen when I went off to university. I'm sorry Mum panicked when she found herself alone with all the responsibility for you and then buried herself in a bottle. I'm sorry you had to look after yourself and her, even when she threw up and passed out – or worse. I know you were only nine, and no nine-year-old should have to know about such things, let alone deal with them. But I can't change it now. I'm sorry. I've always been sorry.' Her voice firmed up, as she added, 'And so has Dad.'

'You don't have to be,' Will said, still looking out of the window, cursing his broken legs for opening the doors he had kept carefully locked in his mind for so long. 'The second you realized what was going on, you sorted it. I'm not blaming anyone – except him. She was his responsibility. So was I. He shouldn't have left.'

'Will, listen.' Freya forced his chair round. 'You're talking about this at last, and that's a good thing, but you have to deal with it and get past it; otherwise, no relationship can work for you. You mustn't punish this woman for making you feel needy all over again. You . . .'

'Oh, stop it, Freya. You really haven't a clue about me.' Will made a vast effort to subdue the billowing words that filled his head. 'Sweet of you to have done all that shopping for me. I know how busy you are, and it's really kind of you.'

She said nothing, so he looked up and was surprised to see

tears in her eyes. Then she turned away before he could comment.

'It's the least I could do. I know you won't listen to me, but whatever went wrong between you and . . .' She laid the photograph down on his table. 'What's her name?'

'Karen Taylor.'

'Between you and Karen, bury your pride and your terror of depending on someone else, and phone her. I'm off now. I'll see you in four days' time – unless you need anything in between. Don't forget: *phone*!'

Chapter 12

Day Three: 12.30 p.m.

'I should have asked for permission to keep Vera out of the interviewing process,' Gilda said as she picked pieces of glass out of Karen's forehead with a pair of tweezers. 'I knew she was still traumatized by what she's been through, but I never thought she'd run like that. It was good of you to go after her. What did she say to you?'

Karen tried to keep still under the heat of the illuminated magnifying glass Gilda had arranged on a stand beside her face. She hoped the tweezers were sterile, and that the glass chips wouldn't leave scars on her face. Already she knew her yellow cashmere sweater would never be the same again. It wasn't just the muddy water from the puddle, which had leaked through the zip of her parka; she'd also dripped blood from the cuts and stupidly wiped her sleeve against her forehead.

'There,' Gilda said. 'Can you straighten up? There's a piece just under the hair line and I need to go in straighter than I can with you tilting your chin up.'

Karen obediently lowered her eyes, relieved to see Charlie still sitting on the windowsill opposite her chair. He was looking intent, as though working something out in his head. A murmur of English speech came from next door, punctuated by bursts of an unfamiliar language. The interviews were continuing.

'What did Vera say to you?' Gilda asked again, just as she tugged out a piece of glass from Karen's scalp, before dropping it in a blue-edged white kidney bowl and grabbing a swab, which she pressed hard against the wound. There must have been disinfectant in the swab because it stung so sharply Karen drew in her breath and blinked hard. But the medicinal smell was reassuring and she was relieved to know her small wounds were being so carefully cleaned.

'Almost nothing,' she said, when she could speak again. 'She asked who we were, and I told her, but I'm not sure she understood. Then she gave me a fag, which I lit. By the time I was ready to hand back her lighter, she'd gone. I followed.'

'Pity you didn't come back and tell us,' Charlie said in an expressionless voice. 'Why didn't you?'

'It all happened so fast,' Karen said, before Gilda pushed her back against the chair once more.

'There's another piece. Here, just to the left of the eye. Hold still.'

Karen braced herself for the moment when the tweezers bit. It came and a second later she heard the reassuring ring of glass hitting metal and felt the warmth of her blood again. Then came the disinfectant's sting.

'You won't need any stitches, luckily,' Gilda said. 'They're all only tiny cuts. And that's the lot.'

'Thank you. You're very deft with those tweezers.' Karen smiled, worrying about scars again.

'I'm a nurse,' she said. 'That's how I got this job. I've done a lot of it in A&E in my time. I don't think you'll be marked. I've disinfected the whole injury site, so there shouldn't be any problem. But if you see any inflammation or the cuts start hurting, go to your doctor at once.'

'I will. Thanks.' Karen looked over her shoulder at Charlie. 'I'm sorry I didn't come and get you. When I saw Vera running away, instinct took over. I went after her. It wasn't till I was face down in the road that I remembered my phone and called you.'

'You were lucky,' Gilda said. 'You could have fallen into the path of the traffic. It goes fast there. Did you see the vehicle that picked Vera up?'

Karen shook her head and felt the cuts sting again. 'A great articulated monster. I didn't get the number plate. It was mainly white with red and blue writing. But I can't remember what it said. Stupid of me.'

'No registration number?' Charlie sounded gloomy. As Karen shook her head, he added, 'Pity. At least you're in one piece. Thank you, Gilda. Can you fill me in on Vera's background?'

The woman's pleasant face creased up into a mask of sympathy as she shook her head. 'We've only had her here for just over two weeks. She was in a bad state when she got here – they often are, as you can imagine – but I thought she was beginning to settle. The doctor prescribed sleeping pills, and she hasn't been wandering at night the last five nights, so I thought she was probably fit enough to answer questions. Obviously I was wrong. Goodness knows what Lady Blackwater will say to me now.'

'I thought she was only a distant kind of patroness,' Karen said, pulling her parka back over her sweater. 'I didn't realize she had any day-to-day part in the running of Clagbourne House.'

Gilda looked a little pink. 'She hasn't. But she takes a real interest, even when she's in Switzerland. And when she is on the Island she nearly always finds the time to drop in and talk to the girls. They absolutely love her.'

'I can imagine,' Karen said with warmth. After being at the mercy of pimps, traffickers and clients like the ghastly Martin Fieny, to be welcomed by a gentle and vulnerable woman, who used her own money to provide them with an escape from a life they hated, could lead to any amount of devotion.

'The idea that I could have missed signs of serious trauma in Vera is going to shock Lady Blackwater,' Gilda said. 'I only hope you manage to pick Vera up before she's reduced to earning money in the only way she can, Chief Inspector.'

'I'm on it,' Charlie said. 'I'm taking Doctor Taylor back to the station now, but I'll leave our colleagues. Send a car for them later. That won't cause a problem, will it?'

'Well?' Charlie said, when they were safely back in his car and on the way back to Cowes. 'What did you really get out of Vera?'

'No more than I said in there,' Karen told him. 'I noticed her the minute we arrived because she looked terrified, but her English was more or less non-existent, and she obviously hadn't a clue who we were. When I said "police", I'm not sure she believed it.'

She glanced sideways at his leather jacket and spiky waxed

dark hair and wondered whether Vera had assumed he was the next trafficker planning to buy and misuse her.

'What are you doing to find her?' she added.

Charlie signalled left to drive down into Cowes. 'I've got Eve mobilizing what little spare manpower she has; warning the ferry and hovercraft operators, too. Are you sure you didn't see any more of the lorry's ID?'

'Sorry. No. But I doubt if she'd have stayed on it long. Charlie, she was terrified. She must have known you'd search for the lorry.'

'Why're you surprised she's scared? Rescued from forced sex work. Probably can't believe she's safe yet.' He clamped his lips together as though determined not to say something he'd regret. Then he said, 'And she won't be if we don't find her soon.'

That afternoon Karen was going through the witness statements Charlie's team had amassed, searching for anything that could give any new insight into Sir Dan's psychology and explain why he had so enraged his killer at this precise moment, and in this precise place. She was still certain that the positioning of the body and the choice of the kitchen table for its bier were of real significance; she just couldn't see what it was yet.

Frustration made her think of Stella and the fact that she hadn't yet responded to the email Karen had sent. Reaching for the phone, Karen called her number, rehearsing the message she would leave. To her relief, Stella herself answered, giving her name with all the authoritative efficiency of a head of department at the university.

'Hi,' Karen said, putting all available warmth into her voice. 'It's me. I wanted . . .'

'Oh.' The single sound was full of disappointment. 'I thought you might be him, phoning to apologize and say it was all a mistake.'

'I wanted to find out how you are.' It was hard to sound sympathetic, Karen found, without adding pity, which would always be an insult.

'Frankly, I feel like shit. As I expect you do, too. They're all fucking bastards, aren't they? All we can do is work, forget that we've ever . . . Oh, you know.'

'That was the other reason I was phoning,' Karen said, still not wanting to talk about Will unless it was absolutely essential. 'You said something the other day about making a site visit to see progress on my house. I was wondering – I'm over on the Island now – if you'd maybe like to meet there, so we could have a look.'

A long pause made Karen wonder whether she had insulted Stella after all, but eventually she heard a long sigh, then Stella's ordinary voice.

'D'you know? I'd love it. Just what I need. To see something good I've been involved in. What are you doing on the Island?'

'Oh, you know: working. I haven't got my car, but I could meet you at Fountain Quay and we could get a cab. How about it?'

'Fab. Really good. I'll come over now.' A much shorter pause was followed by Stella saying, 'Meet you in an hour?'

'Great.'

Karen put down the phone. Her forehead throbbed from the cuts the glass had made and she swallowed a couple of aspirin from her bag, hoping they wouldn't send her to sleep as she tried to concentrate on the human stories and motives behind the formal language of the statements. Reading them had to be better than rushing through muddy fields, cutting her face and ruining her clothes, but she was afraid it wouldn't lead anywhere.

Remembering the details of this morning's fruitless chase, she looked down at her right foot. She'd done her best to clean her shoe and had bought new socks to replace the one that had been soaked in liquid cow dung, but the leather would never recover. Following Vera had been pointless. Karen felt stupid, as well as frustrated. She wasn't surprised Stella wanted to do nothing but work. Karen could see the appeal. Back at the university, she too would be under her own control, analysing, theorizing, and teaching. She was not made for hands-on investigation or physical endurance.

Ashamed of herself, she rummaged in her notes for the photographs Charlie had printed of Sir Dan's body. Wasn't that brutal display enough to make anyone want to help find the killer in any way available?

Her phone rang. Max's name was on the screen.

'Karen?' His gravelly voice held much more urgency than usual.

'Yes,' she said, surprised. 'What?'

'I need you here, at work. Now. Come to my office.'

'I can't, Max. I'm in the middle of helping with a murder enquiry.' She checked her conscience and her diary for a second, then added: 'And I'm not due to see any students today. I know there are essays to mark, but I'll pick them up this evening and do it tonight.'

Karen saw Charlie's dark head lift. She met his gaze and mouthed 'sorry'. He stared at her. Max's voice was even more urgent as it came down the phone: 'Get back here *now*. My office. Soon as you can. Don't say anything else to anyone.' He cut off the call before she could protest or ask questions.

She put the phone back in her pocket, looked at the mess of paper in front of her and thought of Stella getting ready to cross the Solent.

Max had never sounded like that in all the years they'd known each other. And she wasn't doing much good here. She phoned Stella back, quickly explained, and settled with her that they'd have their site meeting tomorrow. Getting to her feet, she grabbed for her shoulder bag, then moved across the incident room to Charlie's work station.

'I've got to go,' she said.

'You can't. I want you here.'

'Tough. That was Max. Something important has come up at the university. I have to deal with it. It's my job; my career; my future.'

'Karen, I . . .' Charlie looked around and saw half the team staring at them. He shrugged. 'Go then. But get back here as soon as you can. Phone me when you know.'

The police station wasn't far from the quay where the Red Jet hovercraft were based. As Karen ran, feeling the first few drops of today's rain, she tried not to worry. Max's unprecedented summons could mean almost anything, but she trusted him too much even to think he could be wasting her time.

Arriving at the quay just as one hovercraft left, she knew she would have to wait half an hour for the next and shuddered, wishing she'd worn her flying jacket again today. The rain wasn't heavy, but it had insinuated itself into her hair and was beginning to trickle down her neck. Coffee, she thought, and set off back towards the town and the good Italian café she'd found, where she knew she would be able to buy some espresso to warm her up and give her the energy to do whatever it was that Max needed so urgently.

She didn't want to risk missing the next hovercraft, so she took the coffee away with her and sat, shivering, as she sipped it. From her seat, she could see the next Red Jet surging towards her, with the muddle of Southampton's less than beautiful buildings beyond it.

Home, she thought, wishing she could still hope to find that Will had let himself into her flat and was waiting for her.

That could never happen now. Even if he wanted to come back, he couldn't get in without her. He'd thrust his set of keys into her hand before he'd gone that last time. The cold hard weight of them was easy to remember, as was the way the barrels pushed into her flesh as she'd clutched them in an effort to hide everything she was feeling. Her fingers curled around the returning sensation in her palm.

It seemed mad to her that she'd ever resisted Will, let alone fought to keep her independence for so long. If she hadn't been so fearful, they'd probably have been married by now and working together to get through whatever problems his accident had brought them.

Karen was surprised to see a light shining through the glass panel in the door to her small, cluttered office in the university building. Outside dusk was already making details hard to see. She longed for the return of summer, when it would still be light at four o'clock in the afternoon.

No one had a key to her room except the cleaners, and

they worked in the middle of the night, not late afternoon. She put her hand in her pocket, checking, and this time the metal heaviness of her keys felt comforting in its familiarity. As she drew nearer to her office, she could make out the sounds of sporadic talk.

Almost certain they were coming from Max and a younger man, she speeded up, hoping against all sense that the younger man was Will. Her hope died when she reached the door. The second voice was much younger than his, and differently accented.

She heard this man say, 'If that's it, Professor Pitton, I'd better get going. I've got a piece of work to finish.'

'I'm grateful,' Max said. 'I'll tell your tutor what a help you've been.'

Karen moved back a pace or two and looked with curiosity at the tousle-haired youth who came out of her office. He barely glanced at her and went on his way, whistling.

She leaned her shoulder against the door and moved round it to see Max, sitting in her chair with his feet up on her desk. He was not particularly tall, and his head looked much too large for his body. She'd often thought that, as a young man, his pendulous chin and large nose must have made him unattractive. Now, at fifty, he had grown into his features and looked magnificent, if odd.

What she had not expected this afternoon was to see all the unmarked essays that had been sitting on the visitor's chair now in a pile on the floor. In their place was this morning's runaway, Vera, tear-stained and very pale, hugging a large steaming mug between her dirty hands.

'Ah, Karen, thanks for coming so quickly,' Max said with heavy sarcasm. 'You know Vera Brovotka, don't you?'

'I do,' Karen said, astonished. How on earth had Vera hooked up with Max, of all people? 'Hi.'

Vera nodded, but she didn't speak. Karen looked at Max again, before staring pointedly at his feet. His unbrushed suede shoes were creasing the top pages of her latest printout of information the FBI had collected and published on post-mortem mutilation.

Max swung his feet off her desk, but didn't apologize or look troubled in any way.

'Who was that boy?' Karen asked.

'The *young man*?' Max said with heavy emphasis, reminding her of the innumerable times she had told him that their female students were young women and not girls. 'He's doing a PhD in comparative literature, but I happened to know he had a Czech background and so I asked him to come to reassure Vera as to my bona fides. I think he succeeded.'

Vera's vigorous nodding caught Karen's eye and for a moment they faced each other again.

'Bona fides,' Karen repeated. 'So you do speak English, Vera.'

'I do. But not at Clag House. Never there.' Vera's accent was still noticeable, and the words were sharp, clipped and fast, sounding as though they'd been fired by a machine working at maximum speed.

'Why not?'

'You have to listen, Karen,' Max said. 'This is important. To you and your investigation.'

'OK.' Karen perched on the side of her desk, half-way between the two of them, but facing Vera. 'So tell me the whole story. How you got here and why, and how Max found you?'

'You give me your card this morning,' Vera said, 'and so I am having access to your address here.'

'But why did you run away from me if you wanted to talk?' Karen's hand caressed her forehead, without her consciously directing it. Her fingertips registered the patches of cut and swollen skin. 'Why not do it there and then?'

'Because I had to check.' Vera uncurled her body and leaned down to put her mug on the floor. When she sat up again, her back was straight and she crossed her legs, looking older and more confident. Nothing could disguise her exhaustion or her pallor. 'At first I think you are one more of them, so I run. Then I see what is written on this card and I see "university", so when I am off this ferryboat, I am coming to make sure.'

'Right. That was sensible. And?'

'And I find your professor and because I am still not . . . not sure that here I am safe, I am pretending I do not speak any English. He asks me questions in French and German and Russian, and . . .'

'I didn't know you had Russian,' Karen said to Max, so surprised she had to break the flow. 'Or Czech.'

'Not a lot of either,' Max said, with a smile that looked more like a smirk, 'but any educated chap knows how to say "good day" in most European languages, as well as to identify the sound of them. I didn't understand Vera's so I hazarded a guess and tried Czech. She nodded. I scoured my memory for a Czech-speaker and came up with young Tom. Happily he was in the library.'

'After he had made me see and understand that he is scholar,' Vera said, 'he tells me all about Professor Pitton here, and then I see it is safe to speak in English.'

'Right. And?' Karen knew she was repeating herself, but these long preambles were beginning to frustrate her. 'Tell me about Clagbourne House.'

Vera's face changed as Karen watched, all the new confidence disappearing as her skin grew even more pale and her eyes widened.

'They do not know. At least they will not believe. But is not safe there.'

'Who won't believe? And *what* won't they believe?'

'Careful, Karen,' Max said. 'You're not cross-examining a hostile witness.'

'Sorry.' She smiled in Vera's direction, deliberately slowing her breathing as she relaxed her lips to calm them both. 'How is it not safe there?'

'There is man coming there sometimes, as workman. But he is not workman. He is called Dev. I know him.'

'Ah.' Karen remembered the security guard dressed as a gardener. 'How do you know him?'

'From last year. I have seen . . . When I was first . . .' Vera closed her eyes. The other two waited while she got her courage back. Without opening her eyes, she said, 'He was working for the people who bought me after I was first brought in here.'

Her English gets better and better, Karen thought as she noticed Vera's accurate use of brought and bought.

'And he raped me.' Vera's voice still sounded as though it had been produced by a machine, even with this declaration. 'When I tried to escape, they found me and brought me back and they used him to punish me. By raping. Before the drugs. They like to use heroin to make you addicted so you are even more in their power.'

'Are you sure it was this same man who raped you?' Karen asked, knowing the question was probably insulting as well as unnecessary. She heard Max sigh.

'Of course. When it is like that, when a man is doing that to you, and his face is inches from your own, you do not forget. And his smell. I know this. You do not forget a man's smell. It is always different in each one. And you do not forget.'

Karen thought of the lemony scent of Will's pillow, and the spicy cleanness of Pears soap and rosemary shaving oil that rose from Charlie's skin. In that moment she knew what Vera had suffered, even though nothing in her own life could begin to match it. And she was twice Vera's age.

'So what do you think he is doing there?' Karen had allowed her words to speed up, well aware now that Vera could understand everything she said.

'I think they have sent him to Clag House so he can find their own girls, the ones they have paid for, the ones they think have been stolen from them. So far, it is only me. The other girls have come from other places. Other pimps. None of them have been at all frightened of Dev. I think he is reporting back to them and when there are enough of their own girls they will come.' Her voice shifted on the last word, wobbling. She stiffened and, with obvious difficulty, added, 'And take us back.'

'So you see, Karen,' Max said, 'why I had to get you back here once I'd heard that story.'

'Absolutely.' Karen could not stop looking at Vera, more impressed than she could have begun to say with the teenager's courage. 'And I must get on to Charlie. This could . . .'

'No police.' Vera's pale greenish eyes widened again until

she looked on the point of fainting. 'No police. You do not understand. They . . .'

'It's OK,' Karen said, softening her voice until it couldn't have threatened a baby. 'You won't need to see any of them, or talk to them. What did you do when you first recognized this Dev?'

'I ask the other girls if they know him. None of them do, as I have said already. Some told me I was making it up. Imagining it because of everything that has been done to me. So then I went to Gilda. And she was very kind and said she is not surprised I am seeing figures from my nightmares because I have this thing, this PTSD, which is giving me the flashbacks, and I must understand that there – at Clag House – I am safe.'

'Why didn't you believe her?' Karen asked, thinking that Gilda's explanation sounded reasonable. Anyone who had suffered what Vera had described could be liable to post-trau-matic stress disorder.

'Because I know she was wrong. I know who Dev is. And when she would not believe me, I . . .' Vera hesitated.

'You?' Karen said, prompting her.

'I was sorry for her that she did not see, that she would not believe, and I try to think who I can tell who will believe me. No one does. When you and these police come today, I think maybe them at last, then I see the way they talk with Gilda and I see they won't believe me either. And if you tell them now, they will try to make me go back there to Clag House, and I will not go. Nowhere near where Dev is. Or has been. Never. *You* will believe me, won't you?' Vera's machine-gun voice was rising in pitch and intensity with every word. 'You will not try to make me go back there. You must not. I cannot go.'

Karen nodded, looked at Max, then said, 'What we have to work out now is where Vera will be safest. If I put her up in my flat, she might . . .'

Max held up one pudgy hand. 'No need.' He nodded at the young fugitive, with the kindest of his smiles. 'We've already agreed. I'm going to take Vera to a refuge I know.'

'A refuge?' Karen said. '*You?*'

Max's face twisted in an expression she found hard to decode. She thought there was hurt in it, as well as a contradictory satisfaction.

'Why not me?' he said, his voice sounding even more like gravel being shaken in a metal bucket than usual. 'I help fund it. So I have enough influence to get Vera in. There's always an extra room kept available for an emergency.'

'Where is it?' Karen was battling with her surprise and trying not to insult him.

'You must know that no one involved ever discloses the address of a refuge for battered women. I may be sure you're trustworthy, but even so. I can't tell you.'

'But . . .'

'Stop it, Karen. This is not negotiable. Now, Vera and I will disappear.' Max looked around the room, his gaze pausing on the piles of unmarked essays. 'While you get on with the work you're paid to do.'

Karen thought of fighting back, then decided to let it go. Max didn't have to be told that she would head back to the Island at the first possible opportunity. He knew her too well to think anything else.

Vera uncrossed her legs and stood up, looking shaky. Still clutching a new packet of cigarettes and a shocking-pink disposable lighter, she walked across the small cluttered space to hold out her free hand to Karen, who took it.

'I wish to thank you,' Vera said with great formality. 'And to apologize for running away from you. But it was not safe for you if I talked to you there. And it will not be safe for you now to be near Clag House. They will be sure that I have talked to you, and they are dangerous. They will go to all lengths to make sure no one knows what they are doing and how they are trying to find the girls who get away from them.'

'They?' Karen said, hearing all kinds of warning sounds in her mind.

'The people who put Dev in there. They will be watching. They are always watching. They will know you and I were alone together in the garden. If you do not go there now and ask too much questions – too many questions – then you may be safe. But be careful. They are ruthless and cruel.' For a second she closed her eyes, then said more quietly: 'You do not know *how* cruel.'

Chapter 13

Day Three: 5.00 p.m.

Karen watched Max usher Vera out of her office. He was twice Vera's width but about three inches shorter. They looked ridiculous together, like a socially uncouth billionaire proudly strutting along beside a leggy beauty he thought of as a trophy bride. But Karen could see how Max's confidence and bulk reassured the Czech, and that made up for any absurdity.

When they'd gone, she picked up her phone to tell Charlie there was a new suspect to find, and a much more likely one than Sheena Greves, then she thought again. She knew she could trust Charlie with Vera's discovery, but if someone on the Island had been sending faked emails around, they could well be monitoring phone traffic too. If there were anything in Vera's fears, it would be stupid to take such a risk.

The landline might be safer than her mobile, but there were still no guarantees of absolute privacy. Karen knew the only safe way of getting the information to Charlie was to give it to him in person. That might also help her persuade him to believe her. If she could watch for the familiar doubts in his eyes and the stubborn thrust of his chin, she would be able to choose the right words to convince him.

As soon as she was sitting in one of the comfortably padded seats of the Red Jet hovercraft, she phoned to warn him she was coming back. His voicemail told her he was on another call, so she left an uninteresting message to say she was on her way, having satisfied Max that she would complete her essay-marking tonight.

Her discretion had worked against her, as she saw the moment she walked back into the incident room.

Annie Colvin looked up, pushing her hair out of her face with one hand while she held a phone in the other.

'Hi, Karen. Charlie got your message, but he had to nip out to do another TV appeal for witnesses before a press conference with the ACC. He should be back in about an hour. But he won't be in a good mood. He hates doing anything on camera, and journalists' questions nearly always piss him off.'

Karen remembered the morning she'd waited for him at the studio before the pair of them had taken the train to London. He had been edgy afterwards, but he'd recovered pretty fast and smiled those secret smiles. But then they had just made love. For the first time in days she thought of the joyous freedom of that night. If only she could hold on to the sense of freedom, instead of worrying about her possible pregnancy and longing to sort things out with Will. What *had* she done to make him angry enough to leave her?

Years ago her beloved brother, Aidan, had abandoned her to their feckless difficult parents when he'd fled to the States as soon as he'd left school. Now Will had gone. If she ever did find a way to hook up properly with Charlie, would he leave her too? If she were pregnant and managed to keep the child, how soon would it be before he – or she – disappeared? Would she ever . . . ?

Stop it, she told herself: you're at work. Concentrate on what matters now.

After a second she smiled at Annie and went back to the table they had allocated to her, covered still with the pile of witness statements. Karen was glad to see, on top of the ones that had been there this morning, copies of the newly transcribed SOCA interviews with the rescued women now living at Clagbourne House.

Twenty minutes later, she raised her head again. None of the statements made any reference to any man called 'Dev' or to anything that Vera had said to any of them. That could have meant simply that the SOCA interviewer had not been interested in either topic, but it seemed odd that no one should have mentioned anything about the woman who had preferred to run away rather than talk to the investigators, who had to be on her side against the men who had exploited her. Karen looked up, frowning, as though she might see something inspiring in the space ahead of her.

What she did see was Annie, mouthing 'tea?'

Karen smiled and nodded, before going back to her work. A few moments later, Annie brought her a big mug of strong PG Tips with enough milk to turn it the colour of vanilla fudge rather than its own undiluted iron brown.

'You don't do sugar, do you?' Annie said, putting the mug precariously on a heap of witness statements.

'No, thanks.' Karen balanced the mug more securely. 'This is great.'

'Have you found anything?'

Karen sighed. 'Nothing yet. I wish I'd been there to ask some questions of my own. These are all . . . well . . .'

'What?' Annie said, pulling forward a chair so that she could sit down beside Karen's table.

'I can see why SOCA are more interested in the trafficking side of these women's experience, but that's not what we need now. There's nothing here about why Vera ran away, for instance.'

'I asked about that, when you disappeared.' Annie's face was full of compassion. 'Gilda said that Vera's at a stage they know well from experience, where the women just can't tell the difference between what has been terrifying them and what has really happened. They're quite used to it at Clagbourne House, and she said it usually takes a few more weeks of therapy and care before it subsides.'

'Did Gilda give you any details about Vera's fears?' Karen asked, hoping that was a vague enough question to satisfy all the promises of discretion she had made.

She was beginning to wonder whether she should drop the paper she'd been planning to write on post-mortem mutilation and concentrate instead on real and false memories. After all, it would have much more general application. Post-mortem mutilation of corpses was rare, whereas assessing the accuracy of memories had to be something the police and courts were faced with every day.

Annie shook her head. 'Only that Vera saw enemies everywhere and she was convinced that someone called "our Dave" was a trafficker. I asked Gilda about this Dave and heard he's a seventeen-year-old A level student, who tidies the garden on Saturday mornings.'

'Oh,' Karen said. Could Vera have misheard the name Dave and been so frightened that she actually believed she had seen – and smelled – the man who had once raped and terrorized her? Memory could work like that in the traumatized, so it was not impossible. 'How did Gilda find him?'

'He's the son of a local in the village. He answered an ad they'd pinned up in the post office for garden labouring. Minimum wage and his lunch.' Annie sounded full of sympathy, adding, 'But in the state Vera's in, she could easily have decided he was a threat to her. Paranoia's apparently quite a normal part of that sort of post-traumatic stress stuff. But you'll know all about it, being a shrink. Oh, look, here's Charlie.'

His face was tense and his expression aggressive, but Karen could not let that put her off. She shut her own laptop and stuffed it in her big saggy shoulder bag, before hurrying over to where he stood beside the door. He was shouting instructions behind him to someone half-way up the stairs. Karen waited until he'd finished, then took his arm, saying, 'Can you come outside for a second? We need to talk.'

Charlie pulled his arm away from her grasp so fiercely that she felt as though he'd slapped her. Hurt and worried, she stepped back, knowing that they had to work easily together if they were to solve the case. Charlie looked at her, surprised, then shrugged. 'OK, but I need time to get those fucking hacks out of my head and . . .'

'What did they do?'

'Oh, the usual: you know, accusing us of wasting time, not using every resource, fannying on about irrelevant procedures. Bastards.' He caught her eye and produced a reluctant grin. 'They calmed down a bit when I told them we were using every available resource, including one of the foremost forensic psychologists, who's a specialist in post-mortem mutilation.'

Karen closed her eyes for an instant. Her academic career wasn't going to be helped by exaggerated claims to expertise she didn't yet have.

'Sod 'em all,' Charlie said. 'I've done all the media training, and I still can't stop them getting to me. Now, you've got something to tell me and I promised to catch Maureen at the ferry stop before she leaves. Can we do this walking there?'

'Fine.' Karen speeded up until they were outside in the dank coldness. She shuddered and was glad to be able to say something absolutely truthful without worrying about how he might take it. 'I hate February.'

'Yeah,' Charlie said. 'The dead month. Debts, hangovers and cold. Nothing to look forward to.'

'Except sorting this case,' Karen said aloud, while adding in silence to herself: and sorting myself out and helping Stella over her humiliation, if I can.

Karen had never been tempted into clinical practice, but she hoped she could use her theoretical knowledge to ease Stella back into her usual sparky confidence.

Charlie produced a humourless bark of laughter, unaware of her internal thoughts. 'If we ever do crack the case.'

'We will.' Karen was holding on to her faith. 'Listen to what I got from Vera.'

'That why you buggered off today – to talk to her again? Why didn't you tell me? I'd have gone into my press conference a lot more happily if you had.'

'She called me. I promised I wouldn't say where she is, but you need to know . . .'

'Can you put your hand on her if we need her?' Charlie's question was abrupt.

'Yes,' Karen said, hoping they wouldn't find that Vera had run off again. 'There'll be one or two cut-outs, but I can pass the word and know it'll get to her.'

'OK. Then it's worth telling me.'

Karen relayed the story of Dev and how Vera was sure he had been sent to take her back to her original owners, adding: 'Annie's decided Vera was actually scared by hearing about a jobbing gardener called Dave. It could be true, but Vera's description of the man who terrified her makes him sound a lot older and tougher than this Dave. If Dev is real and not a manifestation of Vera's distorted memory, he could have been powerful enough physically to have hammered those knives through Sir Dan's joints and into the table top.'

'Right,' Charlie said when she paused. He didn't look convinced. Karen tried again.

'And I've been thinking: if this man does exist, this Dev, his presence here on the Island could have been a coincidence, as far as Vera's concerned. He might not even have recognized her. From what she said, his old employers used rape as a normal means of control. He might not have noticed which woman he was . . .' Karen broke off, hating the thought of what Vera had endured.

Charlie, who had been listening in silence, nodded.

'A man like that does fit with the idea of a contract put out by one of the big traffickers,' he said. 'But if this Dev is the killer, he won't have hung around on the Island.' The muscles in his jaw started pumping, which was always a sign he was worried. 'I'll get back over to Clagbourne now to find out if they've lost any security people, and what they know of them if they have.'

'You mean you don't think he was that bloke who let us in this morning?' Karen said.

'You really think Vera would have run if her rapist had been on duty, only yards away from her when she took off?'

'Maybe not.'

'Too risky. She'd never have done it.' Charlie sounded definite. 'They have a rota of security blokes at the house. I got that much out of Gilda this morning. She's on duty herself from 8 till 8 every day with a relief at weekends, and there's a revolving crew of five men. Eight hours on, sixteen off, three days off in every seven. They act publicly as gardeners or window cleaners so as not to spook the girls or any rare visitors, but make no mistake: they're muscle.'

'I could tell,' Karen said. 'And maybe they can double as carpenters, like the man who could still have been hiding in the house when Sir Dan switched the security system to its night setting.'

Charlie grimaced, nodding.

'Did Mrs Brown manage to provide any descriptions the e-fit people could use?' Karen asked.

'Some. Not enough. We've got to look elsewhere. This lead from Vera may help.'

'You will be careful, Charlie, won't you? Don't let on to anyone that we've talked to her.'

'Am I a fool? Listen, we're nearly at the ferry so there's not much time: you'll be at the incident room when I get back from talking to Maureen?'

'Charlie, I . . .' Karen thought of all the essays waiting to be marked in her office at the university, and the way her breasts had looked so swollen when she'd dressed this morning, and how they ached, and how pregnant she could make herself feel whenever she let herself count the days until her period was due. 'I've a mass of stuff to think about. I need to be back in my flat.'

'OK. I'll come tonight. Nothing to do with the case.' His voice was softer, and held no aggression at all. 'We can't leave it at . . . We do need to talk. You and me.'

Rain slid over Karen's skin, chilling her. 'I'm not sure I'm ready . . . I'm in such a muddle. I need a bit more time to sort myself out.'

Charlie looked swiftly around, saw no one he knew, and gripped her by both upper arms tightly enough to suggest there would be bruises later.

'Didn't you like it when we made love?' he said with an urgency she hated but understood. 'You seemed so . . . so happy about it at the time.'

'I was. I loved it, but . . .' Karen broke off, not knowing how to finish the sentence.

'Not Will again, is it? You said he'd dumped you. Has he come back, yanking your chain?'

'It's nothing like that. I haven't heard a word from him.' Karen was glad her voice didn't wobble. 'I don't expect to.'

'Then what? I . . .' Charlie broke off, gritted his teeth in the familiar way, then said more calmly: 'I can see it's tough for you, but it's hell on earth watching you unhappy like this and not being allowed to help. What's his hold over you? Is it that you think hanging on to him, even though he's trying to bugger off, means you'll somehow put yourself right with your conscience over your dead husband?'

'God, no.' Karen had never analysed her feelings for Will or why she needed to be with him. But there was one truth of which she was absolutely certain: her relationship with Will had nothing to do with her late husband. No two men could have been less alike. And the last thing Will would ever do was get drunk after an argument, roar off in his Ferrari and kill himself by smashing it into a tree, as her husband had done. On the other hand, physically at least, Charlie was extraordinarily like him. But she couldn't say that either.

'I'm just in a muddle,' she said, looking beyond his shoulder so she didn't need to meet his gaze. 'I need to get it sorted before I do anything else. I don't want to hurt you, Charlie. Or mess you about.'

The rain was forcing Charlie's spiky black hair down against his scalp, making him look much more ordinary than usual. She could see hurt in his eyes and doubt, which made guilt burn in her mind. He opened his mouth to say something, and they both heard Maureen's voice calling him.

'Got to go,' he said, letting go of Karen's biceps at last. 'We can't leave it like this. It's too important. I'll come to your flat tonight to talk. May be very late. Stay up for me. You will do that much, won't you?'

The bitterness in his voice almost broke her resolve.

Stella was sitting on Karen's sofa with an empty wine glass in her hand soon after eight that evening. Karen got to her feet to refill it for the third time. As the gooseberry-ish Sauvignon splashed out of the bottle, Stella seemed to notice what she was doing and shook her head.

'Stop! Stop! I've had too much already. And I'll only drink it if it's in the glass.'

Karen straightened the bottle and gently took the glass away from Stella with her free hand.

'Sorry,' she said. 'Would you rather have tea? Coffee?'

'No. It's fine.' She smiled through her misery, adding, 'It's not even as if I loved him. I . . . Oh, Christ! I don't know.'

'What was it?' Karen asked, knowing Stella wanted to talk but determined not to push her into any aspects of the story she needed to keep private.

A huge, squelchy sniff told her how far Stella was from her usual self-control. Karen thought of offering tissues, then decided that would sound critical, and waited.

'I liked his company. Isn't that awful? I *liked* a man who could think like that. It wasn't just showing my bloody mother I could pull an OK kind of bloke. I just liked being with him.'

'What did your mother think of him? I mean, did you introduce them?'

Stella's pale skin flushed, the colour swallowing up her many freckles. 'No. I was saving it. Partly to let her go on taunting me while there was no reason; and partly because I knew she'd find something mocking to say about him and that would knock all the . . . all the shininess off it.'

Karen took a sip of her own wine. She was still on her first glass and it had grown warm while she listened. She put the glass down.

'But maybe her judgment *is* better than mine. Maybe she's right.' Stella put a hand up to cover her eyes, sniffed again, then said, still hiding from Karen. 'Her latest salvo was: you know you'll never become lovable until you stop being so self-absorbed. You have to give love in order to get it.'

Karen planned her answer with care, but Stella had more to say first.

'As if she'd know about giving love, the cow. Both Dad and I could tell her different.'

Stella laughed and Karen joined in, before offering her own take on their relationship.

'Stop me if you don't want the psycho-babble,' she said with care, 'but you have told me you and your father always got on well.'

'You don't have to tell me how hard it must've been for her, watching us. I know why mothers get jealous of their daughters and how they punish them for their own fading into frustrated middle age. Doesn't make it any easier to be the victim.'

'I wasn't actually going to say that.' Karen smiled to take away the sting. 'I was just going to say how hard it must be for a woman to watch the man she loves – or alternatively who's disappointed her – giving double the attention she gets to their daughter. And how most men do it like that because the daughter is half them. When their wife yells at the daughter to tidy her room, he feels yelled at, too. So of course he's going to defend the daughter. So that makes the resentment worse. It's not even psychology. It's common sense.'

'Like that for you, was it?' Stella said, taking back some of the initiative.

Karen laughed.

'Actually no. Haven't I told you? My parents are – and always were – completely obsessed with each other. Aidan and

I were just inconvenient detritus, like rotten coping stones falling off a wall.'

Karen looked sideways at the glass of warm white wine and wondered why her capacity for alcohol had got suddenly less. Her left hand lay across her front. She thought of something Will had once said when he was pressing her to want to have children with him, something about being able to bring them up in love and safety, as children should be, to make up for what had been done in the past.

'Karen!' Stella's voice was sharp enough to bring her back into the present. She smiled and felt her eyes heating up.

'Sorry. I got distracted. How . . .'

'I think we've both talked enough for tonight. Thank you for the wine, and the rescue.' Stella got up and pattered across the wooden floor in her bright pink Peruvian socks. 'I couldn't do without you, you know. Tell me when the investigation's over and we'll make a proper plan to go to the site.' She glanced at the blackness outside the big windows, which were starred and dappled with rain again, 'And if the bloody weather's any better, we could take a picnic and a bottle and have fun. They'll be putting the roof on within the next ten days. Then you'll really see it as it should be seen. It's going to be fantastic. You'll see. Then we can have that celebration you talked about.'

Four hours later, Karen chucked yet another essay on the pile she'd already marked. Enthusiasm for these undergraduate efforts faded when you'd seen the same kind of thing every year for the past six years. If only she'd come across one that showed even hints of an original idea, she could have given more effort to them all. As it was, she noted the points her students had absorbed from her lectures and seminars, ticked them off one by one, then wrote her comments at the bottom of each essay. She pointed out the things they'd misunderstood and the others they should have considered, suggesting further reading, trying always to finish with a question that might set them off on some private research that could lead to an insight no one else had already offered.

She reached for the mug beside her, swallowed and then winced as the cold coffee hit the back of her throat. She must have made this pot at least an hour ago, and the taste was now bitter. The clock on the kitchen wall, which she could just see when she tilted her chair right back, told her it was after one o'clock. If Charlie were coming tonight, he'd have been here by now. He must have been held up and she'd stayed awake for nothing. Her head was aching and she was bored. Time to stop for the night, she decided, reaching forward to click off the angle-poise lamp.

The resulting glow from the tiny star-like halogen spots in the ceiling was much softer. She eased her neck, rolling her head from side to side, then up and down. None of the movements soothed her head. Somewhere in the bathroom should be a box of aspirin. She didn't like taking any kind of drug, having seen how easily any chemical could disrupt the workings of the brain, and she'd already had two aspirin today, but with a pain like this hammering above her left eyebrow, it would be stupid to avoid a simple analgesic.

Having swallowed two more of the small white pills, she emptied the dregs of coffee into the sink and put the mug in the dishwasher, before rinsing out the filter and its matching jug and wiping the worktop. There were no plates or pans to deal with. She hadn't felt hungry tonight. Something lurched in her guts, and she laid a hand on her middle, like a pregnant woman feeling the way her baby kicked.

Don't be stupid, she told herself. Even if there were a foetus, which there almost certainly isn't, it wouldn't be kicking for a trimester or more. Oh, God! What will I do if I am pregnant?

She moved out of the kitchen to take her favourite position, standing in front of the new French windows. The fresh putty the glazier had used smelled of clean linseed oil. It was a scent that usually pleased her but now made her throat and stomach tighten.

The glass was covered with rain again, and the lights of the city and traffic so far below her split and fractured and bobbled through bigger drops.

'Oh, Will,' she said aloud, leaning forwards until her forehead hit the cold glass. The sensation helped a little and she moved her aching head from side to side, enjoying the coolness against her tight skin. Then she pulled sharply backwards.

She'd left his ring on the bedside table, then allowed Charlie to send a total stranger in here to mend the windows without any supervision. How could she have been so irresponsible? She ran into her bedroom and scuffled on the table, pushing aside tissues, book, earplugs, and alarm clock.

No ring.

Real nausea winded her and she sat back on the bed, remembering the night she'd cut her foot and taken the ring off for the first time. However angry and worried she was, she shouldn't have let Will's lavish diamonds go like this. He'd taken such care to find a selection he himself liked and thought might suit her, then taken her up to London to go from jeweller to jeweller so that she could choose from his shortlist the ring she liked best.

All the times he'd irritated her with his control-freakery and assumptions about what she wanted, just because he hadn't taken the trouble to think beyond his own instincts, disappeared in a wave of guilt and longing.

The nausea intensified until Karen thought she really might be sick. In her memory she heard all the times he'd accused her of making a fuss, and all the other times when she'd felt so scarily in his power. She'd always hated that sensation. Was that why she hadn't taken proper care of his ring?

'What would Will do now,' she asked herself, forcibly damping down the hysteria, 'if he'd lost a small valuable thing?'

The answer was entirely obvious and she even managed to laugh before getting down on her hands and knees to look under the bed in case the ring had fallen off the table and rolled there. Nothing caught her eye, so she pushed aside the small wooden table. There, among some shaming curls of dust, was the gold band with its large emerald-cut diamond, gleaming like water.

'Clot!' she shouted aloud, using his word rather than Charlie's 'dafty' or her own 'idiot', before rubbing the dust off the stone and slipping the ring back on her finger. When she'd admired its cool elegance for a moment or two, she slid it off again, having to tug it over her knuckle.

She tore some tissue paper off the sheets that had lain between the folds of the last jacket she'd bought, enjoying the crackle of the thin paper, before carefully wrapping the ring in it. The small package would probably be safest in the back corner of the top drawer in her work table. She tucked it in between the heavy box of spare staples and the hole puncher. No casual burglar would notice it there, she thought, remembering Sheena's photograph of Sir Dan and their son so carefully hidden in the secret drawer of the big bureau-bookcase.

Karen's nausea had receded a little. Probably all she needed now was a hot shower, the quickest way she knew of easing herself out of any kind of angst, especially when she didn't feel like food. She stripped off her clothes, dropping them on the floor by her bedroom chair. They should have gone into the laundry basket, but she was too tired and disheartened to care, and she'd probably have to bin the sweater in any case, if the blood didn't wash out.

When she'd bundled up her hair in the elasticated plastic shower cap, she got into the shower, wincing from the cold of the tiles under her feet. Moments later she felt the pounding water on her head and tipped up her face, revelling in the heat that poured down over her throat and breasts.

With soap on her hands to make them even more slippery than usual, she stroked her flat stomach. It didn't seem possible that there could be anything alive in there.

'Drama Queen,' she said aloud, getting a mouthful of hot water she had to spit out into the shower tray.

A pregnancy so soon after coming off the pill was unlikely, she reminded herself for the hundredth time. Highly unlikely.

She smiled at a mental image of Will's face in one of his rare moments of approval. His grey-green eyes crinkled up when he smiled and the familiar severity of his well-shaped lips disappeared into a friendly curve. For a second, she felt almost as though he knew how she was feeling, and that they were in some kind of communication again. Her own lips curled into a wide smile before she told herself not to be so sentimental.

Through the thudding and splashing of the water came another sound, a hard brisk knocking on her front door.

Bloody Charlie, she thought, turning off the water. Just what I don't need now. How the hell did he get through the street door without buzzing the intercom? Did one of those careless bastards in the ground-floor flat leave it on the latch again?

She dragged off the shower cap, wrapped a huge towel around her body and went to open the door.

Two strangers stood there. Karen tugged the top of the towel higher up her chest.

'Who . . . ?' she began, just as she caught sight of a mass of dark cloth being lifted in front of her.

The knowledge of danger hit her far, far too late. She backed into the flat, pushing the door between her and the two men with both hands and all her weight behind them.

One man shoved a foot in the gap and leaned his shoulder against the door. He was much too strong for her ten-stone weight. The doorknob was forced away from her wet soapy hand. As she raised both arms to defend herself, one of the men grabbed her wrists. She could feel the towel slipping down over her naked body, just as a cloth bag was dragged over her head.

Her wrists were released and she hit out with both hands. One connected so hard it provoked a kind of grunt. Not that the blow helped. Karen felt herself picked up, wet as she was, and carried back into her flat, before being dropped on to what felt like the sofa. Something hard and pointy crunched into her spine. A book? Her arms were held clamped to her side and something pressed down on her stomach. A hand? Or a knee?

She tried to shout, but the cloth covering her face got into her mouth. Pushing at it with her dry tongue, she felt something prick in her arm, and all ability to move or think disappeared in a cloud of powerless terror.

Seconds later, a strange warmth eased over her as something like a mental duvet smothered her fear. She wondered why she'd been making such a fuss, and stretched out her legs, while pressing her back deeper into the sofa's cushions. Whatever was underneath her didn't feel pointy or uncomfortable any more; just lovely. Unbelievable pleasure spread right up through her, lifting her into a mental place she had never known. She wanted to tell the men what was happening as the warmth intensified, and the delight too. No orgasm she'd ever had came close to this heavenly sensation.

Opening her mouth, she felt her tongue rasped by the cloth that covered it and laughed. Something seemed to slip inside her head and her eyes closed inside the bag. Then another surge of delicious warmth flooded through her and she woke again to hear a man's voice with a heavy, guttural accent say: 'She's well away. Let's get going before we waste more time.'

Chapter 14

Day Four: 6.00 a.m.

Will had slept so badly that he gave up the attempt to stay in bed long before there were any signs of light around his window blinds. Levering himself out from under the duvet, he balanced on his sticks and hobbled towards the kitchen to load his aluminium espresso pot and set it on the gas. The smell of the brewing coffee was so evocative of all the breakfasts he'd had with Karen that he closed his eyes and leaned against the worktop, resting his head on the cupboard door, fighting the idea that he might contact her. It wouldn't be fair. Until he knew that he was in a fit state to be with her, he had to leave her alone.

Stiffening his shaky resolution, he got himself out into the small hall, where his newspaper was already waiting on the mat. He bent down with difficulty and managed to scoop up the paper without falling over, which was quite a triumph these days, before carrying it back to the kitchen.

As he flattened the paper on the worktop he saw her on the front page, his Karen in all her glory. It was a terrific photograph, with her standing on the marina at the Island in her

tightest indigo jeans and a skinny striped top. Her blonde hair
blew back away from her face, and her blue eyes looked huge.
All around her were yachts and seabirds, sunlit sea and vast
bright blue cloudless sky. Clearly the picture had been taken
ages ago, and it couldn't have been less appropriate to the
accompanying article.

> *Forensic psychologist Doctor Karen Taylor, who is a*
> *familiar figure on the Isle of Wight (see photo), has failed*
> *to come up with anything to identify the killer of Sir Dan*
> *Blackwater. Sources close to DCI Charlie Trench's investi-*
> *gation say that with budgets being slashed all round, fees*
> *charged by psychologists like Doctor Taylor are unjustifi-*
> *able. See full story on page 3.*

'Bastard journalists,' Will said aloud. They'd obviously
picked the most frivolous photograph they could find to make
Karen look like a ditsy waste of space.

He could imagine exactly how she would feel as soon as she
saw this, and he could also imagine how humiliating it would
be to waltz unprepared into the incident room if she hadn't
seen it. He turned to page three to read the full contemptuous
account of the fruitless investigation into the murder of a big
businessman even he had heard of.

Cold woke Karen. Her whole body felt icy and as though
insects were crawling over it, just inside her skin. In a sudden
flood of memory, she felt the hands of last night's strangers on
her once again, and the sharpness of the needle they'd driven
into her arm.

Were they still here? Watching her?

Keeping her eyes closed for safety, breathing as smoothly as she could in case they were staring at her, she tried to identify her surroundings from the sensations she could feel. The frigidity of her skin told her she was still naked from the shower, but she wasn't wet any longer. No light penetrated her closed eyelids, but the bag they'd put over her head had gone. A tiny lick of her lips told her that.

Her arms and legs were stretched, the joints aching. Was this a hangover from whatever they'd shot into her arm last night?

She had never taken drugs and so she didn't know what the substance had been. But memories of the warmth and the pleasure made her think of accounts she'd read of the heroin rush. How much had they given her? Enough to make her go through life longing for more, like someone forever in search of a lost paradise?

Under her back was something hard, but not like the book on her sofa. This was flat as well as hard, and covered in fabric, like the base of a bed without a mattress. An infinitesimal bounce told her there were springs in the bed base. Tugging gently with her arms, she felt restraints around her wrists. Something hard, like handcuffs, but fabric covered. Panic flooded her, pushing out all sense. She had to fight a ferocious battle to keep her breaths quiet and slow.

After a moment she'd got control of herself, and her mind was working again. She thought she must be spread-eagled, looking like Leonardo's Vitruvian man – or the body of Sir Dan Blackwater before they'd driven knives through his wrists and ankles. Panic surged again. Her fingers curled into the palms of her hands before she could send a thought to stop them. She waited for a voice, a blow smashing into her face, anything to tell her someone was here, watching what she did, ready to punish her.

Listening hard through the thunder of her own pulse in her ears, she could hear nothing else: no traffic, voices, birdsong; nothing at all. Was this room sound-proofed? Why? What were they planning to do in it?

Her throat muscles tightened so much, she thought she was going to choke. Now they must say something, if they were here. She waited, hardly breathing, for at least a minute. No one made any noise. Nothing touched her. She allowed her eyelids to lift very slowly. Still darkness. No one reacted. She opened her eyes fully and felt her lashes catch on something.

Blindfold as well as tied up.

She pulled a little against the restraints around her ankles and felt space between her skin and what felt like plastic ties. But they were loose enough only to allow her to waggle her feet. There was no way she could pull them free.

Tracking her other sensations, she could feel a small pain in her right elbow. That must be where they injected her.

Vera's voice echoed in her memory, fast and machine-like, as she said: 'They are ruthless and cruel. You don't know how cruel.'

Do *not* panic, Karen told herself as all the deeper layers of her mind screamed in silent terror. It won't help. Concentrate, so that if there is a way out you'll be able to find it. Don't panic. Someone will notice you're missing and they'll look for you.

But who?

Charlie had said he'd come to the flat last night, but she hadn't agreed to be there, so he might have thought better of it. He certainly hadn't come by one o'clock. Even if he had dared to knock on the door later than that, he would just assume she was asleep or avoiding him when he got no answer. Or maybe he would have decided that she'd gone back to Will.

Will himself wouldn't come looking because he'd had enough of her. Stella would assume she was busy and away somewhere. So would Max. None of her family were in regular contact. And her students were well accustomed to her absence.

Karen was on her own. Drama Queen, she said to herself in Will's voice, trying to hold down the rising terror. Drama Queen. Don't make a drama. Think this through, and if there is a way out you'll find it. Don't be a drama queen. That's the worst possible. Think sensibly.

But she was tied down and couldn't see. She had no way of getting her hands to any of the ties, so she couldn't cut them, and they were too far away from her mouth for her to try to bite through them. Even the coolest and bravest person would fail to free herself from this.

All Karen had to defend herself were her mind and her voice. But she couldn't use either while she was alone, and she dared not scream for help until she knew who would hear.

A creak warned her that something was happening. Maybe a door opening, she thought. She deepened her breathing at once, instinctively certain that it would be safer to act as though she were still unconscious.

A man's voice spoke in a language she couldn't recognize. He sounded rough but as though he was pleading for something. Another man said something sharper, still in the unknown language. A stronger air current passed over Karen's body, and footsteps sounded. Heavy male footsteps.

Were these the men who'd attacked her last night? Where had they taken her? What would she find outside if she did manage to escape? How would she get anywhere, naked and moneyless like this?

Keeping still took huge discipline. She fought to breathe evenly and to ignore the silent, internal screams that filled her mind. A third man came heavily into the room.

'Why would anyone pay to fuck that?' he said in heavily accented but at least comprehensible English. 'Far too old. No point trying to sell it on. We'll have to get rid of it.'

Through the absolute horror of being tied down naked in front of these men, who could do anything they wanted to her and whom she could not see, Karen smelled a mixture of stale tobacco smoke, sweat and sharp cheese that disgusted her.

A heavy hand landed on her stomach and grabbed some of the flesh, rubbing it up and down. She flinched, unable to control her muscles.

'Fat as a pregnant sow,' said one of the first voices, but now in English. The other two men laughed.

'You're a fool,' said the closest voice. The smell intensified as he leaned closer to Karen and breathed right into her nose. 'These Englishmen like them fat. They've got tits.' The hand grabbed her right breast and squeezed hard, twisting the nipple agonizingly.

In spite of all her determination to keep still, Karen gasped, writhing under his touch, hating it, wincing from the pain.

'She's awake, you know,' the man said. 'Just faking. Like all these bitches.'

The others laughed again, just as Karen heard a completely new sound: the hard slapping of steel-tipped shoes on concrete. The hand squeezing Karen's breast so painfully was withdrawn and the fading smell told her its owner had moved a little way away.

'So what do we do with her?' asked one of the other voices. 'If we can't sell her on, what . . . ?'

'You listen to me.' The new voice was so harsh that Karen could not prevent her eyelids twitching behind her blindfold. She waited for more punishment, but nothing happened.

'You listen and you do exactly what I say before you cause more trouble,' said the man, his shoes slapping the floor again as he approached the bed.

Karen thought she caught a whiff of a woman's scent, Annick Goutal's Eau d'Hadrien, last smelled when she'd been in Olga Blackwater's drawing room with Charlie. Was she hallucinating now?

'I do not know how you could be so stupid, taking this woman,' said the newcomer. 'What were you thinking? How much did you give her last night?'

'A lot,' said one of the other men, sounding as though he enjoyed the memory before adding more seriously, 'We did not want her waking too soon, before we show her to you.'

Karen waited for one of them to admit she was conscious now and hearing everything they said. It came to her that they, too, could be scared.

'*Why* did you take her?'

'Vera talked to her, Dev,' said one of the men, pleading now in a way that confirmed her suspicions. 'She knew too much. We had to . . .'

'You don't know that.' Dev's voice had lost none of its harshness, or its force. 'Gilda said Vera ran away from this woman too. They had no time to talk.'

'That's not right,' said the nearest man, sending another gust of smoke and cheese up Karen's nose. 'Why else would the cop come back here, asking about you, only last evening?'

Why didn't I keep his name to myself until I knew more of what we're dealing with? Karen asked herself as despair welled up, taking away even the last shreds of courage she'd kept. Her fault. Her punishment.

'You said the cop was seen with the woman from SOCA after the interviews,' said Dev, with the kind of passionless irritation a good boardroom operator could always turn on and off at will. 'Vera may have got in touch with them.'

'But . . .'

'But nothing. Anyway, we have to deal with this problem now in a way that won't bring the police back again. She's working with them. This means when they know she's gone they will tear this place apart. We have to make it look right. So listen and do what I tell you. Dress her, get a decoy to bring her car over from the mainland – and be seen clearly on CCTV cameras – put this one in the boot and drive her to the woods near her new house, shoot her full of smack and leave her with all her things: bag, money, phone, laptop. Everything.'

'But why? If the phone's there they can use it to find her before . . .'

Dev laughed with such total ease that Karen felt as though she was being ripped apart and shown her own organs lying in her body cavity.

'If there's no phone and no bag,' Dev went on, sounding

businesslike and not at all vindictive, 'they will know someone took her. She always has them with her – haven't you seen this when you've been following her? Always the bag. Always the phone and computer. But if they are there beside the body, when they find her they will think she's done it herself. The rest of you: clean this place up. Bleach. Everything.'

'No needle tracks anywhere on her,' said one of the first bunch of men. 'I checked. Only ours from last night.'

'All the better. Inexperienced user shoots up, has too much, ODs.'

'But why would she kill herself?' From the sound of nails rasping against fabric, the man who'd just spoken must be scratching himself. He sighed, as though he was enjoying the sensation.

Karen's nightmares of what might happen if she ever put herself in Will's power by marrying him seemed ludicrous now. These men had obviously been watching her, planning when and how to take her. They had stripped her whole life bare, and they were taking pleasure in her powerlessness.

Everything Vera had told her echoed in her mind. 'They are cruel. You do not know how cruel.'

Fear was making Karen sweat now, with a horrible acrid smell she didn't recognize as her own. Then, as the rasping footsteps sounded again, coming closer to her side, she caught another whiff of the expensive delicious Eau d'Hadrien. What had he done to the tiny Olga Blackwater to get her scent on his clothes?

A fierce urge to survive began to burn in Karen, to survive and have these men caught and punished so that no other woman should have to suffer at their hands.

'She has debts,' Dev said, with a sharp edge of contempt to his voice. 'She has quarrelled with her family. Her boyfriend has left her. She has been reprimanded by her employers at the university. Is in the papers for failing to find us. Plenty of reasons for a lonely bitch to kill herself.'

The determination to survive burned hotter, giving Karen back a smattering of guts. She saw that she might have a tiny chance to free herself when they untied her in order to take her to the woods to inject her again. The possibility of surviving made her breathing quicken.

'Leave a bag of smack beside her, and the syringe,' Dev said. This was business and he sounded detached as any CEO while he gave his orders. 'Only her prints on the needle and the bag. Add a few missed shots with the needle to make it look as if she didn't know what to do. Then put the main dose in the same spot you used last night. That way your stupidity in bringing her here will be missed. Get on with it. And don't forget her clothes. No one goes to the woods to shoot up naked.'

'No one goes to the woods to shoot up.' The rough voice sounded much more feeble now, but not enough to help Karen.

'Be sure to give her the overdose before you untie her,' Dev said, sounding now as though he was sure they were cretinously stupid.

Karen's hope died. In its place came a sense of total waste. For thirty-six years she had been fighting all her fears and so nearly beaten them. She'd struggled for love and success and ownership of her own life. Now all that effort and angst counted for nothing. She thought of everything she would have said if she'd known this would happen: to Charlie and Will, to her parents, Stella, Max . . .

'I'll add some acid,' said one of the men as harsh hands grabbed Karen's arm, twisting it painfully. 'In case they do look for her. That way they can think anything she tells them is part of a bad trip.'

A thought emerged in Karen's brain, saving something from the horror. If they hoped the police would think she'd killed herself, she'd have to be unmarked. She began to rattle her handcuffs and waggle her feet as hard as she could, pulling and twisting so her skin would be bruised and chafed. The small pain was as nothing to the possibility that these filthy thugs might be caught and punished for what they were doing to her.

'Stop her,' said Dev, sounding concerned for the first time. 'She's trying to leave evidence. The boss will never forgive us if she does that.'

'How will she know?' asked one of the other men.

Another needle dug into the crook of Karen's elbow and on into the last scraps of herself. A vast loneliness opened its huge dark mouth and swallowed her whole.

The last thing she heard was Dev's voice, saying, 'Don't waste any acid on her. Even if they come looking, they won't find her in time.'

Chapter 15

Day Four: 7.00 a.m.

Will's right leg had wound itself around the left as he read. Now both were aching as though someone had him on a rack. But the only thoughts in his mind were of Karen.

Very little of his certainty that she would do better without him was left now that her career was in such trouble. He knew how much it meant to her, and the snide journalist's assault on it made Will feel responsible for her all over again.

Fumbling on his table, he found his phone, switching on the bedside light with his free hand. Karen's number was still programmed into the phone. He pressed 1 and waited while it rang. Her voicemail cut in after four rings. He tried again. The same thing happened. Beginning to worry, because she always answered her phone, even in the middle of the night, he tried to think who might know where she was.

He had Stella's number in his phone because of her last aggressive call. He rang her.

'Stella, it's me, Will,' he said when she answered, sounding hopeful.

'Oh.' Her voice had changed completely. Now it sounded cold in the extreme. 'What do *you* want?'

'Have you got Karen with you?'

'Why?'

'Because I realize you're right. I shouldn't have . . . I need to talk to her, Stella. Please help. She's not answering her phones.'

'And you're surprised? She'll see your name on her screen, won't she? Why would she bother? Bye.'

'You're wrong,' Will said, even though Stella had gone. 'Karen *would* answer. I know she would.'

Max's number was in the phone's address book, if he could only make his fingers work. They seemed enormous and clumsy beyond belief. Will tapped and tapped. At last Max's number appeared. He rang it. One ring, two, three. Not again, Will thought. At last Max's voice mumbled crossly: 'Yes? What? Who is it?'

'Max. It's Will.'

'What? What the hell are you doing phoning me at . . .' Max's harsh voice hesitated. 'Six-fifteen?'

'Max, where's Karen?'

'I've no idea. For God's sake, Will!'

'Don't play games, Max. I need to talk to her. Haven't you any idea where she is?'

'My dear man, she's probably on the Island. But she always has her phone. Ring *her*.'

'Not answering. I need to talk to her before she sees this morning's papers.'

Max coughed, covering a hesitation. Will felt anger building.

'Come on, Max. What do you know?'

'She's involved with this investigation into Dan Blackwater's murder.'

'I know that. She's working with Charlie Trench again. But why would that mean she's not answering the phone? And don't tell me it's because she doesn't want to talk to journalists because she'll see the call's from me.'

Max coughed again, this time with a disgustingly wet early-morning sound. 'Will, don't you think she might want to keep . . . well, certain aspects of her life private since you dumped her?'

He dismissed the idea at once. Karen would never be so petty.

'I have to talk to her, Max. Find out if she's all right.'

Will shut off that call and wheeled through his address book for the number Karen had once given him for Charlie Trench's phone. The recorded voice told him the number was unrecognizable.

'Fuck!' he shouted, with a violence that shocked even himself.

He hobbled to the desk where his computer stood, fired it up, cursing the slowness of its software loading. At last he had internet access and found the phone number for the Cowes police station. If there were a murder investigation on the Island someone must be answering the phone, even at this hour. There were so many clicks he was terrified he'd get a recorded message, or some offshore call centre, whose operators would refuse to help. At last he heard a human voice asking what he wanted.

'I have to talk to DCI Trench. Charlie Trench,' he said, panting in frustration. 'About the Blackwater investigation.'

'He's not here right now,' said the voice. 'But I'll put you through to the incident room.'

'No,' Will began, but it was too late. Mechanical sounds came again. He wanted to throw the computer through the window and the phone after it. At last he got another voice.

'DC Silver. Incident Room.'

'My name is Hawkins,' he said, using the voice with which he would give instructions during an emergency operation: deliberately calm but filled with the icy determination to get a life saved. 'And I have to speak to DCI Trench about the investigation. I have a mobile number for him, but I think it's an old one. Please give me his new one.'

'Everyone on the team is working together,' said Silver's voice, irritating Will. 'Give me the information and I'll action it.'

'I *have* to speak to Trench. If you won't give me his number, then phone him and get him to call me back. You must have my number on your screen now. If he doesn't phone back within four minutes, I'll phone you again, and then again, until I have him. I must speak to him.'

There was a pause until Silver produced a grudging offer to try.

Will clicked off the call and put the phone down on the desk, so that he could pull out the chair and sit down. He wanted to get dressed so as to be ready to leave the flat, but knowing how slowly he moved he dared not leave the desk until he'd talked to Charlie.

One reason occurred to him for Max's reluctance to tell him where Karen might be. His phone was ringing. He stared at it, then told himself not to be a coward and put it to his ear.

'Will? Charlie here. Have *you* got Karen?'

'I thought you had.' Something lurched in Will's guts, but he controlled it by thinking triumphantly, at least she's not in your bed, you tosser. 'Has she gone missing?'

'I don't know.' Charlie's voice was slow and wary. 'But you do know she's working with me?'

'I saw in the paper just now. Working with you isn't doing her much good, is it? When did you last see her?'

'She went home to do something for Max at the university yesterday afternoon, and I told her I needed to talk to her – about the case. I couldn't get away until late. Very late. I banged on the door of her flat at just before 2 a.m. She didn't answer. I . . . I thought she must be pissed off – or with you again.'

'No.' Fear was making Will's voice bite. 'And her mate Stella doesn't know where she is either. Something must be wrong. She'll have her phone with her. She always does. Even though she's not answering, you can triangulate it, can't you?'

'I could get them to try.' Charlie started to say something, choked on it, fell silent, then added, 'I'll get on with that, while you phone everyone you can think of in case she's there. Try her mother. And that bloody sod of a brother of hers in the States. In case they know anything.'

'Will do. But find her, Charlie. You must find her.'

'Do my best.'

Dread of what might be happening to Karen was eating into Will, like acid progressing through a porous surface, liquefying it. He knew Charlie was right, and the sensible thing to do was to phone all Karen's friends, in case she was staying with any of them. But common sense was no help now. Instead, he called Freya.

She too was clearly still asleep, but she knew the call came from him and she said his name in an only slightly fogged voice.

'Freya,' he said, still breathless. 'I need you.'

'Halleluia,' she said. 'At last. What can I do?'

'I need you to take me to the Isle of Wight. I know it sounds mad, but I have to go and you're the only . . .'

'Hang on, Will. No need to explain. Give me half an hour to sort something out with my clients and warn Julius, and I'll be round at your door. Use the time to eat something. You sound as if you need it.'

By the time Freya drew up outside his flat in her battered Volvo, Will was dressed and waiting on the street, leaning back against one of the pillars that stood on either side of the steps up to his front door. Slung over one shoulder was his laptop bag stuffed with spare shirts and underclothes, as well as shaving gear and a book. He would stay as long as he had to, but didn't want to be weighed down with vast amounts of baggage he couldn't carry. Before his discovery that he couldn't marry Karen unless he could recover total fitness, he would have been able to rely on the spare set of everything he kept in her flat in Southampton. No longer.

Freya leaned across to open the passenger door and he negotiated his way into the car, shoving his sticks and laptop bag on to the back seat. She put the car in gear again and drove off.

'Now you can tell me,' she said, as they turned on to the A27. 'What's in the Isle of Wight? Your Karen?'

'I hope so,' he said, before telling her how he'd woken this morning, what he'd seen in the paper, and what he'd done since.

'And this cop just said: "Yes, I'll look for her"?' Freya was

using the doubting tones of someone presented with a photograph of a unicorn.

'He's a friend of hers. More than a friend really. She works
with him sometimes. Now is one of those times.'

'Sounds like a remarkably interesting relationship,' Freya
said, staring straight ahead at the heavy rush-hour traffic. 'This
is going to take hours. Are you sure you wouldn't prefer to
wait at home until they've tracked her down?'

'Quite sure.'

'OK. Then tell me: if her relationship with the cop is more
than friendliness, where do you come in?'

Will grimaced, feeling a familiar ache in his cheek muscles.
'She chose me,' he said. 'Not him.'

'But you dumped her.'

'I didn't dump her.' He felt injured by his sister's briskness.
'I told her I couldn't commit while I couldn't be sure I'd work
again.'

'So, what do you think has happened to her now?'

'I've no idea.'

Will's phone rang and he grabbed it, saying his name even
before he'd accepted the call, so he had to say it again.

The voice of the head of human resources at the hospital
where he worked asked about his progress and wondered
whether he needed more physiotherapy than he was getting.

Will noted all the signs of stress overload in himself, calmed
down, and spoke with reasonable control as he said he would
ring back as soon as he had access to his diary again.

Signs for Southampton began to appear at the side of the
road, which helped soothe him, then the phone rang again,
sending goose pimples all over his skin.

'Will Hawkins,' he said, briefly catching Freya's eye and seeing vast wells of pity in hers.

'Will, Max here. What's the news?'

'There isn't any yet. I thought you might be Charlie, reporting.'

'Sorry. I've phoned him too, but they won't let me talk to him. They sound . . .'

'What? Who? How do they sound?'

'Woman called Annie Colvin. Karen's talked about her; likes her, I think. Annie sounded . . . well, frightened.' Max coughed again, less squelchily than this morning. 'Where are you?'

'On my way to Southampton, with my sister. I hope we get a ferry slot for her car. We haven't had time to book it.'

'Should do in February. Tell me what happens, won't you? Karen is . . . is . . .'

'Is what, Max?'

'She matters, Will.'

'Impressive,' Freya said as he put the phone back in his lap. 'I heard all of that.'

'I thought you might: Max always bellows so. What . . . ?'

This time the phone had a different ring tone. Freya had a hands-free set, so Will sat patiently listening as she talked to a client, furious about the cancellation of his session this morning. Will was impressed with the way she took the unknown man's rage seriously and managed to soothe him without admitting any kind of fault. He was also impressed that she seemed able to concentrate on her client while at the same time swinging the car into the racing traffic on the M27.

Then she began to allow the car to slow down as her client's voice turned whiney. Will wrenched his neck, looking back to see the panicking expression of a lorry driver, whose vast articulated monster was bearing down on them too fast to stop.

'Freya!' Will yelled, pain screaming up and down his legs as he tightened every muscle. 'Accelerate!'

Chapter 16

Day Four: 3.00 p.m.

Faces hung over Karen. Faces from the distant past and the here and now. The strange Elephant Man, who had been a neighbour when she'd stayed for a while in her grandmother's chalet a year ago, loomed at her. She must be dreaming because he'd died months ago. Her mother had told her so when she'd agreed to buy Granny's chalet. So maybe she was dead too. She smelled mud and leaves and sacking and cooked meat and thought she couldn't be dead. Smell must mean life. Mustn't it?

Time came and went. Sometimes Karen saw nothing but blackness. Sometimes faces. Strangers now. She looked among them for Granny's, which she'd never expected to see again except in photographs. It wasn't here.

Karen felt sick. Hair kept getting in her eyes and in her mouth, however often she pushed it away. Wafts of warm dizziness plaited themselves in with the hair and tangled her in their tendrils, and voices came from far away, then so close they hurt her ears. Someone grabbed her arm and she yelled, but no sound came out of her mouth. She felt the prick of another needle and pulled her arm as hard as she could to get it away from the tightening hands.

'Hold still,' said a new voice, sounding very English, very kind, and very female. 'Hold still. You need this.'

Now the smells were of antiseptic and cleanness and flowers. Floating around in Karen's mind a little later was the word 'naloxone'. This injection hadn't given her the rush. No pleasure now. Would she ever feel it again? Would she be able to resist?

Will was sheltering from the wind on the first available ferry, after an exasperating delay, while Freya tried once more to console her betrayed client down the phone. Karen had always loved this journey and Will tried to find some pleasure in it for himself. They'd taken it so often together on visits to check out the site of her new house. He shifted his body, taking all his weight on his sticks so that he could look over to the muddy woods where it would soon be complete.

If he'd had his way, she would have sold the land and bought a plot on the mainland instead, or even on the other side of the Island, where views and winds were much clearer than anything you got in her gloomy woods. But he knew how much her memories of her grandmother mattered to her, and he could understand her need for the sense of safety they gave her.

His own phone rang. Having now answered it eight times in the hope of news and had none, he was tempted to let the call go to voicemail, but something made him answer.

'We've got her,' Charlie's voice said.

'Where? How is she?'

'In a bad way. In the hospital at Newport. But they think . . .'

'I'll be there within twenty minutes,' Will said, looking at the approaching port of Cowes. 'Or less. We're on the ferry, half-way across the Solent now.'

'Oh.' Charlie sounded surprised, and not exactly grateful. 'OK, right. Fine. I'll see you then. She . . . The doctors think she overdosed.'

He cut off the call. Will couldn't believe it and pressed the button for redial. At last Charlie answered.

'What the hell do you mean by "overdosed"?' Will said, barely containing his rage. 'Overdosed on what?'

'Heroin. Syringe beside her. Various attempts at injections in all the wrong places, marks on her wrists where a ligature was tied to pump up a vein, then in the right place above the elbow and the injection site she actually managed to get right. I can see why the hospital think it's self-inflicted, but I know Karen. She wouldn't. Someone's trying to make it look like suicide. We're checking for prints on the syringe now.'

'Who . . . ?'

'Fuck knows. They found her alone at the site of her new house, bag untouched – money still there, phone, everything. Can't talk to you now. See you later.'

One of the huge seagulls that Karen both dreaded and admired swooped down to stand on the rail, only inches from Will, utterly unafraid. Its long hooked beak looked thoroughly dangerous and its eye was cold, cruel.

Don't anthropomorphize, he told himself, just as the ferry's hooter sounded, a long wailing roar. Even that didn't faze the bird.

Freya hurried towards him, her calf-length trousers shocking pink today, over long socks striped in yellow and green, and flat brown loafers.

'What's happened, old boy? You look dreadful.' She took his arm and he had difficulty not shoving her away.

Staring at the gull, which stared back, then lifted itself up and into a powerful air current, he added: 'The hospital think she tried to kill herself, although the police don't, thank God. I should never have . . .'

Freya put an arm around him. 'She doesn't sound the type,' she said. 'Don't jump to conclusions. Wait till you've talked to her.'

Karen knew she'd gone mad when she saw Will limping towards her through the fog in her mind. This was worse than the Elephant Man. She really had lost her mind in the after-effects of the heroin and whatever else they'd given her. She groaned and closed her eyes, turning her head towards the wall.

The rhythmic sound of rubber-shod sticks stopped dead. She didn't move, hating the way her mind was playing these tricks on her. At least her arms and legs were free now, and she had something covering her body, keeping her warm. And no strange men telling each other what they were going to do to her. She rolled on to her side, wincing in pain.

The sound of the sticks started again, but slowly. After a moment, she began to sense a familiar smell, full of lemons.

'Will?' she said, although her tongue felt like a thick wad of damp blotting paper. 'Will?' She rolled back to see his face hanging over hers.

'Karen.' His lips moved in a small wavering smile, then he said her name again.

'Why?' she asked, blinking to clear her misty vision. 'What?'

'I came . . . my sister drove me, because . . . no one knew where you were. Karen, what happened?'

'Injections,' she said, suddenly pushing both hands down under the bedclothes to scratch her legs, which were driving her mad with their itching.

She felt his hand on her shoulder and smelled his lemony scent. This really was Will. She thought he'd left her. Nothing made sense. A woman stood behind him, a mass of colour and energy.

'Hello,' she said over Will's shoulder. 'I'm Freya, Will's sister. You must be Karen.'

'Yes.' That much was clear. Nothing else was.

'So, he was right. You were in trouble.' Freya turned to Will. 'But do you still need me, or can I get back to work? As you heard, they're yelling for me.'

'You go on back,' he said, not taking his gaze from Karen for one second. 'I'll be fine now. And I can't thank you enough for bringing me here.'

'Pleasure. Any time. You know I'm glad you asked.' She walked round him to touch Karen's hand. 'I'd love to talk properly, but you're too ill, and I'm too busy, now. But soon. Yes?'

'Don't understand,' Karen said.

'Don't worry about it, Karen. I'll be back in a minute,' Will said, rearranging his sticks so that he had one in each hand. 'Freya, I'll come to the lifts with you.'

Karen watched their backs, trying to remember what she knew about Will's family. But her memory was so wobbly and she couldn't think of a single thing. She shut her eyes and stopped trying to make sense.

A quite different smell made her eyes flick open again. This time it was the Pears soap and rosemary shaving oil Charlie used. He looked worried as he hung over her. She put up a hand to stroke his bristly chin.

'Christ! Karen, you gave us a fright.'

'Not my fault,' she said, taking her hand away from his face so that she could rub the top of her thumb over the sore spot on the inside of her right elbow.

'Do you know what they gave you? We know about the heroin but the doctors think there was something else. They need to know what it was. Can you help?'

'Acid,' Karen said, not sure where the word came from. But she was sure it was right. 'Acid. Who found me? Who came?'

Metal scraped across the vinyl floor as Charlie pulled forward a chair and plumped down in it, with all the familiar creaking of his thick black-leather jacket.

'We don't know. Someone spotted you, lying in the woods near your house, and phoned 999. Didn't leave a name, but he was convincing enough to make the call centre organize an ambulance. Can you understand me, Karen?'

'Yeah.'

'Great. I came here as soon as they told me.'

'Why?'

'Doesn't matter. What happened? Can you tell me, Karen? As much as you can remember.'

'Don't remember.' Karen's tongue felt less like blotting paper, but she was sick and itchy, and her head hurt.

Her mind was spongy, and when she tried to see into the past everything was blocked by thick fog. Then another word came into her mind.

'Dev!' she said loudly.

Charlie's face darkened as it scrunched into a frown. 'What? What's Dev, Karen?'

'Him. Giving orders.' More mist parted in her mind and she reached for another fact. Gripped it. 'Smelled of Olga. Her scent. He got her too?'

'Karen, hinny, you're still not quite back with us, are you?' Charlie's voice was very kind and absolutely infuriating. 'The doctors have given you as much naloxone as they can. It's the antidote to heroin. You will be OK, but it'll take time. And if you had acid too, that'll explain why you're confused. Don't worry. We can talk again when you're properly back with us.'

He laid a warm, firm hand on her wrist and let his fingers curl round it.

'Two men. At the flat. Instead of you.' Her mind was clearing. She had to make him listen. Will's limping figure appeared in the space behind Charlie. He looked back over his shoulder, nodded, then faced her again.

'Two men? I see. Don't try to sort it out in your mind yet, Karen. You'll only muddle yourself even more.'

She tugged her hand out of his wrist and went on, pulling the facts out of the mist in her mind and giving them to him: 'Two men. Put a bag over my head. Gave me heroin. Wanted to kill me. Olga too. Check on her. And the others. You *must* get them back.'

'Karen, you're not making sense yet,' Charlie said. 'But . . .'

'You must listen to her,' Will said. 'She knows what she's talking about. Karen, you know he'll do everything he has to.'

She found a way to smile. Will smiled back, asking, 'Where were you when you woke? At the house here or in your flat?'

'Don't know. Couldn't see. Tied to something. Alone. Then the men came back. Dev . . . Smelling of Olga's scent. You . . .'

'Karen,' Will said in a voice so full of aching regret she wanted to reach for him.

'When did you come?' she said, frowning in the huge effort needed to understand everything that was happening. 'Why?'

The shuffling bump of Will's sticks came again as he pushed past Charlie and took his place at her bedside. She felt his free hand smoothing the hair away from her eyes.

'I wanted to talk to you about something in the papers early this morning and you didn't answer your phone. I was worried, so I tried Stella and Max. Neither of them knew where you were. I started to fret,' he said, slowly and clear so that she couldn't fail to understand each word. Even so they didn't make proper sense. He went on, trying to wake up her brain: 'I phoned Charlie and he told me you were missing. I came straight away.'

'You don't want me.'

Blood rushed into his face, staining his pale cheeks a deep carmine. 'That's not true. I just needed time to . . .'

'Never mind that now,' Charlie said, impatience sharpening his voice. 'She's the one who needs time now, to sort her head before you try to put anything else into it. Karen, you'll have to . . .'

A nurse tapped him on the shoulder and he stopped talking, waited, while she whispered something, then walked aside with her. Will took his chair and rearranged his sticks so that they lay in a neat line, precisely parallel with the edge of her bed. This was so like him that Karen started to cry, with silent tears sliding over her cheeks and through her hair and on into her ears.

'Don't, Karen,' he said, as though she was digging red-hot needles under his fingernails. 'Please don't cry.'

She had no more energy to understand what was going on or talk to anyone. A memory of the warm enveloping duvet sensation she'd felt after the first injection, and the pleasure that had come after it, made yet more tears ooze out from under her lids.

'She was right about the acid anyway.' Charlie's voice disturbed Karen again. She wasn't going to react, even though she knew what he was talking about this time. 'Probably explains it.'

'Explains what?' Will had rarely sounded quite so disapproving. Karen shivered a little, but they were too engrossed to notice, or comment.

'Why she's so muddled. Paranoid. They think it could be anything between forty-eight hours and five days before she's completely rational again. We won't get anything useful until then. As she told me only a couple of days ago, memory goes funny when you're under stress.'

'There's no reason why she won't be making sense sooner than that,' Will said reasonably. 'Heroin and lysergic acid can both be expelled from the body within a single day. She's fit and healthy enough to . . .'

'According to the specialist they've consulted here,' Charlie said sharply, interrupting without apology, 'for a naïve user having an overdose like she did, the effects can last days. There's no point me trying to get sense out of her. I'll leave her to you, and be back again tomorrow.' Charlie hesitated, then added: 'She'll need to see a fellow shrink.'

He paused, as though to give Will a chance to comment, but

he didn't. Karen was tempted to open her eyes and join in. But she was too tired. For once, she wasn't going to try to make everything right for everyone.

Then she remembered Olga. Tiny vulnerable Olga. She had to do something to save her.

'Vera told me the men were cruel,' Karen said, still articulating her words as clearly as possible.

Charlie turned back, looking worried.

'They were,' Karen went on. 'But Vera didn't say anything about Olga. I told you Dev smelled of her. Which means he's been touching her. You have to find her. Get her back before they kill her.'

Charlie didn't believe her.

'Find her. Check.'

'You met her once,' Charlie said, sounding kind. 'Only once. And then for no more than twenty minutes. Recognize her scent when you were under the influence of powerful drugs and real fear last night? I don't think so.'

'Annick Goutal's Eau d'Hadrien,' Karen said, amazed the words came so fluently. 'Expensive. Never smelled it on the Island before. Not till Olga. You've *got* to find her.' She was nearly screaming now.

'OK, Karen. Calm down. We'll check. Don't worry about Olga. Don't worry about anything but getting better.' Charlie's voice could have been pitched to soothe a fractious baby. 'They'll look after you here. And in a day or two, we . . .'

'You don't believe me,' she said, feeling more pathetic tears threatening. She was not going to let them out.

Charlie smiled down at her as gently as though she was an aged invalid, then raised a hand to wave to Will and swung away. His boots squeaked against the shiny vinyl floor. There was nothing more she could do to help Olga right now.

Will's hand stroked back her hair again. She let herself smile up at him.

'Thanks for coming.'

'You'd have been OK anyway,' he said, with all his usual determination to play down any excitement. 'Someone else found you first.'

'Thank God,' she said, recognizing the horror of being tied down and knowing she was going to die at the hands of men she could not see.

Will's stroking hand paused, then his fingertips drew half-circles under her eyes.

'You look so tired,' he said. 'I'd better let you sleep.'

'You won't go?'

'Only to the coffee shop for some food. I couldn't eat this morning when I thought you . . .' He gulped, then spoke more calmly. 'But I won't be much use to you if I don't get some protein inside me now. I'll be back here long before you wake.'

The lead in her eyelids was so heavy she had to fight to keep them open.

'They'll come back, you see,' she said, as her hands clutched for his. 'The men who took me. They know everything that happens. They'll come back and try to kill me again.'

Chapter 17

Day Four: 3.45 p.m.

Karen was being checked over by a doctor in a white coat. A nurse stood behind him. He asked her name and where she lived and why she was on the Island. Answering helped her focus. She knew what she had to do, and pushed back the covers.

'Steady,' said the doctor, smiling. 'You need to stay there a good long time.'

'D'you want a bedpan?' The nurse sounded kind.

'No. Phone. I need a phone. Police took mine. I have to phone.' Karen grabbed the doctor's hand between both hers and squeezed hard. 'I need a phone.'

'Get her a trolley phone, nurse.'

The nurse pushed her way out between the checked curtains, answered a rapid question from some stranger and squeaked away.

Karen answered the doctor's next list of questions, then asked one of her own.

'When can I go home?'

'I'd like to keep you in overnight, just to be sure.' He smiled down at her, looking amazingly confident for a man who couldn't be much more than twenty-seven. 'But unless anything unexpected happens, you can leave tomorrow.'

'Thank you.' Karen had understood every word he'd said. She felt reborn and knew exactly what she had to do.

'I'll see you tomorrow morning,' he said and left her with a friendly smile.

He hadn't been gone for more than ten minutes before the nurse was back with a telephone trolley. There was still no sign of Will.

'Haven't you got a phone card?' the nurse said, as Karen belatedly woke up to the fact that she would need money in some form. She shook her head.

The nurse felt in the breast pocket of her uniform and handed Karen a card. 'Pay me when you can.'

Karen hoped her gratitude showed in her smile, as she shoved the card in the slot. A dialling tone buzzed in her ear. Then the fog fell over her again. She couldn't remember Max's number.

More tears leaked out of her eyes and she fought for her real self and the courage she would need if she were to survive. She put a finger on the keypad, then made herself relax. Her finger moved, tapping in Max's number without even think-ing about it. She felt as if she'd climbed Everest without oxygen or even ropes.

Hearing Max's gravel-in-a-bucket voice gave her a spurt of new energy. Her voice was less woolly.

'Max, it's me. I need you. I'm in hospital. On the Island. Can you get me? Take me to your . . . where you took Vera? I was attacked and I'm not safe now, but no one believes me. They're coming after me again. I know they are. *Please.*'

'What about Will? He phoned me. He's looking for you.'

'He can't help at the moment.' Frustration sharpened Karen's voice and firmed up her determination. 'They're coming back for me. They can get at me here. I need your refuge. *Please.*'

'On my way,' he said, asking no more questions.

Karen pressed the button for another call, knowing she should have made this one first, but her need to get to safety had been too urgent to wait. She dialled the number of her mother's mobile, remembering without difficulty this time.

'Dillie Taylor,' came the bouncing exuberant voice Karen knew so well.

'Me, Dillie. My phone credit's running out, so I've got to be quick. You said something about a story you told when I bought Granny's chalet off you.'

'Yes?' Dillie sounded wary, and guilty too. 'What's the matter, Karen? You sound all over the place.'

'I'm OK. Elephant Man: you told me he'd died. True?'

'Oh, darling, why make such a fuss about it now? It's only that I didn't want to distract you when you had such a big decision to make. I thought worrying about a weird neighbour like that, trampling through the woods and pretending to be an elephant whenever it rained, let alone dumping rabbit corpses on your doorstep and all, might have put you off, so . . .'

'Not now,' Karen said fast. 'Just confirm: he *is* still alive?'

'I don't know what answer to give.' A cascade of self-deprecating giggles followed.

'Truth.' Rage made everything worse.

'Oh, well, all right. You could say "reports of his death were much exaggerated". At the time I said it, he *was* in hospital with serious respiratory problems, and they didn't *think* he'd make it, so I thought I was just jumping the gun a little.'

'But he didn't die?' Karen had to have a clear answer. 'It matters.'

'Oh, well, if you must. Yes, he is alive. And still living in those horrid woods you love so much.'

'Thank God,' Karen said.

Now she knew she had seen the face of Roderick, the Elephant Man, before her rescue this morning.

He was just the kind who, if he had found her drugged and unconscious, would have phoned for the ambulance and refused to give his own name. He'd rescued her once before. Now she owed him her life. Everything fitted. The memory of his big, creased face hanging over hers hadn't been part of any drug-induced misfiring in her brain. She was not paranoid or deluded. And Olga was at risk. She hoped Charlie hadn't been lying when he'd promised to find Olga.

Dragging the phone card out of the machine, Karen handed it back to the nurse.

'Better now?' she said, in her soft Island voice.

'Much better.'

Max offered her a grey curled wig.

'What's that?' Will asked from the chair beside Karen's bed. 'Max, what on earth . . . ?'

'Hideous, I know,' he said as Karen stared at it, without taking it from him. 'But it's the safest way to get you out of here if someone is watching you. Put this on, and these clothes I've brought, lean on my arm, hobbling like someone with arthritis, and I can drive you away without being followed.'

'Max, you take my breath away,' she said, more confident by the moment.

At intervals she was still woozy and hung over, and she didn't think her legs would ever stop itching, but she had no more doubts about what had happened, or about what she was going to do now.

'The doctor wants to keep her in overnight,' Will said.

'No fret.' Max frowned at him before turning back to beam reassurance at Karen. 'Will and I'll talk to him while you dress. Come on, young Hawkins. You can do your NHS consultant bit and make them let her go.'

Karen had never seen Will so reluctant, but he allowed Max to help him up and balance on his sticks before walking slowly out of the ward. Once he was on the move, Max pulled the curtains around Karen's bed and left her to dress in private.

She didn't need long, even though her balance wasn't as good as usual, and she was soon sitting on the edge of the bed, fully clothed in a baggy tweed skirt and bobbly acrylic cardigan, with the ugly grey curled wig on her head. She felt spaced out, and a bit fragile, and longed to make her getaway.

It wasn't much more than fifteen minutes before Will and Max came back with the nurse who'd lent her the phone card and who was now holding a discharge form.

'Sign here,' she said, looking as full of disapproval as Will at his very worst.

Karen, who no longer signed any document without reading it properly first, saw she was accepting responsibility for removing herself from medical care against advice. She looked at Will, whose face was white. She could not tell whether it was rage or anxiety that was making him so tense. But Max was all certainty and safety. She was going with him, and she was sure she would be safe. She asked Will to pay her debt to the nurse.

'I'll drop you off at the university, Will,' Max said when the small change had been handed over, 'with the key to my office so that you can make yourself at home. Once I've settled Karen, I'll come back and we'll decide what's best to do next. OK?'

Will did not look happy.

'I'm sticking around here. There are things I need to sort out with the police,' he said, making Karen frown.

She didn't have the energy to deal with him now. Standing upright and walking without a wobble took everything she had. Will put both sticks in one hand to support her with the other. His lemony smell nearly made her cry again.

With one man on either side, Max taking all the real weight, Karen didn't have to do too much acting. The hours she'd spent spread-eagled on the bare bed frame had given her plenty of pain in her joints. Moving stiffly was no problem.

They put her to bed in a tiny single room in the refuge's attic, with a mug of strong tea beside her, a cheese sandwich, and strict instructions to stay there and sleep.

Max had been allowed to escort Karen indoors and explain her presence to the woman in charge, a plump friendly-looking forty-year-old, whose name was Maddie. She accepted everything Max and Karen told her without any sign of scepticism or horror, told Karen she could stay, and advised Max to phone for news this evening, by which time their own doctor would have been in to see Karen.

Before Maddie left the small warm room, she handed Karen

a large key, saying, 'This will lock your door if you want it locked. But don't worry. We have brilliant security here. No one we don't know will get in. No one will touch you.'

Remembering how secure Clagbourne House was supposed to be, and yet how easily the mysterious Dev had got access to it, Karen took the key at once. She knew she would use it every time she was alone in the room.

The clicks of the lock's tumblers falling into place was reassuring. She pulled the key out of the lock and took it with her to the small dormer window. Looking out, she could see no easy means of access. She took the key back to bed with her and held on to its hard edges like a child with a favourite toy.

Lying on her side, with her knees raised to waist height and one hand tucked between them, she held the key with the other pressed against her chest and closed her eyes. But sleep wouldn't come. Her mind was clearing so fast that she couldn't stop thinking now, and remembering, making sense of everything that had happened, and trying to see how best to manage her re-entry into real life.

Once she understood that she'd be awake for hours, she uncurled her body, relieved that she could move in any way she wanted, in spite of the stiffness and the residual pain. She pushed the pillows up behind her back and sat up to eat the sandwich and drink the cool tea.

She had wanted Max to call at her flat so that she could collect some of her own clothes, but he'd refused, saying that if she was serious about being in danger from people who had assaulted her there and kidnapped her, she would be mad to risk it.

Now she was wearing a borrowed Marks & Spencer

nightdress made of pristine white cotton, with long sleeves and a neatly pintucked yoke over the breast, and otherwise had only the disguise Max had brought her and the clothes in which she'd been found in the woods, unconscious and abandoned to die.

The refuge must own a washing machine, she thought, getting out of bed to walk over to the black plastic garbage bag in which Max had transported the clothes. She pulled them out, recognizing the indigo jeans, kingfisher shirt and yellow sweater she had ripped off to shower the night before she was taken. She couldn't wear them, or the underclothes, until they'd been washed at the hottest possible temperature. The thought of those thugs with their hands on her clothes, using them to dress her drugged and battered body threatened her rediscovered sense of self.

She had to get it back, to see herself once more as an autonomous adult, who could safely operate in the world beyond this refuge. Outside, she had students and responsibilities, her own research, work for the police, family and friends, debts and assets. Whatever Dev and his thugs had done to her, she had to get over it.

A small mirror hung in the darkest corner of the room. Karen walked over to it and stared at her small button of a face, which glared back at her from between the long lank strands of blonde hair.

No marks disfigured her face, except for the tiny cuts where Gilda had removed the minute particles of glass. Karen's pupils were more dilated than usual, but that could have been because of her eyes' attempt to see in this gloom. And her skin colour was bad, a greyish cream. Her hair was tangled and greasy. But no one had hit her face.

When she pushed up the cuffs of the nightdress, she saw the marks of the handcuffs. Then she tracked all the faint needle marks and the other scraped bruises, which looked as though the handcuffs had moved up and down her arms, which wasn't possible. The three rows of bruises made it look as though someone had tied three different ligatures around her wrists and forearms. Bending down to lift the hem of the long nightdress, she saw only one set of marks on each ankle, spreading at the edges where she had wrenched her legs against the restraints.

She hoped Charlie was getting somewhere with tracking down Dev. Until they'd caught him and disbanded his gang of thugs, she would never feel safe. As Max had told her, she couldn't go back to her flat. She didn't see how she'd be able to work either. Dev and his men had to be identified and disempowered.

Karen was far too restless to go back to bed, and there were things she could attempt to help Charlie do what had to be done. Reluctantly dressing herself in the pensioner's clothes Max had provided, because they were at least clean, she made her plans. When she had combed her hair with her fingers as well as she could, unlocked the door and made her way down the five flights of stairs, she followed the sound of women's voices into a large bright kitchen.

Maddie was there, stirring something spicy in an enormous aluminium pan on a large range-type cooker, while four other women were sitting around a large table. Each had a mug at her side and a chopping board in front of her, preparing fruit and vegetables.

All of them looked up as Karen came round the door. The

first she saw was Vera, dressed in jeans and a big black sweater with a white apron over the top. She had a pile of red peppers on her board and was slicing them into neat centimetre-wide strips.

'It is you,' she said, not smiling. 'Why are you here? Are you OK?'

Karen shook her head, then corrected herself and said: 'More or less. But you're right about them. I know that now, but the police aren't convinced.'

One of the other women dropped her knife. The expression on her face was quivery with fear.

Maddie pulled her wooden spoon out of the pan, shook it hard but silently and laid it on the tiled worktop beside the stove, before wiping her hands on her apron and walking towards Karen.

'You should be in bed,' she said. 'It's all right, Sue. No one can come here. Here's your knife. Can you manage to go on peeling the apples?'

Tears in her eyes, the frightened woman took back her knife and picked up an apple, concentrating hard and mashing the knife violently across the middle of a soft-looking Bramley.

Maddie looked first at Karen, then Vera, gesturing towards the door with her head. Karen accepted the orders at once; Vera looked reluctant, but eventually followed Karen.

As Vera got up from the table, Karen saw how thin she was under the baggy black sweater, with legs that looked like Twiglets in the clinging leggings.

Outside the kitchen, Maddie shut the door with quiet force.

'You two have obviously met before and know each other's stories. But I can't have you worrying the others. If you want to discuss what's happened to you, use my office. But don't bring your past into the kitchen. OK?'

'Yes,' Karen said, recognizing Maddie's good sense at once. 'Vera? Can we talk?'

'All right. But I get my tea. You want?'

'Thanks. OK. Yes. Milk, no sugar.'

When Vera brought in two steaming mugs of tea, Karen was already sitting in one of the two easy chairs by the unlit gas fire in the chaotic-looking office. She took one mug from Vera and held it tightly between her cold hands, trying to decide where to begin and what exactly she needed to know from Vera.

'What did they do to you?' Vera said after a long silence.

'Heroin mostly.' Karen thought of her hours spread-eagled on the bed. 'Heroin and humiliation.'

The first small smile lit Vera's face. 'Humiliation they are good at. And powerlessness. I know this too.'

'I'm sure,' Karen said. 'When did you last see Olga Blackwater?'

'Who?' Vera's voice was blank.

'The woman who is behind Clagbourne House, whose money supports the work it does rescuing people like you.'

Vera shook her sleek blonde head. 'They have told me of her. She is like saint they say. But I have not seen her.'

'I think Dev has already killed her husband and may have hurt her, too. We have to find him, so I need to know how he discovered where you were. How did you get there?'

'To Clag House?'

'Yes. It seems so strange. I mean, how did you know about the place, and that it would be safe for you to run away there?'

Vera shook her head. 'A man who came to the . . . to where

I was made to work. I thought he was a client, but when I started to . . . you know, he's like "no". This is not what he wants. He is coming, secretly, to rescue girls like me. He tells me I am to go with him then. Right then. And he will get me to safety.'

Karen could not think of anything more unlikely. Why would a woman who had been at the mercy of a group of men who had raped her to punish her for disobedience trust a strange man enough to go away with him?

Once again Vera shrugged. Her face twisted into an ugly mask, in which her eyes looked as cold as a penguin's feet. 'When you have been treated like this and pumped full of drugs and abused in every way every day for months and months, what is worse anyone can do to you? He seemed kind. He didn't want to fuck me. Why not go with him? I had nowhere else. I had to get away from that place.'

'What did he do when he'd got you outside?'

'He took me in his car away from the town, miles down a motorway, and then we drove off the motorway into hotel at the service station. There was a woman with two other girls. He gave me to her and she took all four of us to a different place, where we met other women, who each took one of us away. I don't know where the others go. My woman took me to Gilda at Clag House.'

'And when did you come to believe you were safe?'

'At Clag House. The first night. I ate with others already there. They told me this is true, this is safe house. No clients. No fucking. No drugs. A doctor.'

'But then you saw Dev,' Karen suggested, picking up Vera's changing speech patterns and understanding what they meant.

'Yes. In next week, I see Dev.' Her voice had hardened. 'And I know I am not safe again.'

'Did anyone leave while you were there at Clagbourne House?' Karen asked.

'I don't understand. What do you mean by leave?'

'Well, it's a refuge, isn't it? Like this one.' Karen looked around the small office, with its teetering piles of paper all over the desk, the floor, and the fitted bookshelves. 'I assume that some of the women move on, back into the outside world eventually.'

'Ah, this, yes. I see what you mean. Not while I have been at Clag House. But I have been there only for two weeks. Nearly two weeks. Maybe no one was ready to go yet. They have told me there that there is no set time for staying. We go when we are ready and able to find work or to go home. Not before.'

'I see,' Karen said. 'What will you do when you are well enough to move on?'

A much wider, much more real smile flashed across Vera's lovely face. 'I will go to uni, to take my degree, then to become teacher like I planned.'

'What's your subject?'

'Mathematic. I accepted – I thought I accepted – job for the summer in a bar, to make the money before I study for my exams. My family does not have money.'

Karen wondered whether Vera would ever be able to go back to the life she would have lived, to forget what had been done to her, to have normal relationships.

'Who gave you the job in the bar?' she asked.

'It was a man, the cousin of the owner of a bar where students go. He said he has friends in London who need staff.

He introduced me to someone, who took me to someone else, and so it goes. It does not matter who he was. I was stupid, naïve to believe.'

'Why doesn't it matter? You're in a position to help the police follow every link in the chain, all the men involved.' Karen thought of the way her own life could not begin again until the ring was smashed. 'Don't you want to get them identified, arrested, punished?'

Vera put back her head and laughed. 'And warn them and men behind them that I am free and safe? How would I do this stupid thing? I keep my head down, I change my name, I try to get to a university here, maybe America, and I hide from them for always. I never again accept job from anyone I do not know.' All the laughter had gone from her voice and she looked straight at Karen. 'You must not tell about me to anyone. You must promise.'

'I won't use your story,' Karen said, 'but I have to find them, the men who took *me*. I want them punished and everyone involved exposed for what they are.'

'Then you have to leave here. Is not safe or fair on the rest of us. You have to go.'

Chapter 18

Day Four: 5.30 p.m.

'So where's this evidence then?' Will asked, leaning awkwardly against one of the desks in the incident room. His sticks were propped by his side and he kept a protective hand on them, not wanting to have to scrabble on the floor if they slipped. His leg was aching from the short climb upstairs and he hoped it didn't show.

'I'd have said Karen was absolutely lucid this afternoon and you ought to believe everything she told you. Her delivery may have been a bit slow and the words a bit thick, but she knew what she was talking about. Her mind was working. You need to listen to her fears for this Olga woman and get her into some kind of protective custody.'

Charlie Trench was looking his usual self, in his short thick leather jacket, with his absurd spiky hair. Put him in a striped jersey, Will thought for the first time, and he'd be a dead ringer for Dennis the Menace. Same type of chap, too. More or less. Glorying in his own tough wickedness and despising 'softies'.

'It's not as straightforward as that,' Charlie said, with an air of pity that made Will want to spit. 'She told us she was assaulted in her flat in Southampton, didn't she?'

'So?' Will said.

'She wasn't. She drove herself to the Island.' Charlie's pity was still there. Will wasn't sure if it was pity for Karen being in such a state or for himself for being stupid – or soft – enough to believe what she'd said. 'There was no coercion, and she was untouched then. So I need to know: is her mind affected by the drugs, or is she deliberately lying? Has she been brainwashed into protecting someone? You know, Stockholm Syndrome kind of thing. Or terrorized? Is Olga some kind of decoy, to keep us from getting at the truth?'

'How do you know she drove herself?' Will asked, knowing his own voice was even more clipped and cold than it had to be as he ignored all the questions.

Charlie raised his thick dark eyebrows into little triangles over his round eyes, so pointed they looked almost like perpendicular church windows. He nodded and gestured with his stubbly chin towards a desktop being used by a thin young woman. 'Denise will show you.' He raised his voice to call: 'Den?'

She swung round on her chair, almost overbalancing in the speed of the turn. Will saw that she wore small round granny glasses and a smile of eager attentiveness.

'Will you show Mr Hawkins the footage of Karen Taylor this morning.'

The young woman's face lost its gleam in a tide of self-conscious sobriety. 'Of course. Do you want to come over here, sir?'

Will grabbed his sticks, balanced himself on them and walked across the wooden floor, hearing the old-man's sound of rubber and limp and hating it. He forced his spine and shoulders into their most upright squareness and suppressed the wince of pain.

Denise clearly wasn't deceived because she gave him her seat and leaned over him like a new mother, making sure he felt secure. With one hand on his shoulder, she tapped a few keys with the other and a film unfolded itself on the screen. Will saw Karen, wearing her distinctive jeans, yellow cashmere sweater and the bright blue-green shirt she insisted on describing as 'kingfisher'. He couldn't suppress a smile at the memory of their argument over the term. He'd pointed out that you could just as easily call bright orange 'kingfisher' because the birds had nearly as much of that on their feathers as they did the bright greeny-blue. Karen hadn't been impressed.

The smile shrank as he watched the film of her unlocking the car. This was definitely Karen's bright red Subaru Justy, which she loved for its practicality and its jauntiness, but something was wrong. Will watched the whole of the footage, which followed the car on to the ferry from Southampton, off at Cowes and on through the town, before it came to an end. There were no cameras on the horrible twisting muddy road that led down towards the shore and her grandmother's two acres.

'Were there any other vehicles' tracks on the lane?' Will asked as he pressed the keys to move back to the beginning of the film in order to watch the first part again.

'Plenty,' Charlie said. 'But then there would be. All the weirdos who live in those woods have cars or vans. No other way of getting about. All kinds of tyre marks in the mud, animals, too: horses, cows, sheep, dogs. Lots of human prints. Why? You suggesting someone was following her and shot her full of smack as soon as she parked?'

'No,' Will said, pulling out the long 'o' sound into a message that hinted at untold contempt. He swung round on the chair to face Charlie, understanding exactly why the young constable had so nearly fallen off. The mechanism must have been recently oiled or lost its brakes or something because the chair fairly zipped round. He resisted the temptation to hold the desktop to keep himself safe.

'Hang on, mate,' Charlie said, with a laugh. 'Karen'll never forgive me if I let you smash up your other leg.'

'You know this isn't her, don't you?' Will jerked his thumb back over his shoulder towards the screen.

'What?' Charlie's tanned face darkened as blood rushed up under the skin.

'It's obvious,' Will said, thinking: I may be on sticks and an old crock in comparison to a pugilistic turkey cock like you, but I'm a whole heap brighter. Aloud he added, 'Haven't you ever watched Karen walk?'

'What are you on about? Course I have.'

'You can't have, if you think this is her.' Will didn't even try to suppress his smile. He knew it must be blazing with satisfaction and he didn't care. In this at least he was beating Charlie hollow. 'Watch the woman on the film. She may be Karen's height and weight, and have Karen's hair colour, and be dressed in Karen's clothes. But she's not Karen.'

'*What?*'

'Look at it, man. Karen walks with straight legs, bending

her knee directly forwards. This . . .' Will hesitated, not wanting to surrender any of his superiority in foul-mouthed excess.
'This ringer, if that's what she is, walks with a screw kick.
Watch. Every other step, the right leg kicks out sideways from
the knee. I bet you anything they brought Karen's unconscious
body over in the boot.'

Charlie watched, ran the film again, watched again, and
eventually said: 'You sure? Not just that you're looking at her
from a different angle?'

'I'm sure,' Will said, not looking up at Charlie, who was
now standing over him like a playground bully. 'I know Karen.
I know her in every mood and every kind of movement. This
woman is *not* her. You need to take Karen's account of what
happened a bit more seriously, mate. And then you need to get
hold of this Olga, and sort out some proper protection for
them both until you've found the criminals who did this.'

Charlie was reaching for his phone, when Will added coldly,
'And when you've done all that, you can tell me what the hell
you were doing involving her in something like this and putting
her at so much risk.'

'I involved her to the extent of asking her to sit in on – and
help with – interviews with a suspect in an important case,'
Charlie said with exaggerated patience, truncating his call. He
put the phone down on the nearest table and turned back to
Will, obviously hating him. 'She's an expert, and I was using
her expertise. Paying her for it, too. She didn't have to take the
job.' The patience slipped, and Charlie began to look extremely
dangerous: 'And who the fuck are you to judge me after you
fucking dumped her anyway? A woman like Karen? Get the
fuck out of here.'

Will stood, wanting to hit him, and nearly tripped over his own sticks. The ludicrous idea that he could take on Charlie Trench in his current condition made him feel about three feet high. But he wasn't going to justify himself or explain that Charlie had no idea of how things were with Karen. Or that it was a bloody good thing he knew nothing whatever about her. Bastard.

And now he was jabbering into his phone, setting up crime scene investigation of her flat and house-to-house questioning of any locals who could've heard her being abducted, as though it was he who'd realized the truth for himself. Bastard.

Out in the street, waiting for a taxi and still seething, Will phoned Max.

'Me,' he said when Max had answered the call. 'Can I take you up on your offer of a bed? I need to stick around until this mess of Karen's is sorted and I know she's safe.'

Max said nothing, but Will knew he was there, breathing heavily.

'Why aren't you going to stay at her flat?'

'It's a crime scene.'

'Ah.'

Funny, Will thought, how a single syllable could express so much: enlightenment, relief, satisfaction, encouragement.

'So you made Charlie Trench believe her, did you?' Max added. 'Good for you. Yes, of course stay. Get a cab to bring you to my office and we can go back home together. She's in good hands, by the way. The very best. She'll be safe where she is.'

The next day, when Karen's mind was in full working order, Charlie came to see her, bearing her laptop and phone.

Once again Maddie let Karen use her office, this time lighting the old-fashioned gas fire, which popped and buzzed as it pumped fierce heat into the small room. Charlie looked uncomfortable as he sat in one of the 1950's wood-and-tweed easy chairs. He was dressed in his usual black jeans and leather jacket over a grey-flannel collarless shirt and looked quite out of place in this wholly female refuge.

'Olga's fine, Karen,' he said as soon as they were alone. 'No one's done anything to her, and she has no knowledge of Dev.'

'*What?*'

'I talked to her yesterday and then again this morning. She's had no unexpected visitors or callers. No weird approaches from anywhere. No one hassling her, let alone threatening.' Charlie looked as though he was going to keep his ideas to himself, but after a moment he shrugged and added, 'She knows nothing useful. Nor does Gilda or any of the others at the refuge. They're sure Vera was seeing things that weren't there. All the security blokes who've worked there have photo ID and all the IDs check out. They're all licensed to work in security; they have NI numbers, addresses, dates of birth, passports. They're honest.'

'And you think all that can't be faked?' Karen said, unable to believe he was being so obstructive. 'You *can't* be that naïve. What else did you find out?'

'How the women get to Clagbourne House,' he said.

'What did Olga tell you?'

'That she has a network of volunteers, men, who go round the saunas and lap-dancing places, strip joints, and so on, looking for girls who seem strong enough to deal with the prospect of escape and then giving them the opportunity, if they want to take it. There's no coercion.'

'That's all?' Karen said, shocked. 'If they know which establishments are operating as brothels, don't they . . . ?'

'Give me a chance! That's the next thing. Once they've rescued all the girls they can, they collect photographic evidence – using their phones mostly – and take the information to the local nick. They get some places shut down.' His voice held a certain measured respect.

'Then, I suppose,' Karen said tartly, 'half the men who were running the brothels start up again somewhere else.'

Charlie wagged his head from side to side in the way she knew so well. 'Yeah. That can happen. Depends on the courts, like everything else.'

'So Dev could've been one of the volunteers. Have you thought of that, Charlie? What better way to check out the opposition and steal their best girls?'

'It's possible. Olga's given us a list of everyone who works for her, and Annie and Denise are checking through it now. If the man Vera's terrified of is involved in any way, we'll find him. Don't think we won't. In the meantime, you're safe here. Will you promise to stay?'

Karen nodded. She couldn't spend the rest of her life in Maddie's refuge, nor keep within its walls for the whole time she was technically staying in it, but in principle she would be here until Charlie and his team made the arrests, *all* the necessary arrests.

'Where does Will fit in?' he asked, not looking at her any longer but concentrating instead on the scuffed toes of his heavy black boots.

'I don't know,' she said truthfully. She stared into the popping orange and blue flames of the gas fire, knowing it was still at least three days before she could use the pregnancy test Maddie had bought for her. By then she might have her period in any case. 'We haven't talked properly yet. Max is putting him up and keeping us in touch. He . . .'

She broke off, not ready to tell Charlie she had no idea whether Will wanted to be back in her life or not. Until she knew that, she couldn't begin to decide what she wanted.

'Better be off.' Charlie stood up, looming over her and looking even more scarily tough and masculine in this small female room. 'Stay here and be safe.'

Karen glanced towards her laptop and phone. 'D'you think they're monitoring the airwaves?' she asked. 'Can I use those or will that bring them down on me?'

'God knows.' Charlie's expression was bleak – and frustrated. 'Not worth the risk, though. Can't you wait till we know?'

'What are you doing to find them?'

'Everything we can.'

'Which is?'

'Come on, Karen. You know as well as I do: hairs, fibres, fingerprints and DNA; house-to-house; CCTV; snouts. The usual.'

'Got anywhere yet? It's been 72 hours now. If you were going to find anything, you'd have got it by now.'

'Not true. You never know when someone's going to pop out of the woodwork. I'm surprised none of your neighbours heard anything.' He stood over her. She wouldn't look up, not wanting to see the destabilizing doubt in his eyes again.

'Why didn't you scream, Karen? Couldn't you have called for help at least?'

She thought back to the night when they'd come to her flat, and she tried to answer him truthfully.

'It seems like such an obvious thing to do now,' she said. 'But it wasn't at the time. I know it sounds stupid, but I was so surprised. I thought the knock was you. When I saw it was them, I wanted to keep them out so I concentrated on trying to shut the door. Then I think I . . . I suppose I didn't want to make them angry by screaming. Maybe. It all happened so quickly. Once they'd put that bag on my head, I couldn't make any noise. I tried and I got a mouthful of bag. I . . .'

'All right, Karen,' he said, putting a hand softly on her shoulder. She realized she must have been sounding hysterical. 'It's all right. I understand. No one's blaming you. I believe you.'

I wonder, she thought. Aloud she said, 'Thanks for coming anyway, and for bringing these back.'

He bent and kissed the top of her head, making her want to cry again. She fought the sensation, hating all the signs of weakness she couldn't prevent, except by taking action to further his enquiries.

'Charlie!' she shouted after him. 'Charlie, come back a second.'

She heard his footsteps stop in the narrow hall outside Maddie's office, then come back. He put his head round the door, looking resigned.

'Charlie, I saw them, you know,' she said and watched a new eagerness lightening his eyes. 'When they first knocked on the door, before they put the hood over me. I saw their faces.'

'They weren't masked? In balaclavas? That kind of thing.'
He sounded full of disbelief.

'No. They had naked faces. I might . . . Couldn't I do an
E-fit? If they're the kind of men I'm sure they are, I'll bet they've
been in trouble before. I bet they're on record. And what about
DNA? They probably left some in my flat. If I'd been an ordinary victim, you'd have . . .'

'I've had a CSI at your flat,' he said, frowning at her as
though he couldn't believe she would accuse him of treating
her less well than any other victim. 'All the samples are with
the lab now. OK. I'll set up an E-fit session.' The frown left his
face and a smile, a real smile, took its place. 'Be in touch asap.'

When he'd gone, Karen put her laptop and phone away in
her room in the attic, found the phonecard Max had brought
her and called him from the payphone in the hall.

'Max,' she said the moment he answered, 'I need a new
phone: pay-as-you-go, unidentifiable, and lots of cash. Can
you bring them? You know I'll pay you back. Or you can make
the finance department take it out of my next month's salary if
you don't trust me.'

'That won't be necessary,' he said in a voice that told her he
was not alone. 'Yes, I can certainly organize that. I'm tied up
at the moment. Would six o'clock be all right?'

'Fine,' she said, feeling guilty that she'd interrupted him at
what was clearly an inconvenient moment. 'Fine.' When she'd
put down the phone, she went back to her computer, glad to
feel the freedom with which she could now run up and downstairs. None of the bruises or wrenchings had done any serious
damage.

Upstairs, she switched on the laptop, carefully keeping its

Wi-Fi switch turned to 'off', and typed a list of all the things she needed to know from Charlie and his team, and the others she was determined to find out for herself.

She had to talk to Sheena again, out on police bail and looking less and less suspect with every new development but with plenty of helpful knowledge. Karen knew she should ask her questions face to face. Sitting on the edge of her bed, she looked at the grey, curly wig Max had bought her and wondered how safe she would be if she went to London wearing it.

Charlie phoned the refuge before Karen could make any plans and told her he had arranged the E-fit session for first thing the next morning, in an obscure police station on the edge of Southampton.

'I can arrange to have you picked up,' he said.

'No, don't do that,' Karen said, thinking this would be good practice for the much more alarming trips she would have to make. 'Let me put on Max's ridiculous wig and pensioner's clothes and go in a cab. I'll go nuts if I have to spend my whole time here.'

'But . . .'

'Charlie, let me do this. I have to know that I can operate outside this refuge, even in disguise.'

Eventually he gave in, and she set about her preparations.

Maddie had a safe minicab company she used whenever any of her residents had to get to court or see lawyers, and she called one of their drivers for Karen. He agreed to take her to the police station, wait while she dealt with the E-fit officer, and then bring her back. Max had brought her five hundred pounds in cash, promising more whenever she needed it, and so she didn't worry about how much all that waiting would cost.

The driver was well trained and neither stared at her nor asked intrusive questions. He treated her just like any other passenger and even asked whether she wanted him to escort her into the building.

'No, thanks,' Karen said, smiling at him. 'But is it really all right for you to wait? I don't know how long I'll be.'

'I can wait. I'll park round the back.' He reached into the glove compartment for a card and handed it to her, adding, 'Phone me when you're done and I'll come round to the front to pick you up.'

'Great. Thanks.' Karen walked up the four shallow steps into the brick building, which looked as though it dated from just before the Second World War. Inside, she didn't have to wait. Charlie's name acted as a passport to VIP treatment and she was soon sitting beside a young plain-clothes officer called Jon Blain, watching a screen on which an outline of a face began to build.

Jon was completely unthreatening as he asked his questions about the features Karen remembered. She closed her eyes to shut out the sight of his soft dark hair and earnest expression, trying to bring back a clear picture of the night when she had opened the door of her flat, still dripping wet from the shower and expecting Charlie. All her self-protective instincts were yelling at her to keep the memories buried, but she wouldn't.

Recreating the sensations of damp on her skin and the firmness of the towel she'd tucked into itself over her breasts, of irritation at the idea that Charlie had come so late and disturbed one of her most important solo pleasures, she opened the door in her mind.

'The first one had odd eyebrows,' she said, without thinking about the statement or what it might mean.

'Odd, how?' asked Jon, the E-fit officer. 'Funny shape? Funny colour?'

'They didn't match.'

'That's not unusual,' he said. 'Only supermodels and the staggeringly beautiful have symmetrical faces. Some people think beauty *is* symmetry. Let's start with the right eyebrow then: what shape was it?'

'Like a kind of hairy caterpillar,' Karen said, thinking back to childhood and the way her brother, Aidan, had made her help with his various wriggly collections. 'Isn't there one called a woolly bear? Poisonous spines. If you touch them they bring your skin up in weals.'

'*Pyrrharctia isabella,*' said Jon, as his fingers danced over the keyboard.

Karen was impressed with the neatness of his short finger-nails. Whenever she moved outside the flat her nails seemed to pick up a dark rim of dust. Either Jon had scrubbed his when he arrived in the office, or his skin and nails had some kind of Teflon coating.

His typing produced a change in the face on the screen, and Karen's memories, fears, and determination to get this right were all swallowed up in a spurt of amusement. A woolly curve, black at both ends and russet brown in the middle emerged over the screen face's right eye.

'Not a woolly bear caterpillar, then,' Jon said, removing it at once. His voice was warm with amusement. 'Sorry. Shouldn't have done that, but I couldn't resist. Here goes.'

'No need to apologize,' Karen said, with an edge. 'I'm a

psychologist. I know all about using humour to relax people who have memory problems. You don't have to fake anything with me.'

'Right,' he said, looking chastened. 'Good to know. We'll do it straight then. Here goes.'

On his sixth attempt at an unkempt eyebrow, Karen tapped the desk in front of her with her right index finger. 'That's it. That's the one.'

'I see what you mean about the woolly bear,' Jon said, with a kindly approval she hadn't expected. 'OK, so the left one: less woolly? More woolly? More curved? What?'

'Straighter,' Karen said, concentrating again on the cold and the wetness of her skin and her fear. 'And flatter. It looked darker than the other brow. I don't know why.'

So it went, with Jon puncturing the solemnity with a visual joke whenever Karen's frustration threatened to make her give up and agree to something that did not in fact square with her memory. She admired him more and more, both for his insights into the way visual and oral memory worked, and for the humour he maintained in spite of her bad-tempered snap.

After nearly half an hour, they had still done only the eyes and brows and the overall shape of the first man's face. Jon showed no sign of impatience. Karen looked at her watch.

'Listen,' she said, 'this is taking much longer than I expected. I think I'd better tell my cab to go.'

'God, yes,' he said, his grey eyes popping. 'It'll cost a fortune. I didn't know you had one waiting. I'm sure someone can run you back later.'

Karen fished the pay-as-you-go phone and the cabbie's card out of her bag and suggested he should come back again in two hours' time, asking whether he wanted to be paid now or later.

'Later's fine,' he said, adding with a laugh: 'Maddie's your guarantee. I know I'll get paid. See you whenever.'

'Great.' Karen put the phone away and nodded to Jon. 'OK, let's get on. Sorry I'm taking so long.'

'Doesn't matter. Getting it right is more important than the time it takes. You said something about a scar on the nose. Which side?'

At last the first face was done. Karen stared at it, trying to see anything in it that wasn't right. But she couldn't. This was the man who had raised the black cloth bag and pulled it down over her head.

Whether he had also stood over her when she'd been tied to the bed frame or not, she couldn't say. But she shivered at the memory of absolute powerlessness.

She wondered whether Vera would recognize the E-fit and asked Jon if she could have a printout. He was reluctant. There were rules, he said. Karen told him that, as a forensic psychologist who often worked with the police, she could be trusted with it. Only after he'd phoned Charlie did he give in.

When she eventually got back to the refuge, she felt drained of all energy, ruined by the effort of concentrating so hard and for so long on the faces of the men who had so nearly killed her. She tried to tell herself she would be able to rationalize all the terror, and every other destructive emotion, so that she could work effectively again, but her mind was too full of vulnerability for anything so sensible.

Maddie told her supper would be ready in an hour and promised to send Vera up to her room as soon as the other woman had finished her run on the treadmill. Karen, surprised that anyone as stick-thin as Vera needed to take exercise, stumbled towards the stairs. By the time she got to the first floor, she was hanging on to the banister and couldn't believe she'd run up here so recently.

The bed in her tiny white room was too appealing to resist. She lay down on the bed, still in her weird old-lady clothes, and watched the last of the daylight fade outside her small window. The idea of getting up to switch on the ceiling light seemed too much trouble. She fell asleep, still waiting for Vera to come and look at the two printouts Jon had given her.

Waking was hard, like pulling her body up out of a tank of viscous treacle. Karen was tempted to let go and sink back, but a voice kept tugging her on. At last she opened her gummy eyes, to see Vera hanging over her, shaking her.

'You left urgent message to say you need me at once. Now you are sleeping. What do you want? What is so important?'

'It's OK.' Karen's tongue felt swollen and her brain sluggish, but the panic in Vera's voice sharpened her mind a little. 'It's a couple of E-fits, pictures of the men who took me. I want you to look at them and say which one is Dev.'

Putting it like that was wrong, Karen knew, but it was all she could manage in the circumstances. She threw back the bedclothes and swung her legs over the edge.

'The pictures are on the window sill, there,' she said.

Vera looked at them, peered more closely, then shook her head. Without looking at Karen, she said, 'I not see anyone like these men look. Not in my life.'

Karen had noticed several times that Vera's English deteriorated when she felt stressed.

'Please look again,' she said. '*Please*, Vera. I know it's not like a photograph. It's only the best the E-fit officer could make with the information I gave him. Please look and say if you've ever seen anyone who looks like either of these men before.'

Vera glanced quickly back at the two printouts, then moved towards the door. When she got there, she looked back at Karen, facing her directly. 'I have never seen any men who look like these pictures in my life,' she said, very clearly, articulating every syllable. But the colour had left her face. Sweat gleamed on her upper lip, and she was glaring straight into Karen's eyes.

Karen knew she was lying. And she knew why.

'Vera,' she began, 'do you know the old saying that the only thing that allows evil to flourish is for the good to do nothing?'

Vera stared out of the window.

'What happened to you will happen again and again to more women so young that they are virtually children. It will go on for ever – and get worse – unless someone has the courage to talk to the police.'

'Courage?' Still Vera faced the window. It was dark enough outside for her reflection to be quite clear to Karen, and she could see all of Vera's despair. 'You call it courage? It is nothing like this. It is death warrant. It is invitation to be raped for punishment. It is stupidity.'

'Do you really think that not talking now will make you safe?' Karen tried not to let her enormous sympathy make her voice sentimental. She knew that Vera was dealing with so much of her own emotion that anyone else's would be just one more burden to carry. 'They will be sure you have talked. Your only hope of any kind of safety is to help the police arrest and convict them.'

Vera's head sank a little forwards. She did not speak, but her breathing deepened and caught, stopping completely for so long that Karen worried she might faint.

'Only you can help now, Vera. And that may just be the one thing that could keep you safe. There's nothing else.'

'Safe? You think I am stupid child to believe in this word?'

'I believe that you have been put through more than anyone should ever have to suffer. I know that you are the bravest of the brave. And I wish there was some way I could help you across this last . . . this last barrier. Please, Vera, look at the E-fit.'

'Is no need.' Vera's voice was without expression. 'Neither is Dev. But one I have seen before, when I am first in this country, on way from coast. He . . . he did not rape me; but he give me drugs, forcing me, with needle.'

'Which one?' Karen tried to keep her own voice unexcited, as though she felt no urgency, while her mind was screaming at her, telling her she had to get this sorted. No other woman should be put through anything like it. 'Which of the two injected you?'

'Man with scar on side of nose.'

'Will you give a statement to the police? Please, Vera. They will need it if they're going to get this man into court to answer for his crimes. *Please*?'

Vera peered at her own reflection, then scratched under one eye, pulling down the lower lid to expose the reddened eyeball behind it.

'If I do this thing you will leave me alone after?'

'I will.'

Vera shrugged. 'OK. But now, tonight. I do this thing once. Then I am silent.'

Karen picked up her phone to call Charlie.

Chapter 19

The next morning Karen let herself quietly out soon after six o'clock. The sun wouldn't rise for another two hours, but the city was already bustling. She'd pulled on the wig and old-woman's clothes Max had lent her and took care to walk with a heavy limp, as though every movement gave her pain. It wasn't entirely faked because the thick stockings she wore chafed the unhealed skin around her ankles, where she'd rasped it against the restraints that had tied her to the bed.

There was no evidence to suggest anyone was watching the refuge, but with Vera's terror vivid in her memory, Karen wasn't going to take any risks.

She knew Charlie would disapprove of this trip, but she also knew that she had to take some action of her own. She could not wait, passive and afraid, if she were ever to get back her self-respect and her courage. Charlie and his team would be pursuing their own enquiries, but there were still things she could do on her own, questions she could ask, that might offer signposts he wouldn't see without her.

If that happened – *when* that happened – Karen planned to make the journalist who had dared humiliate her in his filthy tabloid report admit that it was her insights that had cracked Charlie's case. She wasn't going to let a damaging article like the one Max had shown her stand uncorrected for long. This case had cost her enough without damaging her career as well.

The journey back to Wilkes Street in Spitalfields took nearly three hours and when she got no answer to her knock she cursed herself for not getting up even earlier. She knocked again, banging more loudly, and stepped back to look up at the tall house for any sign of movement. At last a light flickered on, then she heard footsteps, followed by the crunching sound of a key turning in a lock. The dark-maroon panelled door opened.

Sheena stood in the gap, still clipping on her left earring. It was made of heavy gold with a single diamond set off-centre. She was impeccably dressed in another pair of wide-legged black trousers. Today's cashmere tunic was a soft bluish grey. She looked very much her own woman – quite unlike the unkempt, vulnerable suspect on the Island. She in turn looked Karen up and down like a prospective employer examining an unimpressive applicant for a menial job.

'I don't want to be rude, but I deal with all my charity donations by post and I do not talk to canvassers. Sorry.'

Karen glanced down at the baggy tweed skirt Max had given her, and the heavy fake-leather shopper hanging over the crook of her arm, and smiled as she realized how effective the disguise must be.

'We've met before,' she said just as the door was closing, and she watched a wary hesitation make Sheena's neck stiffen and her expression harden. 'Karen Taylor. I'm the forensic psychologist who sat in on your interviews before you were released on police bail. I'm only dressed like this to avoid attention.'

She dragged her university pass out from under her mud-coloured cardigan and showed it to Sheena.

'Good disguise,' Sheena said, having examined the laminated plastic rectangle, adding with a faint smile. 'What do you want?'

'Could I come in? It's all a bit personal to be discussed on the street.' Karen stepped forwards, hoping Sheena would retreat rather than push her back. After a moment's hesitation, she did take a reluctant step sideways. Karen took that as an invitation and walked past her into the hall.

As soon as Sheena had closed the front door, Karen pulled off her khaki fishing hat and the grey wig at the same time, shaking out her own blonde hair.

'Sorry about the disguise, but I got nabbed,' she said, trying to use the most informal language she could find, 'by a couple of men. I was lucky, and I was found in time, but I need to know why they took me. I'm sure it has to be connected with Sir Dan's death, but the police don't believe me. I thought you, of all people, would understand how that makes me feel, and so perhaps help me.'

'Why should I?' Sheena said with bitterness. 'You did nothing for me in those interviews.'

'Because I want to find out who killed your lover. And I *know* you had nothing to do with it.'

'That's something, I suppose.' Sheena in turn pushed her way past Karen and opened the door into the kitchen, which, as Karen remembered it, overlooked the small courtyard garden. 'You'd better come in here. I can give you a few minutes. What did they do to you?'

'That doesn't matter now.' Karen was not going to risk her hard-won confidence by recreating what had been done to her. 'But I brought a couple of E-fits in case you recognized either of the men involved.'

'Why would I? I told you I didn't see anyone at the house except for Dan.' Sheena sounded impatient.

'You might have seen them before. At work, or hanging around somewhere. Anywhere.' Karen pulled one of the stools out from under the lip of the island unit and perched on it, uninvited, impressed all over again by the professional *batterie de cuisine* on show all around her. Pans, whisks, knives, copper bowls: everything looked as if it were the most expensive available, and beautifully kept.

'I doubt it. But I'll look if it'll do anything to help. I want Danny's killer paying for what he's done.' Sheena's voice wobbled and she looked out at the tiny paved garden, with its central tree already showing small pompoms of tiny pink and white flowers at the end of dark, leafless branches. Tears oozed out of her eyes as she added, 'And I want my life back. My real life.'

Knowing that could never happen for Sheena, Karen took the prints out of her heavy shopper and laid them on the island worktop, pushing aside a folded newspaper. As it moved, she caught sight of the photograph on the front page, which Max had already shown her, and forgot why she was here in a burst of rage.

'Why did you keep it?' she asked Sheena when she'd

recovered herself, and she watched a rich blush covering Sheena's face.

'I hated you for thinking I could've killed Dan,' she said. 'Seeing you humiliated for failing to get anywhere made me feel better. So I've kept it to reread whenever I get wobbly.'

'I can understand that,' Karen said, not forgiving her. 'But now you know I don't think you did it, won't you help me? See if you can identify either – or both – of these men?'

'OK.' Sheena picked up the printouts and peered at them. For a moment Karen's hopes rose. Then Sheena shook her head.

'I can't say I recognize them. But I don't go round staring at everyone I meet in the street. I mean, they do look fairly ordinary, don't they? I'm sure enough that I didn't see them at work ever. And Dan never brought anyone who looked like this back here.' Sheena put a hand on the kettle and looked round as though she was thinking of offering Karen a drink. 'Did you really come all this way to show me these pictures?'

'No,' Karen said, dumping the bag on the floor beside her stool. 'I came because . . .' She hesitated, wondering whether she would be mad to trust this woman and, deciding she would be, added simply, 'because I need to know more about Sir Dan and his life with Olga, and how they manage their charities. Anything that could give me a clue to the identity of these men and why they wanted him dead. I'm *sure* there's a reason.'

Sheena's dull eyes brightened. Karen saw that it wasn't the effect of excitement, only of more welling tears.

'I've told you all I can.' Sheena walked across the polished honey-coloured stone floor and unclicked the door that led out to the garden, allowing the scent of flowers to reach them both.

Although it was a little like lilac, this scent was more complex, almost peppery, and definitely more interesting than the straight lilac sweetness. Sheena inhaled it, breathing as deeply as a nicotine addict taking her final puff.

'Dan loved viburnums,' she said after a while. 'That's why we put one in here. It's only good for a few short weeks in winter. The rest of the time it's just a dull green shrub, without even being a graceful shape. But he thought that was worth it for this scent in the deadest part of the year. He used to say he'd make a fortune if he got a perfumer to bottle it.'

Karen said nothing. After a while Sheena clamped the door shut on the strong fragrance and turned back to face Karen again.

'What does that tell you about his psychology, Doctor Taylor?' she said with a harsh challenge in her voice. She didn't sound as though she expected a satisfactory reply.

Karen smiled, which was her usual response to aggression in research subjects. 'Nothing in itself,' she said, 'except that he liked scented flowers enough to put up with the tedium of a dull-looking shrub for three-quarters of the year. What does it tell you?'

Sheena looked away, rubbing her left thumb up and down her lips, eventually pushing them apart so that she was almost sucking the thumb. At last she took it out and wiped it on a tea towel, which she then threw into a corner of the kitchen floor.

'That he knew you can never have everything, and you have to accept the downsides in order to appreciate the good bits.'

'You've obviously thought about this a lot,' Karen said. 'Did you apply that insight to other aspects of his life?'

'Obviously.'

So, Karen thought, the patient Sheena can snap like a stapler even when she's not faced with an aggressive man like Charlie. 'With what conclusion?' Karen asked.

'Oh work it out for yourself.' Sheena grabbed the kettle and held it under the cold tap, turning on the water with so much force it sprayed way past the spout and splattered the front of her elegant cashmere tunic. She opened a drawer to take out a clean tea towel and wiped her front with it, before carefully hanging it over the handle of the huge range's oven.

'What was Olga's equivalent of the viburnum's scent?' Karen asked, needing to move the explanation on.

The kettle banged on the worktop as Sheena shoved the flex back into its socket with much more force than it needed.

'Didn't he ever tell you?'

Sheena said nothing. Karen knew she was supposed to go on asking questions; if Sheena hadn't wanted to be made to talk she would never have started this discussion of the viburnum's properties and their relation to her dead lover's mind.

'You must have asked,' Karen added so quietly that Sheena had to lean forward to hear her. 'I know he was loyal to her, and I know you're no kind of nag, but in all the years you were together I can't believe you never pressed him to talk about her.'

The kettle was boiling but Sheena was still holding on to its handle. As the steam built up under her wrist, she suddenly cried out and moved back. Karen could see the red patch of the scald from the other side of the kitchen. She waited while Sheena ran her wrist under the cold tap, before patting the skin dry and then scuffling in one of the kitchen drawers. She brought out a red tube and squeezed some yellow ointment on to the burn. All of which gave her plenty of time to rehearse her answer.

'Didn't you ever feel you had the right to the truth about your rival?' Karen said. 'I know he was very generous to you, but you gave up an awful lot for him, didn't you?'

Sheena bowed her head. Even after his death, her sense of loyalty was too strong to break easily, but this gesture told Karen she'd been right.

'When did it happen?' she asked, hoping a simpler question might act as an emotional hammer.

'About three years ago.'

'What happened? Did he suddenly change his plans so that he couldn't see you when you'd been expecting him?'

'How did you know?'

Karen smiled, a much more genuine smile than the one she'd used to deflect Sheena's anger a few minutes ago.

'Because I couldn't think of anything else that would shake you out of your determination never to give him anything to worry about,' she said.

Sheena's short laugh was more bitter than ever. 'You're right about both. He was here one evening, quite soon after Andy died, and she phoned him and he left. Just like that. I was bringing the food to the table – his favourite fish pie and frozen peas; he had very simple tastes – when she phoned and he just got up and left. I didn't see him again for five days.'

'And when he came back, you shouted at him?' Karen suggested. Sheena nodded, making her hair swing down across her face, hiding her expression.

'I did,' she said after a long, painful pause. This confession was clearly very hard for her. 'The only time, ever. At the start he was as angry as me, but he calmed down first. Like I said to you, he thought anger was a sign of weakness. In the end, he did explain her to me.'

'How?'

'I'd gone off to have a bath on my own. It was the only way I could think of to . . . to stop myself yelling at him even more. He came up a bit later, with a glass of champagne for me, and he sat on the edge of the bath, with his hand in the water, stroking my leg, and he told me about her.'

Sheena stalled again. Karen applied a tiny flick of her verbal whip, and Sheena started once more.

'He told me she'd been a prostitute.'

Karen hid the satisfaction this news gave her. Hadn't she had exactly that idea when she'd first been looking up Dan on the internet? She should have had more faith in her own instincts. Was this the answer? Had some trafficker or pimp from Olga's past become so powerful he had to protect himself from her now? Was he afraid she'd recognized him somewhere and told her husband? Had he encountered Sir Dan somewhere by chance and thought he'd been spotted? Was this why he'd had Sir Dan killed? Could the castration and display of the body in the kitchen – the most female room of any house – have been designed to scare Olga into silence?

'That's how they'd met,' Sheena added. 'He was a client. I hated hearing that. I don't know . . . He'd never told me he used prostitutes, paid . . . You know.'

'I know,' Karen said, remembering how she'd loathed Martin Fieny, Stella's man from the internet dating site.

'Anyway, they fell in love, and Dan . . .' Sheena closed her eyes and tightened her lips. This time Karen knew she would have to wait until Sheena was ready to finish her story. At last, her face relaxed and her lips parted again.

'He had to buy her.' As Sheena's eyelids lifted, Karen saw the expression in her eyes was full of remembered shock. 'When he saw what I thought about it, he told me it wasn't that bad. It was like buying an apprentice out of his contract or something. But I still think he bought her. Like a slave. Nearly.'

'And love died between them?' Karen suggested.

'Not right away. It was good at first, he said. They bought a house and planned a family. But she couldn't have children. Too many . . .' Sheena gulped. 'Too many STDs earlier in her career had damaged her fallopian tubes. She had an ectopic, which they say is usually the result of chlamydia, and then never conceived again. She found life boring, with only shopping and waiting around in one or other of their houses, so they set up the first of their charities, rescuing women like her. Then Dan started to get even more successful and they had to go to some spectacularly grand dinner, and the host . . . the host had also been one of her clients.'

'It all sounds very *Pretty Woman*,' Karen said.

'What?'

'You know, that film with Richard Gere and Julia Roberts.'

'Not at all like that.' Sheena was snapping again. 'That's a romantic fable. Pretty and cheerful. Reality isn't either. Dan said *he* didn't think the host recognized Olga. She looked quite different once she was the rich man's wife. But neither of them could be sure, and after a while she got so she couldn't face it any more: the constant fear of being exposed. That's what triggered her breakdown. She got hysterical and said she could never go anywhere in public with Dan ever again. They'd have to leave the country and so on. He bought her the place in Switzerland, and set up the rest of the charities for her to manage from there, and . . .'

'And employed you to go to the parties with him, knowing you were wholly respectable?'

'That's right. Then the rest followed on from that.' Sheena's eyes now showed nothing but resignation. 'So that night, as I lay in the bath, with his hand touching my skin as the water got colder and colder, I understood them both. And I accepted it all.'

'What did you understand?'

'Why he could never leave her. It wasn't just the breakdown, you see. I understood how she must feel: he had *bought* her. Think of the humiliation. Much much worse than mine, being kept here as his girlfriend, unknown to all his friends. Our relationship might have to be secret, but at least it was honest and equal. I was with him because I loved him. I was free. She never could be, poor woman.'

'But would Sir Dan have stopped her leaving him just because he'd paid . . . ?' Karen began, allowing herself to sound puzzled. 'How could he? Legally, I mean.'

'Dan would never have held her against her will. But she didn't want to go. That was the whole point. Don't you understand? The problem between him and her and him and me. She wanted all of him, but out in Switzerland. How could he live there? Limited geographically and in every other way. His life was his work. He had to run the business. And . . .'

'And there was you,' Karen said. This time she was making a statement, not a suggestion.

'That's right, and on that night – the one when he left here without even eating, just because she phoned – she was in their plane and about to land at Farnborough. Unexpectedly. She phoned to tell him to pick her up. When he came back those five days later, I asked . . .' Sheena shook her head, as though the question was too momentous to remember.

'Whether he'd told her about you?' Karen was back to making suggestions to help Sheena overcome the years of silence.

She nodded, without saying anything, and the expression on her face told Karen what Sir Dan's answer must have been: no.

'Now there really is nothing left,' Sheena said, coming to Karen's side and almost pulling her off the high stool. 'I've betrayed him in every possible way. I need you to go.'

Karen could understand why Sheena's self-loathing expressed itself as aggression, but she could have done with a little less of it. She barely had time to pull on her wig and khaki cotton hat, before Sheena bundled her out of the house. Max's final instruction echoed in her mind: the way you move is a crucial part of the disguise. Think of aching hips and knees and go up and down steps with care, as if your feet can't be sure they won't slip. Otherwise the wig and clothes won't make any difference.

Will stood balancing on his sticks at the window of Max's flat, looking out at the treetops in the small park across the road, waiting for the taxi that would take him to his first appointment with the new physiotherapist. He was going mad with boredom, having no work to do, and he couldn't protect Karen physically while he was disabled like this. All he could do was fight even harder to regain his full strength. He'd pulled in all

the innumerable favours he was owed and a military rehabili-
tation specialist had agreed to see him on a private basis. If
today's session went well, he'd get Max to arrange for him to
see Karen at the refuge tonight.

A sharp beep of a car's horn made him look down to street
level. The driver from Max's favoured cab company was sitting
there. Grimacing because he hated admitting the difficulty of
getting himself downstairs, Will swung round and made his
way out, using the sticks as little as possible.

Frustration made Karen want to squeal as she hobbled down
the shallow steps and looked around for somewhere to sit. She
wanted to get a report of her last meeting down on the laptop
while all the impressions were still sharp in her mind. Spitalfields
was full of restaurants and bars. There must be somewhere
close by where she could find a chair and some decent coffee.

Ten minutes later, to the surprise of a young East European
waitress, who obviously assumed someone who looked like
her would order a more gentle drink, Karen was sipping a
double espresso. After the first wonderful jolt of the caffeine
hit, she sighed in pleasure, before reaching down into the heavy
capacious shopper to pull out her laptop.

All that mattered now was creating a precise record of
everything Sheena had said and a note of all the questions
Karen still needed to ask. She thought the heroin and acid had
been expelled from her body, but she still didn't entirely trust
her brain.

At the end, when she had squeezed her memory like a lemon
until nothing remained but pips and skin, she knew she had to
talk to Olga again. The questions would be painful – and

humiliating – but if they led to the identification and punishment of the men behind Sir Dan's death, surely even Olga would accept that any amount of humiliation and embarrassment would be a small price to pay. Karen's phone rang, and she answered it with circumspection. Her usual crisp 'Karen Taylor' would be stupid in a public place like this, and very few people had the number of her new pay-as-you-go phone.

'Yes?' she said cautiously.

'Karen. It's me, Charlie. Where are you?'

'Oh, here. You know.'

'I've got a statement here I want you to interpret. Shall I bring it to the refuge or arrange for you to come over here? The manager didn't seem all that happy to see me last time.'

'Neither,' she said quickly. 'I'm wigged up and out at the moment. I'll get to you when I can, but what's made it so urgent?'

'Sheena did fake the email.'

'*What?*' Karen had become so sure of Sheena's innocence that this was impossible to accept.

'The email summoning her to Sir Dan's house that night. *And* the one telling Mrs Brown, the housekeeper, that the two chippies were coming to mend the windows. She is involved, Karen. And she's a lot more devious than we gave her credit for.'

'How do you know she's involved?' Karen thought herself back into the kitchen, listening to the sensible, loyal explanations of Sheena's relationship with Sir Dan. Could her own interpretation of the speech patterns and behavioural markers – and common sense – have been so far off-beam?

She also thought of the huge block of very expensive carbon-steel knives she'd seen on the worktop and had to suppress a shiver.

'The techies have traced the emails via all the various cutouts back to an internet café in Spitalfields,' Charlie said, 'only moments from her house there.'

'CCTV?'

'Only of her walking along the street minutes before the original emails were sent.' Charlie's voice had slowed a little in his disappointment. 'The café itself doesn't have CCTV. And the terminals don't have integral webcams. Unfortunately. Where are you?'

Karen gulped and closed her eyes. 'Actually,' she said, 'I'm in Spitalfields.'

'Talking to her?' Charlie's voice cracked like a bullet hitting a wall. 'Karen, you nearly died. You're mad to . . .'

'Leave it, Charlie, please. I can't cope with you being angry with me. I had to do something. And, yes. I have been. I . . . I've got some interesting stuff.'

'You . . .' Even down the phone, Karen could tell that Charlie was having to fight to keep himself from yelling at her. She raised her eyelids, glad she didn't have to face him just now. 'I'm not angry. I'm afraid for you. Get back here quick. And don't go anywhere near her again, whatever you do.'

Karen's eye was caught by a familiar figure, hurrying past the window, talking into a mobile. Sheena.

'Asap, in fact.' Karen used his favourite acronym, hoping it would cheer him up. Then she put a five-pound note on the table, which would easily cover the cost of her coffee, and collected her belongings.

By the time she'd got back out on the pavement, moving far faster than her disguise allowed, she saw Sheena's figure in the distance, turning into a shop. Following as discreetly as possible, keeping her eyes on the place where Sheena had turned in order not to miss her destination, Karen found herself outside an internet café. Looking through the slightly smeared window, she saw Sheena sitting in front of a screen logging on with all the businesslike efficiency of someone completely at home.

Karen took a quick photograph with her phone, ensuring that she got the café's nameboard in the shot as well as Sheena's profile, and then sent it to Charlie, adding a text:

Find out who she's emailing now.

That done, Karen made her way back to Waterloo and the train that would take her back to Southampton and Charlie, hoping her supple rush down the road hadn't caught the eye of any waiting watcher.

Chapter 20

Day Six: 1.00 p.m.

Freed from the need to wear the grey-curled wig by the presence of police officers all around her, Karen shoved both hands up under her blonde hair to fluff it out, before tucking enough behind her ears to keep her vision uncluttered.

'So tell.' Charlie was leaning over her, one hand on the back of her chair and the other on the desk to the right of her keyboard.

Having him so close made her wriggle her shoulders, and look up and back at him. 'I need a bit more room,' she said. 'Why not take the chair?'

'I need to see your screen.'

'I'll email it to you, then you get your own copy. There's nothing secret.'

He peered round at her face, as though checking whether she looked like a liar. Then he slouched his way around the desk and subsided into the chair.

Karen felt better for the freedom, wriggled her shoulders again to get rid of the last of the tension, and reported on everything Sheena had told her, then said: 'Have you talked to Antony Quiggly, the solicitor, yet?'

Charlie blanked her.

'Oh, come on! You have to know which trust it was Sir Dan was planning to alter. Antony wouldn't tell me, but you have to try. Why haven't you? I *told* you to.'

'I did.' Charlie scratched one powerful thigh, the sound of his tough nails on the harsh denim reminding Karen of the moment when she'd heard one of her captors doing the same. She felt saliva rushing into her mouth and hoped she wasn't going to be sick.

'And?' she said when she was sure, allowing much more bite into her voice than usual. Charlie looked up in surprise. 'And nothing. Sir Dan told Antony he wanted to revoke "the trust", but he didn't actually say which trust. Antony says he assumed it would be for Clagbourne House, but . . .'

'Which suggests he himself thought something was wrong there. Could Vera have . . . ?' Karen left the question unfinished as she reached for her phone in the bottom of the big bag. She called the number for the refuge and asked Maddie if she could talk to Vera.

'She's gone,' Maddie said in a voice that suggested Karen was at fault.

'Why?'

'Because you wouldn't stop asking questions and making her look at scary E-fits and bringing the police here, risking precisely the kind of attention we don't need. How long are you going to keep your room? We always have people needing it. You've got it only because we owe Max so much.'

'Pack up my stuff,' Karen said, hurt but easily able to see

Maddie's point of view, 'and put it somewhere. Use the room for whoever you want. I'll find another place to go. I'm sorry. I never meant . . . Did Vera say where she was heading?'

'No. I wasn't going to force her to tell me. Just to phone if she needed us.'

Karen shut off the call, looking at Charlie's dark face.

'What?' he said.

'Vera's gone again. I wanted to know if she could have got in touch with Sir Dan. To warn him about seeing this Dev at Clagbourne House.'

'Why would she?'

'When Gilda refused to believe what she said about Dev, maybe she'd have tried . . .' Karen's voice died. 'Is Sir Dan's involvement in the charity public? I can't remember.'

'There's a bad portrait of him in the hall of Clagbourne House,' Charlie said. 'I'm not surprised your memory's still shot. But it was there when we went there together. Got his name as well as the painter's on the frame's label.'

'So maybe Vera did go to him. Can you check it out?'

Charlie's raised eyebrows told Karen she must have sounded too commanding. She remembered they were surrounded by his team of junior officers and might have blushed at her own tactlessness if it hadn't all been so important.

'Presumably you've got hold of phone records of everyone involved. Isn't there anything in them to show anything that could've triggered the attack on Sir Dan at this particular moment?'

'Sir Dan made no unexplained or long calls on the night of his death, except his regular one to his wife at 5.30 p.m. GMT. Lasted an hour. Nothing unusual.'

'But . . .'

'Believe me, Karen,' he said. 'We are doing our job.'

'What about the content of calls they both made that night?' Karen was thinking that a daily hour-long phone conversation between Dan and Olga didn't square with anything Sheena had told her about their relationship. Had anything Sheena said been true?

'We're not a police state. Content of calls is not routinely recorded. As you should know.'

'Of course I do. But people are listening in to private calls all the time. What about radio hams – hackers, or whatever they're called? There must be some on the Island. It's just the kind of place, where . . .' Karen cut off the undiplomatic thought, remembering how much she owed the Elephant Man, the oddest of all the odd Island characters she'd ever met. After a moment she added, 'Can't you access them, ask if anyone heard anything interesting for the twenty-four hours surrounding Sir Dan's murder? Even if you couldn't use it in court, it might point you in the right . . .'

'We already appealed for witnesses. Got plenty of calls. Nothing useful. So far.'

'And my E-fits,' she went on. 'Have you tried them on Mrs Brown yet?'

Charlie's face darkened even more, and Karen found herself wanting to laugh. 'She recognized them, did she?'

'One of them. He was one of the so-called chippies who came to mend the window frame. The one whose worksheet she signed before he drove the van away.'

'Possibly leaving the other behind to hide in the cellar and come out to kill Sir Dan in the night,' Karen said. 'Don't you see the similarity, Charlie?'

'What're you talking about?' He sounded edgy enough to tell her that the pressures of the case were getting to him. Karen suddenly remembered that he was having to make daily reports to his ACC. She controlled her own impatience and did her best to explain what she meant, without sounding as though she thought he was being dense.

'Don't you see how the intelligence that set up my intended death to look like suicide is so like the one that summoned Sheena to the house here to be the only suspect in the gruesome murder of her lover?'

'Sheena's the one who sent the emails,' Charlie said with a heavy snap.

Karen stifled her instinct to argue in favour of a quiet question: 'Why would she, of all people, do it like this? If she'd wanted to kill Sir Dan, she had dozens of ways, much less obtrusive. Why would she put herself at such risk, killing him in such a dramatic way, in a locked house where she was the only other inhabitant? The only other visible inhabitant, I mean. It's absurd, Charlie. You brought me in to help with the psychological aspects of this case, so listen to me: your theory just doesn't fit with her psychology.'

'She has form.'

'No she hasn't. She may still be suspected by some of your colleagues who investigated her baby's death, but that's not the same at all. Have you seen the records of that investigation?'

He shook his head. 'Not in detail. No time.'

'So you're relying on colleagues' prejudice. Someone needs to go through the list of all the other possible suspects, who weren't investigated because your mates were so sure Sheena did it herself. There must be some.'

'Why?' Charlie could sound cool, too, and very sceptical. 'The baby died accidentally, didn't he? That's what the court decided.'

'Oh, shut up and bugger off.' Karen was afraid she was losing all the confidence he'd ever had in her judgment. 'Listen, I know I'm trying to conquer prejudice with no more than intuition, but at least my intuition is informed by professional experience and . . .'

'You think the investigating officers' "prejudice" isn't? You think they haven't dealt with cases of infanticide over and over again? Commonest cause of death in the under-ones.'

'Although,' Karen said, refusing to be brow-beaten, 'most infanticide is committed by men; usually stepfathers but not always.'

Charlie audibly ground his teeth. 'No time to argue about the causes of child-murder now.'

'No indeed.' Karen nodded in the direction of the two E-fit printouts. 'Have you got either of these blokes on record?'

'One. The one with the weird eyebrows and the scar,' he admitted. 'ABH. Short sentence. Out a year ago.'

'Is he the one Mrs Brown identified?'

Charlie nodded.

'Can you lay your hands on him?' Karen asked, echoing the words he'd used when she'd first told him about Vera. She saw from the flicker in his eyes that he remembered too.

'There's a warrant out,' he said in a softer voice. 'No news yet.'

'Pity. OK. Now, what was it you needed me here for that you couldn't mention on the phone?'

'I want you to have a look at a statement we've taken from Trevor Fieldsham.'

'Who?'

'The accountant Sir Dan sacked for having his hands in the till.' Charlie's expression held triumph and the first hint of laughter he'd shown today. 'You forgot, didn't you? Focusing on all the wrong stuff, see.'

Karen didn't deign to comment, only holding out her hand for the statement.

'Read it, tell me if his story works psychologically, then sit in on the next interview.'

'You mean you've got him here?' she said. 'In the cells downstairs?'

'Yup.'

'Sir!' DC Denise Balker called from the other side of the room. 'I've got it. The email Sheena's just sent to Mrs Brown, Sir Dan's housekeeper. The address isn't her usual one, and nor is Mrs Brown's. These are hotmail accounts. Sheena's is in the name of GreveyS, and Mrs Brown's is HouseyB.'

'Read out Sheena's,' Charlie said.

Karen let the accountant's statement drop to the table next to her, amazed they had access to the emails.

'Like I said, it's to Mrs Brown, but it starts, "Dear Maisie".'

Charlie's head snapped upwards, and his eyes narrowed.

Dear Maisie, Thanks for your email. I'm sorry you're having such a hard time with Olga. It's not your fault Sir Dan organized men to mend the windows without telling her, or that the police have shown you a photo of one of them. She shouldn't have shouted at you. I can't understand why she was so aggressive. How were you to know there could be a problem? You did what you'd been asked

*to do. Don't let her get you down. If there's anything I can
do to help, tell me and I'll do whatever I can. Try not to
forget how Sir Dan always wanted all of us to ignore the
times when she was difficult so we could concentrate on
keeping her healthy and happy. Tell me something, was she
planning to come to the Island anyway, or did she only
come because of his death? Love, Sheena.*

'"Love",' Charlie quoted, pointing at the screen. 'They
friends?'

'They must be, and yet Sheena never said a word about her,'
Karen said, seeing where he was going with this. 'The style
suggests Mrs Brown was giving her a regular update on everything Sir Dan planned and did when he was on the Island so
that she knew all about his life here.'

'So all her ignorance about the house's security system
could've been faked,' Charlie said, with more grimness and less
satisfaction than Karen would have forgiven.

'Is there any answer yet, Denise?' she asked.

'Just coming through, Doctor Taylor. Hang on. Yes, here it
is. Do you want it printed, or can you read it on the screen?'
Karen was already reading.

*Dear Sheena, As always, it helps, just being able to tell you
all this. Obviously I can't say any of it to anyone here. Yes,
Olga was always due to come in that day. Sir Dan told me,
oh, nearly two weeks ago. But there were no guests
scheduled, except for the lawyer coming for lunch. I told
you about him, didn't I? I always thought it was odd. Not
Mr Quiggly coming for lunch. That happened sometimes.*

*But no one staying. Olga didn't usually come here unless
they were entertaining. But no one ever tells me anything,
so I didn't ask any questions. Love, Maisie.*

Karen read the email three times, as an icy lump formed in her
stomach. It looked as though Sheena could have been told well
before the weekend that Sir Dan had been going to see the
lawyer who had drawn up her own trust documents. She was
accustomed to sending secret – or at least private – emails from
the local internet café in Spitalfields. She hadn't shown any
kind of shock or disgust or suspicion in her own email when
she'd been writing about the so-called carpenters who were in
fact her only rivals for chief suspect in his murder.

'Denise, can you get the earlier bits of this correspondence?'
Karen asked, adding to Charlie, 'That's OK, isn't it? I bet you
anything Sheena used the local internet café for it in case Sir Dan
ever looked at the emails on her own computer. If everything
we've heard is true, he wouldn't have liked all this disloyal chit-
chat between two of his employees about his wife.'

'You're telling me. Any bloke would hate it. But that's for
later. Trevor's more urgent. Get on with the statement.'

Karen took the printout to a spare chair and settled down to
read. The statement, which had obviously been constructed out
of a question-and-answer session, had been signed by Trevor.

Yes, it's true, I did take some money when I was working
for Sir Dan Blackwater, but I was only borrowing it to cover
one month's mortgage payment. My wife, who's freelance, had
been ill for six months by then, with ME, and so we had to do
without her earnings, which was hard. I just needed short-term
help. The bank wouldn't extend my overdraft again, so I made

an electronic transfer of money from the business to my mortgage company. It was easy. Just a few keystrokes and a couple of clicks of the mouse. No one knew. I was going to put it back the next month, long before the audit. No one would ever have known. I have paid it back now. After Sir Dan sacked me, I didn't dare apply for another similar job because I didn't want to risk a bad reference, which could mean the end of my career for ever. So I applied for a job as an independent examiner of charity finance, and I got it. By chance, I was used on the accounts of Clagbourne House late last year, and I could see at once that something was wrong. One huge payment had been made electronically and then withdrawn only hours later. It could have been a simple mistake like one wrong keystroke, but it didn't smell like that. I felt that something was wrong. So I started to look into where the payment had come from and I still haven't found the true source. There are so many cut-outs and dead ends that it has to be deliberate. So two weeks ago I wrote to warn Sir Dan that someone was using his charity as a front, probably for money laundering. I should have simply reported the irregularity, but I wanted to do anything I could for him in this way, to make up a little for what I'd done while I was working for him.

Karen looked up, remembering how Gilbert Tackley had explained the urge of many exiled employees to earn their way back into Sir Dan's favour.

'Does it work? Do you believe it?' Charlie asked.

'The story makes sense so far,' Karen said, trying to see how everything might fit together. 'But I haven't finished it yet. Hang on.'

The final part of the statement ended:

I suggested a meeting so I could explain everything, but I never heard back from him. The first I knew about the details of his death was when you came banging on my office door and told me.

'So you went after Trevor after we had that meeting with Gilbert Tackley?' Karen said, irritated that Charlie hadn't told her anything about this part of the investigation.

''Course I did. I'm looking for people with a grudge against Sir Dan. Big enough to kill him and castrate him. Like you said, could've been part of a macho competition. Trevor contacted Sir Dan eight times in the last week alone. Today I got the evidence to show he came over here to the Island on Friday and I arrested him. You still believe the statement?'

'Everything Trevor says here is coherent and convincing,' Karen said. 'But it's more than possible he's recently invented the story of how he'd always planned to give back the money he stole – as a way of dealing with his own guilt.'

'And the irregularities in the Clagbourne House accounts?'

Karen smiled at him. 'That could be wish fulfilment, too. He so much wanted to see himself as Sir Dan's saviour that he invented the problem, or even set it up himself. With electronic transfers of money being so easy to arrange, he could have spent a morning at his computer shovelling other people's money this way and that, you know, without it ever touching the sides or becoming real to anyone whose accounts he was using. It's clear from his statement that he'd know exactly how to do it.'

'*Does* anyone behave like that? Any known examples of it?' Scepticism made Charlie's voice barbed.

'Some,' Karen said. 'Although I wouldn't say it was exactly common. I'd get a better idea if I could see Trevor and talk to him, find out how his mind works. But this story of the dodgy accounts could explain why Sir Dan wanted to talk to Antony. It might not have had anything to do with Sheena after all. Or Vera. Did Antony tell you any more?'

Charlie nodded. 'He said Sir Dan wanted to find out how easy it would be to get an injunction against an unnamed individual he thought could be harassing his wife. He knew all about injunctions and super injunctions to stop the press reporting, but he'd never taken any action against a single non-media individual.'

'Olga again. He'd do anything to protect her, wouldn't he?'

'Seems like it. A really decent bloke.' He raised his voice: 'Annie? Get Trevor up out of the cells, will you. We'll have another crack at him. Karen, you ready?'

'More or less,' she said. 'But there's a quid pro quo for this.'

'You and your fancy languages. You're being paid. You don't get anything else.' The statement could have been aggressive, but it was accompanied by a broad smile and flashing black eyes. Karen laughed back at him, then let the seriousness of what she wanted overtake everything else.

'I need you to get your friends in the Met to hand over all the unused material in the case of the baby's death.'

Charlie hunched his shoulders, turning away.

'Come on, Charlie! Don't you want to know if there is a connection between that and Sir Dan's murder? Both smothered. Both with the same obvious suspect, who may – or may not – be guilty?'

Charlie's expression was that of someone who hears a siren

wailing in the far distance. He frowned, then shrugged, saying, 'I'll think about it. Trevor first.'

The man who was brought into the interview room didn't fit any of Karen's preconceptions about accountants. He was slim, fit, and good-looking enough to earn a fortune as a model, with sharply defined cheekbones, enormous dark eyes under slanting brows and a perfect nose. His mouth would have made most female supermodels ache with envy. She didn't see how he could be more than thirty-four or -five, if as much.

After the introductions for the tape, Charlie nodded to Karen, who smiled at Trevor.

'How did Sir Dan respond to your letter about the irregularities in the Clagbourne House accounts?'

'He didn't.'

'How did that make you feel?'

Trevor blinked, then folded his beautiful lips together, as though he was determined to conceal something highly confidential. Eventually he let them part and said: 'I told myself it wasn't surprising he didn't want to believe it. We all knew at work that he was devoted to his wife, absolutely besotted, and Clagbourne is primarily her charity. I thought he must be looking into what I'd said, getting some kind of confirmation, and that's what was taking time.'

'So what did you do then?' Karen asked, making a silent note about Sir Dan's famous love for his wife. Could anyone who felt as Sheena had claimed he felt have concealed the truth so completely from his staff and colleagues?

'I started phoning, and I wrote again.'

'Did you know he was planning to take out an injunction, to stop you contacting him or his wife?'

As Karen asked her question, she watched Trevor's expression change from rationality and wariness to something that looked like pure hurt.

'He can't have . . .' he began. 'I mean, he must've known I was only . . . I was trying to make amends for what I'd done.'

'I don't think he did,' Karen said, interested in the naïveté that would allow Trevor to think they would believe he cared so much for Sir Dan's good opinion, even though he'd been sacked three years ago. 'When you were working for him, did you ever have any contact with his wife, with Olga?'

The skin along Trevor's perfect cheekbones flushed a deep cyclamen pink.

'But we've been told she never came to the office.' Charlie's protest made Trevor's colour intensify even more.

'She didn't,' he said, looking from Charlie to Karen and back again to Annie on his other side. 'But once there were some papers he needed, and we hadn't had time to finish them before he had to leave the office for a meeting, before heading out to Farnborough to fly to Switzerland.' He paused, then added with a helpful air, 'You know they have their own jet?'

'We know that, yes,' Charlie said.

'It was agreed that once the figures he needed were ready and checked, I'd take them to Farnborough myself and hand them over.'

'Why not email them?'

'Too sensitive,' Trevor said, without waiting to think. 'Some things just aren't safe, however much you password-protect them.'

'OK. I can believe that,' Charlie said, nodding again to Karen. Trevor took the gesture as an instruction and addressed his next remarks to her.

'When I got there – to the airport – he hadn't arrived. I was shown to the lounge thing they have there for private-jet owners, and she was waiting, alone. Lady Blackwater. Olga.'

'Did you call her by her first name?' Karen was feeling her way towards the source of his deep embarrassment.

'She told me to. She said he'd been held up and had warned her I'd be coming. She said it was a good thing because she was bored. She didn't like hanging about for him on her own. She offered me a drink. Champagne. I remember it still: Perrier Jouët Belle Epoque. Vintage. I looked it up afterwards, and . . .' His voice faltered.

'And thought if they could afford that, they could have afforded to help you with your mortgage payments?' Karen suggested, remembering some of her late husband's wine catalogues and the three-hundred-pound bottle price of the champagne Olga had been drinking.

'More or less,' Trevor said. 'Anyway, she poured me some and made me sit down, and we chatted. We'd finished the bottle by the time Sir Dan arrived, and he was . . .' Again, his internal censor stopped his story.

'He was what?' Charlie demanded.

'Furious. Only for a second or two. But I could see it. There was no doubt at all,' Trevor said. 'He asked me for the papers in the coldest voice I ever heard from anyone. She didn't like it either, and she stroked my arm and told him it wasn't my fault and she'd made me have a drink. Then she got all flirty.' The flush on his face was now the dark purple of drying blood. 'It didn't surprise me. I mean, I've seen it before when wives start resenting the time their blokes spend at work, and they want to show that they're still attractive to other men, but . . .'

'But?' Karen quoted.

'Nothing. Anyway, Sir Dan said to her, very courteously, that their pilot was waiting and she should go ahead and board,' Trevor went on, talking as though he had to work hard to get the words out of his mouth. 'When she'd gone ahead, he turned to me and said, with all the fairness he usually showed, "I don't blame you. But I want you to forget this afternoon ever happened. If I hear any gossip about my wife and what she has just said I will know it came from you. Do you understand me?"'

'And you said?' Karen prompted him, when he stalled again.

'I said that of course I understood him, and of course I wouldn't say anything. I meant it, too.'

'Was that the last you heard from her?' Karen asked and watched him looking from side to side as though he wanted a way out. She knew the answer to the first question, so she tried a different one. 'When did she contact you again, Trevor?'

'After I . . . after I'd left the company. I don't know how she knew because she never took any part in his work. But she did know, and she found my private address and she came round one day. I thought . . . I thought she must have brought the police with her to arrest me for stealing the money from work, but she hadn't. My wife called down from her room, asking who it was at the door. I couldn't tell her. She didn't know about the money or me being sacked or anything, and I was desperate to keep it that way. So I just said I had to nip out for ten minutes but that was all, and I'd be back to do all her rubs and help her to the toilet before she even knew I'd gone.'

He closed his eyes and kept silent for just long enough for Karen to get a clear picture of the way he and his wife must have lived. She could understand the temptation of taking just a little money from people who had so much.

'I grabbed my keys and I went with Olga,' Trevor went on with a doggedness that suggested he was hoping to find some relief in confessing after all this time. 'She'd come in an ordinary black cab, not with one of the office chauffeurs. It must have cost a fortune because we live in Sheen. I mean, it's like an hour-and-a-half journey. More in the rush hour. Anyway, she told the cab to wait and she and I walked along the street. The cherry trees were all in bloom and petals fell down over us both like confetti.' He grimaced, as though the memory provoked physical nausea. Karen was curious, but she waited for him to offer an explanation.

'She said now I wasn't working for Sir Dan any more, why didn't I come and work for her,' Trevor added, which still didn't explain his revulsion.

'What kind of job was she offering?' Charlie asked.

'She didn't say exactly, just that I'd be like a kind of ADC, and I'd be in Switzerland, based in Switzerland anyway, and it would all have to be very confidential. She said she'd provide a house and plenty of support for my wife because I'd have to travel a lot.'

'And?'

'I didn't want it, Chief Inspector.' Trevor had regained a tiny measure of dignity, and his colour was beginning to fade back towards normal.

'Why not?' Charlie said with no emotion or judgment. 'You knew how rich she was. You needed money. Your wife was ill. Why didn't you jump at it?'

'I . . .' Trevor looked towards Karen for help, but this time his answer was far too important for her to risk influencing him. He had to say it himself, and without prompting. With his eyes closed again, and his shoulders so tight they rose to touch the bottom of his earlobes, he went on, 'I remembered what she'd said to Sir Dan about . . . about my eyes, and that. And I thought she . . . I thought she was, you know, like a cougar.'

Now Karen understood the nausea. In connection with the confetti-like cherry-blossom, the sexual advances of a frightening older woman, who had already got him in trouble with his hero, could well make him feel sick.

'It sounds vain, I know,' Trevor added, 'but anyway I couldn't think of any other reason why she'd . . .'

'So what did you do?' Charlie said.

Trevor opened his eyes. 'I told her I couldn't. That I was an accountant and that as soon as I'd got together enough cash to pay Sir Dan back, I would look for another job and earn my passage back to respectability.'

'What did she say?' asked Annie, taking an active part in the interview for the first time. She did not look convinced by any of it.

'She laughed at me and said I was a fool. That I'd crossed a line no one ever gets to re-cross. Once you've gone over, she said, no ordinary employer will ever take a risk on you. Even if I paid it all back, and added more interest than he'd have got anywhere else, Sir Dan would always dislike and mistrust me. I'd never get a reference from him, so I'd never work as an accountant again. She said I was throwing away my only chance to make something of myself or earn enough to help my wife recover.'

'And?' This was Charlie again, not prepared to give the man any time to get his answers prepared.

'She left me standing there in the street, with the cherry-blossom petals all over my hair and my clothes, knowing I had to run back home to Katie, who would be panicking because by then I'd been gone a lot more than ten minutes.' Trevor lay back in his hard chair, breathing like an amateur sprinter at the end of a tough race.

'OK. Fine,' Charlie said, watching him with suspicion. 'Annie will get that typed up for you to sign.'

'*Then* can I go?'

'Not yet. Doctor Taylor, anything more you want to ask Trevor now?'

'Yes,' she said. 'I'm curious about the coincidence. How did you come to be an examiner of the Clagbourne House accounts?'

Trevor leaned towards her, eagerness spreading all over his face. 'I thought it was a test. From Sir Dan. You know how charities get to choose their examiners?'

'I didn't.'

'Oh, right. Well, they do. So I thought he'd deliberately picked me to see whether I'd find the anomaly in the accounts and how I'd deal with it. I thought he was checking up to see if I'd . . . if I . . . if he could, you know, ever trust me again.'

'And that's why you took your question straight to him?' Karen said, making a question of it.

'Absolutely.'

Upstairs in the incident room, Charlie surprised her.

'You can't move back into your flat on the mainland yet,' he said before she'd had time to comment on the interview. 'You do know that, don't you?'

Karen nodded.

'If you meant it about leaving the refuge, you can stay here in my flat, if you like.' He looked over her shoulder, as though to check whether anyone else was listening. When he was sure it was safe, he added, 'I'm not making a move. Another move. You can have the spare room. But you'll be safer here, and I need . . . I need you to be safe, Karen. I can't work properly if I'm worrying over you.'

All her residual anger died. As it left her, she felt a familiar griping in her lower belly. She'd always hated the sensation, and the sticky inconvenience it announced, but now she felt only relief. Freed from the need to make an unmakeable decision, she reached out to touch Charlie, then remembered they were at work and pulled back her hand.

'That would be great,' she said casually. 'But I'll need to get some stuff. My work; essays for marking and things. Can you lend me someone to go with me to the flat, in case anyone *is* watching it? I mean . . .'

'I'll do it myself, but not till this evening. Can you wait a few hours?'

'Fine, but I'll have to nip out to buy one or two things now. Do you need me for anything?'

'Not at the moment.'

'Great,' Karen said. 'I'll pick up something for lunch while I'm out.'

'*Lunch*?' Charlie's voice was almost a squawk. 'What d'you mean, lunch? It's gone three.'

Karen checked her watch, surprised. 'So it has. Well I

haven't had anything and it was an early start. I need to eat, so don't expect to see me back here till quite a bit later. When can I have my car again? If they dumped it by my new house, it must still be here, so . . .'

'We've got it,' Charlie said. 'Still awaiting a full vehicle exam. You can have it soon, but we haven't finished with it yet. In any case, they know it's yours. You can't go driving about until we've got them.'

'Sir!' DC Richard Silver's voice blocked whatever Charlie had been going to say next. He waved at Karen and hurried across to the terminal at which Silver was working.

Karen took advantage of their distraction and slipped into the lavatory to pull on her disguise, to make it safe to go out of the police station to buy tampons and more aspirin, before hailing a taxi to take her out to the Goose Inn. She liked the idea of Charlie's need to protect her, but the compulsion to do everything she could to find useful leads was more urgent even than her fear of the men Dev had sent to watch her.

Chapter 21

Day Six: 3.30 p.m.

Peg was talking to a man perched on one of the stools at the bar, but the moment Karen walked in she abandoned her customer and her bar and came round to the doorway to offer a polite welcome, as though to a stranger.

Pleased that her disguise worked, Karen identified herself and watched first amazement then pleasure cross Peg's face. She took Karen by both arms and peered into her face.

'Are you really all right now, chicken?' she said. 'If I'd known you were in such a state . . . You should have come to me. I could've helped. You didn't have to go and do a thing like that.'

'I'm fine.' Karen pulled back a little way. 'How did you know? And *what* do you know?'

'I know it all, how you . . . I know how they found you at your house over the north-west.'

'Then I don't think you know anything at all.' Karen hoped her voice and expression showed how very far from suicidal she was. 'And it can't have been Charlie who told you. He knows the truth.'

'It wasn't. I haven't seen him since that day he came to pick you up here. But you know how people talk here. I heard you'd tried . . . tried to kill yourself. If it's not true, I'm . . .' Peg's familiar dazzling smile flashed. 'You know. What would you like now? A drink? Some food? Your usual table's free by the fire.'

'Thanks.' Karen smiled back, even though she didn't feel particularly happy. She'd wanted to find Peg alone. 'Glass of Sauvignon Blanc please and some of your stuffed mushrooms, if you've got any left.'

'Won't be a minute.' Peg's smile flashed out again. The man at the bar was looking at Karen with direct hostility, clearly believing the price of his drink should have bought him Peg's undivided attention.

Tough, Karen thought, heading off to the loo first. By the time she came back, shivering and aching, she was glad of the flames. She'd taken two of the aspirin, so the pain should ease within twenty minutes or so. She had assumed that when this moment came, the loss of all her heavily rationalized fears of pregnancy would not only make her feel like celebrating but also clear her mind and show her exactly what to do about Will and Charlie. She'd been wrong. She couldn't have felt less like celebrating, and her mind was as muddled as it had ever been.

Will's arrival on the Island made everything look different. Clearly he had not abandoned her after all. Something his sister had said in the hospital seemed important to remember, but Karen couldn't bring it to the front of her mind. And she couldn't be the first to get in touch; not after what he'd said about not wanting to commit himself to her.

Peg appeared with a tray containing an enormous dewy glass of white wine and a hot plate laden with mushrooms stuffed with garlic, Parmesan and parsley. She put it down in front of Karen.

'Thanks,' Karen said. 'I know you're busy, but have you got a second?'

'What is it?'

'We can talk properly later,' Karen said, 'but as you know nearly everything that happens here on the Island, can you point me in the direction of any ham radio buffs?'

Peg's beautiful face looked blank. She looped some of her long, dark-blonde hair behind her ear, showing off a dangling chandelier earring made from seed pearls and tiny aquamarines.

'You know,' Karen added. 'The kind of people who listen in to conversations and police frequency radio and that kind of thing.'

'Why are you asking me?' Peg had rarely sounded so suspicious.

'Because I need to find out about the content of some very long phone calls that were made from and to the Island seven days ago. So you *do* know someone?'

Peg looked over her slim shoulder at the drinker by the bar, who was leaning over his pewter tankard as though he was almost asleep.

'There's a retired farmer, up on the downs above Freshwater. He . . . After his wife died, he went a bit weird, sold their land but kept the buildings. Pretty run down they are too. He kind of camps out in them. He and my ex saw a lot of each other, then. They both liked CB radio, but they listened in to other stuff too. They hid a giant antenna in an old grain silo, and they used to talk about how one day they'd overhear something really juicy they could sell to the papers and live off for the rest of their lives. I don't know if the old boy's still at it, but you could always try him.'

Peg scuffled in the wide pocket of her blue-striped butcher's apron for a piece of scrap paper and a pencil stub, on which she scribbled a name and address.

'He doesn't go out much so he'll likely be there. Don't phone; just go. And be careful because he doesn't like people.'

'Thanks.' Karen's smile was more genuine now. 'I knew you'd be able to help. If he doesn't like people, I'd better take him some kind of present. Does he drink? What does he like?'

Peg's always dazzling smile widened until it filled almost her whole face.

'Green Chartreuse,' she said, laughing at the very idea.

Karen had no difficulty joining in. The thought of an elderly farmer, living on his own in semi-ruined buildings and listening in to other people's conversations while he cracked open a bottle of the expensive, highly sweet, wormwood-tasting green liqueur was hard to credit.

'Have you got a bottle I can buy?' she said.

'I have.' Peg smiled. 'Not much call for it here. How will you get over to Freshwater?'

Karen shuddered at the likely price of a cab right across the Island and back again. She was frustrated by the knowledge of her own Subaru Justy, waiting in the police car pound.

'I'd better have a taxi,' she said, hoping that if she found what she wanted she might be able to persuade Charlie to pay her back.

'Wouldn't it be better to borrow my car?' Peg said. 'You must have insurance to drive other people's cars.'

'Only third party,' Karen said. 'What if I drive it over a cliff – or into a wall?'

'You planning to do either, chicken?'

'No.'

'I trust you. I need it back by six when my bartender comes in and I go and pick up Johnnie. Can you manage that? You should get there in, what? Forty minutes or so. Same coming back.'

'You're incredibly generous. If you really mean it, I'd better get going.' Karen looked at her huge, misted glass of white wine. 'Can you keep that in your fridge for me? I can't drink it if I'm driving someone else's car.'

While Peg went to fetch the car key and put Karen's wine-glass in her fridge, she herself ate the delectable mushrooms, crudely wiping chunks of torn-off bread in the garlicky juices left on the plate, not prepared to waste anything so delicious.

'There's no satnav,' Peg said, as she handed over the old-fashioned Ford Fiesta keys, 'so I've written you some directions. So long as you take the turn by the ruined barn, you'll be fine. There's nowhere else to go once you've got the right lane. He's called Fred Campbell. Good luck.'

'Will he greet me with a loaded shotgun?' Karen asked, trying to decode the full meaning of Peg's 'good luck'.

'More likely he won't answer at all. Just keep on banging on his door, and try the sheds too. He shifts a lot of his radio stuff from place to place, pretending he's operating behind enemy lines in a war and that they'll be sending sniffer dogs and detector vans after him. No one cares what he does, but he'd die rather than admit that.'

Karen didn't think much as she drove west across the centre of the Island, except how wonderful it was to be driving a car no watcher could identify, and how extraordinary the low red sun looked as it sank towards the horizon in the west. But when she passed the turning down to her own house, she shivered.

Would she ever be able to see it as anything but the scene of her near-death in a heroin overdose? One day she'd have to go back, not least to find the Elephant Man and thank him for saving her life. And then she would have to decide what to do about the place. Could she ever live there, even if Charlie did manage to get Dev and his gang convicted and imprisoned?

Traffic was building up behind her and she realized she had slowed down to less than twenty miles an hour. Flushing with embarrassment, she pressed down on the accelerator and raised a hand to her mirror, hoping the driver behind her would read the gesture as an apology.

Freshwater was not far from here. The drive shouldn't take more than another twenty minutes. At the first traffic light in Newport, she picked up Peg's directions from the empty passenger seat, and checked the landmarks she should expect. The mention of Totland Bay brought back better memories from much further back.

As the amber light came on below the red and she put the car in gear again, she thought of the hot afternoons at Totland with her grandmother and her brother, Aidan. They'd always had toffee apples at the beach, and she could feel the hardness of the caramel breaking under her teeth, then the shocking sourness of the apple beneath. Once or twice she'd tried to throw away the apple after she'd nibbled off all the hard caramel, but each time Aidan had caught her and made her eat every scrap. Once that had included the core, and she'd been afraid he'd make her eat the stalk too. Even he had balked at that.

Finding herself able to laugh at the memory of her total subservience to her big brother gave her a terrific kick. She'd loved him and she'd run about after him like an acolyte, turning everything he did to her into a benefit because to think of him as a cruel bully would have been unbearable. There was freedom in facing the truth at last.

She flicked on the indicator and turned left into a lane bordered with broken-down fences covered in ivy, just as Peg had described. There was enough light still to see that much, but the sky was already grey and it wouldn't be long before Karen would need her headlights.

As she drove, wincing for the car's suspension as it bucketed over rocks and ruts in the lane, she tried to decide how to present herself to the reclusive farmer. It would be too much to hope he'd once known her grandmother, so it was probably best not even to try him with that.

A dog was barking, and it sounded very large and very aggressive. Karen shivered. She hated everything about the animals some people kept to scare those around them. As she brought the car to a stop and pulled up the handbrake, she wound down her window, trying to gauge the position, as well as the size and type of dog. The sound didn't seem to be coming any closer, so she wound the window back up again, opened the door and put one leg out of the car.

A tremendous dirty brownish form rocketed towards her, as the barking intensified into a frenziedly aggressive roar. She brought her leg back into the car and slammed the door shut, just before the nude-looking ugly face of the Staffordshire terrier reached her thigh. The smell of its meaty breath filled the car.

The dog withdrew for an instant, then flung its body at the car door with such force Karen thought the panel must bend. Her hands were sweating and shaking as she crammed down the button that would lock the door, then she scrambled over the gear lever and into the passenger seat. The dog whacked the driver's door again, throwing its whole weight into the attack.

This can't be simply guarding, Karen thought. Maybe the old farmer has died and his dog has been starving ever since.

She dared to look as it withdrew for one more assault on the car and knew her guess had to be wrong. This was a well-fed dog.

'Huaaargh.' The incomprehensible human shout made her head jerk round away from the dog.

She saw a man in shabby loose brown corduroy trousers, tied around the waist with thick string, and a jacket that looked as if it was made of sacking, worn over a dark red polo-necked sweater with a huge ragged hole in the front. A heavy chain dangled from one hand. He shouted again. The staffy cast one more malevolent look at the car, and Karen herself, then ran over to the man, who bent down and clipped the chain to its collar. Straightening up, he waited.

Knowing how easy it would be for him to slip the chain off again, Karen was sweating as she got out of the car and walked towards him. She kept her hands held out at either side, the left gripping the bottle of Green Chartreuse by its neck. She wasn't trying to prove she wasn't armed, but it was the only way she could think of to express her lack of threat. As she neared the two of them, the dog strained forwards, barking again. She saw the power of its jaws and the density of its tremendous shoulders and tried not to flinch.

'What d'you want?' shouted the man when she was only twenty feet away. 'And why're you driving Peg's car?'

Aha, thought Karen. That's why he didn't set the dog on me. Peg's my passport here.

'She lent it to me,' she called back. 'Because she knew I needed help and she thought you might give it to me. I brought you some Green Chartreuse.'

'Help? What kind of help?'

The dog's barking quietened into a kind of menacing whine, but it didn't sit or relax any of its fierce alertness.

'I need to know what people were saying on their mobile phones seven days ago,' Karen said, without giving any reason. 'Peg thought you might . . .'

The man took a step forwards and the dog started straining again, as though hoping he might be allowed a bite.

'Who are you?'

'My name's Karen Taylor.' She remembered her old-lady disguise, and she wished she'd at least pulled off the wig. How was he going to believe her, looking like this? 'I'm working with the police.'

Now it was the man's turn to flinch.

'But I'm not a police officer,' she said hastily. 'I'm a psychologist. They don't know I'm here. Only Peg knows that. A man was killed over on the other side of the Island, and I think it's because of something he knew and passed on to someone else. I think the evidence we need is in a call he made the day before he died, or the day of his death, and the only person alive to know is his killer – unless you've got a record of what they said.'

The dog whined again. Its owner suddenly lost patience and whacked its backside with the length of spare chain. The dog shrank against his leg and pissed all down it.

'Filthy beast,' he shouted, pulling away and hauling on the chain to drag the dog towards an old mounting block that had a rusted iron ring sunk into its top. He tied the chain to that. Karen hoped the knot would hold.

'You better come in then, hadn't you?' he shouted at her above the dog's roaring.

Karen followed him into a shed, three of whose walls were more gap than brick, like a particularly hideous kind of lace. The fourth wall, holding up the rest, was in fact the side of his house. Ivy had glued itself to every available surface and thrust its tendrils through gaps in the window frames and around the door. A kind of workbench had been made of an old door balanced on quantities of bricks. On it were bank after bank of receivers, speakers and computers. She put the bottle down in the only spare space.

'I brought you this,' she said. 'Peg told me you like it.'

'You're talking about Sir Daniel Blackwater, I s'pose,' said the old man, with the soft familiar 'oi' sound very clear. 'I been waiting for someone to come.'

'What did you hear?' Karen asked, trying not to sound too eager.

'He phoned . . .' the farmer broke off, just as Karen's own phone shrilled. He grinned at her, displaying several gaps in his yellowed gnashers. 'Better take that, hadn't you?'

Karen saw on the screen that it was Charlie calling her.

'It'll wait,' she said, shoving the phone back in her bag. 'What did you hear?'

'Him telling his wife someone was hijacking their business. Someone he called a Trojan Horse,' he said. 'I reckon the cops need to go after that.'

'I think they might have got there before you,' Karen said. 'Have you got a recording of the call? A disk or memory stick or something?' She looked around the ramshackle shed, trying not to breathe too deeply as she smelled damp and mould.

He pushed his way past festoons of cobweb, making sticky dust fly slowly through the gloom before settling on every available surface.

'Or a tape, maybe?' Karen added, without much hope. 'It could help make their case.'

He bent down, grabbed an old biro with a promotional message printed down one side in gold, and wrote something on a torn piece of paper, which he held out to her.

'My email,' he said. 'You take that to the cops and tell 'em to contact me. If they make it worth my while, I'll maybe let 'em have what I've got.'

'The police don't pay,' Karen began, just as her phone rang again.

'They can,' Fred said. 'They pay snouts, don't they? And experts like you. I can be an expert snout.'

'You'd be lucky to get away without being prosecuted for illegal hacking and recording of phone calls,' Karen said.

'Luckily they know nothing about you – yet. If you give me a copy of the recording, I won't say where I got it.' She put the phone to her ear. 'Yes, Charlie?'

'Where the fuck are you?'

'I'm busy.'

'Get your arse back here asap,' Charlie shouted, before cutting the connection.

'I just had my orders.' Karen smiled at Fred. 'I've got to go. Am I going to send the police here?'

The old man shuffled his feet and looked at his banks of machines, then back at Karen.

'How do I know I can trust you?'

'You don't.' She smiled. 'But you have more to lose than I do. So: are you going to give me the disk or am I going to tell the cops?'

The thinning of his lips and narrowing of his eyes told her how much he hated her. And then he looked towards the dog. Karen's throat closed and she had to cough to make herself breathe again. She was between him and the dog. She hoped she was strong enough to stop him getting to it to loosen the chain.

'Peg knows where I am,' she reminded him.

'And she'll know where you are if I find out you lied,' he said.

'True. So, you're going to give me a copy of the recording?'

He turned away, scuffled on the dusty table, found a disk and inserted it into one of the machines. Karen waited. After four very long minutes, he extracted the disk and handed it to her. She had no way of knowing whether there was anything on it at all, but she'd done as much as she could.

'Thanks,' she said, taking it. 'I hope your dog's chain is safe.'

'Safe enough,' he said, and turned away to fiddle with the dials on two of his bits of kit. An old-fashioned screeching whistle emerged, reminding Karen of her grandmother's hearing aid. 'But don't look into his eyes as you go past. Drives him mad, that.'

'Why did you go charging off like that?' Charlie said as they set off for Fountain Quay. He sounded angrier than ever, but she knew what was really driving him. 'When I *told* you how I need to see you're safe.'

'I had an idea,' Karen said without apologizing. 'So I used Max's disguise. I knew I'd be OK. Let's go so that we can get back to work asap.'

Charlie produced a reluctant grin. 'Don't fucking do it again. I've sent for one of the local uniforms to meet us with a car over at Scumpton. Just in case anyone's watching your place.'

'So you haven't yet got either of the men in the E-fits?' Karen said. 'Or Dev?'

'Not yet.'

'And Olga: have you talked to her about Trevor?'

Charlie closed his eyes and breathed deeply, like an amateur attempting meditation to cool his temper.

'Annie's with her now, with Denise taking notes.'

'And Mrs Brown, the housekeeper? Now you know she and Sheena have been in cahoots all along, and she's the only person around who knows all the security numbers and passwords for the alarm system, so she must . . .'

'She's on Annie's list too. And before you ask: yes, I have got the unused material from the investigation into Sheena's baby's death. You can see it when we get back with your stuff tonight and I've got you safely under my eye.'

The hovercraft subsided on to its dock at Southampton, with a long sigh and a ruffling of its dark rubber skirts. The two of them queued up to disembark. A brawny uniformed officer was waiting beside a small marked police car. Charlie introduced him as PC Reg Fields. Karen shook his hand, then got in the back, while Charlie took the front passenger seat.

When they reached her building, everything was quiet. For once the street door was safely locked. Karen undid it and called the lift. Even though Charlie always walked the five flights up to her flat when he was on his own, he seemed happy enough to wait for the lift this evening. As it bounced to a stop at last and the doors parted, they saw two people inside.

'Hi, Karen!' said her first-floor neighbour. 'Are you OK?'

'I'm fine, thanks, Simon,' she said, smiling first at him and then at his girlfriend. 'I'm sorry for all the coming and going.'

'Oh, don't worry about it. We've all had parties. And you obviously had a lot to celebrate. Sounded like quite a riot last night. I hope the breakages were worth it. We did appreciate the way you turned off the music at midnight.'

The two of them were laughing as they pushed past Karen and her small group. She looked at Charlie.

'Party?' he echoed, with enough menace in his voice to show he shared all her misgivings. 'You want to wait down here while Reg and I . . . ?'

'I'm coming with you.' Karen shut the lift doors on the three of them and pressed button 5. 'Even if someone was ransacking my flat last night, they're not going to be there now.'

They reached the top floor moments later and saw that the

front door of the flat was firmly closed. Charlie held out his hand for her keys. Reluctantly Karen handed them over and waited while he first listened, then silently inserted the Chubb key in the lower lock. That turned easily enough and he used the Yale, too, before pushing at the door.

It moved a foot, then stuck.

'Help me, Reg.'

The two of them put their shoulders to the door and shoved on a count of three. At last the door yielded and they stumbled forwards into the gap, tripping over the body.

Chapter 22

Day Six: 10.00 p.m.

'Vera!' Karen's exclamation hurt her throat.

She put up a hand to cradle her neck and looked down at the swollen discoloured face of the beautiful seventeen-year-old. Memories of her own voice banged around in her head, telling Vera what she should do, ordering her to ignore her fears and her certainty that to talk would mean she'd die.

Misused in every way possible, Vera had kept her nerve and survived through two years of more suffering than most people would face in a lifetime. Now she had been killed. Guilt bent Karen's hands into claws at her side. She knew this could have happened without her intervention. She also knew that she could tell herself the killing wasn't her fault a thousand times a day, but she would never be able to believe it. All she could do was fight to get justice done.

No, she thought, facing herself with brutal honesty, it's not justice. It's too late for that. I want vengeance for every single thing that was done to Vera. And to me.

Trying to distract herself from everything Vera must have

felt before merciful death stopped her feeling anything any longer, Karen concentrated on the technicalities and saw that the ligature around her purple neck was made from electrical flex. As Karen peered sideways round the swelling, she caught sight of a plug dangling from one end of the flex and from the other, her own hair straighteners.

Charlie, who was kneeling beside the body, looked up. 'You sure it's Vera?'

'Completely. I've seen quite a lot of her since I fell flat on my face chasing her. Who . . . ? Sorry. You can't know who did this. Maddie, at the refuge, said Vera had gone when I phoned there yesterday. But why is she *here*? Could she have found something and come to tell me?'

Reg was on his radio, calling in the discovery to his control room.

'Maybe. And maybe someone was waiting for you and made a mistake, Karen.' Charlie's voice was tougher than she'd ever heard it. 'Killed the wrong slim blonde woman. Fuck it! I'm getting you out of here and back to the Island asap. You won't be able to take anything with you tonight. If Max wants you marking essays that's just tough. The CSIs will have to go right through everything here before you can touch any of it. We'll have to talk to your neighbours too, find out more about this so-called party.' Charlie straightened up and raised his voice: 'Reg?'

'Sir.'

'Karen wait outside. But don't go downstairs. OK? Stick in the corridor. And leave the front door open. Don't touch anything.'

She walked backwards through the front door and went to

lean her elbows on the high sill of the window opposite the lift. From here, she could see the docks and the Island, and the lit-up traffic on both land and sea. None of it made much impression. She had no space in her head to think of anything except Vera and what had been done to her.

Karen remembered all Vera's certainty that she could get herself to a university to take her maths degree and live a normal life again, undisturbed by the men who were determined to make money from selling her body or the other men – like Stella's Martin – who thought it was acceptable to rent it for their own transitory pleasure.

'Men,' Karen whispered to herself, thinking of the minds behind the trafficking, and something else she thought she remembered one of Dev's men saying. 'Or women?'

The idea of any woman forcing others, younger and more vulnerable, into the sex trade seemed too cruel to believe, but Karen wasn't naïve enough to think it never happened. There were plenty of female traffickers on the international watch-lists she'd consulted.

Karen thought of the people who might or might not be monitoring her internet traffic and decided she'd be happy for any of them to see what she was going to do now. Her laptop was in her bag as usual. Charlie wanted her here but not involved in his officers' search of her flat. She might as well work while she waited for him.

The windowsill was too high for comfortable typing and so she planted herself on the top stair of the flight that curled around the lift, with her feet on the second step, balancing her laptop on her knees, and began to search the websites that dealt with men and women wanted for their crimes in the sex trade, searching for any names and faces that were at all familiar.

The lift whined and she felt its weight move in the shaft beside her. She listened and heard the unmistakable sounds of a team of Charlie's colleagues, come to assess the crime scene and interview her, as the householder, whose fingerprints would almost certainly be on the hair straighteners and their flex. She braced herself, grateful for his presence and the knowledge that it would stop them treating her as a lying suspect.

Charlie took Karen away less than an hour later and they barely spoke on the short hovercraft trip across the Solent. The water was livelier than usual and the ride a lot more bumpy. Back in his flat, feeling as distant and nauseated as she so often had after a drive in her grandmother's smelly old Ford, she followed him into the bedroom where they had made love. He didn't touch her, merely said she should make herself at home and he would bring her a cup of tea in a minute. This time, he'd had the heating on for long enough to make the ambient temperature perfectly comfortable.

Karen watched him leave the room, then looked all round it and out towards the sea. To her relief there was a heavy mist tonight and the sea had none of the lace-edged satiny look that had seemed so entrancing. She walked up and down the room, knowing she was far too wired to sleep but probably too tired to do anything useful. A memory teased her, of his telling her about some important information he had for her on his laptop, but she couldn't pin down what it was.

'I thought you'd be in bed by now,' he said, striding back into the room with a single mug of tea ten minutes later. He put the mug down on the bedside table. 'Finding Vera's body like that can't have been easy.'

'No,' Karen said, thinking of all the ways she might have described how it had been. 'Not easy' didn't come close.

'When I think how cleverly she'd managed her flight before,' she added, 'and how if it hadn't been for me making her risk herself again she'd still be alive, I . . .'

She wished she could burst into tears, but this was far too important for such an easy kind of solace. The only thing that was going to help was identifying the mind behind all the planning and brutality that had led to Sir Dan's death, and Vera's, and Karen's own assault. It was a mind full of creativity and self-discipline, imagination, fury, and brutality.

'I'm too edgy to sleep,' she said to Charlie, and felt her memory opening up with the words. 'You said you'd let me see the unused stuff from the original investigation into Sheena's baby's death. Can I have it now?'

He frowned and took a step towards her. 'Karen, you have to get some rest. Look at the stuff in the morning. You won't . . .'

'Don't *you* start telling me what to do,' she said, with the irritation making her voice much spikier than usual; louder too. 'I've *said* I can't sleep yet. I might as well do something useful. Even if I'm not at my best, I can't do any harm by looking.'

He hesitated. She saw how heavy his eyelids looked and some of her impatience disappeared. 'Come on, Charlie. Hand it over, and get off to bed. You're the one who's knackered, and I know you've got to start again first thing tomorrow.'

'Have it your own way,' he said as though he was still angry, but there was a hint of smile in his eyes as he brought his laptop and set it up on the table in the window. He bent over it, clicking and tapping; then he pulled right away from it.

'Here you are. See how I trust you. Don't stray beyond those files, will you?'

'You know I won't,' she said, barely able to refrain from stroking his exhausted face. 'Get off to bed. If I find anything, I'll leave you a note. Night.'

He looked as though he might try to kiss her, but in the end he didn't, just wheeled round and walked out.

Karen moved the tea so that even if she knocked it over, she couldn't flood his laptop or her own. She pulled hers out of its bag and switched it on, reaching for her mug as the computer went through all its normal checks. The first sip of tea made her gasp. Charlie must have left the bag in the hot water for much longer than she would have. This was so strong the tannin scraped at the skin of her palate. But it gave her almost as much buzz as an espresso and she drank greedily, staring at the screen over the thick pottery rim of the mug.

She waited until Charlie had had time to get to sleep, then she slid Fred Campbell's disk into the side of her laptop, turned the volume low and began to listen as a crackly but vigorous voice emerged from the tiny speakers:

'Olga? Me. Just wanting to make sure everything's all right for your flight tomorrow.'

'But of course, Dan, my darling.' Olga's husky voice sounded full of affection. 'I can't wait to see you. And I'm sure we can get all this sorted out. It seems incredible to me, absolutely incredible, that anyone could have put some

kind of Trojan horse into the work we are doing at
Clagbourne House. Who would be interested? Why would
they care enough to do such a thing?'

'That's what we need to find out. The first thing is to
break the trust and cut off the funding and get our names
right away from the charity before the balloon goes up.
Which it will. That has to be part of the plan.'

'But whose plan? Dan, darling, why would anyone . . . ?'

'Plenty of people want to discredit us, my love. Could be
political, or someone planning another raid on the business. Anyone. That's why we've got to shut everything
down right away, then investigate.'

'What about the girls? They are too vulnerable to
abandon. You must not just send them away, Dan. Not on
supposition alone. Only if . . . only when you have proof
that one of them is involved in using Clagbourne House as
a front for something illegal.'

'We can't take the risk of waiting. We can find somewhere else for them, on a temporary basis. That won't be
hard. There are plenty of refuges of one sort and another
around the country. As I told you, I've asked Antony to
come to the house at lunchtime on Saturday with all the
necessary documents to revoke the trust. I'll need you
there, too, to countersign the papers. I know you don't like
the Island in winter, but this is too urgent to . . .'

'But why now? And why won't you tell me who has
been bothering you with all this stuff about hijacks and
Trojans and so on, making you so worried when you have
much more important things to occupy you?'

'That doesn't matter. What does matter,' his voice

continued, 'is that something is very badly wrong at
Clagbourne House. Neither of us can afford to be used by
criminals, however unknowingly, or to deal with the kind
of press attention that will follow if it becomes public. We
have to pre-empt that: find out exactly who is doing
precisely what and get them into the hands of the law. But
the funding is the first thing. Antony can help advise on our
legal position while he's here. Then we can then take what
we know to the police.'

The voices stopped. As simple as that, Karen thought. She
tried to see how she could share the disk with Charlie without
jeopardizing any future trial. The recording had been made
illegally and she'd had no right to acquire it. Somehow she had
to think of a way of getting the information to him without
specifying how she'd got it.

While she tried to come up with something, she extracted
the disk and shut down her laptop. Reaching for his, she set to
work on all the unused evidence from the investigation into the
death of Sheena's baby.

Four hours later, Karen had two blurred CCTV pictures of
elderly women on her screen. Both were bent over wheeled
walking frames at the entrance to the small park where the
baby had died. There were no cameras inside the park itself;
only this one, perched on the notice board that gave the opening times and the local bye-laws, recording those who came
and went.

Karen wasn't surprised the police hadn't bothered with
these photographs at the time. If she herself hadn't recently

been disguised by an old-fashioned permed grey wig and instructed to limp arthritically as she leaned on her stick, she would probably have missed their significance too.

She grabbed a sheet of paper and noted down the reference number of the file, before clicking back to a statement an investigating officer had taken from one of the children who had been playing in the park on the day Sheena's baby had died.

'I didn't see no one go near the baby's pram except for the old woman who was stroking the dogs and talking to all the babies. The foreign one.'

'Are you sure she talked to this baby?'

'Yes.'

No wonder no one took that seriously, Karen thought, as she added the statement reference to her note, drew a long dash and then wrote: *See if you can get this photograph enhanced. I think the wig is fake, the clothes are fancy dress, and the walking frame's a theatrical prop. I think this is the woman who was following Sheena and the baby and took her chance when Sheena fell asleep on the bench, smothered the baby with its own pillow, then turned its body so that it was face down.*

Karen switched off Charlie's machine, then rolled herself up in his duvet and slept.

Next morning, over breakfast of black instant coffee and stale, soggy Ryvita smeared with the last scrapings from a jar of ancient, crystallized honey, Karen asked Charlie if his colleague from SOCA had come up with anything from the interviews at Clagbourne House.

'Nothing relevant to our enquiry.'

'So it's down to us. Did you see my note? Can you get that photograph from the files on Sheena's case enhanced for me?'

'Doubt if it'd be worth the money.' Charlie poured more coffee. 'But I can try, if you've got a good reason for wanting it.'

Something in the way he spoke warned Karen that he was too preoccupied to concentrate on any of her ideas.

'What's bugging you, Charlie?'

'We've picked up a man we think is Vera's "Dev".'

'*What*? Charlie, that's amazing. How? Who? Where?' Karen sucked the last of the honey off the end of her knife, too relieved to care about her manners.

The possibility that the man in charge of her assailants was now in a cell took away a lot of the terror that had gone everywhere with her since her return to consciousness in hospital.

'A sharp-eyed PC in Dover spotted him, driving on to a car ferry. Bloke pays attention to his work and will go far – unless he shows up too many less effective senior officers.' Charlie laughed. 'Watching for a particular terrorist suspect, he notices a Merc with a registration plate that looks dodgy and familiar. Turns out on checking to be the one from the stolen red Fiesta that was used on the white van with the two carpenters Mrs Brown admitted to the Blackwaters' house the day before Sir Dan was killed.'

'How could Dev be so stupid?' Karen asked. 'He must have known you'd have a record of the registration plates.'

'Probably panicked when he saw he'd killed Vera at your flat instead of you. Maybe he had the usual low opinion of traffic cops and thought he'd get away with it more easily than nicking a new car or plates,' Charlie said. 'Whatever. Dev was

brought back here to the Island overnight. He's been proc-
essed. A brief's due to arrive in ten minutes. You ready to see
if you can identify his voice?'

'You bet.'

Charlie put both hands on her shoulders and held her still,
about eighteen inches from his face. His eyes moved slowly as
he examined her.

'How's your mind now?' he asked, letting her go and moving
back. 'In hospital you weren't sure your memories were real.
What kind of guarantees can you give me now?'

'I'm confident, if not absolutely certain – if that makes
sense,' Karen said, fighting for a legalistic exactitude because
only that, she felt, could keep the memory of panic from rising
up again and making her doubt herself. 'Obviously I can't
guarantee anything, but I'm sure that, if this man is one of the
ones who talked while I was blindfolded and handcuffed, I will
recognize his voice.'

He watched her in silence for a moment, then said: 'Great.
Let's get going – unless you want more coffee.'

'One more slug,' she said, needing the caffeine. 'Thanks.'

Karen drank the last of the horrible coffee, wondering
whether to share with him the new – incredible – suspicions of
Olga's part in the story, which had come to her since she read
the files on the death of Sheena's baby.

'Charlie?'

'Yeah?'

'Have you wondered why Olga hasn't said anything to you
about Trevor and the suspicions he took to Sir Dan?'

'Mebbe she didn't know about them.'

'I don't think that works. Think about it: Sir Dan summoned

her and told her Antony Quiggly would be coming to lunch. She must have wanted to know why. It wasn't a regular occurrence. Sir Dan must have told her something, so why hasn't she said anything to us?'

'What are you getting at?'

'Maybe she's scared,' Karen said, wanting to steer him to see it for himself so that he was more likely to believe it. 'Maybe if we could talk to her again and tell her that Dev is now safely in custody – and talking – that could be enough to free her to tell you what she knows. She has to have some idea of what's been going on.'

Charlie took his time thinking through the implications, then nodded. 'Makes sense. Get your coat, while I stuff these in the cupboards and then let's go.'

Karen pulled on her flying jacket and leaned against the kitchen doorway while he cleared up.

'You got any ideas about exactly what is going on?' he asked over his shoulder.

'It's way outside my competence,' Karen said, amused to see that at some level he knew what she was doing, drip-feeding her suspicions into his mind, 'but if you really want to know, I think that – whoever they are – they're distorting the original purpose of the charity, so that although they *are* collecting the reluctant prostitutes from the saunas, massage parlours and lap-dancing clubs, their motive isn't rescue but the ruin of rival businesses. I think when those ravishing young women leave Clagbourne House some – if not all – of them go back to doing their old work, but now for Dev and his boss. Vera told me it was the tough women, who looked as though they could protect themselves, who were picked. I think it's even possible that Dev's boss is looking to fill more senior roles in a burgeoning sex trade. That's why I wanted to know what SOCA had discovered.'

'Senior roles, like what?' Charlie had turned, his hands dripping with foamy water, so that he could face her. He was frowning as though he didn't believe a word, but this time he wasn't trying to stop her sharing her ideas.

'To collect the girls from their homes in Eastern Europe in the first place, bring them here, manage the clubs, help build the empire.'

Charlie put the last of the cutlery on the draining board, dried his hands and pulled his leather jacket over his shirt.

'Let's go.'

Chapter 23

Day Seven: 10.00 a.m.

Karen sat in one of the interview rooms, facing DC Silver and Charlie, as they played tapes of a whole series of male voices with a variety of un-English accents. At first she was too tense to recognize any of them, but on the third round she felt her heart beating much faster and harder than usual.

She listened until the end of the recording, then looked across the table to say, 'Could you play number eight again, please?'

Neither man was unprofessional enough to show any sign of pleasure, but there was an extra watchfulness about them that made her think she could have picked out Dev's voice. She listened again, and once more, then nodded.

'That's him. That's the man who stood over me while I was tied to the bed and told them not to waste acid on me because you'd never find me in time before the heroin overdose killed me.'

'So, those bits of glass left no scars then,' Gilda said cheerfully a little less than an hour later. She looked closely at Karen's face as she stood beside Charlie in the hall at Clagbourne House. 'You must be very healthy.'

Sunlight was pouring in through the open sitting room door, and the scent of hyacinths still filled the whole building. Breathing it in, hearing the gentle domestic sounds of a washing machine sloshing in the distance, along with kitchen clattering, and soft cheerful female talk, Karen couldn't help doubting her own ideas about what was really going on here.

Charlie was glaring at her. She nodded briefly, regained some of her sense of being part of the investigation rather than a victim, and turned to thank Gilda with an unwavering smile.

'It's down to your neat work with the tweezers and the disinfectant,' Karen said, wondering how much Gilda knew about the men who provided the muscle at Clagbourne House. Could she really be the kindly innocent woman she appeared? 'I know perfectly well that if I'd left those bits of filthy glass in my skin while I got myself home, I'd be a mass of infected lumps and bumps by now. I owe you.'

'It was nothing,' Gilda said, smiling easily at them both. She looked as wholesome and practical as ever, and her clothes were impeccably clean and pressed. 'What can I do for you both this morning?'

'Just a small thing,' Charlie said, taking the photograph out of his pocket. 'I'm sorry to bother you. We're on our way to see Lady Blackwater, and I just wanted to check some details of this bloke with you first. Have you got his employment records here?'

Gilda took the A5 print of the man with the scarred nose and pulled up the spectacles she wore on a plastic chain around her neck.

'That's Pavel,' she said at once, showing no anxiety whatsoever. She let the glasses drop against her bosom again. 'His file will be in the office. Would you like to come with me?'

'Why not?' Charlie took the print back. 'Pavel what?'

'Dankovitch. Some of the girls called him Donkey, but he didn't mind.'

Karen wondered whether that was because he knew what 'hung like a donkey' meant.

'Always popular with the girls is Donkey.' Gilda's tone was cosy enough to suggest that she did not know, which seemed odd. 'I often wish he worked full time instead of just putting in a few hours here and there when he feels like it.'

'What else does he do?' Karen asked casually, as though the question was trivial. 'I mean when he's not here?'

'Building work mainly. And goes back home a fair amount.' Gilda showed them into her sunny office, which overlooked a neat yard where wet sheets billowed off rows of washing lines. 'You know how they come over here to work under EU laws and then go home again when they've had enough, or made enough cash, or someone in the family needs them. Yes, here we are.'

She took a sheet of paper from a fat red cardboard file. 'We do it all by the book, you know, record everything we pay, even when it's to freelancers who take their fees in cash. He was last here a few days before your first visit with those people from SOCA.'

'So you'll have a home address then?' Charlie said, giving no indication to Gilda that the timing of 'Pavel's' departure held any interest for him at all. 'If you do it by the book.'

'Oh, yes.' Gilda turned to another file, copied some

information down on a piece of paper torn from a spiral note-book and handed it over.

'What work does he do when he's here?' Charlie clearly wanted everything pinned down before anyone suggested to Gilda that discretion could be in her best interests.

Gilda's smile looked a little self-conscious. 'We call it house maintenance, which fits with his building experience, but in fact it's security. Because of the places these girls have been held in, and the kind of men who've run their lives, we have to be sure we can keep them safe. All our "maintenance men" are fully qualified and registered security guards.'

'I see,' Karen said. 'Did he have any other nicknames besides Donkey?'

'No. Except from one of the girls, who's Russian. She did sometimes call him Pasha. I gather that's the usual diminutive for Pavel over there. It means Paul, you know.'

'Yes, I know. But did . . . ?'

'That's all for now, thank you, Gilda,' Charlie said quickly, taking Karen's arm in a grip so tight she knew he was telling her to shut up. 'We must be off. But you should know that Vera – you remember her?'

'How could I forget that dramatic flight?' Gilda's stiffening voice suggested she disliked Vera. 'What's she done now?'

'Died.' Charlie said, watching Gilda with interest. 'We've found her body over on the mainland.'

Her face showed a barely acceptable amount of shock, mixed in with a puzzled frown.

'Who . . . ?' she began. 'I mean, how did she die?'

'We're still investigating,' Charlie said. 'Part of our enquir-ies will involve a search of this building. Vera's room. Any stuff she left here. The team's waiting outside. Here's the warrant.'

He offered her a piece of paper. Gilda confirmed all Karen's ideas about her efficiency by reading it with care, nodding and then handing it back.

'We will, of course, give them every facility,' she said with great formality.

'That's good. And we'll need to take DNA samples from everyone living, working and visiting the house now,' he added. 'For elimination purposes. Coming, Karen?'

Back in the car, watching as Charlie's searchers spread out around the house as well as entering it, Karen rubbed her bruised arm. 'You still don't know your own strength, do you?'

'Sorry about that,' Charlie said. 'But I didn't want you raising the spectre of Dev until we've got further with this and picked up Pavel Dankovitch. We need Mrs Brown to confirm her ID of him too. She should be waiting for us back at the nick. Annie's taken the first statement off her.'

He drove back the way they'd come, swearing at the slowness of the traffic that clogged the outskirts of Cowes. For once Karen didn't care about the delay. With rare sunlight gleaming on fresh white paint and making the seagulls look like advertisements for washing powder against the brilliant blue sky, she was happy to look around, while her subconscious played with different ways of running the forthcoming interviews.

They reached Charlie's designated space in the car park behind the police station at last and he rushed ahead of her in through the back door of the building, calling for DS Annie Colvin.

She emerged from the lavatories, still drying her hands on a paper towel.

'What's the matter?' she said. 'You sound as if the building's on fire.'

'In a hurry. How d'you get on with Mrs B?'

'She confirmed her identification of the man with the scarred nose as one of the two window-mending carpenters at once. No problems there, so you can relax.'

'Did you let her go?' Charlie looked as though he wanted to grab Annie's arm just as hard as he'd held Karen's.

'No. You said you wanted to talk to her. She's getting agitated about not being at work. Olga didn't want to let her leave the house in the first place. But I said you had to talk to her and I couldn't let her go until you'd had a chance. She's in interview room 2.'

'Come on, Karen,' Charlie said without bothering to thank Annie. She exchanged 'isn't-he-the-pits?' glances with Karen, then went back into the lavatory, still wiping her hands.

Mrs Brown looked exhausted as she sat waiting in the interview room, with a junior member of Antony Quiggly's staff beside her to watch over her interests. She was dressed in a suit so beautifully made, and yet so tight, that Karen was sure Olga must have handed it on to her when she'd finished with it.

'Thank you for identifying the carpenter again,' Charlie said as he sat down. 'I now need to ask you something a bit different. Your emails show that you and Sheena Greves know each other well.'

'She worked for my employer, Sir Dan Blackwater.' The tight voice gave away as little as Mrs Brown's small face.

'There was more to your relationship than sharing a boss,' he said.

'I don't know what you mean,' Mrs Brown said, as a dull purple flush mottled her cheeks. She twitched in her seat, as though she was trying to get physically away from the lawyer.

Karen leaned forwards, saying gently, 'He won't report on this, you know, Mrs Brown. He's *your* lawyer, bound by duties of confidentiality to you, not to Olga.'

The housekeeper bit her lip and looked at the floor.

'Are you afraid of her?' Karen asked, then cursed herself as Mrs Brown raised her eyes and revealed an expression of pure stubbornness.

'You don't work in this kind of role for as long as I have if you let demanding employers frighten you. Lady Blackwater has many problems and any kind of inefficiency, or noise, or mess can trigger a crisis. So I'm always careful to do everything I can to keep her calm. That's all. And it's why . . . why I tried . . .'

Mrs Brown flicked a wary glance at her young solicitor, then looked back at Charlie.

'What did you try to do?' he asked, sounding a lot kinder than usual.

Karen wondered whether Mrs Brown reminded him of someone he cared about.

'I tried to find out everything I could about how Sir Dan was at any given moment and what he might need when he arrived on the Island so that I could have everything just so for him. There was an occasion a few years ago when he arrived in very great distress. I had to know why. So I emailed Sheena. That's how our . . . well, our friendship, began.'

'And you found Sheena was able to reassure you, comfort you, whenever Olga upset you. Did you do the same for her?'

Mrs Brown shrugged. 'I hope so.'

'Do you see much of her?' Charlie asked. 'Olga, I mean.'

'Not a lot. She seemed to lose her liking for the Island something like four or five years ago. Recently she came here only when Sir Dan insisted. I never told Sheena that. It seemed unfair to burden her with . . .' Her efficient voice faded into silence.

'What about Olga's charity at Clagbourne House?' Karen couldn't resist chipping in again. 'Didn't she have to come here to deal with that?'

'Not on a regular basis.' Mrs Brown looked at the solicitor, then back at the other two. 'She flew in sometimes to talk to the girls, about the kind of work they could do when they were – what would you call it? Rehabilitated? – yes. That's it. And sometimes if there was a crisis.'

'What kind of crisis?' This time it was Charlie who interrupted.

'I don't know. But sometimes I'd get a text warning me to have her room ready at nearly no notice, and then when she was here I'd hear her on the phone. It was always obvious when something was wrong. At first, I used to think it was my arrangements in the house, and that she was complaining about me to Sir Dan, but then I realized it wasn't anything to do with me or the house.'

'Did Sir Dan always come when she was here at times like that?' Charlie asked.

Mrs Brown looked surprised. 'Never. Those times were nearly always on weekdays, and he spent his weeks in London.

He'd get here on Friday evening in time for dinner and stay until first thing on Monday.'

'How did Sheena feel about that?' Karen was genuinely curious.

Mrs Brown smiled a little, and made herself more comfortable on her hard chair, with a movement that suggested she might have enjoyed feeling a certain superiority over Sheena, if only in this. 'In a role like hers, you have to put up with a lot you don't like.'

'The rewards outweighed the rest for her, did they?' Karen said.

'Must have, mustn't they?' Again the housekeeper's voice betrayed satisfaction. 'She's stuck with him all these years.'

Charlie turned his laptop round to face Mrs Brown, and clicked on 'slideshow' to show her a succession of photographs of short-haired, bullet-headed men of East European appearance, saying, 'Can you tell me if you recognize any of these men?'

'I've already done this with DS Colvin,' she protested.

'I know. But humour me,' Charlie said, at his most charming. 'I like to see the moment when a witness identifies an important figure in any investigation.'

Mrs Brown shrugged, but she watched the succession of twelve portraits in silence, then asked if she could see them again, nodding briskly at one moment.

'That one – number four – is one of the two carpenters who came to mend the window last week. Like I said before when you showed me the E-fit, and again when DS Colvin showed me these photographs.'

'So you're sure?' Charlie said. 'No bossy lawyer in court will be able to shake you?'

'I'm sure.'

'Great. When did his mate leave the house?' Charlie's voice held no suggestion of criticism, but Mrs Brown flushed again. Karen thought the mottled colour made her slab-like cheeks look like old salami.

'That's what I don't know,' Mrs Brown said. 'It was the one with the scarred nose I saw getting back into the van. I signed his worksheet and watched him drive off. At the time I just assumed the other man was in the van already. But I never looked to check.'

'So it is possible that he was still somewhere in the house when you left at the end of your day's work, the last time you saw Sir Dan?'

'It's possible.' Tears welled in her eyes, and she sniffed hard. 'But I don't know whether it's true.'

'Thank you.' Charlie smiled at her and nodded to the solicitor. 'That's very clear. Now I have some more faces for you to look at.' He clicked on another slide show. 'If you see anyone you recognize, tell me.'

Mrs Brown watched in silence, without moving, as face after face crossed the screen in front of her. But Karen knew at once when she recognized one of them. Her eyes sharpened, and her breathing changed very slightly.

'Him,' she said.

'When did you see him, Mrs Brown?' Charlie asked.

'He was the other carpenter. The one I'm not sure I ever saw leaving the house.'

'Are you sure?'

'I said so,' Mrs Brown snapped, displaying the first sign of temper Karen had ever seen in her. 'So am I free to go?'

'You're not under arrest, Mrs Brown, as your solicitor can confirm,' Charlie said with a deliberate blandness Karen assumed was designed to provoke her. 'Of course you're free to go.'

The young solicitor picked up his briefcase with one hand, then offered the other to his client to help her out of the chair. When they'd left the interview room, Karen said: 'That has to be how it was done: Dev holing up in the basement until the house was quiet. They were lucky Sheena was so unhappy she took sleeping pills; otherwise she'd probably have woken as Dev started hauling the body around and he'd have had to kill her too. Presumably they'd factored in the risk and planned to make it look like suicide. Did your CSIs find anything in the house to show Dev had been?'

'How would that help?' Charlie demanded. 'All he'd have to do is admit to the window-mending, and maybe looking around the house to check if any others needed work, which could have left his DNA all over the place. We'll need a confession. Two confessions. One from Dev and one from whoever's behind him. Let's hope Rich Silver can pull it off.'

Karen was glad to see that he'd now dropped all his suspicions of Sheena. But there were still things he had to be made to see.

'Have you got the security tapes of Sheena's arrival on that laptop?' she asked.

Charlie pressed a few more keys and Karen watched the films again in silence, before saying, 'It's what I remembered: at first he is *really* pleased to see her. Even though she's here on the Island, where she was never supposed to be and Olga was due next day. Sir Dan's happy to see Sheena here. Then she shows him the email she thought he'd sent her, and everything changes. As she told us, he gets angry. Then, as we know, he won't let her go upstairs with him, and he orders her not to come down in the morning until she's dressed. What does that tell you?'

'You're the shrink, not me,' Charlie said. '*I* don't do guesswork.'

Karen ignored the insult, with all its echoes of Rich Silver's contempt for her profession.

'I think Sir Dan's making absolutely certain,' she said, allowing her voice to bite, 'that no hidden cameras can record anything that looks as though he's in collusion with Sheena or having an affair with her or anything else that could be used against either of them. He knew he hadn't sent her the email, and he must've been suspicious that the person Trevor warned him about, the one who's been hijacking the charity and turning it into a front for crime, was behind Sheena's arrival.'

'Poor bugger,' Charlie said. 'Afraid he was at the centre of a massive scam and didn't know who to trust any more. Maybe not even Sheena. You must . . .'

His phone rang. Karen knew he'd have to answer the call, but she was still irritated to have their talk interrupted. As she watched his dark face, the taut muscles under the skin relaxed. He thanked the caller and put down the phone.

'Tell me again about the room where you were held,' he said.

Karen forced herself back into the feeling of complete powerlessness that had been her worst nightmare for as long as she could remember, then she talked without thinking at all until she'd given him everything her memory could provide.

'That figures,' he said. 'They've been searching Clagbourne, and there's a sound-proofed room in the basement. No bed there now, but marks on the floor consistent with a metal bed frame about four-foot-six wide. The whole place has been cleaned. Stinks of bleach. So there won't be any DNA, but that's suggestive in itself. They're bringing Gilda in, and all the other women. One of them has to know something.'

'And my car?'

'Results not back yet from the vehicle examiners. But with everyone involved in Clagbourne having been DNA-tested, we'll soon know if the tall, blonde driver we saw on the CCTV was one of the inmates. We still don't know if they brought you over in the boot or in some other vehicle earlier. But we will get there. I promise.'

Karen couldn't understand why Charlie looked so uncomfortable. After a moment, he shook himself, like a dog emerging from a river.

'You're right about Olga. We have to get everything she knows. But if she's been scared into silence it could be hard. Will you help?'

'Of course.' Karen smiled as though she was simply glad he wanted her with him, but she was silently cheering at the opportunity to test her own suspicions of the ultimate boss behind Dev and his men. 'Have Annie and DC Silver got anything from Dev?'

'Bugger all so far,' Charlie said.

'You should have let me in on the interview.'

'Dafty,' he said. 'You know you can't be part of the team interrogating a man you've accused of attempting to kill you. You ready?'

'I'm ready. But I'd better read everything Mrs Brown gave Annie before we go.'

Karen sat in silence as he drove with all his usual impatient efficiency out of Cowes and through the soft, pretty countryside to the big white-pillared house, where Olga reigned when she was in the UK. Mrs Brown admitted them, with a frosty politeness that told Karen she hadn't forgiven Charlie for treating her like a suspect.

Olga was waiting for them in the cream-and-gold drawing room, surrounded by the magnificent paintings, and still looking so fragile that Karen wanted to urge her to sit down before she fell over. She was wearing black again, but this time it was a dress rather than a suit. The cut was miraculous, showing off the sleekness of her body. Her hair was loose today, hanging just on her shoulders and making her look even more vulnerable. Her make-up was so soft it was barely there.

'Chief Inspector Trench,' she said, holding out her hand for shaking. Charlie took it. 'And Doctor Taylor. Please have a seat.'

As Olga gestured towards the low comfortable sofa, Karen smelled her ravishing scent and knew for certain that her memory hadn't lied: Dev had most definitely smelled of this when he'd stood over her and instructed her captors in the best way to kill her. And now she was fairly sure she knew why. She had to make sure that Charlie came to share her understanding in time.

Once Karen had despised people who lusted after physical vengeance. This morning she understood their need. She felt as though only watching this woman, as well as Dev and the rest of them, in terror of their own could take away the horror of the hours she'd spent strapped to the bed and the two forced drug overdoses. Trying to control herself, she looked towards Olga, ready to say something polite. But she needn't have bothered. As before, all Olga's concentration was on Charlie.

'You said you have at last collected some evidence of who killed my husband,' she said, arranging the full skirt of her expensive dress around her impeccable knees. 'Does this mean you will soon be taking away this well-meaning but exasperating Liaison Officer you have dogging my footsteps?'

'Soon,' Charlie said, pulling his laptop out of his bag. 'But before we get to that, I have to ask you why you didn't tell us about your husband's suspicions of someone involved with Clagbourne House.'

Olga shrugged, her delicate shoulders distorting the line of her dress and making it cling so tightly under her breasts that the seaming of her bra showed through the fine fabric. 'Why would I waste your time with anything so absurd? There is a crime here, isn't there, called "wasting police time"?'

'Doesn't apply. This is a motive for your husband's murder. You must see that, so I don't understand why you never mentioned it to us.'

'It could only be a motive if his suspicion was based on anything real, Chief Inspector, and of course it is not real.' Olga would not meet his eyes, looking at the photograph of her husband instead. 'I did not want to distract you from the search for my husband's killer by talking about this nonsense.'

'Are you sure it's not that you were afraid?' Charlie said gently.

'Afraid?' Olga sounded astonished and insulted. 'Why would *I* be afraid?'

Karen could think of several reasons but she waited for Charlie to speak and give her the opening she needed.

'Because the people who have been using the Clagbourne House charity as cover for their illegal activities are ruthless and violent. Have they threatened you, Lady Blackwater? Is that why you haven't told us the truth?'

'Threatened *me*? Certainly not.'

Watching her carefully, Karen noticed a flickering in her eyes and a slight downward turn of her lips, as though she'd produced her answer too quickly and now regretted it.

'What made you so sure your husband's suspicion was not justified?' Karen asked, holding down her hatred with all her strength. 'You can't have had time to investigate every aspect of your charities here on the Island.'

'Because it was too stupid. A fuss about nothing other than a fantasy produced by a disturbed young girl. This you call "crying wolf", I think.'

'Hardly that,' Karen said. 'Can you tell us which young girl you're talking about?'

Olga shrugged again, but her eyes looked wary and her colour was rising.

'My husband had told me he had been contacted by our latest refugee, a teenager called Vera, with a wild accusation that one of our security guards was a criminal, one of those who had misused her before we rescued her.'

'And that was all?' Karen kept her voice pleasant and chatty.

'But yes. What else do you expect?'

'He didn't tell you that his erstwhile accountant, Trevor Fieldsham, had been inspecting the Clagbourne House accounts and found some serious anomalies?'

'Most certainly he did not.' Olga's wary expression hadn't changed, but it hadn't intensified either. 'But then he knew I have no interest in – or knowledge of – finance.'

'I doubt that,' Karen said and realized her tone had been much too sharp when she saw Charlie's surprise. The last thing she wanted was to make him feel like Olga's champion. He'd never see the truth then.

He took over again.

'Vera has been murdered, Lady Blackwater. Whatever the truth of what she told your husband, she did not invent the threats against her. Are you *sure* no one has been trying to intimidate you into silence?'

Olga's expression hardened so that her face looked as though it had been modelled in wax. Karen was sure Vera's death was news to her. She saw a way forward and opened her mouth to ask another question, but Charlie pre-empted her again.

'Because you do not need to be afraid any longer. We have the chief suspect in custody,' he said. 'It is safe for you to tell me everything you know.'

Olga's impeccably threaded eyebrows twitched. 'I am glad you have them. But I have never been afraid for my safety. Who is this person you have?'

'Goes by the name of Dev. We expect a more accurate identification shortly.' Charlie looked down at his notebook, as though checking his facts. Then he glanced up again. 'The other chief suspect is known as Pavel Dankovitch, who has been working as a freelance member of your staff at Clagbourne House.'

'Hardly *my* staff,' Olga said, well in control of herself again. She added a light laugh. 'You cannot expect me to know the names of every tradesman who does work for one of my charities.'

'That's fine.' Charlie smiled. 'We have all the identification evidence we need. Vera gave a statement before she died, identifying him, as well as implicating Dev as the man who had raped her a year before she escaped from her traffickers to your care. We also have an identification of both men from your housekeeper, who admitted them to the house last Friday to do some work here before your husband's arrival. And we have a sworn statement identifying Pavel Dankovitch as one of two men who assaulted Doctor Taylor here.'

For a second Olga didn't move, then, perhaps realizing that no reaction would look more suspicious than anything else, turned her head as though having to force it through some lake of molten metal. When she was facing Karen, she spoke as formally as Charlie had just done.

'I am sorry to hear you have been attacked. What did this man do to you? Was it a robbery? A mugging?'

'Neither. He and a . . . a colleague abducted me,' Karen said, as though she was talking about a trivial shopping expedition, 'brought me to a sound-proofed basement room in Clagbourne House, and, in the presence of Dev, and at his instruction, injected me with an overdose of heroin designed to kill me.'

A small bubble of laughter escaped between Olga's faintly reddened lips. She pulled out a lace handkerchief and pressed it to them, before apologizing.

'Please forgive me. I should not laugh at such a terrible story, but it is just so impossible to believe. On the Isle of Wight! These things do not happen here. If this man and his confrères meant you harm, they cannot have been very efficient. Not exactly master criminals.'

'Unlike your husband,' Karen said pointedly, reminding Olga that violent crime was not unknown on the Island, 'I was rescued before their activities could kill me. Quite unexpectedly. And the doctors got the naloxone, the antidote, into me quickly enough to prevent any brain damage. My memory of the hours leading up to the overdose is clear. It is my captors' bad luck that I was fully conscious as they were discussing what to do with me.'

This time Olga did not hesitate, smiling easily as she crossed her legs and said, 'That must have been . . . unpleasant.'

'It was,' Karen agreed, 'but it provides me considerable satisfaction, too, because it gave me the pointers I needed to identify the mind behind all the clever stratagems that have been played out around your husband for several years now.'

'I do not think I understand what you mean.'

Now it was Karen's turn to laugh. She felt suddenly filled with the kind of lovely confidence that she'd felt only once or twice before in her life. It was almost as pleasurable as the heroin rush she knew she could never allow herself to experience again.

Ignoring Charlie and the fact that he had no idea what she was about to do, and the risks she might be taking with both their careers, she carried on.

'I think you do. I think you know all about the seemingly elderly woman who smothered the baby your husband had with his press advisor Sheena Greves, just as you know all about the faked email that warned Mrs Brown that Dev and his mate would be coming to mend a window frame here in this house, as well as the one that summoned Sheena to be the obvious suspect when Dev had killed your husband and placed his mutilated body in the kitchen here.'

'What is this nonsense?' Olga sounded untroubled, but Karen had gone too far to pull back now.

'This is the same intelligence that planned my "suicide", selecting from among the inmates of Clagbourne House the one who would look most like me on the CCTV cameras recording her as she brought my car over to the Island.'

'All this is very interesting,' Olga said, wiping her lips again. Even from where she sat, Karen could see the pink smears on the fine linen. 'But what is any of it to do with me?'

'You don't need me to tell you that,' Karen said. 'It won't be long before Dev has made it clear in the statement he is giving DCI Trench's colleagues at the moment where he got his orders – and why he smelled of Annick Goutal's Eau d'Hadrien, the scent you always wear. The two of you must have been physically extremely close for him to smell so clearly of it. Anyway, never mind that now. I wanted to come to talk to you because I feel so sorry for you.'

Charlie winced, but Karen would not let him distract her.

'How dare you?' Olga's voice was brittle with disdain.

'You see,' Karen said, 'I know how you met Sir Dan and how he had to pay your pimp to buy out your contract; I know how you met another of your old clients in a social situation when you must have thought you were secure for ever. I know how humiliated you felt, how much you loved your husband and how terribly you resented his preference for a woman who is so very ordinary in comparison with you – in looks, in character, and in experience.'

Olga turned slowly to Charlie. 'I do not understand why you have brought this woman here, but I would be grateful if you would remove her at once.'

'I can see exactly why you felt driven to wreck the businesses of the kind of men who had enslaved you – and the others like them – and I can sympathize with that,' Karen said, hurrying to get it all out before Charlie found a way to stop her. 'Where I can't sympathize is with the way you set up a rival business, using other young women as you yourself had been used.'

'You are *disgusting*; a disgrace to your profession.'

At this first hint of passion in Olga, Karen knew she had to push hard to take advantage of the weakness.

'I can understand your psychology, of course.' Karen offered a light laugh of her own. 'You had learned to despise yourself for the way you had allowed those men to victimize you and so you had vengeance in mind, an urge to punish not only them but also every other young woman who was weak enough to be used the same way.'

'You are mad.' Olga's back was absolutely straight and her feet were both planted flat on the floor, as though she was taking strength through it.

'The strong women you picked off to become your couriers and managers,' Karen continued, 'bringing them here to Clagbourne House for training, and the weak ones you shipped straight off to your own clubs and brothels.' Karen paused, collecting her scattered ideas and instincts.

'But it hasn't made you feel any better, has it?' she said, with spurious gentleness. 'None of the money you have made, probably far more than your famous husband, has helped at all.

Nor do your works of art or your beautiful clothes, the aero-plane or the skiing trophies, the adulation, or the fear you arouse in almost everyone who works for you.'

Karen waited for five distinct beats, then said into the icy silence: 'So much anger, so much hatred, so much money, so much nothing. You must be the loneliest woman I have ever met.'

Olga's rigidity was like that of a steel joist. Karen had thought she might well be one of those people to whom an accusation of unhappiness was more insulting than any allegation of murder could be. If so, she was hiding it too well.

'And then your husband found out that Clagbourne House was not the benign charity it seemed. He hadn't amassed the evidence that would betray you but you knew he would. He had told you he would go to the police, and so you had him killed.'

'Do not be ridiculous.'

'Karen,' Charlie said. 'Karen, you have to stop. *Now*.' His phone rang. He pulled it out, glanced at the screen. 'Lady Blackwater, I have to take this. Karen, keep quiet until I'm done.'

Olga was on her feet, ringing the bell. When the door opened and Mrs Brown appeared, no longer wearing the elegant, too-tight suit, but her usual blouse and skirt, Olga said with frigid distaste: 'Doctor Taylor and the Chief Inspector are leaving.'

'Not quite yet, Mrs Brown,' Charlie said, slipping the phone into his pocket. He glanced at Karen and from the glitter in his eyes she knew he'd heard something that made him believe at last in what she'd been doing. 'You were in Sir Dan's confidence, weren't you?'

'I liked to think so,' Mrs Brown said, carefully avoiding her employer's eye.

'You told us this morning that about five years ago Sir Dan was in great distress. What was it about? Do you know?'

Mrs Brown licked her lips. Karen hoped her courage wasn't going to fail. They needed her now. As Olga repeated her instruction to show them out, Mrs Brown stared right past her, squared her shoulders and said quite calmly, 'He looked terrible that night. His eyes showed he had been crying. I asked if I could fetch him something, and he said there was nothing. He told me that he was trying to believe it was better to have tasted perfect happiness and then lost it than never to know what it was.'

No one said anything for a full minute, then Charlie asked, 'Did you know what he was talking about?'

'Not at the time, but I emailed Sheena later because I was so worried about him, and she told me about their baby and how he had died in his pram in the park.'

Karen watched Olga's face as her employee revealed the full extent of a whole new shame she had known nothing about. For the first time Karen felt squeamish, understanding how humiliation had always driven Olga. Then she thought of her own hours shackled naked to the bed before Olga had ordered her to be pumped full of heroin and dumped to die.

'Who else knew about the baby, Mrs Brown?' Charlie asked.

'Only my husband. We did our best to look after Sir Dan all through the trial, which was a terrible time for him.'

'Did he ever talk to you about his child?' Charlie's voice was soft, but Karen could see that each word hit Olga like a punch.

'Of course not. He didn't know we knew it was his. He was

a very private man, you know, and he hated to have any hurt mentioned.'

'Thank you, Mrs Brown.'

The housekeeper left, and Olga never moved.

'There's no way you're going to be able to control the publicity now, you know,' Karen said to her, with a pity that was not entirely faked. 'Once the trials start, all the journalists you've silenced over the years will get their revenge. You know what they'll do. Nothing will be spared: your attempts at IVF; the sexually-transmitted diseases that caused your infertility; your past as a prostitute. You'll be pilloried everywhere. Everything will come out, including the way you faked the email that brought Sheena to the Island to be the only suspect in your own husband's terrible death. The lawyers won't be able to help in the long term. Your only way of containing any of it is to plead guilty to conspiracy to murder your husband so that the evidence doesn't have to be pawed over in court.'

'Evidence?' Olga spoke at last, her voice hoarse with strain. 'What are you talking about? You have no evidence.'

'We have a signed confession from Dev, implicating you in everything he has done, including the murder of your husband,' Charlie said, still holding his phone.

'And it doesn't stop there,' Karen said. 'There's the other killing.'

Charlie frowned at her, but she couldn't stop.

'There's the child your husband had with Sheena Greves. The police will be enhancing a photograph taken of a slight, short woman dressed up to look elderly, who was seen interfering with your husband's baby five years ago.' Karen paused to allow a protest or a question, but Olga sat still and silent.

'All the DNA samples will still be available for retesting. You must have left some DNA on that pram and that tiny corpse. You see, although you have been very clever, you have not been quite clever enough.'

A siren sounded in the distance. Charlie cocked his head towards the window.

'That's my officers with the arrest warrant. How about calling your lawyer, Lady Blackwater?'

She stood unspeaking for four long minutes. Karen timed them on the gilt clock in the centre of the mantelpiece. At last Olga looked at Charlie.

'Whatever,' she said, before walking towards the sofa, where Karen sat.

The disparity in their heights meant that her head was only about a foot above Karen's, but she still had to look up to meet Olga's eyes. They blazed in her lovely face.

'This will happen to you, you know, Doctor Taylor. Whichever man you choose – this policeman or your crippled surgeon – he will betray you. When he does, I want you to remember this moment. Will you have the courage to do as I have done?'

Karen couldn't answer. She felt as though Olga's knowledge of her most private dilemmas had smeared dirt all over her.

'Of course you won't,' Olga continued. 'You would always prefer to ruin someone else's life than fight for your own.'

Words poured into Karen's mind as she thought of everything Olga had done to assuage her own hurt: the lives she had ruined; the young women she had put to work as prostitutes; the people she had had killed; and the child she had almost certainly suffocated with her own hands. Karen thought of her own terror when Olga's men had taken her and through those memories understood what all the others had endured.

'Karen,' Charlie said, urgent and worried. She turned to smile at him.

'Don't worry, Charlie. Nothing this woman could say would even touch me. Not now that I know she will be exposed for what she truly is, taken to court, and punished for it.'

Chapter 24

Day Seven: 8.00 p.m.

Mario poured the wine – his ordinary Chianti – into the big glasses in front of Charlie and Karen as they celebrated Olga's double confession, and Dev's.

'Is on the house, *Dottoressa*,' he said. 'To welcome you back to Mario's.'

'You are too generous.' Karen raised her glass to him and drank appreciatively, planning an enormous tip.

She looked around the friendly little restaurant and wished Stella had agreed to come. One day she might be able to see the place again without shuddering, but it hadn't happened yet.

'Thanks, mate,' Charlie said with a smile that meant: and now that's enough; we want to be alone.

As Mario moved away, Karen raised her glass again.

'Thank you for what you said to the press,' she said. 'You didn't have to.'

His smile reached right down to the coldest, darkest spaces in her mind.

'Yeah I did. If I hadn't told them about you in the first place, they'd never have run that piece with the sexy photo of you, claiming you were screwing up the case. I like to pay my debts.'

'With huge interest in this case,' she said. 'I've already had three calls from other police forces with tricky investigations since they read this morning's article.'

'You going to work for them?' Charlie asked, looking across the guttering candle at Karen with an expression she couldn't quite understand.

'I'm not sure yet. Why?'

'Because you're mine. I saw you first.' He paused to swallow some wine, then added, 'And I know I'm going to need you again. When we were with Olga I saw how you really do know how minds work,' he said.

Karen drank some more wine, glad her taste for it was back. She knew he was talking about more than work, and she wasn't sure what was coming next or whether she should pre-empt it.

'Other people's minds. They're a lot easier to understand than my own,' she said, noticing the way Will's large watery diamond caught the flickering candlelight.

Charlie was watching it too.

'Yes,' he said, 'we've got to talk about that, too.'

'Maybe it would be easier not to say anything,' Karen told him. 'We could just let it ride. Kind of go back to where we were before?'

Charlie lifted his eyelids. His dark eyes stared straight at hers. She thought of the way the black sea had looked when they'd made love and knew he was also thinking of that night.

After a while he shrugged, as though he didn't agree but was prepared to accept what she'd said.

'Have you told Will?' he asked.

'No. Did you?'

'No. I didn't know where . . . what you wanted.' He made a face that reminded her of the story of the Spartan boy with a biting fox hidden in his shirt, then he pointed to the big diamond on her finger. 'It's him you want now, isn't it? That's why you're wearing that rock again.'

'Yes. Charlie, I . . .'

He wouldn't let her say it. 'I knew, I think, when he and I were watching the CCTV film of the woman driving your car.'

Karen's eyebrows snapped together. Whatever she'd expected him to say, it hadn't been anything like this. 'What do you mean?'

Charlie looked over her head towards the hot, noisy kitchen through the wide-open hatch.

'*I* thought it was you,' he said. Then he let his head drop a little so that he was looking at her again. She thought she could see sadness in his wicked black eyes, and apology, and something else that looked like guilt, which did surprise her. 'But *he* knew right away that it wasn't. That told me . . .'

Charlie broke off, picked up his glass again and produced a laugh intended to tell her he was going to be fine.

'Told you, what?' Karen asked.

'Where to get off.'

Next morning Karen checked the address Max had given her when he'd confessed that he'd ordered Will to stay well away from her until the case was over and she had had a chance to recover from everything that had been done to her.

Certain now that she had the right place, she looked up at the tall, barely modernized old industrial building. Through the thin drizzling rain, the only entrance she could see was a pair of rusted, grey metal doors, with no bell or knocker visible anywhere.

Not at all sure what she would find inside, she pushed at both doors. One gave under her weight and creaked open. A long dark passage extended ahead of her, and she felt as though she was in the kind of dream that includes an unending journey with no point and no arrival. Walking down the corridor, listening hard, all she could hear were her own footsteps and her own heartbeat.

Then she heard a thud just over her head and a short sharp curse in a voice so familiar she stopped for a second, with her left hand pressed hard over her speeding heart.

'You can do it,' said another voice, a deep voice with a heavy Hampshire accent. 'You're nearly there as it is. Come on now, Will. You can do it.'

Karen allowed herself to smile and headed on towards a faint increase of light just beyond a right turn in the corridor. Rounding it, she saw a concrete staircase and ran up it. The two voices were more distant again, but she could hear their owners talking.

Another pair of metal doors confronted her, this time freshly painted and without a speck of rust anywhere. She pushed again and, as the door yielded, she was faced with a brilliantly lit space, floored in pristine boards, covered with a whole range of rubber mats, step machines, bench-presses, rowing machines, and all the other paraphernalia of the fashionable gyms she'd known. Only the lack of disco music, screens and flashing lights told her this was no leisure palace.

A man in army camouflage trousers and a tight khaki

T-shirt, with very short hair and a very rich tan, looked up from the prone body on the mat at his feet.

'Can I help you?' he demanded in a voice that meant: what do you think you're doing in my space?

'I was hoping to speak to Will,' she said, pointing down towards his back.

Will raised his head at once, looking up and over his shoulder. His face was so covered in sweat he could have just emerged from a shower. His fair hair was dark with it, pressed hard against his scalp, showing off the perfect modelling of his skull.

'Karen,' he said, rolling over to grab a towel. As he wiped his face, arms and head, he added, 'Meet Sergeant Birkin, who's getting me back into shape.'

'Hi,' she said, moving forwards with hand outstretched. 'I'm Karen Taylor.'

Birkin looked at her, then down at Will, who was struggling to his feet, then back at Karen. 'We could do with a break,' he said, as though he grudged the admission. 'I'll get water.'

As he moved past her, she could see how fit he was, and how neatly he moved.

'Tactful,' she said to Will as the metal doors banged behind him.

Will dropped the towel and balanced himself on both feet with care, before walking forwards with no visible limp at all and no recourse to either of his sticks.

'Charlie told me,' she said abruptly.

'Told you what?' Will's tone was chilly.

'That it was only you who knew it wasn't me on the CCTV footage of the tall blonde woman who drove my car.'

A faint flush coloured his spare cheeks. 'Ah, that. I couldn't exactly miss it.'

'And you knew when I needed help,' she added, finding this exceptionally difficult but knowing it was too important to allow any embarrassment stop her saying what had to be said. 'And you came. Which makes me think . . .'

She broke off, feeling as though there were something in her throat that had to be swallowed. She coughed instead.

'Will, I can't do it like this, all rational and analytical. I've got to say it straight out. I miss you like hell. If you can't bear the thought of getting back together then I need to know now because I'll have to find a way of . . .'

She stopped talking because he'd grabbed her and kissed her.

'Why d'you think I've been working so hard with Birkin?' he said as he pulled back. 'I have to know I won't be a drain on you. He thinks I'll be fit and ready to work again within two more weeks. If he's right, and if the hospital let me go back to work, then you and I can get the wedding plans in train again.'

Karen leaned forwards until her forehead was resting in the hollow of his neck. His arms tightened around her and he didn't stagger as he took her weight.

'If you ever do anything like that to me again,' she said seriously, 'I think I will probably kill you.'

Envoi

Four hours later, Karen sent a text message:

Dillie, U can order polyester frills now. 28 June. CU Karen.

N. J. Cooper
FACE OF THE DEVIL

Suzie Gray is only fifteen when she is stabbed to death
within metres of her uncle's yacht on the Isle of Wight.
Her body is found in the blood-smeared arms of Olly
Matken, a family friend who grew up with her.
Schizophrenic and vulnerable, he presents a serious
challenge to the police.

'I didn't hurt her!' Olly protests. *'All I did was keep her from
the devil.'*

DCI Charlie Trench turns to forensic psychologist Karen
Taylor. She knows she should ignore his call, but she
cannot. Curiosity and, although she would never admit it
to her partner, Will, a dangerous attraction to the
brooding detective, push her into a deeply troubling
case.

Is Olly capable of murder? His own psychologist doesn't
think so, but his father does. The only way to find the
truth is to identify Olly's devil. And Karen has demons of
her own.

ISBN: 978-1-84983-286-1

N. J. Cooper
LIFEBLOOD

'If you ever talk about this, if you ever identify me to anyone, I'll find you and kill you. Wherever you are, I'll find you. And I will kill you.'

Five years ago Randall Gyre was convicted of the brutal rape of a young student, Lizzie Fane, on the Isle of Wight. Handsome, rich, slick-talking, Gyre had avoided prison for years before that, despite a string of accusations from other young women, who had been sadistically raped.

Forensic psychologist Karen Taylor is sure Gyre will attack again, and this time he will probably kill. She's prepared to stake everything - her career, her reputation - to protect Lizzie and any future victims. But Lizzie has vanished. Karen believes everyone involved in putting Gyre away could be at risk. She must warn DCI Charlie Trench - her friend, and the detective responsible for Gyre's arrest.

Soon people who gave evidence at the trial are murdered. Has Gyre started to kill, as Karen predicted? Has Lizzie herself turned avenging angel? Or is there someone else here, pulling the strings?

ISBN: 978-1-84739-423-1